Crawl Space
&
Other Stories of Limited Maneuverability

by

Richard Krause

For information contact:
Unsolicited Press
Portland, Oregon
www.unsolicitedpress.com
orders@unsolicitedpress.com
619-354-8005

Cover Design: Kathryn Gerhardt
Cover Photo: Bruce New
Editor: Caitlin James and S.R. Stewart

ISBN: 978-1-950730-81-0

ACKNOWLEDGEMENTS

These stories were published in the following magazines:

"Urban Tales" *Scarlet Leaf Review*

"The Firing of the Music Teacher" *ink&coda*

"The Handkerchief" *Red Savina Review*

"Jockey Underwear" *Gnu Literary Journal*

"A Piano Story" *Subtle Fiction*

"Raising Cain" *Dodging the Rain*

"The Curtains" *Descant*

"Beets" *Umbrella Factory Magazine*

"Waiting" *Wind*

"Hawking" *Flash Fiction Magazine*

"The Liver" *Headway Quarterly*

"The Paddle" *Northwest Indiana Literary Journal*

"Art" *Eunoia Review*

I wish to thank S.R. Stewart for her courage in selecting this collection.

TABLE OF CONTENTS

Crawl Space
&
Other Stories of Limited Maneuverability

URBAN TALES

WHEN IT HAPPENED, she went downtown to the funeral, for the child she never had. Well, she did, but farmed him out before he was one, then finally when he was ten placed him in an orphanage. She used to recount how her own mother of six children, who died when she was thirty-seven of tuberculosis, sympathized with the poor Japanese when the Russians took Sakhalin Island, the mighty Russian bear swallowing up the territory of that small country.

Mary spoke with her friend, also named Mary, about placing the boy in a school in Pennsylvania. It was the practical thing to do, her friend told her. Everything is paid for and "he'll be out of your hair." Though the boy never really lived with his mother. He remembered being left in Port Authority bus station for hours on end waiting for her to return, imagining the boy was safe in full view of so many strangers. She took him to visit her one room apartment at the top of the building in Washington Heights. He remembered her pinching him to get him to do something. She wasn't necessarily good with kids, but visibly attracted to them on the street, in the subway, or in stores, noticing their beauty, smiling and making faces at them all the time.

She finally did place the boy in the orphanage, five hours drive from New York City. On her first visit she took him to department stores in nearby Harrisburg to buy him a red turtleneck sweater and a black leather jacket, saying to the houseparent when she took him out that he wasn't dressed warm enough. Actually at the homes he had stayed at before, his caretakers always worried about the boy not getting enough to eat, for Mary ate irregularly, didn't think three meals a day was necessary, and growing up in the Depression always stinted with money.

"Mary" she insisted was the name of the mother of God and should be treated with respect and reverence. Of course when the boy returned to the group home that first time, all the clothes were confiscated since he could not be dressed differently than the other boys.

The ride to the orphanage the boy would never forget, or the jungle film he watched that afternoon hoping it would never end and she'd never turn up, but she did, and in the long silence of the Greyhound bus ride to Pennsylvania he uttered not a word. He had a tiny, clear plastic gun with small candy colored balls that gave him a sense of confidence just in case he needed them, not as live ammunition of course, but something his appetite could fall back on if all else failed. The mother hardly visited the boy after that, intent on living her own life, taking art classes, getting her degree at the Fashion Institute of Technology, doing Bible studies, dance classes, jazz and ballet, and acting classes at Actors Studio, but her career in fashion went nowhere and so her nursing continued. She worked in pediatrics and spent her nights sketching young babies in their cribs.

In her two-room apartment on Audubon Avenue where she moved, the clutter was staggering. She had dozens of dolls of every color and nationality. She had always told her son that she wanted a daughter. She wanted to write and illustrate children's books, and so there were boxes upon boxes of clippings from magazines and newspapers of children and the scenes she wanted to draw, also boxes of her poetry. It was a cornucopia of ideas and dreams and interests stacked to the ceiling that were never quite realized outside the thousands of drawings she made, lamenting always that she didn't have enough space, and how she couldn't break into the art or publishing world since they wanted young people.

Mary never really found another man, a "Sugar Daddy" she called him, after the boy's father died. There was Giuseppe, the doorman, who called himself Steve, whom she privately referred to as Bozo whom she used as her tool. Other than that, and despite all her forays downtown to Christian Science lectures, especially Raymond Barker, and finally to Ron Hubbard, the scientologist, and out to her brother's and sister's houses on Long Island during the holidays, she lived an extraordinarily lonely life.

She always claimed that she was mistreated by her father who because of her red hair called her "Cockroach," and made fun of her freckles. He kept her and her sister Sarah up in the attic away from the other siblings and rationed out the food kept in a locked trunk under the bed. That is why her apartment was ringed with cans of food on the floor, and stacks of jars that sealed all manner of comestibles to insure she would never go hungry again. Often she had no school lunch and wore cardboard in her shoes to cover the holes.

So when it happened, she was ripe for the visit. The time had come to mourn, and she never considered how it pointed right back to her. In fact, the whole city seemed to collectively grieve, and with Mary it wasn't knee jerk, but her whole life had been building up to it. In a sense you could say it was almost planned from the sympathies of her mother for the tiny country of Japan. Just such a horror brought everything into focus in her own life, spotlighted her father who kept her and Sarah in the attic away from the rest of the children. What happened to that little girl she never had was mobilized around Lisa. She could dispense with the disappointment of having a son by rerouting it to the unspeakable horror that now occurred.

Sadomasochism must come from the anger of our stupendous solitude, to erase the barriers to our painful differences from each other, to bridge that gigantic gap. It is nothing more than an overexpression of love that somehow is not enough until the other person finally stops breathing. Those with inadequate love will go downtown to at least pay their respects, as if to celebrate the horror as an excuse for their own grief. Traveling underground, Mary could draw out her thoughts in poetry and sketch exactly how she saw the world to the clatter of the train tracks when her ideas would come so freely.

She could already see Lisa playing with such pleasure, skipping through the city streets, over puddles after a rainfall, sailing boats in Central Park, what Mary never had in her own life, that the past and her strength of personality had kept away, her Catholic upbringing, the Irish privation, her father, the sudden death of her husband, all that would produce the little niños in the Spanish she studied, words too she tried to get her little boy to repeat after her on the subway.

WHAT WOULD SHE find with Lisa but her own lost opportunities, the absence of the little girl she never had, feelings that poured out of her for those shunted into art, feelings engaged in constant study that her son never received, living with others early on, living her own life in the city, bettering herself with everything but to give him her time, languishing finally in an orphanage in Pennsylvania, virtually unvisited, but he didn't want to see her anyway. For she was so unpredictable, making comments about strangers within earshot.

"You don't want to be like that guy," she said once when they were walking in Parkchester, and the man turned around and said, "What's the matter with you, lady?"

The tension wherever she was, was almost palpable, in restaurants where the bread was always stale, the meat uncooked, her drink unrefreshed, or on busses or in theaters where she was never comfortable, or never had enough room.

She was now traveling downtown to Lisa's address, for the past now that age had caught up with her, realizing her blue eyes and red hair could no longer grab attention like when she was younger.

Her talent too she realized required youth, and in truth she never learned to speak to men, the easy banter, the flirtatious give and take, but instead thrust herself into someone's lost opportunity. All her feelings extended to the little girl for whom she dressed herself up as if she were a family intimate, for everyone was family to Lisa, the whole city fascinated by the treatment of that little girl, as if people took it personally; this most powerful revulsion in the world, harming a defenseless six-year-old, such innocence, fascinates us, for our own throttled assault somewhere in the darkest recesses of our mind, what we'd never dream of, but still is there under the crust of each of us, inevitably in the midst of our outrage towards someone else; we are unable to help ourselves, or call out for help, because we are sure no one would be listening, and our own past is deaf, carrying all the violence inside, the desire to strike out past the solid impediment of each other; the hand, arm, and shoulder are reflexive to overcome the sheer stupefying loneliness of whom we are, making our bodies almost always doubly, trebly ours, all that governs more than most of us, that is, the universal contagion of the self. We are all catching from each other, even though wisely we try to keep our impulses to ourselves, mollify them by rushing downtown. And that is just how we deal with them, by going on the attack, making pilgrimages, addressing the horror of what happened. At the altar we are standing before we know it, and the train is rattling to get us there.

How it starts we don't even realize. First by admiration, the worship that lowers the defenses, then circles in the dark while the smiles are up front, at a cocktail party or seasonal gathering of coworkers, or maybe it is just in a park on a sunny afternoon in spring, the seduction of a polite word, or his sense of humor. You go home alone changed, or with each other, go through the dance of courtship, employ courtesy at first, knowing sometimes how to talk to the woman, be gentle, cadge to get what you want, but it is somehow you find in time never enough, neither of you can get close enough. Your bodies are wonderfully there, but then they are the obstacle; you can break down the resolve, erase the boundaries, the sky's the limit, but the breast that is so attractive is one day openly bruised, the black and blue turns yellow; the head snaps back at first, and you don't know what just happened. It is not you, but it is. Or your teeth one night get out of hand, the biting that first time leaves you confused, but goes right to your partner.

"Ouch!" she says.

She gets angry, may even hit you. You like that too, are surprised at how much, and so there is almost a mutual escalation. You can't withhold yourselves, but all your past pushes you, urges you forward. There is something you need to resolve, the love that never occurred, to erase the past cruelty, the favoritism, all the attention your sisters and brother got.

Then one day you see the evidence of someone who did push past. She's lying before you. You know beauty is the most unfair element in the universe, the diamond beside the coal fields, the gemstone in ordinary rock, the transparency that one day is scratched, devalued, you can hardly imagine how it happened initially. A diamond, a diamond, what did I do, left the bruise, a mark, the scratch on her!

Hedda before and after. Who can look at her? It throws you for a loop, dizzy you look at what happened to the face. The transformation each time escapes your notice. You are not reeling like the first few times when you were even sick yourself in the morning looking at her. But the face infinitely fascinates you, the alteration, your handiwork, the absolute horror of what has happened, beaten to a pulp that you deny it is just the opposite of the Creator. She brought it on herself. She was your partner, participant, playmate. You can't take it, beauty destroyed. She revolts you, totally apart from anything you have done. You only cooperated.

The rectangular glasses, the cold unfathomable look of Joel, the alternate scenario of even Lisa's death shrouded in lies, but the look of Hedda is too true to comprehend. Joel is in absolute denial. Where did such a monster come from? Hedda could have done it when Lisa was caught rooting round the medicine cabinet, overturning bottles that smashed on the tile floor. Hedda did it, except for the punching bag she had become.

The black eyes, the split lip, the absent bridge of her nose, that's what gets you about the photograph. A collapsed bridge? Just where is that going to take you? Where do such beatings lead? To throwing yourself off the railing beforehand to stop your own breathing? The cartilage it is reported even protruded, the frizzled hair she stopped combing, the beauty transformed, a forty-year-old looking like she was sixty. The life extinguished from her eyes, more a hunted rat, a hunk of battered meat constantly tenderized by Joel, eventually defaced. How could it happen? How can we be so lonely, so alone, so angry, reach such cruel disregard?

If you know about escalation we build ourselves up to it, slowly draw what's inside further along, after one bruise, a too strong hold, then the next, and the next, until there is a discoloration, then a mess of them that doesn't look like an arm, but a withered appendage, an excuse for an arm, finally a dead tree limb. Maybe the first time I am sure it startles us, but that is only the beginning you got to admit, we are all well-intentioned, but we get away from ourselves. We do.

"Oh, I'm sorry. I didn't mean it, Hedda. What came over me? It won't happen again."

But each time it does, more and more frequent, and so do the apologies that after first being elaborate empty themselves of meaning, as the lines between the couple blur. They become one flesh. Though he manages to keep his shape, in fact his lines are sharper, cleaner by the day due to the intent of being himself, being clarified in his body as her lines disappear, the bridge is flattened, eyes blacken and smear, sinking in their orbit, the lips split, the face is a mass of pulp, Joel's blender. Joel, the brilliant lawyer still has his place in the world. He goes to work every day. Hedda gradually withdraws further and further from the children's books she wrote and enters the horror of her own fairy tale in the dim light of their apartment. Something Grimm, which started out with such hope, does not shy away from the worst in us. Innocence can bring that out, as can beauty, and then not knowing how to deal with it vis a vis our feelings, those creepy crawling things that multiply dizzyingly until swat, what we think swats them only multiplies. The goodness cannot last.

Brains confer advantages, can erase the boundaries with the right argument, split hairs so combs don't pass through them anymore. They became like Shredded Wheat, Hedda's hair. Look, she was in the apartment for ten hours with Lisa before she called the police.

He became a lawyer again, with legal arguments eclipsing human nature, the stupefying, bottomless cruelty with rational arguments, discovery, contrary evidence reestablishing what happened, all the twists and turns we have at our command that don't need to dig, or expose all those corpses in the backyards of our family tree that sometimes come to us in our dreams, why the night is so difficult to get through; we don't want to fall into what we really are, fearing sleep will bring it out.

And what strikes you are the intentions. Yes, we all have the best intentions in the world for motherhood, for childhood. That's how we are made. Or is it? Are there contrary principles at work?

Hedda wrote children's books, and Mary did too, at least she gathered all those clippings, examples for her own art, watercolors of dolls and stuffed animals and little girls. What remarkable intentions to end like this. You can easily imagine all the anxiety Hedda had waiting for her children's books to appear. How could things go so awry? That is what Mary was going down to see, past dumping her own child in an orphanage, past the fact that he was just a boy, and not the girl she wanted; she was coming to pay her respects to her own vision of motherhood. How they can unite, the good intention of mothers the world over, band together, what a force to be reckoned with!

Mary could openly criticize the George Washington toll bridge operator who did note the bruises on Lisa, fault her for not reporting it immediately, or did she? Perhaps Mary was coming to rectify that, even if it was too late, or at least pay her respects now to the dead six-year-old who only wanted to go out to eat with her Daddy, and was whipped for it. Let me say, Joel took on Lisa to find her a home for five hundred bucks but decided to keep her himself. No, he wasn't her real father.

Men, Mary would say, faulting them, overlooking pinching her own son that he later dubbed the pinches her caresses focused. Do we all have the capacity to focus so that we strike out at what we can't control, what doesn't love us enough, or feelings we ourselves can't show. Are there no lines, only nets we are all susceptible to being caught in? Are we the loose fish of each other? Is that what Mary was traveling downtown to authenticate.

Hedda tried to get out of the relationship, missed work, though she was seen often enough that her facial changes were too gradual and noticed piecemeal so the overall effect hit no one until they saw her face in the newspapers, or on television. At first the sexuality depressed everything in secrecy, the newly opened vistas of pain and the portals of pleasure. Through it all Hedda left six times, but ultimately identified with Joel and came back, her life outside the beatings curiously incomplete. She became part of him, that one flesh often talked about in marriages, her beauty totally absorbed into his power finally disappearing because of it. And she grew malnourished, buried the pain of the broken bones, the collapsed bridge of her nose, the lost weight. She stopped going out. Joel did everything. Lisa was her only solace, her saving grace. Her book *Plants Do Amazing Things* no one saw as a reference to her life with Joel, or *Animals Build Amazing Homes*, how it now applied. What an unspeakable gulf between the actuality and the warm comfort of cuddling rabbits or anything in its den against the dangers outside. Outside! The dangers within are the unspeakable ones, the muteness, the apartmental silence in the end where only the walls could talk about the heads that smashed against them, the unchallenged cruelty where everyone is afraid to speak, or look the wrong way, fend off the charge of cross-eyedness, for fear of the fist, of being thrown against the wall, or commanded to drop down on all fours to crawl and eat off the floor. Joel didn't even want to be pleased by her any longer. He was long past that now. She repulsed him, he told her.

Maybe we shouldn't live together. Isn't it cleaner to attack, gut, skin the other member of the species, like a trapped animal, rather than this slow erosion of ourselves living with each other, sharing our intelligence, dreams, talents, and then the absolute horror of when they are all drained away, and we are left alone. Beforehand he was so nice. What happened to that woman, to her beauty, where did it go? It makes us angry. Beauty some of us would die for?

That is why Hedda Nussbaum is so fascinating, because she shows us the potential of what any of us could become. And the breathtaking study of beauty disappearing overnight. Oh, at the start never, who'd think of that, but the tiny escalations, the baby steps before the long march, before the trampling goes unnoticed. Who knew we are all toddlers taking our first step with each other, or who admits the appearance of the boot and the sheer number of kicks we can endure, or that the soft resistance of the human body is absolutely amazing. Only public outrage can force the boot back into hiding. How two of us tolerate each other together without jealousy, without appropriating all the other has, their talents, their laughter, their pleasure until in the daily erosion of the personality, the one absorbs the other and how she or he disappears from the other's regard is a mystery. Until one is finally null and void and the other flourishes. They are ours, the scoldings, the scratches at first, later the punches, the battering, until even the face that we admired is no more and we privately, unknown even to ourselves, revel in our own strength, or the truth slips out and we call ourselves "a piece of shit like me," as Joel said, surprised at a guy one day who said that he was glad to meet him. Better be on the veldt or in a savannah where we can attack an entirely different species, in the jungle or a forest, than worst of all in the same urban household. The grip we imagine outside is really inside, our already knotted intestines over bruising her arm the first time, then regularly leaving black and blue marks all over that she covers with scarfs and long sleeves. We get the dents in the wall repaired, the broken glass is swept up, Mama's cherished vase or a favorite figurine that shatters where you forced her to walk barefoot. Better a wild animal be brought down, the jaws clearly on the neck, the power displayed all in one leap, the decisive spring of the haunches, or squeeze of a trigger, one clean shot right through the heart felling the beast than this weakening of the heart muscle gradually, than the violence inherent first in the language of just wanting to live together. Who knows in the beginning that they want to remove the body, the obstacle to loving ourselves standing in front of us. Melt it right there, even if it means bruises, black eyes, and a caved in nose, superficial signs of not gutting her outright. It disappeared in Hedda so that her wheezing went with her gravelly voice and poor Joel couldn't on some nights get any sleep himself. Her books too were totally absorbed by him, reduced to nothing by a thousand silverfish. Hedda was underwater, no longer worrying about simple breathing through her collapsed bridge.

And the monster that Joel was pictured as, placed in protective custody so he would not be attacked, only emboldened him. He claimed it was consensual, that Hedda was his partner and enjoyed "the roughhousing," the broken bones, the total domination where sex became blows to every inch of her body. Remorse was alien to him, for he remained the lawyer saying his own defense lawyer Ira London had "his head up his ass"! Freebasing cocaine could be blamed, but wasn't it more than that?

Joel had absorbed Hedda, his striking out became routine, the tick tock of his own heart muscle. He beat her like clockwork. It was his morning workout and his midnight sleeping pill. She was his heartbeat. That's it. They were finally one flesh. That's us, simple breathing, in and out. The whole species rolled into one ball, the gender resolution. One person, one pulse, our differences extinct all at once. And the staggering blow he gave to Lisa that made her brain swell sealed the deal; it was only the result, the old-fashioned Joel's way of rewinding.

Hedda's limp, too, Joel began to imitate. Some thought he had actually injured himself. Poor Joel didn't know sometimes if he was coming or going, mimicking, mocking, or mauling Hedda. The ice baths that he forced Hedda to take at first to reduce the swelling finally came to naught and must have added to his own numbing. The rituals we can only imagine, forcing Hedda on all fours to crawl and eat scraps he threw down for her.

Lisa too picked up the bruises. At St. Vincent's Hospital they noticed marks all over her body, as if Hedda's flesh was extended to the adopted girl at Joel's feet. Joel was indeed a piece of work. His military duty he felt the press overlooked, his connections to the Phoenix program where over forty thousand Vietnamese were killed, brutalized before Hedda, for democracy, for self-rule of the people. Maybe Joel thought like in Vietnam it was all for the collective good, the single-headed monster marriage could be. That each would benefit in the end, that there was no limit to pleasure or pain and the light was at the end of the tunnel. One body, one head had to deface the rest, Hedda's included. How is love to survive except by this triumph, total possession of the other, so thoroughly until the beloved is no more; that is true love, no different than the narcotizing effect of living uneventfully forever together. This oneness requires the disappearance of the other. We are left absorbing memories of those forty thousand eliminated for love of country, of the facial disappearance of a beauty that drove us out of our mind in a love that finally had to erase itself the way love always does eventually, only not as in this case so dramatically. That is not love, you say. Then what is it but such erasures? Time does its own devouring of beauty. Joel was only accelerating time, spearing the beautiful speckled trout, accelerating the shocking difference the years make by trumping time in a matter of short years, creating the appearance of an old woman almost overnight, showing the children's books are a charade of the monsters everyone grows up into. Yes, the wild things are here and now. Maurice Sendak was right. It is no joke what we should be afraid of.

Steinberg even wanted his lawyer, Ira London, to be "more aggressive with Hedda." In fact Lisa was not hit for wanting to go to dinner with Joel, but Hedda herself could have done it, he maintained, over her cosmetics on the bathroom shelf out of Lisa's reach.

"She wanted to go with her Daddy," Darnay Hoffman, Joel's attorney speculates; "she wanted to 'make herself up' to accompany her Daddy to dinner. She knocks over the tray and Hedda, already jealous of the six-year-old, goes into a rage and smacks her against the wall and there you have the fatal injury when her head hits the tile. Hedda is paralyzed by the blood and there you have it," Hoffman speculates.

Anything can be speculative. We don't know where to stop, we can like Swift says of lawyers make black white and white black. She is passing on what Joel did to her, "violence she shared in their sexual life, that she too enjoyed, folks, but now she takes it out on Lisa and Joel is only the fall guy."

"Poor Joel, getting a bad rap," Hoffman concludes and adds, "Joel is your grandmother. If you let him be demonized and receive an unfair trial and distorted coverage, as happened, your relatives are next!"

"I rest my case."

Who has a rebuttal for that outside a burned down courthouse. No wonder the stretch limo was sent to prison upon Joel's release, the Lincoln town car, the height of emancipation, "Darnay's prom ride." Joel was only a kid, really. Where's his boutonniere, and Hedda, well, she's no longer his date. Look at what she had done to herself? It's her handiwork, too.

Her looks, "They were nothing but 'title fights' folks. She enjoyed being hit, some do," Hoffman said.

"A man can be factually guilty, but legally innocent. Then who is ultimately guilty?" Just those in harm's way, for being there, sitting in the park, or in a café, or on the subway when they are first noticed? Isn't this what they deserve? That's love, folks. We may not want to face up to it, but there it is!

*

TAKING THE A train was a descent into herself. Her talent, her latent abilities, her sympathies flourished underground. The sturdy steel structure gave her support, absorbed sound in a way that even when the oncoming and passing trains were deafening, it left her with a peace of mind she could never find in her cluttered apartment filled with countless dolls and knickknacks, paintings and boxes of news clippings, art from magazines, not to mention all her sketches. All were a charade of the life she found down in the subway that calmed her. Every race made its appearance; it was a United Nations ensemble that one person had gathered in the small, sad apartment where she lived alone except for her son's occasional visits.

It was down there that something else overcame her. One could see the transformation as she entered the yellow light of the subway system and descended the steps of her psyche that led not only to herself, but to that communion among all people that above ground and finally in the solitude of her own apartment she never had.

"I can't work here," she said, "it's too cluttered. I need a separate room for my artwork."

In fact as she paid the fare and went through the turnstile, she descended a second set of steps into the most unexpected studio that in a few moments would come well-lit and on wheels. She sat down and waited, and always had a book. The loneliest of lives reads the most books, knows how to people their solitude, though her relationship with people was never ordinary. She never mastered those social graces attached to the uninspired, everyday contact between people. No, she always kept that edge where the caustic remark, the curt brusque reply, would sit precariously on her tongue.

As the train came the doors opened and she stepped into the lighted car and took out her sketch pad, pencil, eraser, and gray shading stick. She looked into the distance and picked some figure, often a black person for the train passed through Harlem. She delighted in the richness of their features. The generous spread of their noses, the large wings, the expansive nares, the broadlined flatness so easy to draw, she'd say. And the lips, so richly sculpted and with thick, beautiful curves, on each person as distinctive as their fingerprint. And the largest eyes, dark and reflective in the yellow light of the train. The warm yellows that seemed to go with the skin entered the discolored whites of their eyes, and that was one of the reasons that she favored them above all other races. For she loved color and its powerful effect on the emotions.

Coming from northern European ancestors and not having the same access to her feelings, she could appreciate the warmth in others where she found it so visibly and did her best to transfer it to paper. Sometimes, too, she'd go home and add watercolor. And the hairstyles as they became more distinctive intrigued her. The woolly black and brown hair, bushy and in corn rows, and the powerful athletic figures, or the steatopygous hips on the women. Or those tall svelte figures to offset the motherly and expansive. But most of all it was the old men. Those with dignity and snappy dress, with two-tone white and gray or beige shoes and straw hats, and the poor, the broken old men whose bloodshot eyes mapped a life of hardship. How the athlete's frame would turn into these unrecognizable figures as frail as hangers upon which the clothes were hung was a mystery she tried to capture with her pencil. How the body grew resigned, how work or the lack of it had sapped the vital energies. But how the women kept coming, rich and fertile, the very picture of fecundity, how they welded the family together, sometimes it seemed just by their own body mass.

She sketched them all, the mothers with arms outstretched around their children. And the children's faces she adored. In fact when she worked in pediatrics on the night shift, more than once she was reprimanded for drawing the babies in their cribs, accenting the long eyelashes in their sleep that was so peaceful. Or the children on the subway, their eyes so alert and inquisitive. Even the sauciness, then the scoldings from the mother, the quick slaps, she caught the aftermath of all that on paper. The child's lowered eyes nursing the sting in front of everyone. And the young boys, she tried to capture their jauntiness, the pride in their developing bodies, their postures and carriage before it turned menacing.

Mary's art career never took off in fashion, and so she had to continue nursing but still drew. Drew the faces, the mixtures of people that were now changing the complexion of the city, drew the features blended through intermarrying. She often raved over the beauty of the Spanish women. Caught the stiff dignity of some, the slouching lassitude of their boyfriends, or how they held their bodies. She caught them sleeping on each other's shoulders, the amorous scenes they now engaged in more openly, the petting and caresses, all that her pencil followed.

She tried to sit far enough away to capture them without their seeing. But sometimes people came up to see what she was doing and asked her if they could have the sketch and she always tore it out and gave it to them without hesitation. For there were so many trips on the subway and so many faces she had captured. She had finally taken to using scraps of paper to draw on, old envelopes, and the back of used stationery, for her drawings stored in boxes were getting to be a problem in her small apartment. She was happy to give them away, and glad for the pleasure on people's faces.

This one day she took her seat as usual and started to sketch even as Lisa's face kept popping into her mind, when she noticed a group of younger girls at the other end of the car talking animatedly. She had caught their attention and they glared back at her. From experience she paid them little mind and looked elsewhere to draw someone else. They grew louder and it seemed they were discussing the old lady.

"Who does she think she is?" was one comment.

"Damn white!" another said.

Suddenly the subway car froze as an electric current went through everyone. There must have been four or five girls--the lines of hatred went out from them sharper than the point of the old lady's pencil that kept on mechanically drawing. The sound of the subway was deafening, and more easily allowed riders to look away. From the 1950s to the 70s, and now the 80s, it seemed to get louder, ever more strident.

Just before 125th Street the girls approached and stood by the old woman who was looking down at her pad moving her pencil, drawing now from memory. As the station came within sight, the one girl reached out and smacked the old lady across the face that her glasses flew off. The other girl grabbed her pad and threw it down. The old woman dropped her pencil and clutched for her handbag that had fallen out of her lap.

Another girl stepped on her hand, "Think you're going to draw us?" she screeched--as she drove the fragile bones of the old woman underfoot.

The doors burst open and the girls jumped out and disappeared into the crowded platform.

The woman sat dazed as she reached for her things. Her one eye was swollen, already black and blue.

A large black woman came and stooped down to pick up her pad and gave it to her and said, "I'm sorry."

The old woman's nose was cut. Her nose, as sharp as the tools she used to pare her pencil points, looked flatter as the bridge seemed slightly pushed in, broadened by a discoloring bruise. Her lips that were as thin as the lines on her paper, where she always smeared large daubs of lipstick to thicken them, now were enlarged and swollen. Her disheveled hair was curling over her forehead. And the dark facial discolorations of her skin that had come with age, and a blotchiness of tan pigment also on the backs of her hands, were now duskier as the light of the subway flickered. People stood above her and stared down at the old woman who had tried to capture the richness of a race that no longer wanted to be enslaved by even the admiring pencil of a white woman. They wanted to be free of that too.

We can imagine how Mary continued to the stoop at 14 West 10th Street cluttered with pictures of the little girl, candles, notes and flowers, but all is uncertain. She claimed she attended Lisa's funeral like many other New Yorkers who in their own way look out for each other, but in Mary's case for the mother she never was to a little girl, we can still picture her standing there.

THE FIRING OF THE MUSIC TEACHER

NOTHING CHANGED. The campus went on as before, everybody quiet as a nun concerned only about their own private vows. That's the way it is with people who regard themselves as religious. They wear nothing on their sleeve but their own souls.

Nobody was visibly burned up. That was for monks decades earlier to protest the war in Vietnam, not something that occurred in the backwaters of Kentucky along the Cumberland River where the terrain is hilly, and the hollows exist inside each of us.

Yes, I include myself too.

It is only one music teacher, so get real. Despite the firing it is only his livelihood we are talking about. And kids, he doesn't have any yet, only his music and his girlfriend. Girlfriend! It's what most of us don't have. What a luxury to not be married yet! To have that freedom. We've already made our decision. Our wives are already in our homes, our lives determined, fixed, mostly stale.

Tom was too fresh anyway, and never showed the President the proper respect it was said. At the time we didn't know how much she needed that, how quickly she took offence, how she never forgot, could hold a grudge against any of us that we didn't even notice it until years later when all at once out of the blue we'd get the shaft and a score we didn't even realize would be settled, not the head-on assault against the music teacher like when she first arrived.

She was new then, and so we couldn't tell why she came down on him. Like a ton of bricks someone said, the cacophony was so strident, unmusical to us that we had all we could do not to clamp our hands over our ears and run out of the room.

The rumors spread like wildfire about Tom Donne. They said he was finished. At the time that was beyond us. His music was intimidating to some. Tom was in his own world. He felt a stunning ownership of his field akin to the only real estate on the block, not so much space as he never complained about not having the best office like the rest of us, but the very air we breathed, its vibration as we were out walking is what he controlled. The notes in it, the melody of breezes through the trees, the sounds only he registered as he walked along. The mice scratching along the baseboards, the musicality of their appetite. That's what was beyond us that he caught. Tom was always composing when he walked and talked; even the lilt he had in his voice was musical, or the agitated drumming of his fingertips on a table or the tapping of his shoe, or at the end of what you said, the rising intonation he caught, then the deep base of something Beethovian, the bottom feeding of Dat dat dat dah! He always added to something you'd say about music, about the divine reach of Mozart soaring like a bird scattering droplets of light on every bush as it climbed to the heavens; he set to music even the shiny chrome off a car racing by. Tom wasn't all there for anyone who couldn't appreciate his enthusiasm for the world around him. His mind was lightning fast encompassing the sounds of everyday life, or the beautifully emergent melody of a Chopin piece through an open window, freed from earthly constraints, played to the hilt, not unlike Excalibur only a few could remove.

We privately suspected the President was tone deaf like so many people in charge who respond only to the sound of their own voices. We imagined she heard only what she perceived to be her own melody, but she had the power of the gavel, its concussion as judge, jury, and executioner. She never included the rest of us in the conversation of who'd stay or go. She eventually gathered around her yes men who all repeated the same refrain. That was the only music she heard.

We did have a meeting only because she was new. Holly Hock was her name as if in Kentucky the flashing hooves raised in the air exhibited the perfect picture of a thoroughbred. After all she had come from Mississippi and would bring us Southern culture, but we didn't realize it accompanied the incendiary art of firing.

Music was out and visual representation was in. How things looked trumped anything heard. The beautification of the campus never involved the music teacher.

She wanted someone to paint her, lionize her as Napoleon on a horse, the ultimate equestrienne performing at the international games in Lexington, and the only music permitted were the trumpets announcing her arrival and the clop of hooves, nothing that reached for the heavens. Yes, Tom Donne was finished and she newly hired was just getting started. It was a tableau vivant she envisioned that froze her in a perfect representation of the Commander-in-Chief.

BUT THE QUESTION was why she had come to the meeting. What did she have against him? we all speculated. He himself had only arrived a year earlier. Couldn't she use him at least for background music?

The meeting was scheduled for Monday morning with the Humanities Division. She'd entertain questions about the firing, put nicely the letting go of Tom Donne; his contract just wouldn't be renewed, it was said.

We were quite unwilling to believe, too, all the fires in town that someone pointed out. We questioned who set them. Were those mysterious house fires no one knew about until the article in the *Commonwealth Journal* came out a coincidence? Were the fires connected to rumors of Tom's firing, like a drumbeat to the flames on campus, capturing their essence. Was Tom the culmination of the crackling sounds that reached the next village, rumors that because the music teacher was being fired art instructors all over should make ready to apply, that sound was out and silent portraiture was in? Was someone marshalling opposition against the decision by starting these fires? Little did we know as we sat in the room with the President what else would come of her decision.

Was it faulty wiring that caused the fires, a short circuit, a stove left unattended, a cigarette in bed after some illicit lovemaking? Did it affect everyone's private life, the firing? Was it sexual! There you have it most of the time. Some shenanigans going on in the workplace that spills over into the community bedrooms, not generated by official policy in a firing. Of course we don't call it that. Who'd want the conflagration of mass layoffs to follow, so we start one at a time. Who'd get back up from that but a tone-deaf public who claimed they'd heard nothing.

It could certainly be the student body. Some passion its youth inspired that the music teacher took advantage of. After all, he only had one girlfriend. Why not two, or three, or a whole class of them? Did the music teacher, I hate to mention it, affect everyone that way? Was it a contagion, and not a conflagration? Was the wildfire already on campus, the burning up of students' sensibilities, flames of Beethoven, Mozart, Bach, and Chopin, or Tchaikovsky or Scriabin, or all those smug marches? Okay, admit the charred remains of a student body that no one recognized, burning with private passion, with the naked desire of the ear to the ground for every vibration from Tom, for every high note that he hit? For the administration, Tom Donne could be secretly named Black for the dithyrambic orgy of mass burning of not books but bodies. The faculty sat there unwilling to say anything, too fearful for their own jobs to speak up.

One of us schemed to be out of town taking his child to his first day at college, another claimed illness, a third just forgot, a fourth wouldn't interrupt her sabbatical, but I was there, and it fell on me. I didn't mind the ton of bricks, had the illusion I was broad-shouldered, but it could be called outright stupidity. For I too was admittedly tone deaf, but loved what I wasn't skilled at, enraptured by sound, how it etherealized everything then brought home the thunderous clap, how it matched nature in all its violence and brutality, then the absolute majesty followed by the tender whisperings of a brook, exquisitely attuned to the small things in life, to the bee buzzing, to the warm sunlight and a clear running stream. Yes, I was seduced by the discipline. It was titanic and breathlessly gentle by turns as to be beyond words and even pictures. Painting I loved, but music beguiled me and that is why I defended Tom to the hilt knowing he was led by a different drummer, had access to sounds I didn't, and so I cocked my ear around him to share in what I considered the distant clop leading to the music of the spheres. He was the instrument that brought the best out of us.

We sat at the rectangular table to hear about his fate, but nobody was willing to break the silence.

"We just want to know why," I finally blurted out. "Why is Tom being let go, why is his contract not being renewed? Do you have something against him?"

"Jack, if you knew me, you'd know that would never be the case. It is something I cannot discuss, for Tom's benefit. It's a private matter."

"I don't understand. How are we to accept something that is not clear. I've talked to Tom and he says he himself doesn't know the reason."

"It's confidential, Jack."

"But if he doesn't know what it is, how are we or anyone to understand, or address it?"

"Is it something actionable, legally?"

"Tom just isn't a good fit for our school. Yes, he's is a talented teacher, but his abilities will be better served elsewhere."

"What exactly does that mean?"

"I mean he just doesn't fit in with the plan we have for the future of Cumberland College. I'd like to say more, but I am not at liberty to say. Jack, my hands are tied."

"But if he has to have done something, certainly he should know what it is to address it."

"I think he knows, Jack."

"Then I am baffled that he wouldn't tell me. He says he doesn't know. Have you talked to him?"

"Yes, and no."

No one else spoke up. The silence was palpable, speechless at the ambiguity.

I continued questioning the President, but she was not forthcoming with any more information, only insisted it was not personal and repeated that Tom was not a good fit.

One Division member claimed Tom left her church as choir director.

"That's his business," I said. "This is a nonsectarian institution."

"There were problems," she said, "but I can't discuss them."

It sounded as if Tom was being railroaded. Perhaps only I could hear the train whistle at the other end of town, the marshalling of rustics gathering their most dangerous tools to descend on the harmless music teacher. Perhaps they blamed the firing on him. Maybe they knew about the seductions of whole classes, how the teacher mesmerized students. Maybe it was the editorial about the fires in town that roused them. Who knows what anyone's passion for their field might inspire, others setting fires out of sheer jealousy? Maybe Tom was more a threat than we knew about.

After the meeting when the President left, two faculty members came up to me and expressed their sorrow over Tom's dismissal. One was in tears, blubbering that she was going to miss him.

I wanted to say, why didn't you speak up, but swallowed my words.

Why was the firing? Who started it? we were always trying to find out. Did Tom have a secret enemy? Would the art teacher hired find out it was like Orozco's ceiling in Guadalajara that sent the music teacher up reaching the church ceiling where for the initiate the sounds of music incorporated the crackling flames. Who collected the faggots that led up to it? And is this also what happened to those poor women in Salem? Did some consider all screams musical, as the flames devoured the bodies, splintering bones and burning fat, a choral ensemble transported heavenward, and was it something Tom was to expect, that hadn't happened yet in the simple announcement of the firing? Who fed the fire this time, gathered the kindling? Who poured on the gasoline, lit the fuse, sent Tom charred out of the student body, and identified all those student witches? Did a bevy of them accompany him at a naked rally? Would the remains be found at the side of the road? Some beautification!

Still we were waiting to hear. What would be the result of the firing? Tom turning on himself. After all he was already fired. Did that stop the music and usher in the flames?

Was this modeled on a town in Spain, involving the Grand Inquisitor himself, that placed Tom at the stake, the tone deaf cone hats that hate melody busying themselves gathering wood. But again, we are only a backwater college. No open repentance was required, no disavowal of faith. Tom had directed another choir in town after he left the one church. Apparently, he was still in demand.

It could have been the burning at Mill Springs, reviving the battlefield. Johnny Reb's revenge on Tom who came from Ohio, not the Mississippi of the President. The South still needed protection from the Northerners, Yankees. Who knows what will filter down if you let it flourish?

It could have been someone guilty over a missile in Iraq or Afghanistan, its whistling before it took out a wedding party. The high-pitched sound of that participated in this firing. The President probably had helpmeets, and in our own Division, with different agendas. Or the thirty-five Middle Eastern celebrants, was Tom to rectify their remains? Was only Tom's music left to right that wrong, had he all the danger of a free spirit that might highlight that tragedy? Maybe his notes, the starkest melody would capture the slow lugubrious tread of the student body moving around campus unchallenged, implanting the ghosts of the wedding elsewhere. And Tom himself had to be taken out to remove that overseas horror from coming to our campus. Why should we suffer for what was done thousands of miles away? Removing Tom would remove the instrument that might make that happen.

Could it be that the President was afraid that Tom with his composing abilities was the prime culprit who'd educate everyone to what exactly happened, that his music would capture the grief of all those innocent civilians? The President and her cronies were the prime suspects in the drop in enrollment, in the frightening away of students so they fled to other institutions. Could the screams of the innocents after that bombing be on their minds and confused with the loss of students on campus, especially the Provost's whose son had recently returned from Iraq. Surely the music died, erasing the girl in Vietnam running naked down the road after her village was napalmed, her facial grimace the very mask of tragedy. Did the fear of resurrecting that contribute to Tom's removal? Did Tom possess the danger of all free spirits for just what they might set to music? In all our minds it was young girls moaning from pleasure, but in reality, could it be something entirely different that could change to shrieks in a second?

It could have been the Iraqi villagers' guns firing in the air that got them bombed. Tom discovered the mistake musically, exultant peals of laughter, then a staccato melody, identifying the syncopation of running steps, and then the explosions, the screams, and all the charred remains.

One note took in an arm, its reach cut short, another the rubber mask of an emptied face with no bones inside, or a foot poised taking a step without a body.

I remember Tom exiting buildings on campus bursting into song,

"Oh, what a beautiful mornin'

Oh, what a beautiful day

I've got a beautiful feelin'

Everything's going my way"

That would have been the perfect timing for the explosion, and you knew his volatile nature could capture both and put them together, the exultant joy and then the horror that erased everything. Perhaps we had to get rid of anyone who could do that.

There were no limits to his exuberance. Maybe that was the problem, how at all institutions we set limits on each other, weed out with tenure the excesses of anyone who can't be controlled by others, college campuses that can't reproduce the horrors abroad in pictures, not even musically. Tom had to go. We didn't understand it at the time. One doesn't shine before others. Even a star with his talent had to be plucked from the firmament, especially if its rays needle us. No, he wasn't a good fit.

Tom ultimately was undeterred by the firing.

The President admitted he was a talented man and would "do well taking his talents elsewhere." She got no objections from most of us.

I quizzed her what that meant, but I never got a straight answer.

What I didn't like was that there was no outright courage to burn him at the stake like in the past, only the whispering that something was wrong. The weak rumors of the cowardly who protested his not being choir director at a local church any longer. It was their own idea of character assassination, those who had never protested the killing overseas were probably fearful that Tom would compose a dirge that would sting their consciences, or reproduce the horror of the actual killing and the earsplitting lamentations that followed.

They were afraid of actually setting the teacher on fire, an actual burning ceremony, for no one wants to hear fat sizzling, or see skin peeling off, experience the smell or screams, or pick up the crumbling remains afterwards. Maybe the art teacher would come and paint that, the gruesomeness, or transform it to some domestic scene, a marshmallow roast.

"It's easier to hear the truth than see it," someone said.

He was quickly shushed.

It was mentioned that there was already talk about Tom in the community.

"It is spreading like wildfire."

"Did you see the mole above his right cheek?" one asked.

"And the supernumerary dactyl?" another added.

"His contract said they could terminate him at any time, smoke out the termite."

"Termite?"

"He's not a good fit, even if he is just trying to make space for himself."

"In the structure of our buildings on campus! They could collapse!"

"He's positively unstable. He must go!"

"Yes, his passion will hollow everything out."

"You think holocaust, the big burn swooping too close to earth. We got to get rid of him."

"I like that, 'the big burn'! You imagine him singeing us along with himself," someone added.

"Yes, he's got to go."

"I got a bad feeling that the firing is going to affect us too. The crackling sounds will drown any pretense to music."

"Flames have their own cadence, you know."

"That's not funny."

"The arrogance that thinks it can control our sensibilities with music has to be stopped. Thinks he can connect the present with our past crimes! He's the one who has something to hide. What do you think he is doing with the students?"

"Seducing them, that's what he's doing."

"Yes, they could be our own daughters, or sons!"

Noisemakers will always win when we need a sacrifice; they can always find it with the drum rolls. Who needs a music teacher for that?

Will the tears of the choir members, or his students over his firing, put the fires out? Streams of them running unabated down their cheeks, collecting in the mouths of his persecutors like deluges. Will the water level rise and drown them all?

"Someone in the administration claims he beat his wife with a broomstick."

"He probably did, he's in his own world."

"But he has no wife," another said.

"That's my point."

"He's free to do what he wants to anyone and there will be no consequences."

"More than one house was mysteriously burned in the community over the weekend."

"Jason, statistically it is only another fire. Don't try to put them together and call it a conflagration."

"But it's not his fault," someone said.

"What do you mean? The man is dangerous, I tell you. Anyone is who thinks he has the freedom to seduce his charges and produce anything he wants. He's dangerous. We have to put an end to it."

"Thank God the President already did."

In fact, I imagined it started one night from a simple bonfire I saw behind St. Mildred's when I was walking late. A group of men were gathered, big burly figures silhouetted against the flames. I thought they were up to no good. I thought of medieval Spain, and afterwards the houses started to burn in town. Unexpected fires cropping up everywhere I knew would be the result. No one would be able to explain them. The imagined increase of fires made us all pause, seek for an explanation. Feel a little guilty about our hand in the lone firing. Could that too be something the President wasn't at liberty to expose, reduced to what sparked the rest around town? Was it indeed a conflagration? Or could it be Tom himself, how he represented the singular firing, multiplied by the good citizens. Certainly it wasn't one class's response, their reprisal over the firing. Tom's spineless colleagues whose lack of courage also made up the local citizenry, who had heard his enthusiasm conducting local choirs, playing the piano, had heard the exuberance of his compositions. They had done nothing.

His firing should have sparked more of a review. But nobody spoke up, all are protecting their own turf, even though fire is no respecter of turf.

"Didn't you recognize false notes in his defending himself?"

"He mounted no defense."

"That proved he was guilty."

"But of what."

"Creativity! Not being like us, going around doing what he wanted, bursting into song everywhere."

"But do you have proof?"

"The President says she can't talk about it."

"That's a police state."

"No, Arnold, that's the war brought home."

"She's complicit in this too."

"How?"

"Her secrecy. Her political affiliation."

"He had to go so there won't be a holocaust in our community, a mass firing on campus, that's why we couldn't speak up. So he wouldn't provoke student unrest. We had to protect the student body from that man, especially the female students. Who knows, he probably lives with one! He stepped down from the Church choir and we don't even know why."

"Someone saw the light of the stained-glass window, how its eerie red colored his face. He looked positively infernal, they said. It was as if they caught him in the act, red-handed. How could there be any other conclusion?"

"But what did he do? All of us could have been colored by that same light!"

"I don't know, but it must have been something.

"But what?"

"Something he did, Buster!"

"What's that?"

"That's what I want to know."

"'We don't know yet,' the President said that, didn't she?"

"It's confidential!"

"The red light looked like he'd already caught fire when he stepped out into the sunset. The President wasn't responsible for that, was she?"

"For what?

"Firing him," someone said.

"Look, when he was conducting the choir, there were too many colors. He went too many places and that made people uneasy."

"But that enriches the music."

"Yes, with the devil's touch," someone said.

"You know he talked about the wedding parties in Iraq and Afghanistan."

"We are supposed to be academics!"

"No, we are Medievalists!"

"Yes, we can tell when someone's possessed!"

"With a name like Donne we'd all be finished if he stays around. It sounds euphonious but its terminal and Tom, he should be drummed out of town!"

"That's not music, that's a threat."

"You've heard of spontaneous combustion, haven't you? It can happen at any time."

"It's happening now, Jennifer. Because the President's brave. She sticks up for the rest of us."

"Who wants that when she can't control the blaze."

"Bank him."

"Yes, he'll get severance money."

"The President's right."

"He's gotta go."

"He could have gone up in flames himself. All that passion. She jumped on him at the right time. To save us all from conflagrations down the road and to save him from immolating himself just like those Vietnamese monks."

"I don't know what you saw at St. Mildred's, but it's not a good sign."

"They are just ordinary house fires that take place in any small town."

"Right. Just like what he's done is an ordinary rumor."

"Will you stop, Mathew."

The faculty rarely got exercise, were largely sedentary, and slow to action.

One needs to be fired for everyone's health, the faculty decided, to insure their way of life would be unmolested, not upset by disturbing notes, melodies not heard before, or suggestions of state crimes that could be set to music, not to mention their own domestic indiscretions.

Yes, melody and malady are the same thing to the unimaginative. You have to be on your guard.

"His passion was two-headed, each ignited his classes, and who knows if that would set everything aflame, an antiwar movement on campus, or late one afternoon when no one was looking there all at once the sunset took over, and we were all paralyzed by the beauty and convinced that we needed an art teacher to replace Tom. Maybe the President was on to something, the way light struck them all at once. Maybe the conflagration of dying colors was confused with the simple firing that they now didn't know how to respond."

"You can't do what you want, say what you want, without suffering the consequences. Nobody can march to their own drummer."

"Honest, folks, it's a parade we are all part of. Everything, even the truth, becomes lies if we all go our own way. He's just like Magritte's lost jockey. It may make a fine silhouette, but musically it will not work. Everyone will be running out of the theater with their hands to their ears. The race will be run without them. Poor wandering Tom! Eventually like in *Lear* he'll have to travel in disguise and live in a hovel. That's just the facts of life, folks. The President's right!"

"He'll end up in Hell," the Baptists among us insisted, mindful of his losing his position in the local church choir when nobody knew the reason. But they especially were suspicious. And what is suspicion but what there is about someone else that does not redound to our favor. We always claim it must be rooted out in others, what doesn't promote us.

"But we are a college, a secular institution," I claimed.

"Nothing's secular, son," as I got stared down.

"Nobody should have that much passion. Something's wrong with him."

"I have caught him not even looking at us," someone said, "just whistling to himself."

"Yes, just the other day he passed me as if I wasn't even there, like I was invisible."

"No, he's not a good fit, not at all!" others repeated. "The President's right."

The blaze at dawn or sunset was so brilliant you couldn't imagine a newly hired art teacher not capturing it, nor Tom not somehow disappearing into its remains so that in the clear light of day he was no longer seen at all on campus.

"He cut off his nose to spite his face, didn't respect the President enough, put his music first."

We all knew Pinocchio would catch fire eventually. Tom is just wooden kindling for the tone deaf. Yes, we cried for him, and that was by design. Our nonsupport, our tears damped the ardor we couldn't duplicate much less admire after the criticism. No, he wasn't a good fit. How could music be when it escapes us and his singing all the time got on our nerves. It would irritate anyone that didn't want to take part in his musical performance.

Bring on the art teacher, that's what we'll hire next. Appearance is everything, appearance is reality, not these escapable notes no one can understand. Bring on someone to reproduce us. Not those abstracts, but something that looks like us that we can see and appreciate and most of all understand. Bring on the realists who know how to live in the real world and not let their passion get in the way. Those that will provide a photographic reproduction of, yes, even charred remains to assure us that Tom Donne is elsewhere, truly fired.

THE HANDKERCHIEF

OULDN'T THE BLACK boxer have come out of him and given it to Alvin Dark? Alvin was the best fielding shortstop in the league, but didn't have the courage to face the pitcher, or stand in the batter's box and take his fastball right down the alley, and so his dream of entering the majors ended in legion ball.

Ingemar Johansson gave it to Floyd Patterson that first time and he took it. Lightning speed he had, and charm, a broad smile, modesty, and enough friendliness to be dubbed an Uncle Tom. There was nothing fake about Floyd either, and so from that alone, and his black namesake, Floyd Patterson, you'd have hoped the punches would have been thrown at Alvin Dark. How could Alvin Dark get the better of him if he possessed the smooth black limbs, with all the quickness, the nimbleness of his namesake? Wouldn't that be enough to scare Alvin away, and the power of Floyd's own punch that the name threw in everyone's face? No matter this Floyd Patterson was small, white, with tiny timid eyes behind the metal frames of his thick glasses.

Like the boxer he'd never laugh at anyone, never sting like a bee, float like a butterfly, transcend the ring. Could some of the speed and dedication have rubbed off on Floyd, did he have to come from Patterson, New Jersey for that?

You can't leave your name once it has stuck. Floyd Patterson of New Jersey, a small white boy with thick Coke bottle glasses in an orphanage. The wrath of the bigger, stronger boys would come down on him and he had to defer to the boxer. The quick black man with lightning-fast fists, handsome and winning.

Floyd the rodent-faced boy, no glistening off the sweaty film of his shiny black muscles under the incandescent lighting, not a heavyweight world champion, the stuff of *Ebony* magazine, on the cover of *Boxing World*, no, this Floyd was instead a punching bag.

At first the little boy fought back and was hastily beaten to a pulp. Like a pomegranate crushed underfoot, he lost a few teeth until he stopped resisting. The bloodstains on his shirt got him a special reprimand. He was squashed like a bug, stepped on, pushed, gouged, poked mercilessly.

Finally he gave up, saw it was useless to fight back, but kept the saving vision of the black boxer as he was being punished, clenched his fists in his mind. It was devastating when Johansson beat him. Floyd was crushed and took it personally, as if his own defenses had collapsed before the Swedish boxer and he was even more vulnerable around the boys. But he secretly plotted revenge, though he was never able to carry it out like the world champ who met Johansson a second time, still he was emboldened in his mind.

The night Patterson lost it was like those white handkerchiefs young women flutter in the air then have to daub their eyes with. Floyd was all sniffles, sensing his own vulnerability. And when Sonny Liston beat him, Floyd was broken. He'd come back against Ingemar, but the big bear, the ex-con was too much. Floyd tried to slug it out, like the fighter in his mind, but the power of Liston, of the more powerful Alvin Dark was too much. He saw that was impossible and he just collapsed to the chagrin of all his fans. Floyd never put up serious resistance after that and Alvin Dark was all over him whenever he pleased.

AND SO WHEN Jack heard that the Alumni Association paid six thousand dollars to get Floyd to the Homecoming, dressed him in the best of suits and tie money could buy, new Alfredo Fortini shoes, flew him and his spouse first class from their home in Shreveport, the wheels started to turn to heavyweight boxing, an association Jack had never made before with the ears pinned back in fear, the tail between the legs, to Alvin Dark, the would-be Giant who lorded over the smaller Floyd, the namesake of the famous black boxer.

Simon put his large head close to Jack and whispered in his ear in low but confident tones bursting with pride, "It's great, Jack, what we did."

"What, Simon?"

"To get some of the guys back. Over seventy-five after all these years is a record! Guys that had never been back. You know, Jack, some don't even have the money. Floyd Patterson didn't."

Jack thought of all the awards for helping people, the mania of community service, the rampant cliché "to give something back."

"Americans are a great people, Jack, so powerfully kind!"

Jack pictured uppercuts, body shots, head butts, left hooks, jabs below the belt; his own head feinted not to collide with all the goodness of Simon's enlarged cranium. Simon had been nicknamed "Head" in his youth. Jack remembered his sawed-off shotgun body exploding from the line of scrimmage against Cedar Cliff for seventy yards.

Simon could barely contain himself. He couldn't wait to tell Jack everything. He was positively bursting with the good deeds, like an Easter bunny his pockets stuffed with jelly beans, colored eggs, chocolate rabbits, yellow marshmallow chicks, or a Santa Claus with a sleigh full of presents and a full stomach that he'd have to let out another four or five notches of his black belt to accommodate all the goodness in him.

"Truly, Jack, you don't know how good it feels, the impact we can make on people's lives! You know, not everybody's well off," he chuckled. "It just does your heart good. You can't imagine the satisfaction when you see the guys return, the tangible rewards of helping less fortunate classmates, giving them the red-carpet treatment!"

Floyd down the dimly lit basement with Alvin Dark over forty years ago flashed through Jack's mind. His own ear glued to the radio, straining for every syllable from the Patterson and Johansson fight, the fight with Sonny Liston, getting his own ears boxed in by older boys and the radio taken away.

They tormented each other as youths so exquisitely, along every nerve, that it is only natural that they'd shell out six thousand dollars years later. Simon wasn't there, but something similar must have happened at Vian.

The flesh over time keeps its rawness, the flies stay away from what's preserved in our minds, the memory doesn't decay, turn flyblown, maggoty, but remains on the plate signifying the lost appetite of our treatment of each other, beaten as we were to make ourselves tender, or hard for the rest of our lives until we could pay for it, correct the horror with smiles, handshakes, the good will of a fortieth class reunion.

"Jack, you just don't know how good it makes you feel!"

Did Simon know? Intuitively he must have known. Maybe it was the hangdog look that Floyd still wore, as if he'd been beaten by Liston and Johansson on the same night. But it was the endless nights that he was forced to perform in front of the other boys.

Were they all guilty as their munificence amply testified, paying for those who never returned, sensing they were implicated in the hangdog expressions, in the cautiousness even as an adult, Floyd's pack-rattedness, all he accumulated against their assaults, secreted in his pockets for consolation. The fact that he had nothing all these years shows how he was stripped of pride, confidence, the zest for life that they were now trying to buy back.

"It makes you feel good!" Simon whispered a third time stretching out his arms as the conversation was going nowhere.

"Floyd, over here!" Simon on tiptoes waved. "Someone I want you to meet!"

Jack pictured Floyd being sent the money, his surprise at opening the envelope, his purchase of the suit, tie and shoes, and the first class tickets, renting a car for the first time, entering the luxurious suite at the Hilton.

"…that you can do something for one of the guys," as his belly shook and his eyes twinkled as they locked on Floyd walking towards them just as he had distanced himself the last forty years.

"You remember Jack, don't you Floyd!" Simon said.

"Yeah, Jack Dooley, how are you doing?" and he put out his hand.

Jack looked down at the hand and a split second later was clasping it. There was a clamminess to his limp handshake. Floyd had stopped making a fist altogether by graduation after the farm home of twenty-one boys had rendered him defenseless.

Floyd and Jack made small talk, asked where each was living, quickly ran out of conversation. Floyd was doing some kind of maintenance work, seemed a little dazed, lost in the rotunda, the high dome dedicated to the Founder of the Home, all the space above oddly connecting the past to his standing there exchanging pleasantries after the unexpected goodness of the alumni committee. It was like the unintended consequences of an electroshock that everything came back to him. Beneath the calm, his eyes had a wild focus, as if someone might appear from any of the numerous wooden doors lining the circumference of the rotunda. He couldn't grasp the leap of forty years, the newfound dignity. It could have been the surprise at the familiarity that now seemed part of the six thousand dollars.

After their conversation broke off, both wandered separately over to the easels where returnees of each class signed their names and Jack saw Floyd again.

He approached him and said out of the blue with Floyd's back to him, "I talked to Alvin a few weeks ago."

Floyd turned and gave Jack a blank stare, as if he had not registered what was said. A punch-drunk look appeared on his face, the dazed effect of the two boxers who had KO'd his namesake. Jack brought his hand up for emphasis, but Floyd didn't flinch, just blinked through the thick lenses of his glasses. Maybe it was the rope-a-dope that dazzled him, a memory of the footwork of a successor.

Through the largess of the guys, the blue silk threads shimmering in Floyd's tie, the brown pheasant design and impeccably tailored suit, through the airiness of landing in Hamburg, despite the reality of the engines, the red carpet, the rented car, the luxurious hotel room, he was transported back to the past.

The wives of the alumni committee had come with balloons and met him at the airport. But that was swiftly punctured; at the mention of Alvin darkness lowered, spicules appeared, the air was let out, the tension that always holds the present in the rosiest grip was gone and Floyd stood in the lonely glare of headlights on a country road.

"Alvin Dark, you remember him, don't you?"

For a moment Jack thought there'd be a feral animal with a snarl, the snort of the sharpest teeth, but no, Floyd's spine had been broken years ago, and he was simply preparing for another bout standing there.

"Alvin, you lived with him at Rolling Green!"

Floyd had a large chin, small eyes, and a glass jaw that jutted out precariously.

He was frozen at a standstill when Jack mentioned Alvin. It was as if the past had come armed with a powerful bat. Floyd thought he heard something shatter in the distance forecasting his appearance.

He who had flown first class, stayed in the best hotel, had suddenly come down to earth and wondered why he was there. Had he come all this way for the shock of having Alvin's name mentioned?

"Alvin, you know him, don't you?" Jack insisted.

Still there was no response.

"Alvin Dark, you lived together at Rolling Green," Jack repeated.

Floyd's eyes still had a glazed look. Alvin Dark tumbled from the recesses of all the doors that had shut behind Floyd for forty years, the screams, the banging, his young body behind them as he waited once again for Alvin to walk through.

"Oh...yes," he stumbled. He had ducked down in the basement again, been ordered to stand up after hunkering with both hands behind his head, been forced to admit he remembered.

"He's not here?" Floyd murmured.

"No," Jack said.

"No?" he repeated, looking as if he no longer knew whom he was talking to or why he was there. He looked quickly around the rotunda at the doors to see if one would open. This small man who hid behind visions of a magnificent black boxer with lightning quick moves was sluggish, more unprotected than ever.

Floyd with thick glasses was now beating back the past. He was ruminating as Jack spoke to him, his jaws worked nervously in tiny little bites, a mouth empty of all but chewing motions. He swallowed compulsively sucking air as if in the giant rotunda there wasn't enough oxygen. Once again, he was depositing stains on the salty, tear-stained towel in his mouth so he wouldn't yell.

"Oh, yes, Alvin Dark. Where...is he?" And the black hole drew him spinning, whirling back, passing out, getting up, his thighs, his hands slimy, through the glare of the bare light bulb, the boys egging him on.

His darting eyes told everything. They didn't have the wide-eyed remembrance of old times, but retreated, furtively checking if Alvin was in the rotunda.

"No, he's out in Vegas," Jack said.

Jack knew the story of the handkerchief. It leaped to mind when Simon mentioned "the generosity of the guys." How they "banded together" to help. "The guys are great," echoed in his mind.

"It gives you goose bumps," Simon had said.

The stickiness of the handkerchief stayed, the one strong spermatozoon breaking through ahead of the others to rescue Floyd from the basement at Rolling Green. The "guys are great" reverberated in Jack's mind as he shook Floyd's hand, again felt his loose grip.

"No, Alvin has a weight problem, he's a little self-conscious."

The scene repeated itself, the way Floyd was forced to do it each night into the handkerchief in front of the others. The permanent tic it left, that twitching of his left eye, the constant swallowing when he was eating nothing. He was instructed not to leave a mess, swab the last drops, keep his clothes immaculate.

Jack was introduced to Floyd's wife who stood back, spilled punch on her dress backing up that Jack quickly got out his handkerchief to wipe it off. Floyd winced as if his glasses experienced a sudden magnification.

Alvin Dark was the master of ceremonies, the baseball wannabe who hadn't the courage to face pitchers because of his fears of the hardball crushing his facial bones, crushing his temple like a paper lantern.

He was the instigator who produced the soap and had him clean off the smell, and after the second, third, and fourth rounds, had him dispose of the handkerchief.

"How is he?" Floyd asked vaguely.

"He's fine, living in Vegas, doing a lot of betting on sports."

"Maybe he'll strike it rich," Floyd said as if he lost a boxing crown he had nothing to do with outside being a punching bag himself.

Sexuality is a weighty matter with twenty-one boys and no girls around. They didn't see them for weeks.

How is it to express itself? There were no handbooks. It was only natural that they'd turn on each other.

Floyd stood there as Jack imagined an uppercut, jab, left hook decking Alvin, the real Floyd Patterson this time, who didn't need the alumni's six thousand dollars. Simon must have known.

The guys should have come to his rescue years ago. But they piled on instead. Stood back intrigued knowing Floyd was not the boxer his name evoked, but the bottom of the barrel, the SOS of his white handkerchief sticky in his hands.

"It makes you feel great what you can do for your classmates!" Simon says, swollen with pride, spit forming on his lips tiny white balls of goodness.

His tormentor should have been decked, left flat on his back there under the dim light of the basement, not become this optical illusion of a little boy standing as a broken adult decades later nervously looking around the rotunda.

Jack looked down and saw Floyd had bitten his fingernails to the quick.

"He's not back, is he?"

"Alvin?"

"No," Jack repeated. "He's worried about his weight, couldn't come but still bets on the fights," as Jack too looked at one of the doors of the rotunda to open.

CROSS COUNTRY

H E WAS ALMOST an old man, even though he had a boy who just turned eleven who was running his first year in cross country. This was State, the tournament for middle school. His boy was in sixth grade and the father was surprised at a boy so young running competitively.

Boys love to run like deer, but when they are compelled the drudgery sets in and takes all the joy out of the sport. His son had not reached that point yet. It was still a novelty and his times dropped with each race. Although he was in sixth grade the boy was the first in his middle school by the end of the season.

It was early November and the weather was in the low sixties, crisp without a speck of cloud in the sky. The lines of parked cars were endless as the man and his wife walked towards the runners.

"I feel I could compete," the father said.

They had not had cross country at the schools he attended. Track only started in his last year of high school, but he had loved to run as a child.

"I could run today!" he repeated foolishly to his wife half-listening, ignoring anything that smacked of a joke.

She was still angry at having gotten lost, and him taking over the driving and finding the way by asking. He had no shame about being lost. In fact, he imagined that was the condition of most people and why they found comfort in finish lines.

As they got closer to the colorful tents, there was a roadblock manned by young girls who demanded five dollars from each. The man paid the one young girl who with a magic marker drew a black x across the back of his hand. The man looked at the x as symbolic.

The array of tents and runners of all sizes signaled the importance of the tournament. The boy's 5K race was to start in twenty minutes.

The man and his wife approached the starting line where the loudspeaker announced middle school boys were to report in the next ten minutes.

They glimpsed Coach Jack Terry, an expansive, large man who loved children, and who appeared not to have run a day in his life. He was always huffing and puffing to catch up with the runners at turns in the race and the parents privately were afraid he'd have a heart attack.

Coach Terry shook the father's hand with the solid grip men use to establish a sense of place. The father's return squeeze confirmed this weaponless community among males.

Jack Terry looked squarely into the father's eyes as if to ferret out the exact depth of his enthusiasm and gauge how much he had relinquished the tutelage of his son.

Though the father loved his son deeply, he possessed none of the urgency of Coach Terry. He loved athletics but was careful not to push his son in anything, careful not to spoil his son's enthusiasm. He demonstrated his interest by being there, but oddly enough when his son was running, he was tightlipped and couldn't even yell out, "Come on Jason," like his wife, or Coach Terry who bellowed, "Gut it out, son!"

The father was curiously inhibited, growing up when people didn't freely show their emotions. Perhaps like a flock of pigeons in the sunlight overhead this doubled the aesthetics of what was felt. Maybe growing up in an orphanage too had placed a damper on the father's feelings.

The father was warm enough and loving to his son, hugged him regularly, but for the most part acted properly out in public. After all, other people were watching. They would chatter on about anything given the chance.

The whole world waited for unseemly behavior and so to avoid that the father was silent; for who knows what might be revealed. That became the main thing, not to reveal yourself, keep close to the vest. Who can calculate the laughter that might follow were anything unseemly to surface? And if this happened in front of one's own son, it would be withering. Who could abide the laughter, the shame? You might even find out something about yourself that's dangerous, something that once revealed you couldn't suppress. Then who'd be there to put the cat back in the bag? Heavens knows, some deep dark recess could be illuminated that you'd spend the rest of your life atoning for. It'd open a Pandora's box, or maybe there'd be an immediate arrest, permanent incarceration, so you had to keep your hands to yourself, keep your ideas private, keep things under wraps. Give away nothing and be the perfect spectator.

As a child brought up a couple of decades after the Lindbergh abduction, children were warned not to talk to strangers. There was something implicitly frightful about adults. This dampened the father's personality and he kept his hands pocketed around people and his opinions to himself. He remembered too the charge of playing pocket pool by his scoutmaster. In fact, sometimes he didn't know where to place his hands. It was such a balancing act. Most would say the father had no visible personality, though he could squeeze the proffered hand in a handshake hard enough.

Dave, the father, was nondescript and blended in with the other parents. The gray in his hair bothered him, but he stood there straight with enough dignity that his little boy was not at least embarrassed. Certainly he was not proud either, for you can't try to impress a son too much, or he'll turn on you. The father learned this with his over-the-head foul shots in basketball. The boy called him a "show off." Though he told his mother when his father made ten foul shots in a row, but mostly the father was lackluster, fading into the woodwork. In fact, he stood there little different than the tall trees in the background, as mute as their dried leaves. Of course, he didn't have the stature of the oaks; he was more like the stunted yellow birch in his own backyard that was always peeling.

Dave had never gone anywhere athletically when he was a youth, but perhaps now following his son he was making up for that. His son sometimes threw his body against his father or buried his head in his lap and he'd stroke his hair. When he was sick the father seemed intimately to know to do that. But as his boy had grown a few inches this didn't seem to happen as often.

After shaking hands with Coach Terry, the parents stood awkwardly silent looking at the hundreds of runners, searching for their son in the crowd. The brilliant colors, the sheer energy and power of youth electrified the autumn air.

Coach Terry left, then drifted back to the father who said, "I guess it'd be nice if Jason placed in the first half."

"Yes, it would be," the coach said.

"Three minutes to starting time," the announcer said. "Line up, runners!"

The boys toed the line, holding their breath until the gunshot sounded when all five hundred runners took off.

The next moment the runners were stopped dead in their tracks with a second shot. Someone had fallen and the rules required the race be restarted.

The parents looked at each other as if to voice a complaint but said nothing and the runners lined up again.

The gun went off, and then again, a second shot stopped them. There was murmuring through the onlookers that someone had gotten a false start, but this time the parents were told to step back and give the runners room.

The runners lined up again and the gun required no other shot. The beauty of all the colorful uniforms, of so many pumping legs, gave the crowd a shot of adrenalin as it hurried towards key junctures where the runners doubled back. Many parents didn't know the course but followed everyone else like clouds of gnats.

Runner after runner passed until finally the parents saw their son. He was the first for his school, but around midpack. Second was the tall boy Josh whose mother was the assistant coach for the girls who were training for high school Regionals the following week. Josh was just behind Jason. He was in eight grade and long and lanky with a shock of blond hair over his blue eyes. The much smaller Jason had been passing Josh in recent races and Josh's legs had begun cramping up.

Jason's mother spotted the tall Josh first, and then saw her son just ahead of him. She then called out to one of the last runners from her son's school, "Come on, Christopher!"

After the runners passed, the parents made their way to a lookout on the next leg and saw the leaders' confident, machinelike strides apparently achieved from years of long practice.

"They look really good," the father said to the mother.

"Yes, they do."

Then after three minutes or so their son came.

"Come on, Jason!" his mother yelled.

But the father couldn't yell out; a native shyness, the unseemliness of any open enthusiasm hampered him as he watched in silence his son pass.

Why? he thought to himself. Why was he so inhibited? What was blocking him from yelling words of encouragement to own son? It'd only be right, natural, but still he left it to his wife.

Was there something unseemly about displaying emotion? Did something in his childhood interfere, the friendliness of a stranger at the bus station in Philadelphia who asked him up to his apartment, or Father Gallagher's pass at him at DeAngeles restaurant when he sought him out for spiritual guidance, or the scoutmaster in the orphanage who shared his sleeping bag with the other boys?

Yet he had no bitterness even though his personality had gone underground, had deflected the passes of adults without apparent scars. But what is the personality doing, never having the courage to yell from the crowd? There must be something wrong with him when he came to think of it. He was quiet too at his girl's basketball and softball games. Never once did he yell, "Let's go Cindy!"

He was mute. Something was obviously missing. His wife got angry at the referees, but he just sat there the like a block of wood. "Dull Dave" the other parents must have labeled him. He'd be the last to bring down a Goliath. That's why I hesitated to give his name, a name that should amount to something if biblical history is any precedent. Otherwise, why call him Dave?

He should get back in his hole, not waste space not cheering his son on this beautiful fall day. His son probably didn't even see him, and certainly never heard him.

Sometimes Dave thought Coach Terry avoided him for being such a mouse. Little did anyone know he could disappear in the middle of the field they were crossing right into a hole, a regular Alice, field mouse par excellence. He certainly wouldn't be missed by his son, or any of the other runners.

As his son passed the last time and his mother shouted out words of encouragement, Jason turned his head slightly, but Dave wasn't sure he saw him.

Maybe he was eyeing stones on the ground for his father, the rounded ones to protect him from the Goliath of all the other runners with their millipede legs, or from feelings his father surely had but could not show to anyone.

He'd never be his son's hero. He wanted biblical stature, but had almost no musical ability; his son even tried to teach him a song on the piano he had picked up from his sister's playing, but Dave couldn't learn it. He just looked on in amazement at his son's ability. He was the head of no tribe, not even of his own household where his wife ruled the roost.

He taught high school where his students were just short of throwing paper wads at him and playing jokes on him. His voice was so low and self-effacing. Where he found the courage to shake Jack Terry's hand so strongly even he didn't know. Mostly he didn't like to shake hands for the germs involved. He'd hold his hand down at his side away from his body afterwards, his skin absolutely crawling at the touch of another human being. His wife, too, didn't like to be touched lately. She left Jack high and dry, sometimes wondering what marriage was for.

"Touch, ugh, call the police, please, right this moment!"

"Will you keep your hands to yourself," she'd yell at him.

"Don't touch yourself," she'd yell to their son. "Get out of my sight, stop licking me. Go to your room, now!"

Did someone say that to Dave when he was growing up? He didn't remember.

In fact, he didn't know why he was so unassertive, so willing to take a back seat in everything. Why was he chagrined at human contact? His daughter hugs every other boy in the school but doesn't hug him. She's too old to hug now, he thinks

He never criticizes his son, only tells him to touch himself in private when his sister cries out, "Pervert!"

The parents followed the runners congregating around the finish line to receive their awards. The first twenty got medals, and the next eighty ribbons.

Dave and his wife searched for their son, then finally ran into the coach who said Jason finished first for their school. Dave didn't know what to say knowing Jason was only among the first 250 runners. The parents then spotted their son with Josh, the tall eighth grader. He was quiet as usual and pale.

"It was a tough race," Dave said to both boys, but Josh didn't seem to answer.

Jason then asked his mother if he could get a shirt with the meet logo on it, and Ida said yes.

Dave wanted to go and eat, but instead Jason trotted off to get in line. Dave went over to Coach Terry and told him they planned to eat and return for a three o'clock race. Both parents went separately to look for Jason, but he wasn't in line.

They then came upon an enclosure with a small trailer. Coach Terry and two medics were with two boys; Josh who was sitting in a chair was beside a tow-headed boy. Both boys were pale.

Josh was shaking with chills.

Ida, who was a nurse, bent down and took his pulse. It was 120. She said it should have slowed by now.

Coach Terry asked Josh if he was all right, but he barely answered. He then got on the phone with Josh's mother.

In the shade of the trailer Josh sat with the other boy. The coach was trying to get him to drink liquid, but one of the medics said, not if he doesn't want to.

Josh sat there shaking and Dave thought he needed touched, but there were the two medics and his wife, who had just taken his pulse, and the outspoken Coach Terry whose voice boomed with authority whenever he spoke.

The one medic was asking Josh how he was. The other boy's condition stabilized enough so his coach came and walked him away.

Dave, biblical rock thrower, expert at sling shot, at the harp, stood there misnamed, King of nothing, with not even a voice that had the courage to yell encouragement to his own son. He stood there half-miffed at his wife for indulging their son with another shirt so they couldn't go eat and watched the four adults looking at the shivering boy and asking if he was okay.

Josh appeared too weak to get up and walk, and trembling all over hardly answered.

Dave looked and could barely keep from doing something but being a mouse, who hardly made it across the field without falling into a hole in the ground, did nothing.

What did he know about the tunnels, the crevasses in human behavior, the danger spots, or alterations in body temperature? The cooling system in his own house was a constant challenge. He'd rather call the HVAC man than get involved with the chills in the body of another human being, not to mention his own home where temperatures were controlled by others. Everyone was always too cold or too hot, and his preferences were rarely consulted.

Stay above ground, don't let out a peep to give yourself away, you sorry mouse, and despite all the impulses in the world, do nothing, Davy boy. That's your style.

Finally the two medics lifted Josh's chair into the sun.

Still Josh didn't look up and continued to tremble uncontrollably even in sunlight, hanging his head on his chest.

Finally Dave said, he couldn't help himself, to his surprise at even opening his mouth, "Do we have an extra sweatshirt?"

I have one Coach Terry answered.

The coach got it out and Dave draped it over the front of Josh's body and then suddenly without thinking he reached out and rubbed Josh's arm up and down as if with the protection of the shirt it was all right now to get some warmth back into the boy's body saying, "You'll be okay."

Dave then touched Josh's head and rubbed his hair back and forth past all the warnings about strangers in his childhood, past all the bus stations he was approached at as a youth, past the scoutmaster sharing his sleeping bag, or priests propositioning him in restaurants, past the twinges of self-consciousness when he himself placed his own hands under his son's blankets at night to adjust the sheets so the cotton covered him between the blankets. He'd feel self-conscious in his own house, with his own child whom he loved, sometimes even touching bare skin to cradle his whole body closer to the pillow to rest his head, afraid he'd awake and suspect something. He'd kissed his daughter in her sleep when she was younger more than she'd ever be kissed by anyone in her lifetime.

Past all this Dave ran his hand through Josh's blond hair and onto his slumped body to stop the trembling. Up and down and around his shoulders, he tried to warm the distraught boy.

"You're gonna be all right," Dave kept saying as he rubbed his arm.

He readjusted his sweat shirt that started to drop exposing his bare skin, then asked Josh if he could put it on and Josh did while Dave continued rubbing his body.

"Just relax and you'll be okay," Dave said.

One of the medics now said breathe in and out.

Dave sensed instinctively that the boy needed contact plain and simple, uncomplicated by the thousand and one prohibitions of a litigious society.

He remembered being in tears over the shoes that pinched his feet as a boy of eight in West Virginia waiting for the bus to Clarksburg. He only wanted for his mother to hold him, instead of making such a fuss over his cousin, Betty Lee.

"His mother's coming," Jack Terry said again.

But Dave continued touching the boy.

"He's going to be all right," he said, to reassure Josh.

"Do you feel better?" and Josh nodded as the trembling slowed.

The four adults watched Dave laying his hands on the boy after a lifetime of warnings and feeling awkward around children, youths, even his own flesh and blood. Fearing that he'd discover a latent desire in himself reaching out to comfort others. He forgot all that now as he ran his hands over Josh's body and the hair on his head to soothe the youth, remembering how the sound of the roots had calmed him. Everything he'd ever heard about child abuse and inappropriate touching disappeared under the watchful eyes of the others, though it was uppermost in his mind even when everyone was absent, alone in the privacy of his own home, or in his children's bedrooms. His timid personality didn't help either, nor did his not yelling out words of encouragement even to his own children. The very last thing in the world would be to touch someone, but now that was all gone, brushed away so simply and surely. Where did the certitude come from? How had he so thoroughly left everyone motionless while he broke through barriers that had been built over a lifetime of strictly observing social taboos?

Dave had brought down the frowning giants of his childhood that ruled even his adult life as somehow untouchable, preempting the medics, the nurse, the blustery coach. A stranger in this boy's life, field mouse that almost didn't make it to the finish line himself, who could have been permanently disabled by the hole in the ground and not have returned even to his family, but he made it, though his anxieties had almost gotten the better of him, feeling so small and about to be swallowed up by the excitement around him, by the shame at not cheering his son on, showing feelings that everyone has, for we are all a cauldron of emotions just waiting to bring comfort and love, not always best identified by the noise we make, but sometimes more effective than anyone realizes if we'd give ourselves half a chance. But that is usually taken away by the vociferations of others and our own lack of courage, by the yellow streak running down our backs more concentrated than the sunlight ninety-three million miles away. Dave had smothered his fears to touch the young boy.

"You are going to be all right," he said and remarkably the boy stopped shaking and grew calm and the color reappeared in his cheeks until the medic who had been joking and who must have felt left out asserted himself, fearing his position was being usurped by Dave. He told Josh to stand up and looked at his pupils and shook his head.

"We'll take him to the hospital," he said suddenly.

At that Josh sat down and started shaking all over again, worse than before, looking immediately weaker and pale, as tears now ran unchecked from both his eyes.

Someone produced a towel to daub Josh's cheeks.

"You'll be all right," Dave said trying to calm him as he glimpsed the golf cart that had already arrived. The coach and medic lifted Josh up into the cart.

"Coach, you better go too," the medic said as the machinery of society was once again in full motion.

"I'll tell his mother we're taking him to the hospital," Coach Terry stuttered.

Dave and Ida had forgotten about their own son.

Though Josh was gone, Dave felt he had crossed over from a country where most of the population keeps their hands to themselves.

He understood all the misspent opportunities and how they multiply by each person in society, but he had caught a glimpse of what might be if we don't all stand around like bumps on a log, even though there are always hospitals to be taken to and emergency rooms testifying to the fact that we don't touch each other enough.

JOCKEY UNDERWEAR

WHO CAN IMAGINE being in the saddle? Its soft leather contours, the supportive rump, the smooth horn you can hold onto. The vast security that almost contrasts with the random stains to white cotton, as if you'd been splashing through mud, or battling branches and upsetting the yolks of newly laid eggs with the reinforced supports.

That the underwear lets you breathe is the claim, and so you imagine riding breakneck on an unshorn heath, but once in the woods air is trapped.

And the hemorrhoids the underwear absorbs with a double thickness of cotton at the crotch almost allows you to bleed with freedom and no longer worry about your clothing. You are naturally sedentary, so being up in the saddle should be natural.

The mount beneath you takes all this in stride. You pull the reins on her when you feel too much bleeding, as if the bit in her mouth, the bridle, acts as a ligation on your own backside that hugs the saddle as you squat rounding the bend.

And your other body processes are squeezed off as you get deeper into the heat of the race. In fact, you forget the staining and imagine instead the prize. The beautiful girl at the end with her horseshoe of roses to drape round you in the winner's circle.

You feel beads of sweat forming as the elastic band hugs your waist. You bend lower on her, hug her neck, clasp her belly with your thighs, spur her on to keep up with the rest.

So proud of her are you, the blond mane blowing in your face, the rich chestnuts, the stainless white teeth when she whinnies, pleased at her morning sugar cube she noses for in your pocket. You try not to notice the green bubbles, the alfalfa stains, and concentrate on the pink beauty of her lips and the gray of her velvety nostrils, those hot air vents that raise the temperature all around her.

In fact, you are even half-attracted to the comforting warmth of her manure as the steam rises in the peaceful atmosphere of the stable. It makes you think of your white underwear, and her teeth playfully pulling at them, pacifying the fears you have about yourself. You always marveled at the continent types who could wear white pants. Though you'd have to admit you never got a close look at them, since the brightness always kept you away.

How the whitest teeth and underwear come together always bemused you as you hug her. But the next moment you are being passed on the outside!

"No one is going to pass us, girl!"

She's the prettiest, the fastest, you think, ever since you began wearing Jockey underwear, ever since you've starved yourself to settle atop of her, light as a feather, as if no one were there, only someone light-boned, barely attaining puberty, a wisp of a lad to give her all the added power she needs to keep up with the rest and surpass them down the stretch.

She is being passed on the turn and you "giddyup" for all you are worth, lean into her, become one with her powerful withers, her haunches. Like the most beautiful suspension bridge her vertebrae enables you finally to travel to yourself. You don't want to use your switch, but know she likes it from time to time to show that you are the master.

She's being passed and so you, bloody hemorrhoids aside, yellow stains aside, embrace her and kick her, dig down into her fur, putting out of your mind all thoughts of alfalfa gasses; your rowels prick her distended belly, her forelegs kick faster and her haunches pound the track numbing her to the pain in her sides. You don't know if you are getting through to her, for she's not yet making headway. Both horses for a moment seem at a standstill.

The horse on the outside is now nosing further ahead. You kick her for dear life. You can feel the skin being scraped raw, breaking, the fissures deepening. The blood in your own backside is oozing through the cotton shorts. You can feel the stain spreading. Your shoes seem slippery, your legs wet with her body fluids. She too must be bleeding, yet you keep kicking her, hugging her closer.

"Come on, girl, come on!" burying your face in her mane, like a tight fistful of lice you cling to her, hug her neck, her belly, until you are one magnificent galloping unit.

"Flee, girl, flee," you yell to her, champing down through her fur to her skin to draw blood. Love bites that'll get you both to the finish line pop into mind! You'll be embarrassed for her neck.

Suddenly the strain, the tension atop her causes you to start to bleed faster, staining beyond your underwear. You imagine the saddle darkening, a pool of blood.

She must only be a filly, so why are you putting her through all of this? Why does she have to win each time, why do you have to hug her so for your personal victory? What's won? Why a jockey anyway? For another day of imaginary protection in soft white underwear?

There is something lost about you in this underwear business, like Magritte and his jockey miles from a track racing through the woods. Why do you always have to end up with people cheering, nosing out the competition? Why can't there be something grazing about wearing stainless white underwear? Something boll weevil, at least. Or a flower print instead of sordid stains on pure white, the fascist yellows, browns, reds that plague most all of us throughout the day with an unspeakable authority all their own.

But the alternative travels in your blood and has you going into training, hidden in a camp in the Catskills in upstate New York with a whole entourage just when you are walking around on the street alone. You clench your fists over it, think of the lost protection of Jockey underwear. You are already sparring, worrying about the freedom between the legs, the dangling between jabs and uppercuts, the enormous vulnerability to low blows, not to mention the escaping body fluids. Where will they go when they trickle unhindered down your legs and are not absorbed by the soft cotton from Egypt? There will be no leather saddle to hide in for support, no belly to hug or kick to stabilize your own bloody backside. You will be alone on your own two feet before all those people. Not on a race track, but in a ring having to rely on your clenched fists and the lard on your chin, cheeks, and forehead to deflect blows, on the desperate whisperings of your trainer.

At least you won't be sitting, except for spells between rounds, and so the strain of bleeding should not affect you. The cuts on the opponent's face will draw attention away from the stains. But you know the tight fists can't be good. The sphincters will suffer after all, and you'll have to relax eventually, continue the leaking yellow incontinence you've had all your life, the bubbly gases that escape from the foods you've eaten, so demonstrably visible underwater. In the end you prefer the saddle, even if Jockey underwear doesn't let your anatomy breathe.

Boxer shorts you fear will give you entirely too much freedom, not to mention the added strain from always having to duck to avoid punches.

THE TYPEWRITER

T HE TRIP TO New Orleans was delayed due to being nearly beaten to death.

He had a feeling she might still be there but didn't check. Her clothes were laid out on the bed in such neat piles for the trip, like his mother used to pack, arranging the loneliness of her life for hours, days even.

She never made it because she was *nearly beaten to death by the idiot who was to watch my dog.*

Idiots sweep down out of nowhere in the night, even the ones she placed enough trust in to watch her dog, the dog she said she saved in the car wreck risking her own life.

"The bitch likes men," she said as the dog pawed at Jack's pant leg and then curled up on the bed.

"She's afraid of rain," she said.

Jack always thought her treatment of her small dog was the best part of her, revealed a warmth and kindness she otherwise hid.

The fact that the guy was an idiot reminded Jack of his mother. "Bozo" was her Italian boyfriend. She never had respect for him either. He was her tool. Maybe the idiot sensed her contempt and answered with his fists, with the strength we all have to relieve ourselves. Idiot is primed for sex. The naked charge through closed doors turns into violence at the fickle contempt.

"Not now, not now," but idiots don't take no for an answer.

It is obvious how men take the word 'NO,' she writes.

Clarissa must know how open the second letter is. The "N" stands guard but only on one side. To get to the point of saying "No" lets her guard down. You'd think contempt would be a ring of sentries, but it is mere papier-mache. It provides all the structure in the world along with the rings in the ears, nose, lips, but all that is in the end no defense at all.

"No" inflames the passions, erects the obstacles, doesn't have the easy access of "Yes" that has us falling asleep right afterwards, and sometimes before, losing interest and instead drooling on our pillow.

"No" gives the world meaning, establishes value, proscription, promises a treasure at every turn.

"Yes" makes everything too close for comfort. We struggle for fresh air.

She writes that she hopes Jack is in New York or going there; at the funeral she recommended he attend while she was busy with her own *nearly beaten to death*. She then adds how she dislikes asking a favor, but she is *struggling for a bit of sanity*.

She needs cleaned up after the attack; he imagines the clothes so neatly piled were swept off the bed. The luggage is in disarray. The apartment furniture is overturned where Jack stood only a few hours before. Her hair she had done just for the trip is mussed up.

She hadn't wanted to see him for almost two years. He had dropped in and couldn't get over how good she looked after all this time. He thought he'd find her wasted on drugs, but she had gained weight, wasn't stick thin. Her eyes were not sunken; there were no indigo circles. She wasn't at death's door.

"I gained twenty pounds," she said.

She needed assistance finding an *old typewriter with round keys*, but that functions. She can't *pay a lot*, she wrote.

He wants to write to her that if getting an old typewriter will stand in her way she shouldn't be writing. That's when she said she's *struggling for a bit of sanity*. The keyboard she thinks will do it. It'll stave off the attack after it's taken place, remove the repeated humiliation, give the memories the unreality of fiction. The smooth pounding of the keys will remove the incoordination of his fists, his nails raking her flesh, the belt he tried to get around her wrists. She dreams of the machine evoking a rhythm of ideas charting every movement of the attack into her own recollection. The keys aligning the letters represent the bodies responding to her touch, unlike the crude attempts at sex, smothered in violence, the crash to the floor, the "idiot's" hands at her throat. She likes women too doubling the violation of the man's hands on her, his trying to enter.

"Not this time, Buddy!"

She likes men though she warded off Jack earlier in the evening.

She tries to analyze herself, get help. She visited another Jack in Texas, her therapist. He agreed to see her for a week of intensive therapy. She saw him but "he couldn't fix me. I am too damaged," she said.

She claimed this Jack, the visitor earlier in the evening, recipient of the email, was damaged too, just like her.

He had never thought about it, at least to the extent that he needed repair. But thinking you are damaged makes you produce something. He told her she wanted self-pity.

She denied that. Her exterior is so tough, because inside she's a pussy cat, so kind to her little dog, kind once to Jack. Outside her language is withering, vile, salty, as if there were wounds in every sentence. She was going to do "a hanging" once for some friends in Lexington. "It's sadomasochistic art," she explained. Her own universal wounds appeared every time she passes the city road crews with their truckfuls of salt to melt ice on the roads, spreading them to make her feel the pain. The salt gives traction in people's lives, but she needs to feel more than anyone ever felt because her sister got killed in an automobile accident. She turned to drugs and alcohol, to beatings to dull that pain when up popped the typewriter.

Can you help me?

He was always a stationery person, using heavyweight paper and thick-nibbed fountain pens. The machine stands between the horror of the beating and ushers it to the background. All writing is theater that depresses just what it doesn't want to bring out in real life.

Can you get me a typewriter? Her bouts of creativity came between what happened to her sister. A part of her was already dead she insisted. She was a zombie.

I can't pay a lot.

The typewriter sits on the bruise precariously balanced. A Salvador Dali irrelevance that tells of every purple discoloration without accompanying fingers, the existence even of the closed fist even before the first keys are struck. Their rhythm is better than sex, than the black and blue marks; the nails that rake the white skin Jack discovered she was so proud of, and her "green" eyes, she corrected him that very evening, were "not blue." Her vanity knew no bounds.

Our appearance hangs suspended like an albatross. It is too big to walk with, to carry every day through life, and flying is out of the question. Coleridge's bird that could only exist in the poem passed into real life. Clarissa was now wearing it. Her appearance was like Baudelaire's bird awkward on land. Beautiful skin and hair just fixed for the trip, the green eyes ready to go. Wow them in New Orleans, and she looked rested just before packing. She ushered Jack out about eleven. The clothes on the bed made him not want to disrupt her preparations, a life in order, all the pleasure of an anticipated trip.

"I'm leaving in the morning," she told him the Saturday he dropped over unexpectedly.

But now the clunky typewriter was sitting nowhere. As a request. He was charged with getting it to release behind the keyboard what had happened that night, shrouded in speculation of the events after he left, or had he left? Do any of us leave, or are we not in the end constant shadows of each other?

All the ones I find in antique shops are dead. Code words again. She'd be dead by thirty she had predicted. Was she symbolic of the nonfunctional typewriters?

Was that a way of getting back at the fate that took her sister in the car crash? Every week she visits the cross she erected by the highway, maintained with fresh flowers. Once Jack came upon her in the dark by the side of the road. She'd just come from the cross.

"No, I don't need a ride, my car is just over there."

This circumlocutious way of saying the trip to *NOLA was delayed due to nearly being beaten to death* threw Jack. The keys are not pounded, there is no rhythm. Neither with the idiot as she is all bruises for resisting him.

The typewriter must bring it out, or *if I don't write, I'm going to implode, explode.*

She said she can't use her computer *because my head injuries this time worsened my vision more so than the wreck.*

The idiot hit her in the head.

That'll do it, smacks in the head and under the chin, that's where he left the biggest bruise. Did he use his fist there? Is that what snapped her head back and worsened the vision? Will the typewriter alleviate that?

"Just get the typewriter, just get the typewriter," he imagines the urgency of her request.

We think art will accelerate the healing, capture the horror on paper, alleviate the pain and humiliation. Scorning help is one way. Intensifying the pain is another.

Please do not pop by unannounced.

Just like the idiot popped her in the chin, Jack is not to come by. Pictures are enough. Getting hit is bad enough, but the shame of having it observed. Who wants that? Jack has always been impressed by the dying pet retreating to the sack of potatoes in the basement, but she's not there yet. She wants a typewriter.

Did Jack bring on the attack? He remembered her peering through the blinds for someone she thought she heard outside when they were talking books.

The idiot worsened her vision. Jack imagined the uncoordinated bumping of her head on the floor, the sheer animal urgency. Even a little tap can alter eyesight, much less real bumps.

She was so glad he was there. She showed him her altar. The many candles for her sister. She took death hard, everyone's death. She suddenly flared up that he should go to the funeral.

She showed him pictures of her parents.

"That's the one time my mom held me. Usually Clarice got to sit in her lap."

She showed Jack pictures of the saints, an assortment of devotional paraphernalia. It showed a whole life of remembrance that informed the present. Uncles, cousins, grandparents, friends, every death she chronicled.

"Elizabeth's spirit will be around for seven to ten days, so you have to go to the funeral," she urged by way of commanding him, as if there were something elusive about her own sister's funeral.

I'll attach some pretty pictures, the email said. *He made me a real doll.*

Jack had to download the attachments. There they were. Two head shots. The first was a side shot of her face, her ear and jawline, part of the mouth and her eye partially closed. The shame as white as her mottled skin, her jawline harsher without make-up. Four scratch marks extended from her ear covering half the cheek to the corner of the mouth. Multiple bruises were on her neck and face. In the next picture her chin is held up to supply maximal visual exposure so you can only see the mouth and part of the nose. There is a large plum-colored bruise just off center under her chin. Splotches of red suggest the hemorrhaging provided a visible sequence to the effort to control the head. The marks all over the neck clearly show the struggle to cut off her breathing. The third and fourth pictures are of the backs of her right and left hands outstretched separately in a sink. They both have bruises down from the wrists and one above the wrist. The right hand has a tattoo bracelet. Both are severely mottled showing a struggle. They are splay reminding you of claws, the extension of the bones of a lizard.

He made me a real doll.

The perverted fantasy and the sheer unreality of the comment disgusts Jack. He is nauseated by the realization that the attack turned her into something she wanted. The irony of what she looks like without her make-up makes him dizzy. The sheer nudity of skin violated shows the blood came to the surface time and again, and the specious reality of bruises she's already turning into something else horrifies him. The rag doll she swung as a child catches up to her. As horrifying is that she won't answer his calls, just sends the pictures.

Dolls fall off every shelf every day in every young girl's room across the country, get bruised falling down. Bruises are expected. What dolls want, dreaming, just sitting there in rooms unmolested, and no matter how many piercings through the ears, lips, nose, tongue, they are no substitute. She's become instead a cutter. The scars on her chest she showed Jack and on her arms, the longitudinal ones where she meant business and the horizontal attention getters. Then the tattoo covering her whole shoulder, a creature of some sort with wings and talons, a severe beak and large mounted eye making her upper arm a strut. She knew early on her twin sister was the doll in the family while she only aspired to flight.

She continues, *Don't get all weirdly noble or concerned on me and come by.* Jack can't even fathom *weirdly noble.* Yes, she knows we're all the same. With two words she threw him into the pit, the pendulum moves ever closer to his chest for all the imagined wrongs in the penal colony we all inhabit. Jack's as guilty as innocence can be. It doesn't matter he's not caught red-handed. Everyone knows it. Jack does too. The guilt oozes out of him like body secretions, exudates, everything is poised to run, we strangle it to keep it back, pin it down, hone our righteous indignation. It makes us wince, what we don't have a stomach for; we grow outraged for what others do. Noble! Who do you think you are, all self-righteous? You are just like them. The rats come with their tweaking, pushing their pink noses, sucking the fetid air to tell you. Noble as a sewer. Why go on a crusade? I don't need it, Jack tells himself. Did she sense the complicity right off? Is that why she emailed him the pictures, to make him feel guilty too? Did he? Was it shared drugs, a deal gone sour? Was there something Jack didn't know about? They must have been in league. Not noble but a peasant taking what he wants, that's what she can't get through her thick skull.

You're the same, Jack, something whispered in his ear. You stupid Jack-o'-lantern, the same burning eyes, the same bad teeth and collapsing mouth. Your milksoppish concern gives you away. You shouldn't have that name. You're not a lumberjack. You can't chop him down; you'd expose your own trunk. She's in his branches if not his arms. Don't you see that? *Don't get all weirdly noble or concerned* is meant to take the wind out of your sails, make the axe impossible to pick up, instead spikes the tree you want to cut down.

Jack's not noble, nor a lumberjack. How can he clean up this mess if he has only half the story?

Jack knew the police should be notified, or she should at least talk to him. He calls and she doesn't answer.

The next day she hangs up twice. Did he do something he doesn't remember?

Was it him? Is there something he doesn't know about, but she sees clear as day? Is *weirdly noble* confined to a castle. Jack's old-fashioned. He doesn't know beatings are de rigueur, more commonplace than he realizes. Mock-beatings too. Did it turn real? He winces, gets angry, frustrated, feels left out. *Don't get all...concerned* echoes from the email. She's on top of things. Yeah, tell me another one.

Jack left her that evening and hugged her on the way out multiple times. He was gentle but clasped her to him and she hugged him back just as tight. She had offered him something to drink earlier in the evening, all the catching up they had to do, but he didn't take it. She went out to the kitchen between cigarettes and drank straight from the bottle of whiskey, then came in and sat down beside him and continued talking. He thought she was showing off, acting for him. No, she doesn't take so many pills, she said when he cautioned her. She likes alcohol too much, she said. He had called her an actress before. She had told how she shocked her teachers and classmates. But despite the whiskey she acted with decorum.

"You better go," she then said as he held her in his arms. "I have to leave tomorrow."

That's when he stood up, wanted to kiss her on the mouth, but she pulled back and turned her head. He kissed her on the cheek, then the neck, and she kissed him a peck on the cheek.

He pulled her towards him with all the arm strength he could muster considering the short distance between their bodies, clamped her to him, felt her body through the silk robe.

He tried to touch her, but she pushed his hand away.

"I'll hit you," she said, "if you touch me there," and he tried again but she pushed him away.

"What a waste," Jack said. "You know, I'd like to touch every inch of your body," he said.

"I am off all sex," she said. "I can't handle it."

"Well, I had a nice time. It's been great seeing you."

"It's been more than excellent," she said.

He hugged her again hard. And she did him, pulled him towards her.

"But you got to go," she said.

"Okay," he said, and at the open door they stood and still talked. She looked out and then at him.

He felt her loneliness but didn't know how to penetrate that save with his intellect. She was smart, so living was never easy.

He stepped down, trying to go, but they hugged multiple times.

"Such a waste," he repeated.

"Yeah, well. I can't handle it now," and so Jack went home and took care of things like she suggested.

I'm grand, really, and armed and batty and pissed, her email read.

She had put in words that meant and didn't what they said. The sheer stupefying opposite of "grand" he could barely stomach. All the inflated insincerity of it, the crashing opposite left everything in miniature and Jack revolted not knowing what to do. His very helplessness between the false inflation of "grand" punctured something in him. But she recouped after the sheer disappointment of the loss of her sister, walking into the middle of Jack's class one day, the same one her dead sister had taken, with her black leather and chains, and strolled to the back of the room. Jack was shocked that they looked so alike. She even got the job her sister had just to soak up that atmosphere. But then the bravado of *armed and batty and pissed*. She had told him of once attacking friends with a knife, and the respite from turning the blade on herself, she had the scars from that.

Her leather and chains and all the piercings and getting the tattoos was the best part. She relished the tattoo artist's needle, and the pounding women take from men, the sheer machinery of the act, the soreness for days, then the awful pretense of pleasure they are so tight-lipped over. The men were always stranger no matter how well she knew them, no matter how many times she was used; it was always a new aggression, but the violence of the act got old and drove her to drink, pills, to a lower self-esteem, to women, finally to art, flowers around the house, and now to old typewriters. *Writing will keep me from imploding, exploding, get me one*, she says.

I just thought I'd take a minute to ask, she prefaced her request. Yes, she took a minute out for Jack after almost two years. A precious minute it was that Jack would not be answered as to what happened.

"Look, don't bother me, just produce the machine," Jack heard.

I don't like being in anyone's debt at the moment, she wrote.

Did Jack go home after all, leave her standing in the doorway, or did she let him back in. Did he force his way?

Is Jack the idiot, who can't take no for an answer? All men are, headbutting to gain entrance, using their fists, their nails to rake a woman's cheek, strangling them to get what they want, popping them with uppercuts to the chin. Wasn't it him, or his proxy? Someone to avenge all the humiliations of refusals. Did he headbutt her scrambling on the floor to get what he wanted, or did he hit her outright? He thought when he left maybe she wanted him to just take her. After all she told him she had been raped twice by the same man as a teenager. The authorities had done nothing then too. And when she'd done it with Jack the first time she was rough at first, as if she wanted to be manhandled herself, subdued just like she was doing to him. He was tender though, until he got them in position.

Did she need to be violated? Was that the only way it was acceptable?

Jack felt guilty. Was his short-term memory going? Did the email express his other side, the caring, the loving concern of the *weirdly noble*? Was that her way of exonerating him, establishing that he was not like all the others, was not there that evening, but a shoulder to comfort her even though she refused his calls? Could he have composed the email to himself? Sick individual that he was! Is this the way to settle being at odds with himself? Did she know him deep down, quickly identify the idiot in all men and that's all they were, indistinguishable from each other, and the definition of his upper body was not his alone; the strong shoulders, chest muscles, the visible abs were tools of all men. *Weirdly noble* aside, *concerned* aside, we all want just what the idiot did. Character is a false façade. Underneath we are all the same, it's one muscle. But the violence, the hitting her was baffling, but who knows what might escalate. Did she scratch him, bite him, hit him in the balls, laugh in his face? Big bad Jack. Did he have it in him? Did it come out that night? Did the whiskey bring it on? The free, uninhibited conversation, her extraordinary intelligence could go anywhere, and his was not off limits either. Did that all make for a brew whose fumes made him forget what happened, forget himself, made her forget it, hence her email to him, Jack, the perpetrator. Did she intentionally now not accuse him so he could accuse himself all the more? Did her not making him accountable ensure his sense of guilt for what was done to her? And the therapist in Texas, was that Jack too each time he talked to her trying to get into her pants through words? What a toxic brew trying to do the best for people, how it stands everything on its head to expose the genitals. Sometimes we will even garb ourselves in robes, in a priest's surplice and cassock, and imagine a high-ceilinged cathedral so that our small pleasure is at the mercy of a stunning architecture that places screams beyond anyone's reach. It is all closer to heaven with good advice, so nobody hears. Why can't we just give ourselves and be done with it? But then would we cherish it as much? The other Jack in Texas wanted what was best for her; he was making her better, trying to fix her, but the fact is that he couldn't because he was the perpetrator and healer all rolled into a toxic embrace. This Jack here who knows so much about literature and philosophy, she only half-trusts him. She wasn't ready to give her judgment over to anyone, or her body, as she said of those she reserved to mitigate her loneliness, calling those around her house "stalkers."

She doubled as funeral director and master of resurrection of this horrid violence. She had pictures, four of them.

"How do you want to proceed, ma'am?" he imagined the policeman saying.

She's sent the pictures to Jack, there they were, and he enlarged them, the pink skin, white really, but with red and purple bruises, some darkening to indigo. All manner of marks in graphic detail. The police should know. It should be reported. He'd send her an email, saying he'd already forwarded all the pictures to the city police. He wanted to take a baseball bat to the guy. Whomever it was. He needed his brains bashed in. But was it him? Did Jack do it? Could he stand to hit himself, much less rat on himself? He knew what all men felt, she did too.

Of his advances she said, "It's not your fault," and pulled him towards her while pushing him away. She exonerated him beforehand. Is that why she didn't answer the phone, wouldn't speak to him? Did she hit him so that he'd attack her? But he doesn't have bruises on his body, no scratches.

You go see Elizabeth, she ended the email as if she'd follow the dead woman who was like a mother to Jack, so she'd be dead by thirty as she predicted. Does she want false pity? She'd taken overdoses, was on suicide watches already, dropped her classes after the automobile accident.

All Jack was concerned about was her welfare. Sure, he wants her, but her health is his overriding concern. That's all that matters, he tells himself. She wasn't convinced, didn't trust him, but respected him, knew about idiots, about *how men take the word 'NO.'* She knew her own complicity and the sheer insult to the body that women endure all their lives. How do most sort that out and live with it?

Jack was up in the air. He couldn't storm over there. She was *armed*, and she told him three times in the email not to come and he knew deep down he'd do nothing though the guy deserved to be beaten to a pulp. The idiot had beaten him to it, got to her that night like Jack had wanted.

She got what she deserved for denying both of them. A shameful thought! The idiot just did Jack's dirty work! Assuming of course there is some other idiot! That too she was throwing in his face with the email. Her mincing behavior with him having succumbed to blow after blow later in the evening. Did she calculate that? Jack felt looking at the pictures, No, he couldn't have done that! In fact, maybe she half-wanted Jack and the idiot smelled the vulnerability already on her from earlier in the evening. So, Jack was partly responsible. Or maybe Jack didn't leave after all, took his place beside the long run of idiots; insofar as every man is complicit in wanting to beat up, punish a woman for all the rage and humiliation of denial that they suffer? But he couldn't watch women being hit in films, that's one thing he couldn't watch. But is that only because it struck a chord in him? Still he must have felt the absolute rage in all men for being denied so often. Both sexes are angry, it is a miracle more don't explode like rigged tinderboxes over the lifelong humiliations. The idiot just estranged something in him hitting her, made himself more acceptable despising what he had done. The equivocal, dismissive tone of taking things in her own hands in her email mystified Jack. Maybe she felt guilty, was on his side, on all their sides, co-conspirator like all victims. She probably went back to his apartment and smashed the window after she thought better of what he said, "I expect payback for this," and tried to kiss her. Maybe she felt the insult and tried to get her dog back. Maybe he wouldn't let her back in and mocked her holding the dog in the window and that threw her into a rage. Maybe the glass was so tempting over her sister's death that she relishing the pain could already see her arm bleeding. Nothing shatters so pleasurably as glass. And a broken window made the jagged entry poignant. One wonders what else she wanted broken for what couldn't be fixed in her. Who wouldn't rake the skin on their own arm to get their dog back?

"Leave go of my baby! You Bastard, give her to me!" Maybe he laughed at her.

The "pissed" may be no more than the trickle down her leg trying to do it standing, match the males, but the "batty" thinks she is holding a baseball bat, though armed with only her nails: still in the end she'll be no more than Venus de Milo. For all the lack of tenderness, for all the aggression, there is something totally unarmed about women. All the erogenous zones end unprotected and there is no resistance even to a body of art.

She had to end with the request for a typewriter to record it all, so she'll not implode. She probably was stepped on before she left. Did he piss on her to get her so pissed off? We cannot be humiliated enough once we start on that track and in the end even the windpipe is crushed. Is that why she won't answer the phone? Was it that the smell of his urine didn't go away? Is that all pissed means? If it doesn't, perhaps the pain of his kidney stone one day, the crystallization of the minerals secreted deep in his body, not passing, affects her with a kind of pleasure, combats the tendency to nurse him.

I figured you could help with the typewriter business is how she ended her email. Maybe he didn't beat her up, but was so much the recipient of the pain not allowing him to vent that he imagined he somehow delivered the blow to her chin, choked her, raked his nails over her cheek. After all, she wouldn't oblige him, yet pulled him so tightly to her, what was he do? Just leave?

I'm a man, after all, he thought, primed for this sort of thing.

"Clarissa, that will teach you how to leave me for someone else on the same night! Otherwise how am I to recoup my manhood but by staying there, get you to imagine you were with someone else. Get you to imagine a real man that was going to take you no questions asked. What did you drink the whiskey for but to give me the courage to attack you like you wanted deep down? But I left it to someone else to do my dirty work. See, because I am a gentleman, *'noble'! 'Men,'* you say, placing them all in one basket. They are pretty ghastly, I know, almost as ghastly as women who tiptoe around us with more grace than we can pin down even with all the beauty of mutual compliance."

THE HANGING, FOR NOT LEARNING THE ART OF SMALL TALK

T HE FATHER PICKED his son up at the YMCA. He had asked if it were all right if his friend Kevin came. Kevin was an exchange student from France with an improbably Irish name. The father had met him once before. He was friendly and very talkative.

When the father arrived both his son Abel and Kevin got in the car. Abel spoke right off the bat, unlike his usual silence punctuated by occasional monosyllables. There seemed to be intended openings for the father to talk, but he said nothing, and the openings soon passed. He thought hard of something to say as they approached the brief stretch of highway, just as they passed the huge First Baptist church that looked as large as a small arena. But on the brief stint on the highway, the father could think of absolutely nothing. He indeed reached for something significant to say, about French literature, e.g., Stendhal, Hugo, Balzac, Baudelaire, or Proust, even LaRochefoucauld or Chamfort. He thought how the pages of his separate books of *Remembrance* were now brittle and crumbling, of Gide, Genet, Camus, and Sartre. He thought too of Henri Michaux, even of Jules Michelet and his original 1859 copy of *L'Amour* at home on his bookshelf, of Barthes' study of him, of Robbe-Grillet and Michel Tournier, of Alain Badiou, but sensed the boy wasn't intellectual enough for him to bring them up.

Kevin and Abel were now talking about some computer game that the father was unfamiliar with as they pulled up to Max's Village Pantry. It was now permanently closed. For years it had been a marker for directing people to their house. Everything changes, the father thought, and as with most changes we have little to say about them. Somehow the store closing reinforced his inability to say anything. Things just happen and we suffer the consequences. The father had done that most of his life, buried the past so that looking at him driving his son and his exchange student friend from the YMCA you'd suspect nothing happened. It was just another day of shuttling his son, nothing to stoke the flames of the past for. After all, the Inquisition was hundreds of years ago. It had no effect today. The present after all is a gift and we only drag as much of the past as we can without a grimace on our face. All of us are triumphs of the moment that have gotten us to where we are. So it was with Jack Kunkel in his easy maneuver of his ten-year-old Toyota van onto Jaeger Avenue. He was not the hunted anymore, but up-to-date, modern, in control of the steering, of his life. He didn't need to talk. In fact, he knew he was little more than a chauffeur for his son, irrelevant to his son's preoccupation with his iPhone and weightlifting. The father was indeed marginalized and daily bathed in his son's silence save the grunts and groans from pumping iron.

Right now his son and Kevin were carrying on the most animated conversation, and this surprised the father, but even in the gaps the father struggled to find words but he was at a loss. No thought came to mind. Small talk was not his forte, for that assumed a friendliness that comes so easily to others but was a positive chore for him, heavier than any weight he could lift; it was a desert to him that made his mouth dry and his brain stretch over expanses of abandoned terrain empty of syllables even when he wanted something to pop up. He was so totally alone about communicating the small things, the incidentals in life, that it gave the impression he was alienated from everyone, not simply at a loss for words.

Still the boys spoke and the father resigned himself to a growing silence that couldn't get a word out. The pressure of their approaching their home only increased his incapacity. He was speechless after they finally pulled up to their long lane, less than fifteen seconds left and still nothing came. You'd expect something from the father, that he'd blurt out something clever or amusing that told that he not only had the steering wheel but also the situation, his own language, under his control, being an adult in his sixth decade who understood people, someone with a smidgeon of courage who knew tactfully, humorously, how to break any silence, but nothing, absolutely nothing came as the seconds ticked away. He felt it almost an Olympian event as they pulled under the carport with tenths of a second left and still he said nothing as he brought the car to a halt stepping firmly on the brakes.

His son jumped out of the car after gathering his things and Kevin followed more slowly. Jack knew they wanted to get away from the adult supervision of this questionable silence, the total irrelevance of the father, for who knew what he was thinking. It was better to just get away. Who could calculate the consequence of an adult not saying anything? Perhaps he had a history of saving his words and then issuing a stinging rebuke at the right moment. Little did they know that the right time according to the father had passed long ago. He was simply tongue-tied. What an ugly picture that made for the father, that poisonous expression, the multiple folds in his mouth, his own tongue an infinitely enlarged knot, choking the opening, barring even food, letting the stomach shrink over nothing to say, the whispered syllable blocking, hiding the bunched tongue between his teeth.

The father followed the two friends into the house. His house, he thought, but he knew nobody owns anything they don't feel in possession of.

Finally something issued from out his mouth.

"Do you watch the winter Olympics?"

That's all the father could say after all this time. It took almost fifteen minutes of rumination, of studied thought behind the ever-growing blankness, but here it was, he had asked a question, gotten over the camel's hump, relieved his dry mouth. He had finally broken the silence. The question hung in the large kitchen with all the windows, under the one skylight, totally unmolested by the scream it probably hid. The terror at being with each other hiding behind the apparent coolness of just giving the boys a ride.

Kevin nonchalantly replied to the father's triumph of asking a simple question. "Yes, but I like the summer Olympics better."

The father even after mentioning the Olympics racked his brain to think of something more to say, bring up any French athlete in the Olympics, but couldn't come up with one. He was on the verge of thinking of the ice dancing pair, but that too faded before he could get it out. The fact that he had heard earlier in the day a sports show host say the winter Olympics weren't really a sport, resonated in his mind, bothered him, but again he was silent about that logjam of indignation and couldn't form a relevant response to an argument the boy probably knew nothing about. The words simply didn't come as Kevin after giving the father just enough time to reply followed his son into his bedroom leaving the father more speechless than ever.

*

JACK KUNKEL STOOD there in the empty kitchen absolutely alone and thought about the consequences of his silence cutting off his airway with an almost frenzied effort to speak, turning his face in his mind purple. Still nothing came. What are words for but to shame us, he thought. So little of what we say is ever triumphant, he tried to rationalize.

Over fifty years had passed since it happened. Maybe it wasn't totally a lack of courage, or the complete absence of personality, or being dumped in a home with twenty-one boys. The shy gene has a way of creeping onto the tongue, thickening it so it doesn't move, so it says nothing when it is supposed to. *Kuchi omoi*, the Japanese say. Heavy tongue. That described Jack exactly.

The older, bigger, stronger boys, some were four and five years older than Jack, used his head as a "cuffing dome" on the bus whenever it pleased them. They'd sneak into his room in the dead of night, gently remove his covers, and punch him on his thigh while asleep as hard as they could. Big boys whose two hundred pounds packed a wallop. He'd wake up moaning and complained the next day of a Charley horse, at first not knowing what hit him. He remembered too having to "play army" in the barn, crawling through the wet manure in the cows' drop. He had heard one of the boys on another farm had placed a live hose in a cow's rectum and killed it. In their own farm the worst they did was add stone dust to the feed, or occasionally kill a calf with a bucket for the animal acting up.

80

The father clearly remembered that Sunday sitting in the church service. It was a large auditorium in town with clouds scudding overhead and with pinpoint lights twinkling like stars. They had sat beside him Mac's girl whom everyone knew he liked. They probably foresaw the effect of the seating arrangement, but still acted surprised so they could make good on the consequences; their threats were a tonic to the slow Sunday mornings.

Her name was Gail. She was a darling local girl with the prettiest face and the largest brown eyes. Mac would call her from the phone booth at the bottom of the hill in Union Deposit while Jack would stand by mutely listening to Mac's every word. Mac this Sunday sat up on stage during the service while Jack sat beside Gail. Jack had accompanied Mac to the phone booth every time he called. It was the high point of Jack's week. Occasionally Mac made brief reference to the younger boy there, before Gail even knew his name; he was so excited when Mac told Gail who he was. But still he never said anything, even one time when Mac asked him if he wanted to talk to her on the phone, for he was too shy.

Well, during the long service Jack said nothing, yes, nothing to the pretty girl he sat beside. It was not that he was even searching for the words, but he was just enveloped in a thick fog of shyness.

Occasionally one of the boys would poke him, or whisper "Talk to her."

"Say something," but Jack was mute as his shyness got the better of him.

"You're disgraceful, Kunkel!"

Jack felt smaller than ever as his cowardice, his shyness, only enlarged.

He hid in what he imagined was underbrush like a rabbit fearing to expose himself. Even the hymns that they all had to stand up for didn't offer any relief. He couldn't utter one syllable. His tongue was literally tied, caged, and he didn't even look over at Gail though he felt so keenly her presence. It was as if something would come tumbling down if he uttered a word, a syllable that would cause the whole building to collapse. So, he remained silent.

Imagine that, the whole service he couldn't look at her, and probably had no idea of her own beating heart while his thumped wildly in his chest that he imagined it would split open at any moment. It could only be slowed by his continued silence. Who knows what ugly frog might leap out of his mouth the moment he opened it?

"Cold fish!" one boy chided, and then when the service ended Gail left and Jack the next moment was showered by taunts and jeers until he found himself on the bus. He didn't even know exactly how he got there, only that he had said nothing to Gail when she left.

"Kunkel, you're a disgrace to all of us, to your sex, to the whole world! You should be ashamed to sit there beside that poor girl with your mouth closed."

Even Injun Joe, bullied in his own right for his big ears and his unusually large teeth, but older than Jack, jumped on him.

"Yes, a disgrace!"

Dan Hunt said, "Yeah, you shamed us, our unit."

"It's embarrassing," another said.

And Weaver, like Hunt, a heavyweight wrestler, a football player, recently suspended from the team for smoking, said "You should be hanged, Kunkel!"

Even the effeminate Mays said, with enough size to hide that effeminacy, "Let's hang him when we get back."

"Yeah!" others seconded.

Jack shrank in his seat, took any number of smacks to his dome, and said nothing, his nose moving in fear with tiny sniffs to catch his breath.

Finally they reached the farm home. Union it was called. They changed from their Sunday best, struggled out of their ties and suits, changed their shoes, and everyone eagerly converged upon the basement to see if the threat would be made good.

"Come here, kid!" said Gingrich who was soon to go into the army after graduation and return in green fatigues and high-top boots. He grabbed Jack like he was already a prisoner .

"Wait, I'll put the rope on him," Injun Joe said as Weaver made the knot and Bailey adjusted the noose.

They placed it around his neck and told him to step on the chair. Weaver tied the rope to one of the overhead pipes running across the basement ceiling.

"This is what we do to anyone who disgraces us, sits there the whole time and says nothing! Nothing, not one word out of you, you little coward! You make me sick!" Bailey said.

Mays then added, "You couldn't even look at her, just straight ahead the whole time. You yellow belly! I saw you."

"You're never gonna be a man, but a mouse, Kunkel! Hear that, a mouse! You shamed all of us!" another said.

"Someone with so little courage doesn't deserve to live, and should be hanged, posthaste!" said Weaver.

"Are you saying your prayers?" Denike chimed in.

"Tighten it around his neck," Bailey said.

"No, you can leave his hands alone," Weaver advised. "Maybe at least he'll have the courage to fight for his life, coward!"

"What a disgrace," and someone pulled the chair out from under him.

Jack started to fall but reached up in time with one hand and grabbed the pipe, clenched his fist and tried to untighten the noose with his free hand. His face turned purple. The rope was burning his neck as he held himself to keep from falling.

Suddenly a couple of younger boys ran over and held Jack as he finally worked himself free.

The older boys stood around and continued to call him coward, disgrace, mouse, making tiny squealing noises while sucking up air, and then "baak, baak," chicken sounds one after the other.

"Maybe that will teach you a lesson," Mays said.

"Yeah, not to disgrace us," Bailey added.

"Or you'll be hung for good," Weaver said.

Perhaps it was only a mock hanging, but the brush burns on Jack's neck were real so that his teachers asked about them at school, but he never told anybody what happened that day.

Jack never really learned to speak to women, but managed to make his way in the world without being hanged again, though, as evidenced by picking up his son and his friend at the YMCA, neither did he learn the art of small talk.

THE MIRACLE OF JIMMY CUTLER

I MEAN WHAT brought him back? The heart had stopped. He was clinically dead. The head of the hospital Dr. Blackstone asked Dr. Barnard why he had operated. Nobody knew. He certainly looked dead even when he came back from surgery. We coded him, but the nurses never gave up.

"Jimmy, Jimmy," we shouted, urged, pleaded with him, and whispered repeatedly, "Jimmy, come back, come back," and gave him CPR.

Then we yelled louder and louder, "Wake up, Jimmy, wake up!"

Like the time when he was hit with a mortar shell in Vietnam and lay unconscious and his buddies yelled to him, "Stay with us, Jim." It was the first of his Purple Hearts. He then stirred and suddenly came back to life.

"He has nine lives," Nurse Emily said when he suddenly moved.

"You'll get out of this, Jimmy," his buddy John Stoltz had said when he had seven pieces of shrapnel lodged in his two legs. That was the second Purple Heart. "Hold on, man," John said and Jimmy did survive.

"The women are all waiting back in the States for you," he had said, "don't leave us now, Jim!"

The shrapnel had also been embedded deep inside his chest, but the medic arrived in time. They had taken heavy fire and even after Jimmy hit the ground dirt continued to pile up and rain down on top of him burying Jimmy and his buddy, but Jimmy escaped and manage to be redeployed again.

The last tour he was awarded the Bronze Star for valor when he rescued Reginald Buckholz. The letter of commendation said Jimmy had carried Bucky fifty yards under enemy fire. Jimmy Cutler from Hail Knob, Kentucky. Imagine that. He had also thrown his body over his buddy, Joey Palumbo from the Bronx and a bullet meant for Joey ricochet off Jimmy's canteen. For that he received no commendation, but the canteen that saved Jimmy's life now rests on the mantel of his living room.

"Jimmy, wake up!"

The room was filled with nurses and aides, while Doctors Blackstone and Barnard reviewed Jimmy's chart.

"Don't go, Jimmy," April whispered with a voice as soothing as a night of Kentucky rain.

"Don't leave us," Emily said,

Jimmy owned a bar in Tennessee just across the state line. Everyone knew him back in Carter County. The local paper called him a businessman referring to the *Wooden Nickel Tavern* in Breckinridge, Tennessee. Three years before three people had been indicted for attempted arson. Walter Johnson 50, Ken Hamm 45, and Sue Ruhe 53, all of Scott county were caught trying to burn down the *Wooden Nickel*. Brad Biggs, the patrolman on duty, discovered small fires at the entrance and beat back the flames with a fire extinguisher from his car. His assistant Tony Stringer also battled the blaze. After it was put out the two officers found accelerant in the crawl space in the back of the establishment. The two males served two years, but Sue Ruhe though charged at first was later released.

Jimmy apparently had enemies but everyone in the county knew him and that gave him a kind of immunity.

"Jimmy, wake up," and at that Jimmy moved and opened his eyes. Dr. Barnard walked over to him relieved.

"How are you doing, Jimmy?"

Jimmy seemed to answer faintly.

"Dr. Bernard, you performed a miracle!" someone said.

"Jimmy's back from the other side!" Tammy exclaimed, and another two or three repeated that muttering to themselves.

Suddenly everyone in the room broke into applause chanting, "It's a miracle, a miracle that Jimmy's back!"

Nobody knew why Dr. Barnard operated, except that he was curious, nurses had always said. He wanted to discover what secrets were closed up inside Jimmy's uncut body. The MRI and x-rays were never enough for Dr. Barnard. He considered them inaccurate compared to the naked eye. The secrets of the human body were always a challenge for the doctor and an incentive to operate on what others had given up on, patients others had pronounced irrecoverable, throwing their hands up exclaiming nothing can be done.

Not Dr. Barnard. He instructed his team to prep for the operation. Sometimes he was overridden by the astonished looks of nurses and even doctors but being the chief cardio-thoracic surgeon in the hospital, most of the time he had his way. He rushed in where others failed to go and gave grieving families hope. Dr. Barnard with his skillful knife glittering fiercely under the operating table lights carefully separated every layer of skin, teasing fat and mesentery away, clamping the arteries, and leaving as best he could as many nerves as possible unmolested though some tiny white threads were inevitably cut when bathed in so much blood that it interfered with the doctor's visibility.

When the chest pains started, the Breckinridge city jailer did not believe Jimmy's complaints at first. Jimmy had been arrested intoxicated before and though banged up this time from a fight outside the *Wooden Nickel*, the jailer dismissed his complaints as the ramblings of a drunk who needed to dry out. That's why Jimmy was clinically dead when he reached the hospital.

Who knew a miracle was about to take place at the hands of the Chief Surgeon whose curiosity about even ordinary patients was well-known, much less anomalies like Jimmy Cutler who had already escaped death multiple times. What was there inside the chest that caused the fist of heart muscle to clench permanently and Jimmy go limp after yelling out that he can't breathe, doubling over and collapsing in his jail cell? Only then did Sheriff Howard call an ambulance.

Once again Jimmy was left unconscious like he had been on the battlefield with Joey Palumbo before the medic came. Twice Jimmy had escaped in wartime. Three times if you counted the incident with Joey Palumbo. Now Dr. Barnard cut him open, used the high powered saw whose astonishing acceleration cut clean though Jimmy's sternum revealing his unprotected heart, the same heart he had given to his ex-wife Lulu, and to his 25-year-old mistress Lisa who the nurses at first thought was Jimmy's daughter.

Lulu came even though she and Jimmy were separated. She imagined the saw cutting through Jimmy's bone, winced at losing Jimmy even though they had lived apart for the last two years when Lisa came into the picture. But now they too had separated and Jimmy lived alone with his canteen with the bullet hole above the mantel in his living room.

Dr. Barnard after the sternum was separated saw the aneurysm, as big as day, the swelling vessel all ballooned up. He immediately reduced the swelling though Jimmy had almost no vital signs. He inserted stents and stitched up the artery. It was like Dr. Barnard was sewing up a corpse, but he worked as if he could save Jimmy.

Lulu had said to the staff that Jimmy had seemed too alive for most of the people around him. It was obvious that she still loved Jimmy, the consummate joker, the life of the party who drew people out with laughter. His disarming flattery put everyone around him in a good mood. He was a hopeless chaser of women even though he appeared happily married, or even while he had a 25-year-old mistress.

Jimmy stirred weakly and said, "I'm back," and everyone in the room suddenly clapped as a smile unwrinkled Jimmy's weatherworn 66-year-old face, and his eyes shone brightly like a light was ignited inside him. There was something persistently youthful about Jimmy's appearance that when his eyes lit up a mischievous deviltry appeared that defied his age.

"Truly it is a miracle," the newly hired Dr. Choctaw said. "The hand of the Lord is in the room."

Sara bleated, "Praise the Lord," but Nurse Emily said, "Bless Dr. Barnard!" and everyone began to clap again as a tear gathered at the corner of Jimmy's eye, found a seam and promptly rolled down his cheek. Everyone from the nurse's station appeared at the door and their eyes too grew moist to see Jimmy and how the room was so affected.

"Jimmy was saved for a reason," someone said standing by his ex-wife.

Lisa said two purples hearts in Vietnam didn't get him, or protecting Joey Palumbo, so "Jimmy is not going anywhere."

"The Lord works in mysterious ways," Dr. Choctaw intoned.

Dr. Barnard normally bristled at such talk, but affected by the mood remained silent, despite being an atheist himself. He didn't believe in any of this despite the fact that he himself had performed what everyone thought was a miracle.

"Praise the Lord!" Dr. Choctaw, an understudy of Dr. Barnard, repeated as if he were at a prayer meeting. "Dr. Barnard brought Jimmy back to life, from the other side to be with us today. Praise the Lord!"

You couldn't tell if Dr. Bernard was cringing before Sara said, "Yes, the Lord has big plans for Jimmy. He hasn't yet finished the Lord's work."

"Thank you, God," someone said.

No one in the hospital knew about Jimmy's private life except for what they could glean from his visitors, but all agreed bobbing their heads that the Lord had plans for Jimmy. This was the Bible belt where belief provided a sturdy foundation for everyone's daily life. Jimmy's life was not going to end at North Thumberland Regional Hospital if the Lord had other plans.

"Jimmy's too stubborn," Emily said.

"Yes, he has nine lives," April, a tiny spark plug from Eastern Kentucky, chimed in echoing Lisa.

"Dr. Barnard is a healer, a man of God," Dr. Choctaw said.

It was hard to tell if Dr. Choctaw was mocking Dr. Barnard's lack of belief, or just openly challenging it with his own idea of a miracle.

"He is curious what goes on inside a man's heart," April said. "That's what we are all sent here for."

"Jimmy has work to do," another nurse said. "His life is not going to end here. It is a healing for the Lord. Jimmy will set things right. We just witnessed a miracle, folks. Let's everyone give Dr. Bernard another hand," and the room broke into applause as if everyone had already been together too long and didn't know what else to do.

"Yes, the Lord has big things in store for Jimmy," Emily said and all seemed to agree.

By now everyone knew of the drinking establishment in Breckinridge, Tennessee, the *Wooden Nickel*, just across the state line, but this was the real thing, the genuine currency, hundred percent proof that everyone cared about Jimmy and his work, and the Lord was by no means finished with Jimmy Cutler. Nobody knew what the work was, someone said, but they knew that the whole hospital staff was instrumental, especially Dr. Barnard and his team, in furthering that work.

"We are all tools of something larger," said Emily.

"Tools of the Lord!" Tammy chimed in. "We are all doing his work every day at North Thumberland."

"Maybe Jimmy will not go back to his bar," another said. "Maybe he'll seek a new life, a higher path, make amends for all the fighting and drinking and womanizing."

"Maybe he'll be cured of drink or dispensing it to others," Dr. Choctaw said, "not burn his candle at both ends!"

"Yes, close his bar and open up a mission in Honduras," Sara said.

"Maybe that's why we saved him and we are all part of a larger plan!" and everyone looked around the room and smiled to each other.

"Maybe the *Wooden Nickel Tavern* will inspire an alabaster house of God, not of drink but to dispense holy water to baptize all the young children in Breckinridge, and to bless ourselves with, and just think, all this started at North Thumberland," Tammy said as if amazed herself at the consequences of the miracle that had taken place.

"Yes, this doesn't happen every day," April said. "The Lord is with us."

"Patients are not just brought back from the dead like Jimmy. How did Dr. Bernard do it?" someone said, but everyone looked around and Dr. Barnard was nowhere to be seen.

"There'll be prayer meetings conducted by Jimmy and everyone will be cured just like Jimmy of their ways. Lost lambs on both sides of the state line will be brought back to the fold. Jimmy will be our shepherd."

In fact, the pale fellow on the white bed sheets had plunged into a deep sleep. He looked like a ghost, an emanation from another world, as he had no permanent color in his cheeks despite the glow from the sunlight breaking in around the blinds.

It took weeks of hospitalization for Jimmy to recover his strength before he was finally discharged. By that time all the nurses had gotten to know Jimmy and some were eager to get him on their shift. He was determined to return to his old ways, however, he said defiantly to the nurses on duty, but they thought he was only joking.

Dr. Choctaw, especially, thought after such a scare that surely the miracle would open up a new chapter in Jimmy's life. He personally never lost faith in Jimmy.

"God Bless," he always said to everyone on parting. "The Lord works in mysterious ways. We did something good. Who knows what will come of it? Jimmy Cutler may end up being a credit to North Thumberland and reward all our efforts. Maybe he will purchase heart monitoring equipment that will help save the lives of others. One day we may be repaid hugely for doing the Lord's work."

Dr. Bernard, the rationalist, if he had an opinion kept it to himself. He opened Jimmy up not out of any humanity and certainly not to do the Lord's work, or because he thought of himself as a savior, or even a healer, but because Jimmy was a conundrum, a scientific enigma who needed to be investigated beyond even the capacity of the most advanced machines to supply answers. In the end Dr. Bernard thought that nothing could compare with the judgement of the naked eye, or the precision of a skillful surgeon's hands. Could he get the heart working, regain the synchronicity and make the nodes fire again, that was the challenge. To do that he had to overlook what he considered the inexact imaging of magnetic resonance, avoid entirely getting approved for robotically working the probe and scalpel, and its consequent stitching. Could he discover what was wrong and then restore the heart's remarkable electronic rhythm, he'd have to do it his own way. That according to Dr. Barnard had nothing to do with God so much as the deepest impulses of life inside ourselves, a man's vanity and the simple curiosity to find out. A muscle lodged in our chest that fires remarkably all our lives 72 times a minute occasionally needs the intervention of men like Tom Barnard. That's what attracted the good doctor, undeterred by the violence of the high-speed saw, by the profuse bleeding in the almost still heart of Jimmy Cutler. Nothing deterred Dr.

Barnard from breaking through the sternum to reveal what has to be done and get an open look at the heart. Only then did he properly detect the ballooning artery in Jimmy's body. North Thumberland Regional Hospital was his own battlefield where Dr. Barnard won a Silver Star for valor, a star that twinkled in a firmament all of us could see.

*

ONE NIGHT A few months later, Dr. Barnard received a call from Jimmy Cutler's ex-wife. She had thanked him profusely for saving Jimmy who nevertheless apparently did return to his old way of life, not a life of missionary work building a house for the Lord in Honduras or Breckinridge, Tennessee, or of donating new machines to the hospital; in fact he returned to the *Wooden Nickel*, smoking and drinking and carousing, but as Lulu now informed Dr. Barnard, someone had slipped into Jimmy's house that Friday night in Hail Knob. She said she felt the need to tell Dr. Bernard since he had brought Jimmy so miraculously back to life. Jimmy had been stabbed multiple times in his bedroom, and his body was set on fire and his house burned.

Firefighters were dispatched to the house when they received a call that Friday. Detective Billy Wheeldon determined Jimmy was the victim and despite the burnt condition of the body he counted thirteen stab wounds. The suspected weapon was not located, nor was an obvious motive determined. Jimmy she said knew everybody. Dr. Bernard expressed his sorrow.

Detective Wheeldon praised the Hail Knob fire department for their quick response.

Newspapers reported Cutler's body had been transported to the state Medical Examiners Office in Frankfort for an autopsy.

In the *Hail Knob Chronicle* it said Cutler had lived alone in the house for about a year. It mentioned that he was the proprietor of the *Wooden Nickel Tavern* in Tennessee and that he was a Vietnam Veteran who had been awarded two Purple Hearts and a Bronze Star for valor.

Detective Wheeldon said Jimmy had been released on bail that same day. He had been charged with a DUI and first-degree possession of a controlled substance and six other traffic related offenses.

No arrests have been made and funeral arrangements are to be handled by New Brothers Funeral Home.

So ends the saga of Jimmy Cutler and the astonishing miracle at North Thumberland Regional Hospital. The stabbing of Jimmy Cutler surprised everyone at the hospital, especially Dr. Choctaw who searched for an explanation for the shocking outcome of Jimmy's miracle. He couldn't understand the random stabbings that so contradicted the precise cuts and exquisite stitching of Dr. Barnard that had miraculously saved Jimmy's life for what he thought would be the Lord's work. Nevertheless, Dr. Choctaw's faith remained strong, as if Jimmy' fate was only a brief hiccup that a drink of cold water could address as he added, "Jimmy's in a better place."

Three weeks after the first responders found Jimmy Cutler in his home, a surveillance video at a local Marathon gas station shocked everyone. The video showed Jimmy's stolen truck at the gas station thirty minutes after the fire at his residence was reported. A woman was seen getting out and buying a soda from a vending machine, then getting back in the truck. Police reported finding the truck a couple of days later burned, but they have so far been unable to identify the woman, or who else was inside the vehicle.

The neighbors have not been able to breathe easy and Jody Speaks who lives right across the road from Jimmy said, "I know that there's horrible people that can come back and do this to any of us."

Little did neighbors imagine the miracle that had made such a tragedy possible.

A PIANO STORY

SHE DIDN'T SEE the outline of his face. It was so big, a solid imposing mass just like the rest of his body. It seemed gray with almost no identifiable features except the ears and the long nose. The comparatively beady eyes she never even noticed as looking at her. His tread was so light, but powerful enough not to be disregarded. What matter to her his movements, his sense of smell, his looks? He was like the rest that she had to be indifferent to, or they'd interfere with her music. Her beauty was a magnet that drew them all. And when she played some thought they were in heaven listening for the first time in their lives to a celestial music here on earth.

So she had to ignore them, keep them off her back, where she couldn't imagine them anyway. She'd be crushed by their weight alone. The size differential always amazed her. How could they be so big?

It was simple, by being ignored their size enlarged mincing its steps, pretending so much bulk is not there. It can sneak up on beauty and surprise it with birthday gifts so pink that they are compatible with the grayness of the world that they highlight. And if their tongue is noticed, its pinkness too resembles the gift, but out of modesty it'll quickly retract it.

Beautiful Maria never distinguished her admirers, especially the larger ones that formed a frightening contrast with her petiteness.

It is amazing how creation can accommodate both the large and the small, though the vivid contrast at times was laughable. Maria didn't even want to get into that, and so avoided all her gray suitors that made up the bulk of a faceless humanity. Maybe they should have harbored some anger towards her. Perhaps they had visions of lifting her up so easily that their own size became a supportive asset, a suspension for all time, an overcast cloud suddenly brightening. Maybe it was the pink dresses they wore at masquerades trying for the duration of the ball to pass as petite themselves.

You'd imagine them forgetting themselves, crushing little agates like Maria. But that was the furthest thing from their mind. They dreamed of a lightness of foot that buoyed their whole body as if it were floating, airborne like the divine notes that came from Maria's piano. She was reflected in the polished black wood transforming her deeper into the souls of her admirers that she could never be extricated, not even with the sternest rejection.

And there were probably so many of them that Maria couldn't hope to pick after all. She was just one woman who could only with her performances satisfy the appreciative dreams of multitudes. In fact, her personality developed enough coldness and indifference to ward off the constant train of suitors who even with gifts in hand knocked on her recital door. The shimmering pink ribbons and every pastel color under the rainbow, the silver entreaties, especially the gold of the iris that took on the stock color of bright ribbon, all eliminated the frightening eyeball and the threatening lashes.

"Lashes!" the word was alien to Maria, born with a silver spoon in her mouth. The closest she got were the scoldings from her piano teacher when she missed a note. But they were administered with such a velvet glove to ensure that the teacher would not lose his commission. In fact, everyone was careful not to upset Maria and tiptoed around her or gave into her laughter. Their abjectness brought out a mean streak in her.

Needless to say Maria controlled every aspect of her environment that she became destructive. She couldn't take a compliment; in fact, they no longer inspired her playing. She lost all appreciation for those who constructed her instrument. Even for the weavers who had produced the red felt that covered the keys. In the polish of the wood she dismissed the elbow grease that brought it out. Maybe she imagined the carpentry that fashioned the piano's beautiful shape competed in some odd way with her, so she ignored it. It is strange how objects can so displace us, diminish us. In fact her face was so distorted as she played that her whole upper body when she wore a white dress emerged like white flowers from the underworld and sank back into it. This sustained her with a kind of companionship that she never had in real life.

She was drawn to the piano just to see this reflection of her white dress in the polished wood, see its energetic movements, forget herself even at a crescendo, then catch herself on free fall as the music would trail off to a pianissimo and she'd be left on the black surge of polished wood that threatened to box her up like it did the keys every night.

When Ray Rice came into Maria's life she never imagined at the outset all the implications. She was caught off guard. He was such a big man, too big really to look at. One of the gray mass of admirers that followed her. His every movement seemed sprawling. But oddly enough her petiteness was kind of a bulwark against his size. It staved off bigness with that compactness that miniatures always possess being so self-sufficient. And to have a grand piano at her disposal and to be able to play it with such virtuoso accomplishment gave her a completeness that didn't need a man in her life, certainly not the likes of Ray Rice.

He played for some band or other, had a cousin that knew Maria and so was introduced. As I said, his size for Maria was a gray sprawling amorphousness that suggested some dim childhood memory, or vague outline that Maria couldn't place, whose face hardly came into focus. It was doughy with beady eyes, and multiple corrugations at the shaft of the nose that grew more pronounced with every joke. For Ray Rice was given to practical jokes and unexpected outbursts of laughter. Maria overlooked the joking, saw the bulk of Ray Rice as her sounding board, something oddly enough felt through the fingers. Saw in comparison with his grayness, herself already reflected in the smooth polish of the dark piano in a white dress though she had not sat down yet. How could Ray Rice compete with that? It was as if he claimed no illumination, beyond the honeyed colored trumpet in a band she knew nothing about. Or his short hair, could that have had something to be harvested, a shower of rice falling on her at a wedding? If Maria had had such thoughts she'd have cringed and locked her doors, not have met him like her cousin suggested, not actually have gone out on a date with him.

It surprised people that she did. Maybe there was something she was making up for, the long gray line of suitors that she had rejected. Maybe a woman rejects so long that she privately begins to think that something is wrong with her, that her counterpart will never emerge from the piano with such white mystery as she herself sitting at it. It is physically impossible she concludes, and so exasperated turning on herself she finally gives someone a chance. Out of the indefinite grayness of all the prior suitors comes Ray Rice. He had their emblematic light-footedness, their combined nosiness, their beady eyes comparative to their body size. Like the rest he wants to know everything there is to know about her. He minces in his walk to affect an elegance he doesn't have but is ultimately an entertainer. He could be in a circus, Maria thinks, or in vaudeville, just at the moment the gold buttons on his blazer seem about to pop from another belly laugh.

He'll wear little party hats too and blow paper whistles, and as was mentioned give those pink ribboned presents.

"Ray Rice!" Maria repeats laughing to herself, forgetting her fears in the novelty of the name, at going on a date with this band man! What does it mean she asks herself, the saccharine quality of those wind instruments compared to her divine piano?

Ray is there puncturing the ether like the first light struggling through the morning haze to assert itself. Maria is shy and retreats to a silence at Ray's antics. He amuses everyone but Maria, and that redoubles his efforts. Still she sees him as a buffoon.

He accompanies her home, insists she should play the piano for him, that he's heard so much about her playing.

Maria is flattered, but repulsed by Ray Rice, sensing something short of disgust in herself.

But he is so focused on hearing her play, as if he has found the path to her. The notes in air that he knows she will never leave written, he'll grasp as a kind of pledge between them.

Maria looks at him, at his bulkiness, his gray insistence, as the embodiment of all men, pushing themselves on her.

The disparity of size actually stupefies her. How could she ever accept such a big man? What in the world could be the connection? Her mind reels, flounders. She reaches out as if she is already playing and finds only harsh notes, discordance, disgust with Ray Rice's spiel.

Still she offers him tea in her best china. So odd she thinks to herself sitting beside his bulk. His chubby fingers are too big for the ring of porcelain on the teacup. He holds it by the lip. She warms the teapot, puts it in the cosy and sets it down.

She has tiny biscuits that are too laughably small for the appetite of Ray Rice. She knows that he could shovel in everything on the plate if she turned her back. She fears he is only getting started.

The wedding rice occurs to her and she shudders.

Such an oddity as she catches a glimpse of them both in the piano, looks down at the claw feet holding it up.

What is there about the piano, what secret connection between her and this behemoth of a man?

"I'd like you to play, Maria," Ray Rice says as the tea warms both their bodies.

Ray Rice now is no longer the buffoon, behemoth, band man, flatterer, but he's shrunk to the size of Maria's enlarged vanity that takes all of Ray in, contains him in her smile, in her nimble fingertips.

Maria goes to the piano, opens the fallboard, takes off the red velvet and sits down. She catches a brief glimpse of herself in the dark polish and imagines except for her white dress a whole continent of mixed emotions purified by her playing where wildlife roams freely and poachers are unheard of, where the musical notes tame the breasts of the most savage animals.

But just as she is going to hit the keys the horror strikes her. The horror of what she has been doing all along, the horror of keeping the Ray Rices of the world at bay.

The wear of countless hours of playing has never occurred to her, the yellowing over time, an unfathomable passage of her fingers on the keys that has led back to him. It floors her just sitting there looking at Ray Rice, but she is a continent away having seen for the first time, having heard the eerie screams of separation, the thundering herds, felt the vibrations of the earth beneath her, the deafening sounds of the giant gun, the penetration, the bleeding, the gaping wounds, the sores that will never heal, broken collar bones that deprive the head of movement, the unearthly extension of the struggling pink tongue.

The gray mass of Ray Rice sitting there, the aggrieved herds of suitors rebuffed by her petiteness, all gather in her mind as if in reprimand for what was so intimately taken. He seemed so indulgent even as she had repulsed him. How otherwise could she live with herself? She couldn't admit it. Who could do otherwise for such divine music? She had created a world unto herself, become ironically so thin-skinned. What a luxury so as not to be identified, tracked down, have your own family broken up.

There he stood, leaning over the piano, the accusatorial leer of Ray Rice not knowing himself what he was emblematic of, the unspeakable slaughter of all those who never forget, waiting for her surrender. Forget the prominent nose, the ears almost fanning his body to overcome the effects of the hot tea, her fingers are frozen in horror. She is too ashamed to sweep them over the keys. The unspeakable theft must have been simultaneously realized by him. Just what was done to bring that huge instrument to her, those keys surrounded by the polished black wood that mirrored her, that challenged her consciousness of such a violent theft with the sweeping grace of the nimblest fingers burying all thoughts of what was stolen. The actual theft Ray Rice must have felt in his loins.

The repeated blasts from the gun, the animal wobbling, dropping to its front knees, the river of dark blood streaming out of such a huge body, the tilting gray trunk arching up in the air, the concussion of the head, the mighty collapse heard in the next village. The death throes as the herd screams back. This goes on for hours until it finally subsides. Already large humpbacked birds are gathering, waiting, the hyenas are massing, and thousands of flies are already at the sticky blood. When the last spasms are over, the saws are produced and the grating sounds that disturb sleep. The only consolation is that they are destined to be replaced by Beethoven, Mozart, and Chopin.

It should take anyone's breath away, and it did Maria's, but Ray just stood there as if frozen himself by her realization, sensing now her vulnerability, how something from him had been taken. His bulk was so emblematic of the theft, yet he was there to advance the plunder, stalking this little slip of a woman as if to demonstrate how things would come full circle.

All the earlier certainty of those modest little keys now brought out the crude grating of serrated edges, what since has been banned internationally, so little women sitting before polished black pianos all around the world could play their hearts out free of the dangerous interruption of behemoths who gone wild could easily trample them to death had not the thundering herds been depleted for their ivory. Over and over the elephant guns had been thoughtlessly shouldered after the deed was done and the booty collected. All big men must feel the menacing tragedy of that. For as Felisberto Hernandez has said, "The piano keys had been tusks," as Ray Rice's unwitting stare now bore down into the terrified eyes of little Maria Pendergast.

A BULL STORY

I TROT INTO the ring as brown as the little drum that signals my arrival. All the fanfare of the male, that you'd almost think the hump on my back came from little bursts of the accompanying bugle, and not everyone's expectation.

I snort and race to position myself in my newfound freedom. I've come of age and am only now allowed pursuit.

And they dress up for me, so womanly and pink, almost flamenco dancers they flit and strut, and stamp their feet. The silver threads on their outfit are meant to gleam in the sun, while the pink curiously repels the sun's advance.

They walk about unaffected, throwing their hips up high as if they were haunches, chest out as if they had breasts. They toss their heads, so I imagine a mass of black curls; in their darkness they imitate me, as if to say we are already one.

I stomp my feet at them heedless of their mockery and charge toward one after another in the most picturesque and politest of terms. They hide behind wooden posts of convention, jeer and taunt me from there. I never give away, despite their already diminutive size, how small this is of them.

Sometimes they will take their hats off and wave them at me titillating, brushing my nose even as if to say, here follow, when they are safely behind the strongest wooden parapets, when they have all society on their side; they who could have hundreds, thousands like me and just as horny.

I butt sometimes against what I know to be useless, the conventions that close ranks on me each time, like the doors to their houses that keep me out.

I snort, flare my nostrils wider and gather the hummock of muscle on my back. So much would I just once like to sink my horn into their bodies. I imagine something almost reproductive and mythical, a new birth to my maleness.

But they only feint, as if waving lace handkerchiefs at me. The insults of their perfume I have catalogued, as if to attract only what they ward off. And so face proud are they, their hair tied behind their heads, every feature telling me that I am crude, an animal by comparison, not dainty and mincing like them. They develop their wiles; the dress to show off their shape will add another layer to mystify me. They swirl, sweeping their skirts past my face, brushing against my nose, going into a frenzy of dance just when I tire.

Maybe it is not all their fault, but my own indecision. I never know which one to take, which one to butt, when to mount. I think they want me, that their badgering approach, their withdrawal, their feints and sidesteps are by design, that secretly they want what gores, want my maleness, but just when I think they do, when my head is down and I am most defenseless traveling at such breakneck speeds having put every ounce of my body into contact with them, the ultimate union that everyone clamors for, has come to watch me lift them high up in the air, out of this ring, this performance for something more productive, something that sits securely on the sharpness of my horn to end this taunting, feinting, this abuse of my desire for them, just then they avoid me.

But what makes me put my head down again and again, go into such a rage? Do I imagine I am routing some salon, some china shop?

I run after them, humiliating myself, but they plot against me, too. They'll choose a favorite it's true, but until they do, they will tire me out. I'll run to one, and imagine I hear tittering behind my back and she all pink and silver will hide, play peekaboo, as if she is not involved in my being quartered, as if they all don't have an eye on my ear.

They are not above first whispering sweet nothings or blowing hot mocking air back into my nostrils.

Why will I then run to the other who now comes to the center and teases me, but who runs quickly and hides behind a post, unless she aspires for more than my attentions, unless she is one who wants to be loved by the crowd, one who wants her name in lights for humiliating me and my kind.

She'll take a chance with me. I rush blindly to seize, ravish her, but she twists and turns, throwing me only the empty pink flounce; at every pass the crowd applauds. But if I get too close there comes out another, draws my attention away. They are all in league, know my weakness for their colorful garb, my indecisiveness.

Sometimes it is only one I want, and then so many crowd in the way, making my eyes wander, eyes large and amber, reflecting this circus of hooting and jeers, this mincing and affected courtship that mocks in its dress the color I want, this prissy pink, as if they are only young school girls that don't really understand bleeding, or its consequences.

They tire me out. I think I am at some ball, that this is a dance I am forced to perform, a ritual courtship, that the applause is somehow for only my own movements, my speed and hindquarters, my thick neck, the hump that my desire for them gathers to bury myself in their bosoms out of rage and incomprehension, to stop the taunting, the applause, and just let me have my will without all the fanfare, this undignified appeal to my sense of color.

I don't know myself which one to run to. They dress so similar, the hair coifed the same, their bodies svelte, the mincing strut so much alike. They, the imitations of each other, adopt movements from me at their will, bowing their heads, scraping the ground, snorting. I end just wanting to get one, but rush around, making beelines to the timbers they hide behind, butting them.

I finally stand stock-still, dazed, confused. The heroics of my entry are long since past, having given way to fatigue. The applause has ceased, unless one of them makes a fool of me. My tongue hangs lolling, a long and exhausted gray. I so much want them, know they've dressed up for me, know the drums and fanfare are for this desire in me, for the pirouetting in them, for their dress and pretty movements, for the female in them. Sometimes I think the crowd almost favors me, but finally it is the affectation, the gaudy pink display that captures their imagination.

I stand there and it is quiet for a second, hushed, the four of them as if by agreement recede, huddle together, casting side glances, talking me over. How I comported myself, as if they don't know my kind. They think they do know, but that's when they'll get caught. They think all of us come at them with our heads down, thinking of only one thing. They think they know the angle we will take, every thrust and tilt. They imagine they control the power of our flanks with their svelte bodies, and the gathering of muscle in our shoulders with a twist of their wrists.

The drums roll, the little bugle blasts, and I imagine their suitors, or chambermaids perhaps, astride horses. I have nothing against them. Their long poles are to keep me away. I don't get close but wait for the pink ones. They confabulate as is their wont. I stand in the middle alone. On each side the chambermaids stand adjusting their long staffs. The horses stand innocent of any wrongdoing.

They smell me, my sweat, my anger, my humiliation, my frustrated desire, my fear. The crowd is hooting, urging, jeering, but I stand in the center immobile. One of the pink ones comes towards me, pirouetting, does her dance. I am reluctant to rush her; I stand aloof, distant.

It seems a trick, but her body turns so colorfully and she shouts come-ons, coos, drops hints, wiggles her backside, minces, twists and turns again and again, that finally my maleness wins out and I charge blindly.

She works me ever so closely to the horses, around and around in a diminishing circle. The ring is a miniature of this turning, the running around that they want me to do, to finally lose my bearings, my footing. She feints, gives me more material than my horn can ever catch and get a grip on, than I can ever hope to pin the body underneath, but I thrust and push, run, halt, lunge and twist, trying just once to catch her and just when it seems I will, I am in the ambit of the long pole. It reaches towards me so gently, almost will-less. I can't imagine its purpose. The chambermaids because padded seem little more than attendants, servants inclined to gossip, but knowing their chores. And so I find myself within range of the one. The pink skirt has fled all of a sudden behind the horse.

I stand there uncomprehending, confused at what will come next.

Did she want to leave me with her lady-in-waiting? Though stout, bullish, dressed like a man almost, but with so much protection, not modest or mincing, wearing a dull white with silver ornament and a bit of gold braid, almost not a chambermaid.

Why am I standing here with my gray tongue foolishly hanging out? The horse is silent, doesn't once whinny. I stand fatigued and sweaty. The sun glistens on my back. My haunches, my shoulders seem like rocks, immobile and unsexual. Everyone's attention is off the pink now, so is mine.

Suddenly the lady, the manservant, now I see—my eyesight is so bad—raises the long pole and I just stand there not knowing what to expect. Slowly he moves it into place, so undramatically it hovers over my head, is lowered between my withers. His mount is side-stepping towards me. The next moment a sharp pain rushes down my back, as if a giant horsefly has bitten me, but quickly a second time I feel a sharpness dig into me, and push, push, as if I'm being violated, as if I am not the male and don't have sharp horns and powerful shoulders to work my will.

The manservant twists and turns the sharp instrument around and pulls it out bloody; quickly I back away enraged. I feel dripping down my sides and a flash of pain zigzags through my body.

Without realizing what I'm doing, I charge the horse. The manservant tries to poke me again, but I lunge into the animal's belly and lift, lift, but he has so much protection that I can't pierce him.

The manservant is almost unseated and tries to thrust again but misses the mark. I spin around and rush to center ring.

My own sex is for a moment confused. I don't know whether to charge or stand still to get poked again. The ground moves beneath my feet brightly colored. I throw my head back to staunch the dripping. I stand all alone trying to stop the wetness, shake my body, ripple my skin to shake the drops off, take two steps back and notice a piece of skirt on the ground, as if I am losing what the women wear. The next instant there is a fanfare, both manservants have disappeared with their horses.

The drums roll and out come another two more manservants on foot, no pink dress, just colorful streamers on sticks. They talk and the one circles toward me, and when he gets close enough so I can butt him he arches his back and steps high on his tiptoes raising the colorful sticks whose streamers hide their sharpness.

I swat my head at the horsefly I am trying to get off my back, where the moisture has caked and begun to crack in the sun. I swat my head; he on tiptoes whirls around and nimble as a woman takes the two sticks and plunges their blades into my shoulders, one hits bone and falls out, the other dangles but stays in.

I throw my head round again and again to dislodge it. The biting won't stop. I low loudly, and before I notice he is on top of me sending two more blades into my body. I shake my head at the red capes, and flounces that I splash about. I run aimlessly round the ring bellowing, not realizing what is happening, not hearing the crowd applaud the two direct hits. The three sticks in my back, the colorful streamers divert the flow of energy from me. My mouth dries like the earth, I foam, and my gray tongue protrudes further than my horn. My whole face is twisting toward my tongue.

I bellow again and again my incomprehension. I forget completely the pink dresses, when a shout of applause for the nimbleness of the manservant rises up again before I realize that the last two sticks are in my back, the one streamer hanging down into my eyes, blocking my vision.

I bellow with all my might and swallow a gargling of blood. Where are these tittering creatures who have led me here, who I've yearned for? Why are they doing this to me? Sent their men. Is this the end for all males, slaughtered by their own sex? Are these the bastard children, the youth they haven't had by me that now sink these sharp knives into my back, that the crowd is now applauding?

I breathe so deeply that at every breath fresh blood streams down my sides. My gray tongue lolls, swollen, bitten so many times. I can barely get the air in through my nostrils, so choking am I. The saliva is again dripping and turns to a white cream on my lips. I stand there in the shade huffing and puffing when she comes finally into view.

She's in the center of the ring with more silver on than the rest, in a more striking combination of colors, precious metal catching the sunlight, and with a calmness and confidence that the giddy ones in pink don't have. Her dress is blood red and she shakes it in front of me, first very slowly, without effort, almost without interest. She is not in a hurry, knowing that I have strewn the ring with capes of the same color.

She taunts me as if to say, "Come on, you think you're a man. Come on, prove your stuff!"

My saliva drips again in one long continuous line, spittle conterminous with the ground that I seed unproductively.

"Come on, prove you're a man, the male of the species, that there is no doubt."

She flounces, waves, and shakes her dress before my eyes, hikes her backside. All I see is the red of her; mandrill, I think privately. All I feel is her body already underneath my horn and my driving it up with the most powerful thrust of my neck through the stadium and out into the most quiet pasture imaginable, where afterwards there will only be the softest sunshine and the buzzing of bluebottle flies.

Oh, to lift her out of this ring and me out of my misery. The pain and fatigue, the dripping saliva, the perspiration and blood, all are as if galvanized liquors that move me back from her to stamp my foot, not in anger, but with a curious male confidence again.

I lower my head and the crowd goes wild at my seeming to have controlled my rage. Before I know it I am rushing towards her dress, her bloody, unperiodic red dress, the dress in which she loses none of herself, but which she claims to give me all. There must be a body behind so much movement, such grace, such titillation and flirtation, so much mincing and taunting, a body that wants the horn it sidesteps.

I charge and at a gallop am all shoulders, all head, all penetrating horniness, proven male, bull-necked and egged on by the female who knows my color weakness, my smell, the female who is always there until I thrust and jab and twist my horn up through her dress and then she's gone.

I reach to hold and grasp and am left in mid-air with the crowd jeering, shouting for more, and she does this again and again to please them. She twists and turns, pirouettes and dances, half, quarter steps, mincing little minuets, and I bellow and lunge and cry for her, lust and twist every ounce of my body.

She's bathed at the belly with my blood, the color of her cape. She struts and the crowd roars. I can hardly stand on my feet. I am wobbly.

She parades proud and menstrual, parades at her periodically shedding the blood I give my life for. She struts around the ring after the charade of giving herself to me and always withdrawing at the insistence of my horn, compelled to follow her and skirts like hers all our lives.

I'm numb, dazed. My vision grows double, multiplies her. She approaches again, this time with an extra flourish that she pretends to keep from me. She shouts like a fishwife now, "Come prove you are a man!"

I have no more desire for her. But she taunts me, and the old juices mixed with a blinding anger get the better of me. Still mad enough to gore, I rush and she turns her dress in a swirl, almost trips, turns her back to me completely that I graze her backside.

She tames me in a number of turns as if this is a dance. At one pass both our bellies touch and I smear her again with my blood. The crowd applauds this; she now seems redder than I am.

I don't know how I keep on my feet, but I do. She walks up to me and scolds me for my fatigue, grows almost tired of me. The crowd is waiting.

She goes over to the ladies in pink who give her something. She approaches with it beneath her cape, walks right up to me and taunts me, then pulls out a long sword from the extra flounce and in a halfhearted gesture away suddenly changes direction and sharply plunges it into my neck up to the hilt.

I can feel it penetrating, feel the intimacy of her will inside me. I give off a blood curdling bellow. I try to shake the blade out, do a *danse macabre*, a frenzy of throwing my head up and down to mimic the plunge as if I did it to myself, thinking I'll free myself that way and we can start all over, me goring this time. My tongue is now choking, protruded, as if my body can't absorb any more penetration.

He calmly walks up to me to retrieve his sword. I see him now dragging his cape freely behind him; he is not a woman! She, they all are males in disguise!

I grow dizzy as he pulls the sword out of me and shoves it in again. I think of my own acute maleness, the exemplum of all others; the haunches, the neck muscles, the horns, are all a charade, that nature has tricked me. The color I am attracted to, the skirts, the bodies, the mechanical charging, the thrusts I am bound to, all tricks to end in this!

The five are now surrounding me, closing in. Four females again in pink dresses, the only color I see they wave in my face and I, cornered, turn my head this way and that, my tongue lolling, gray and longer even than the stroke of a clock almost run down. They close in. The blood red, his body smeared with me, claims the closest, most intimate contact, this sterile unproductive relationship he thinks will win him a family of friends and admirers, lovers; he thinks he'll imitate me, but his future he doesn't know will be the same. His vital powers will run down like clockwork and be cornered one day by the youth and vitality that will dance disguised in front of him and finally run him through one last time, even pull out the blade and clean it off on him. Finally, he will be brought to his knees and collapse to the applause of the crowd.

His cohorts now move in and pull the sharp instruments out to use on the next animal. One takes a small dagger from his waist and thrusts it into the base of my skull and twists it a hundred and eighty degrees gritting his teeth.

Everyone will think back to my animated, bold, fearless entry, their cheering at my being innocently unaware of the show, the timely execution by the pink ladies, their timid maidservants, the nimble attendants, the disguised lover in red. Somehow it seemed improbable that it would end like this, that so much bulk and majestic animal spirit could be brought to its knees. The audience is stunned by the collapse; though they've seen it a hundred times, they are always surprised.

As I lay there on my side, a team of three white horses with bells on and little Spanish flags sticking out of their harness comes rushing out. The stadium attendants hook me up. I barely feel the retainer of the one in red come and with a knife slice my ear off to hold up in display.

The homosexual! I want to say, as I am dragged away across the dirt ring leaving a trail of blood, when I realize that nobody is homosexual, and everybody is. That sex is a disguise to behave cruelly to one another to prove finally what we are not.

I am dragged in a swirl of blood that will later be raked indistinguishably into the dust and sprinkled with water for the next male pride that thinks it can overcome the odds of so many disguised females.

STANDING AT A URINAL IN
YOKOHAMA

T HERE WERE PEOPLE when I went in. I know there were people, the cleaning lady and more. I stood against the urinal. There were about twenty on one side alone and the station was big. The lavatory was newly built. It was Yokohama Station and had just been renovated. There were two sets of urinals on each side. I don't remember the toilets. In the back was the raised tile floor with more urinals. A line of wash basins divided the lavatory in two, and new mirrors were at each basin. On the wall at eye level were gray silhouettes of birds in flight; the blue tile background came through as sky.

As I said, I walked in. Usually I take the last urinal furthest from the exit. I don't like to be watched, as I suffer from tenesmus anyway. And usually I close my eyes, too, trying to relax. Nerves, that's what drives me there half the time, rather than any physical need to pass water. And if I have a newspaper, or bag, or my coat is long enough, I use them as shields so nobody will look. I'm careful though if it is my coat to keep it out of the way of the water I am making. Though I can't help thinking that sometimes I must wet myself, as there is a curious curl to the ends of my long blue coat. But it smells all right, so maybe it is only the moisture it picks up.

Anyway, I walk in and go to the very first one. Normally the first urinal in Japan can be seen from the station outside the lavatory. The people passing can look right in. But also it is the first one that people will line up behind. So I never choose it as a rule. Well, this time I did because about five or six of the neighboring urinals were vacant. Sometimes I use the compartments. They are ground level and I can pass water in peace there, away from prying eyes. And my body is relaxed enough that even if I don't have to do anything something comes.

Well, I'm standing there, you see, with blinders on like a horse, going about my business. "Doing my duty," so to speak, as this old woman I knew would say of her dog when he was "good" and the walk had been successful.

I, too, was doing my duty, standing there, minding my own business. And no, an arm didn't touch my shoulders, or circle around from behind. In such places men's eyes don't even look at each other. And my eyes are so circumscribed within the arc of water I'm making that I don't know what's going on outside. (This is important.) And no, I didn't find out anything about myself that I didn't know, or did I?

See, I'm standing there not looking at anyone, minding my own business. Not even thinking about her (You never think about women in such places.), the deep sadness that suffuses my body, my life. My heavy heart that not even a visit to a john makes more buoyant, but it does make me forget myself for a moment, forget her. (Why I've come to Yokohama.) What she's done to me again. My feelings. I know they are luxuries, that there are more important needs in life.

"I got to go, I got to go," my mother used to say rushing unceremoniously from a group of people.

Maybe it was a weak bladder, or some void within her, that had her always rushing off. Anyway, it makes you forget for a moment. And in Japan, I'm a foreigner, and there's a sense of visual curiosity that mounts in a toilet, becomes more highly charged. You can feel the electricity there in the air. You'd hope people would be more polite, not stare at you, but some do, especially out in the country where I live.

But here I am standing at a urinal in Yokohama minding my own business. Out of the corner of my eye I catch a glimpse of an old man, well-dressed, wearing glasses. He's standing very erect, overly erect now that I think of it, though at the time only my eye registered the erectness. And so I continue doing, as I said, what I'm doing. My bladder has dilated. I guess I do have a thing about going. For my mother's a nurse, and she would tell me about the catheters inserted into men's urinary tract when they couldn't go. "It's the most painful thing," she'd say more than once. "How those men scream!"

I remember how often I winced just thinking about what she said, and the curious funny sensation I felt running down my leg.

Well, my bladder is opening up and a nice straw yellow stream is passing into the white urinal. I had always prided myself on my diet, the water I drank. The color I kept it. The little chance poisons had to accumulate in my body.

I never looked at myself, of course. That was a relic of my Catholic upbringing. Sometimes that made things messy. And no touching, no, I never touched myself while going, just opened the zipper, gave a little pull to my underwear and there it was, hanging, ready to do its business. All I had to do was give it a shake once or twice to assure myself of its freedom. And to put it back, too, I didn't even need to touch myself, just grabbed hold of the zipper lightly and pulled up the one side and it went right in with a little jerk upwards of my hip. Two times was enough. (I remember, too, the admonition of my scoutmaster who said, "If you shake it more than two times, you're playing with yourself." That I would never be accused of.) I pulled the elastic portions of my jockey underwear down through my pants pockets and I was on my way, like nothing had happened. Another success, having done my business. That's how it usually happened.

And all this water ritual doesn't come out of nothing. For I remember as a child the adults out at the kitchen table with company playing cards, proudly calling out to them, "See, I can go without touching myself!"

They all got a big laugh out of that, and told me to close the door.

Well, there I am standing in the middle of having fully relaxed and having caught a glimpse of this man out of the corner of my eye standing erect. The next moment I'm back looking at the gray silhouettes of birds on the wall in front of me, eyes straight ahead, at attention, and I hear many short steps. I look over and the man is falling backwards in short choppy steps (just like a Japanese woman walks forward), as if he is losing his balance, but it is accelerated by his erectness. It must be because of his effort to walk forward, to keep his balance, to stand up straight. But his head is perched high. And before I realize what's happening, he's lost his footing completely and he is falling so fast that I can only turn helplessly and look. I blamed it later on my bad eyesight, then on the blinders I wore minding my own business, that studied indifference even a westerner learns in Japan, giving away nothing, not tipping his mitt, so to speak,

Well, he's falling, and I can do nothing. His hands are outstretched like wings stripped of their feathers, helpless against the weight of his body. You imagine him a stubborn, or at least proud, old man whose effort to walk forward has rendered his fall that much more forceful, for the complete loss of balance threw him almost angrily down. But not his body, not his body. That was what was so awful, and my just standing there helplessly halfway through my business, frozen by what I saw. His head was as if dismembered, with a coffinesque stare, as if the body had already abandoned it. It was suspended taunting me with the fact that I had not a chance in the world to catch him and break his fall. I did stop and whirl around. It was only me and him. We two in the whole bathroom, in Yokohama Station. Imagine it, one of the largest stations in the world, and its biggest john, and about three-thirty in the afternoon.

I turned around and groaned, "Oh, my God! My God!"

At that moment his head crashed to the floor, only his head, his whole body slapped him down. The pride in his step, or whatever it was that rendered him mute and made him so erect, slapped him down with a vengeance.

Like an eggshell the skull cracked, but no, like a coconut I thought to relate the story, but, no, not that even. It was so loud, and a man's head, that I can still hear it now, the sound on the upraised lavatory tile and the way it bounced, as if it weren't even attached to the body. The glasses flew up and shattered, and the body seemed not even to absorb the impact but leave it all to the head. The body froze. The one arm didn't go limp but went rigid and perpendicular, just as a man might reach out at a formal occasion to let a woman grab his arm.

His eyes were open, and I ran over to him, "Oh my God!" I said choking. His eyes were open, but he was unconscious, rigid. "Oh, my God!"

I didn't know whether to hold his head up or what. I was going to run to the exit, call someone, but the cleaning lady just then came as if she heard the fall. I pointed to the man. She let out a little scream and hurried over to him and started to say something.

"No, no," I said. "*Atama, atama*" (Head, head), and I smashed my fist in my hand again and again with a loud sound.

She understood and quickly went out. A train conductor in a uniform came in and walked calmly over to him and bent down to speak. I was surprised how measured his walk was. I was standing back, wincing.

"No, no, *atama*," I said and clapped my hands together loudly. He looked at me a little irritated and left.

People were now filling up the entrance. I left in physical contortions for the sound I had heard. I winced like a catheter, or something, was in my own body. I shook my head to get the sound out. My stomach grew nauseous.

What's life worth, just slapped down like that? No chance. And the more stubbornly he wanted to walk. A hunk of meat rigid with not even time to get cold, the mind in a second penalizing the body for not doing its will.

And I told the old lady I was visiting that night the story. I wanted to call her up then, to show her I could talk about something else.

"Why did you tell me? Why did you tell me?" she said.

And later while we were eating tangerines around the kotatsu, I sat screwing up my face.

"What?" she asked.

"I can still hear it. It was so loud. And the head!"

"Don't, don't," she said. "No more!"

I woke up from my sleep and heard the sound, went to sleep with it in my mind. Privately, however, I took a kind of pleasure in it. For the next day I saw her. She was more beautiful than I had ever seen her. She was meeting me to tell me never again would she see me. Never again. The finality of those words, I was crushed again by her, slapped down. My body a will-less rag stiff with resentment. Old man already. Years ahead of his time.

Soon after the initial awkwardness I told her about the old man, involuntarily. It was such a relief. Something to fall back on, not having to talk about us. The old man's fall was an ace up my sleeve. My wild card. Something I could rely on.

She laughed at first not understanding the gravity of the fall. The sound I had heard had not gotten through to her yet. The whole life that would probably never get up under its own power again. How could it, he had hit his head so hard? Everything in life there crushed! How could she, her beauty, begin to understand? Yes, like an eggshell, so unprotected against tile.

Only later did I realize I delighted in telling the story, in not talking to the old woman immediately about her. The old man filled the need so completely. He was a blessing in disguise, as only the misfortunes of strangers can be. She, the old lady, was jealous of her anyway.

"She'd be hard to live with," she said.

"You didn't like her from the beginning," I said.

"She looks unhealthy," she finally admitted, "and so skinny."

And later the hardness of her falling for me, the obduracy. She had married. I had wanted her, gave all I had, didn't even keep my pride, though I had tried to walk erect around her, correct my stooped shoulders, but was slapped down by her. There was nothing left for me either. Everything froze with the refusal.

I was like the old man giving her my arm on this last formal meeting walking to a coffee shop. She'd tell me she wanted to stay with her husband, that visiting me last weekend was a mistake, that she believed in something more than love. But why had she dressed up so beautifully, worn so much perfume and make-up? We sat there sipping coffee.

She could have had anything she wanted from me, what in the world I was able to give. Yet she was to cast it away. I was nothing, had nothing. Only a head that I would see fall on someone else.

She wrote in English two pages for me.

"It's all in the head," I said. "*Atama, atama.* Intelligent, yes, but in the head, not the heart. What do you feel? The head and body must work together. Be one. If they don't support each other they both fall. This shows me your thinking, your intelligence. I want to see your heart."

She looked at me. Her eyes showed me feelings I could never get her to admit. Two thousand years of culture, reticence, passion I hadn't instruments sensitive enough for. And all this repression, I suppose it's good. It gives the edge she needs, makes life interesting. Mine too. All head, all thinking about her, all physical sickness.

The sound yesterday was a relief, I realized. His banging his head was a relief. But not until this next day. Crushed, dashed, my brains I realized were not scrambled, but the one sound, the loudness of it, after blaming myself for not catching him in time, then convincing myself I could do nothing, that it was fate.

We both were alone in that well-attended lavatory in Yokohama in mid-afternoon for a reason. That sound, the excuse of that man's head smashing so decisively on the tile floor, was a message. That's why I was so eager to tell it, and over and over again.

Of course I felt badly for the horror of what could happen to an old person crashing down on his head, or taking a nose dive like I had done with the woman I wanted to spend my life with. It could happen to anyone, anywhere, anytime. I was already doddering at the rejection. But it forced me from myself into his body. The fall became my own. Of course the age was different, the nationality, the hair and eye color, the glasses, but the fall was the same. Not a fainting like women do.

The pain had already stiffened me. My body defenses had already seen to that. The paralysis had set in. There were no tears this time like last week. Though she looked for them at our parting. I knew too intimately from the day before what man's fate was. It got me free for a moment, and later the solace of what's love and the feelings to say when I have just heard a man's head crack, and only today does the word "crunch" occur to me. That was exactly the sound. Before yesterday I couldn't have believed it of the skull. What's the sound of the heart breaking compared to that?

CHIKA CHAN

"SHH...CHIKA CHAN is sleeping," she said.

Startled I just looked at her as she continued reading *Crime and Punishment* I had gotten her to buy. And every once in a while, she would look up, but never at me directly, just down at Chika chan. It seemed Dostoyevsky was our only connection, the common ground that she periodically turned to, otherwise eliminating me, as she looked at Chika chan motheringly, making me wonder how and why things had come to such a pass.

I tried to scan my behavior to see how I could be the cause of her attitude toward Chika chan. Maybe I should have accepted it as normal, or myself anticipated the problem of a threesome. I had always traveled alone, had never to contend with balancing favor; an only child I was used to getting my way and the attention of adults whenever I wanted it. Perhaps I was spoiled and that was why her behavior so startled me.

I had thought that she was all mine, that I was the center of her life, but here in Mexico I learned differently. Chika chan interfered, and I could accept that up to a point. I can understand a woman's need to tuck a child into bed, to care about how she sleeps, that she isn't cold, or hot, needing to wash her clothing and brush her hair and arrange her little braids, to dote upon her. I know every woman has such needs, so why should I kick against them as if something in me always needs to be born. I've been given my chance. I know way must be made for others, that there are more people in the world than just me, Jack. That's what I was told when I got selfish and unbearable as a child and would be reproached with stern looks, or quick slaps, for showing off. I should have learned back then, it is true.

But everyone has a right to be surprised, don't they? Life can't all be planned out, not even Raskolnikov's murder of the old woman went as expected. He didn't mean to axe her the way he did, did he? Unexpected events do occur, and especially in another country, under such a hot sun. Here in Mexico there were revolutions, so why not complete turns in a person's personality? It doesn't always have to be a whole nation on the rise. It could be just one woman, the one you are traveling with. It could be the high altitude, the much vaunted climate; it could be the incredible dryness and the striking colors that gave rise to the dress of Chika chan that could have won her over, and away from you. Or it could have been you, or more uncharitably her.

She opened up a world, perhaps out of spite to be in competition with the book you had gotten her to buy, a world that you never thought you'd have access to, that was learned by your feelings for her. They should have been enough, your traveling together, enjoying the climate, the country, the food, each other. Why need there be more? Why did the little one have to come between, insinuate herself? She herself was Japanese with big eyes and the smallest feet, with a daintiness of movement and gesture, and a mind that you felt could absorb *Crime and Punishment*; in fact, now you realize she would use it against you like a court and jury system. You realize that you should have given her, due to her age and innocence, "A Gentle Creature," but no, no, though the situation is the same the scenario ends too violently, as the girl finally jumps out the window.

No, you have to accept things, take them in stride, as you look over at her in the other bed adjusting Chika chan to a more comfortable sleeping position, plumping her pillow, fondling her, fixing her night dress, pulling up her underpants, and smoothing the hair from her forehead, giving her a look of love while, and this you can't understand at all, barely looking at you, as if you are not there, totally out of the picture, as if there is a huge gulf of resentment larger than the lake out the window that space cannot bridge, as if you are on different planets, not just sharing time in a strange country. Maybe she doesn't even have to look at the lake to sense the strong undercurrent of resentment in you towards Chika chan.

Now I don't know quite how to refer to Chika chan, the position she has in everything. The word "usurpation" immediately comes to mind. Those first tentative steps into both your lives were at first welcomed, a sign of love. You had held her arm and drew her closer, but living alone for so long you never had experienced how children come between adults, how so thoroughly they can fulfill the need of one partner, and leave the other absolutely stranded. The little hugs she gave Chika chan went ungiven to me, and the kisses grew louder and, I imagined, more spiteful by the day. The attentions she used to show me, to lavish so thoughtlessly, now were transferred.

It was Chika chan this and Chika chan that.

"Chika chan are you hungry? Are you thirsty? Are you comfortable? Do you want me to straighten your little arm before it gets caught in your dress? Shall I fix your blouse, tie your shoe?" which she even had me do. All the attention she used to show to me was now hers, and I was left high and dry, hardly able to get a syllable of concern out of her for me.

Why I didn't insist on her sending Chika chan to her grandmother soon after she arrived and started to come between us, I don't know. The airlines would take care of everything and I'd have her back all for myself, not dividing her sentiments. Division! It was not even that! I was cut out altogether. There was something spiteful like the alternating mind of Raskolnikov, of generosity one moment, then stinting behavior that surprises even the reader that human beings can possess both natures, and change so, yes change so rapidly! And that's it, possessed! That's what she was, possessed! And I was simply discarded like an old hat worn too many times, kicked out of the way.

"How do you like the book?" I'd ask, and she'd give me a vague answer, or an ambiguous smile that I could only read as having found something in the novel that uncovered a strange aspect of my own behavior.

My behavior! I wasn't the strange one. But how could I tell people? She was just over twenty and had every right to show mothering impulses. It was in all their genes, who can deny it?

Maybe she wanted me to give a more paternal look, be more loving, doting, then slip my hand in hers over Chika chan, win her that way, seduce her by paying attention to the child. Maybe that is the way husbands with patience do it in her own country.

But it was my own fault, too, I know. I had been told, had seen enough with my own eyes how the husband is treated, how in Japan the child sleeps between the parents for months on end, years in the same room, how the lovemaking stops altogether, how the man goes off on imaginary golfing trips to other Asian countries. I had many lessons from friends, but I never thought they pertained to me, for I was somehow exempt. The freemindedness of both of us I thought obviated the maternal impulses I now saw, if that is what they were.

I know there is something I am trying to deny in myself. Maybe that is what this Russian novel business is all about, the step out of the daylight, away from basics, to the dingy underside of life that refuses love and a woman, and most importantly children. They are only grown up in Dostoyevsky, young boys already; Kolya in *The Brothers Karamazov* after whom I named my Siamese cat. That was as far as I got being reined into loving a child, that literary creation, and so I could easily afford sharing the bemusement of Dostoyevsky himself over why children suffer, how a Deity could allow that to happen. But now it was I who was suffering!

Why? How was it possible? How had things gone so wrong? Was I such a bad person? Didn't I have love for her? Wasn't I kind enough, didn't I try to improve her mind, wasn't I warm enough, giving enough? Why had she turned on me? Why a third person? Why always a third person to keep us on our toes? Nature's trump card. To get a rise out of the one, or the other. Why always this leavening as the staff of life? Why must people be nourished this way on jealousy? And it doesn't even have to be an adult, someone tall and darkly handsome, someone who is athletic, a man of her dreams. That's what I was prepared for more than Chika chan. That is what every man is prepared for, and does push-ups for, tries to keep his body trim and in some kind of shape for. And then one day a child comes, or even a dog, or a slinking cat, anything that draws from us. Just her overly worrying about feeding the animal will make us starved for attention.

Why are we made so? I couldn't understand it as they both lay in the bed across from me in the dim light of the hotel. What had I done to deserve this, why had nature and my emotions tricked me? Why couldn't the bridges I thought Dostoyevsky would build to her psyche sustain the structural deficiencies of two different sexes? Was it because of my preference for twin beds, that she now claimed she too couldn't sleep without them, was that what started it?

My mouth dropped as she said, "Chika chan is getting a draft, I think I'm going to close the window. You don't mind, do you?"

And I didn't answer, thinking this had been carried far enough. Instead I slipped down in bed and under the covers. She never liked to be the last to have to turn out the light, and me with my nervous temperament who took everything to heart, the possibly unlocked front door, its chain, the stove still on, having to relieve myself one last time or put the finishing touches on my look in the mirror. I was always the last one up, but this night I dropped under the covers hoping to draw her to my bed that way.

But instead, she said, "Chika chan are you more comfortable now?"

Why couldn't she ask me once? That I couldn't understand.

I slumped down and reviewed her behavior recently; her straightening the legs, combing her hair, talking while seeming to maintain her interminable silences with me, telling Chika chan when we were going shopping and out to eat, how much she was going to like Japan, and all about her grandmother. And the way she fed her in the restaurant made me uncomfortable, getting food on her mouth, or dribbling it, and promptly having to wipe it off her dress. Giving Chika chan her breakfast before she started in on mine or raising her little arms to try and get her to feed herself. At all this I sat back and looked in amazement.

One day she even spanked Chika chan and I sighed with relief that maybe she was making her way back to reality. The next, however, she bought her candy and put a piece up to her mouth and said, "Here Chika chan."

When she took a drink it was always an occasion to ask Chika chan if she wanted a sip, and she'd stain her little red mouth till the water bubbled and ran down her chin. Or sometimes out walking, for once alone, she'd say suddenly, "Maybe Chika chan is waiting for us." And we'd hurry home. Or before leaving she'd put her out of the way of the maid "so she wouldn't be stolen," she'd joke, or say because she was so small she could fit in the safety of her shirt pocket in the closet.

Even I couldn't help adding, "But will she get enough air?"

She at once grew friendly and disposed towards me for recognizing her feelings for Chika chan, and acted normal and loving for a time, put Chika chan in her place. So that I felt I had her back again, that there was only the two of us, not the specter of a threesome that looms over every couple in various degrees of outline till it clearly materializes in their lives one day, and pushes out the one to place itself in the affections of the other.

But it didn't last long, for I couldn't help myself again, and keep up the charade of being content with her present, with being the odd man out so to speak, even if that did dispose her more kindly towards me. I made no comment when she brought back food for Chika chan, when she looked for little bits of jewelry, or colored string she would embellish her wrists or ankles with. I just kept what I thought was a dignified silence. And when she'd give Chika chan a little shampoo, I didn't say anything or mind her using my Breck.

I knew of her tendency to go off and play with the children when she'd meet my friends. She was always great entertainment for them, so maybe I should have had the imagination to suspect this or something like it might happen someday. But you never know who you are traveling with. It could be a blood relative, a friend, or even a lover that suddenly with one purchase reveals a side of themselves you never remotely imagined.

And when she grabbed Chika chan one day, apparently angry at me, I didn't get upset. I have nothing against corporeal punishment. It wasn't my child as much as she probably wanted me to assume a kind of paternity, or at least make a show of it. I thought too she wanted to punish me by having her hopes acted out, come between me and my love for literature, after all I had gotten her to buy the book, was it now to punish me for it?

So I lay there and thought how I had left her sleeping in the room that afternoon and passed Chika chan for the first time on the blanket, and bent down to her and noticed how well-made her fine features were and her little braids, and the colorful Indian outfit, the bright reds and purples and black and white and blue, the yellow and oranges, and the flawless dress she wore. I quickly asked her when she came down if she wanted it. And we went over and looked at the display, and then she bent down and picked up another, but finally chose Chika chan, and I got it for her.

I was the cause of everything. Yes, the father of all this you might say. Though, true, it was she who picked out the name and elaborated a pattern of behavior that I could only marvel at, no matter how disconcerting. I went over in my mind how every day she grew more distant from me and more attached to my purchase, a purchase designed to bring her closer. And I tried to compensate in a thousand ways, tried to distinguish her breathing from a doll's, as I lay in the darkness after she switched off the light with a tension the night breeze should have dispelled, but refused to.

Instead we lay waiting for the first one to break the silence and call for the other to come to finally abandon Chika chan or join her. The first who spoke would have the choice where Chika chan would stay, until one day she could have a real child of her own.

RAISING CAIN

THE SWEETNESS OF Cain was so connected with the earth that he loved the sheer pleasure of overturning the soil, working it between his fingers as he broke the smaller clods with his thumb. The earth was cleansing, the way it seeped through the filter of his skin as nutriment almost. The furrows he made were like in a woman. His Mother Earth. The seeds he dropped in one by one, the plants he lovingly tended until the first green shoots, shiny and fresh, burst forth, absorbed him with infinite delight. So rich and sumptuous was the bounty of nature. The bright berries, the shiny apple, the succulent fig, the swelling pumpkin, the deep purple grape was all a riot of color. The drooping bean and many tendrilled cucumber, the long zucchini and incomparable eggplant, the private potato and the hidden white tunics of the onion all held their secrets that he unearthed. They were planted, raised, and picked with such loving care, that the world was good.

Cain even in time took advantage of his own sweetness with duly planted brakes, tall stalks that would one day be turned into refined sugar, as if man had found his bliss renewed by morning sunshine and the afternoon rains.

When his brother was born it was such a joy to have another tiller, another child of the generous earth. But Abel was to become a man of many parts, powerful and moody. The domestic plants weren't enough. The grape didn't make him blush, the glaucous clouds on the newly minted fruit only affected him when it was fermented, when the juices turned to rich syrups or intoxicating liquors, for his blood was thicker and more demanding than Cain's. The taste of apples didn't predispose him towards life and its bounty, neither did the sweet interior of the fig, or the berries that were too small for his fingers, and the mighty pumpkin inspired no fairy tales. He overlooked even the sharp radish, the dull bean, the suggestive pendulousness of the eggplant, or the tomato calling for brightly colored attention, turning from inexperienced green to bright red overnight.

No, Abel was not a flower child. Cain alone appreciated the blooms as much as the actual fruit, the pink apple blossoms, the delicate pear, the yellow cucumber, the remarkable lavender pink of the sweet pea. What a delight of florescence!

Abel herded with his staff and had no sympathy for a parallel tendril curling into a double helix. Abel loved challenges well beyond the rooted vegetable, challenges whose screams sought the open air. He relished his place in the order of things, powerfully treading the earth. Naturally hierarchical, he moved from the lowly worms that he pulled from clods to more complex forms of life.

Abel played with ants, put together the red and the black, started fights, then whole wars. He pulled the left appendages off grasshoppers to watch them crawl in a circle or calculated their length of life in the baking sun. Butterflies he'd reduce, the more striking, royal, the better, not the cabbage moth so much as the Viceroy, the Monarch, even the pale lime Luna Moth; he'd bring out the caterpillar in them pulling off every appendage down to the wriggling torso.

Cats, he cut their whiskers off to watch their disorientation, and fish he fooled by removing their fins until they lost all mobility. Birds he blinded with hot pokers and then kept them around for their song. He finally was drawn to sheep. Maybe it was their hot breath. I'd like to say it was the cuteness of the lambs, their soft wooliness, but he thoughtlessly sheered them, then slaughtered them with pleasure for the meat.

The first time he cut the neck and the warm blood spurted out a rain of tiny droplets smearing his arms and legs, Abel's senses quickened and he knew he had found his vocation. He panted over his labors like never before.

Not even his fights with Cain brought such pleasure. The bloody noses, the cuts above the eye, the vision reducing blows, the split lips inspired Abel, but nothing gave him pleasure like the entrails of sheep and the stickiness of their blood on his hands. Abel's taste for blood was unslaked that one day he even tried to lick the drops from under his brother's nostrils.

Their Father's love for Cain was steady, had that uneventfulness that reduces love to the humdrum, cyclical expectations of the seasons and the crops produced. It had a shallow rhythm, despite deep roots in the soil, but it never achieved the same blessing. Perhaps it was controlled by the future culpability, the history destined to be made.

The true love was reserved for Abel.

It came to a head one autumn when the sons made their offerings to their Father. Cain once again brought a rich cornucopia of fruits and vegetables, the proud harvest of all he had planted. The burnished skins of grape, the berries, apples, tomatoes, figs, plums, and pomegranate bulging inside their taut skins didn't arouse the Father like Abel.

The Father's voice thundered as from the heavens approval for Abel who instead carried his sheep on his back; like Atlas he balanced the old man's universe. The salty blood of the newly slain animals covered his son with a stickiness that renewed the blood tie to his Father's love. Cain's fruits and vegetables seemed watery by comparison; they had no beating heart, no circulatory connection with the old man. There was something about the visionless eyes of the sheep that sharpened the Father's eyesight. The animal hoisted on the shoulders of his son and dropped before his Father infused the old man with renewed youth. He looked on astonished at how easily his son could cut the throats of animals. Perhaps he sensed the protection Abel offered. Sweet pea tendrils would never grow around anyone's neck while sleeping, but a rampaging ram could butt a man high up into the air. In fact Abel introduced eating the complex organs, developed a taste for the grainy liver, the stubborn kidney, the rubbery heart with its chewy chambers, the curved necks with the tender flesh between the vertebrae, and the scrumptious sirloins which imparted a potency to the old man's declining vigor.

No wonder he selected Abel's animals over the peaceful produce of Cain. Even the brains Father and son ate imagining a triumph over the sheep's friskiness, gamboling in the evening pasture, or the benefits of added vision from sucking on a salty eyeball, inspiring a contentedness that came from the sheep grazing in the dewy grass and the shepherd watching.

All this was laid at the Father's feet as he surveyed Cain's colorful crop that hadn't sacrificed one live animal.

The rush of power from Abel's offering, the bleeding aftermath at his feet, energized the old man. This was life circulating through him dismissing the heap of vegetables. The excitement of their pushing through the ground, their colorful erectness in the sunlight, could not hold a candle to the evening slayings, the wheezing throats slit, the bleating beforehand, the baa cut off in mid-utterance, so different from beans being snapped, or zucchini cut. How could that compete with the outside air rushing in the windpipe to preempt the animal's breathing with the corrosive effects of oxygen? The animals lay there, testament to man's future. What could a son do if a father was pleased by that?

Cain was devastated when his Father ignored his produce, showed so little regard for his hard work, but bestowed his blessing on his brother Abel.

Days after Abel taunted Cain over his Father's choice as he worked the land, bent over his hoe. He called his brother a loser for sweating in the hot fields, working his fingers to the bone, while he lay dozing all afternoon under the shaded trees tending his flocks.

"The whole world is mine," he said. "The future's mine!" he taunted, bending down mock bleating into Cain's ear, "Father loves me, not your dirty vegetables and dull fruit!"

At that Cain rose up with his hoe and struck Abel with the accumulated grip of all the thankless years spent tilling the soil, trying to win his Father's approval. His brother didn't have time to resist. The blow was so decisive that his legs crumpled beneath him like empty husks of corn and there he lay.

Cain left off work and it wasn't until the evening meal that his Father asked, "Cain, where is thy brother, Abel?"

Cain, normally sweet, upright, and open, his father's favorite until the birth of his dynamic shepherd brother, said he didn't know.

Cain left after the meal and went to the field and saw his brother lying cold on the dewy earth. He lifted him up in his arms under a bright round moon and brought the body back to the house.

His father saw him carrying Abel just as his brother had carried the offerings of so many sheep and goats. Like the animals Abel had killed, he too became a dead weight. Cain set his brother down before his Father. The blood was caked dry at his ears and mouth.

The Father wept and buried his son.

Afterwards Cain worked the land, but as was forecast the land yielded little and he was forced to flee and wander the earth a marked man. His attentiveness to the soil lost heart, the desire he infused the ground with and its loving reciprocation was gone. Nothing would grow for him. Cain left home doomed to earn his living tending flocks, inspiring a bloodline of shepherds and butchers who slaughtered a variety of animals for food, clothing, and the approval of their fathers.

PELICAN

THERE IS A storybook intimacy with a pelican. Maybe it is over its oddness. The squab body, the almost flightless wings, short in our minds except when extended by force, the knotting of opposing muscle that accounts for flight. But most of all it is the bill. The long bill little different in its ramrod straightness from a horseshoe crab's tail. But with a difference. A pouch of flesh that seems almost like a placenta, to itself be a membrane of life, merged with the child it carries tied with the overlarge kerchief in our mind, almost a stork, but as I said squab, an oddity after all.

Maybe it is the flesh that attracts us. Something like the webbed feet of ducks that'll make us uneasily spread out our own hands to look at the webbing between our fingers; you'd imagine if a light were trained behind the pelican jowl, like a delicately translucent wattle, the network of veins would map out a pulse of blood and pinkness that would make us as onlookers blush at the comparison with our own flesh. And the small eye is mounted above the bill, beadily surveying the potential load, the burden of carrying such a bag of flesh, of rendering it airborne. But the wings are deceiving, as I already mentioned. In a moment they'll spread larger than a man's outstretched arms and the pelican will have raised the oddity of himself with the most graceful motions. Or the sack will sometimes go yellowish brown, or gray white like the more unattractive variety found in Mexico, along the coast, a town like Puerto Vallarta, for example.

One such pelican was beneath a bridge, dove-brown flecked with black feathers, the belly an overcast gray, just the opposite of the too bright Mexican sunlight. The blue and the white morning clouds seemed almost a reproach to the pelican's overcast coloring, an unkindness, in fact. Not even the humanizing gray white fold of skin could redeem the pelican, you felt, from the severity of a clear day.

You wondered if the brilliant day could accept in the small stream that he flapped, splashing the water with his wing, his pouch of flesh. The waterproofing of his feathers you'd imagine kept him from getting immediately soaked; if only he could fly away, prove himself a bird. Then the morning light could accept his overcast coloring, glisten on his wings with little prisms of water making him a bird of the heavens, free of the bad weather of his wings, not this oddity up close, the bearer of almost human flesh that a hand would feel compelled to grip.

Maybe it was the flesh that brought out such impulses, the flesh mercilessly seeking out flesh, and the unsupportive anomaly of frame, or the very lightness of the hollow bones compared to the man. Or maybe it was the beady eyes, that contact couldn't be made, that they were too far from a bird of prey, from the hooked beaks that in one stroke could bury themselves in entrails. No, the pelican at best skimmed the surface, was a fisherman, innocuous on land. Maybe it was his very harmlessness that made the fist twist its beak, loop then rotate the whole body around the wrist. After all, that's what a man is given a ball and socket for, to twist pelicans. Its body is too odd for the man to do otherwise, its beak too much of a handle not to grasp.

And could it be when it did try to fly away, flap its wings, that it didn't know that the rope around its foot would pull it back into the water? Or is this what it wanted? To get closer to the man, within striking distance. But the slow motion of its beak, the way it opened like rusty oversized scissors, and almost harmlessly closed, mocked the power it didn't have compared to the man's forearm that he purposely put all the way into the pelican's mouth to show how ineffectual its bite was. The bag of flesh was enough to give away its incapacity early on and only amused the man whose laughter echoed many times beneath the bridge.

The bird's futile pecks only encouraged him. Such a big bird, but so helpless that the man let go of the beak, and as the bird beat his free wing the man grabbed it too and twisted the animal around again and again. Every time the bird came up with his bill to peck, the man put out his arm and laughed. And when the bird tried to fly, the man promptly pulled him back.

That the man was up to his waist in water didn't seem to matter, that his white shirt was wet didn't bother him; he was having too good a time tormenting the animal to worry about his appearance. Maybe he was out of a job. He'd set the bird free and when it would rise completely out of the water, he'd yank it back, then go to work on the beak again.

I looked away and at that moment the pelican brought the point of his beak around with a thrust of his neck. Whether the eye was its target was hard to judge, whether the bright sun conspired to blind the man to this possibility, or the sheer pleasure of tormenting the bird got the better of him, we'll not know. All we know is that the bird's beak found its mark. It could simply have been the angle at which the wing was held, the twisting that snapped the beak toward the man, or maybe the bird saw his own loose feathers floating downstream. In any event he sank his beak with one swift stroke into the eye of the man till it reached bone, as if the eye was not there at all.

The man quickly threw his arms up to his face and blood drenched his fingers and the pelican swooped away with two, four giant sweeps of his wings that left the man screaming on the bank, his body wrenched, twisted toward the eye with blood pouring out all over his white shirt. I imagined the pelican trailing the rope that held him like a thread the further away he got.

So when I did turn back the broad grin on the man's face seemed to slit his eyes protectively, as he now taunted the bird with language I couldn't understand. The bird was wetter and less airborne than before and his efforts to peck were pathetically slow, that you'd think the man would have tired by now. But he kept up as vigorously as before, twisting the wing, first this way then that, then the beak, giving the bird ever more rope then yanking him quickly back again. Maybe it was because the man had an audience.

At that moment I could stand it no longer and leaped over the guardrail and down the hill, splashed into the water towards the man and bird. The man kept laughing, bellowed, his evil mouth yellow and blackened by teeth, teeth he should have had removed. Maybe that was the problem, the pain in his own mouth; all the dark empty spaces seemed a tunnel that I was entering under the double shadow of the bridge. In one leap my fist reached the man's face that I could feel under my knuckles the cartilage of his nose give way as he threw his arms out and splashed backwards into the stream. The bird stunned for a moment swam towards the shallows and shook himself, and the next moment was aloft flapping its large wings, taking the almost human flesh under its beak further away from the man. The bird soared into the sky smaller and smaller until its freedom could only be identified as a speck.

The man got up and sneered at me but lacked the courage to attack. Maybe it was my size. Instead he yelled a torrent of Spanish as I climbed up the bank to the deafening applause that I didn't realize was only a carriage going past as I left the bridge that the further I got down the road eclipsed the man and the pelican from view.

I tried not to hear the laughter of the man and what I imagined to be the shrieks of the bird, despite that bag of flesh that seemed to mute its vocal cords. The bird through it all had been curiously silent, as if he expected that of the man. Maybe it was his bird.

The further away I got the more I felt the bird should have shrieked, whined, barked, meowed, not have been a bird, reptile almost, maybe then I would have bounded over the rail, not have let the man continue, not have walked away. Not have recalled the eye the bird didn't peck out, or the punch not thrown, when one winter day years later in Japan I'd find an enormous jack rabbit on the beach, the skin torn off its hind legs, the musculature exposed to the white bone, the abdominal muscles clearly visible, the source of spring gone. Tufts of hair scattered about like feathers. In its giant head one eye missing.

That reminded me of what the pelican should have done, and that I had walked away saying to myself, "This is not my country. I'm only a tourist."

TEDDY BEAR

CHILDREN SQUEEZE THE life out of their teddy bear to make sure that he'll never leave, that he'll stay with them another night. They hug him to sleep in mock hibernations underneath the covers curled up as if inside a giant log. Maybe they'll let the head peep out for the visiting parent, as the bear is clutched tighter after their departure.

The bear will stay even if one of the parents won't. It will keep an eerie silence as the couple argues in the other room over money, infidelity, the future. The bear will have nuts, berries, honey, peanut butter containers at campsites to comfort the child before he succumbs to sleep. The bear's absent cubs the boy dreams about, and sparkling streams full of speckled trout scooped up by a giant paw.

The boy slips down under the covers at every disturbance, at the sound of thunder, or rain, at the hooting of an owl under a too full moon, ever closer to the brown bear, to his own reflection in the pupil, to the black spokes of an amber iris, to the stitched line of mouth leading from the nose, and the large ears that take everything in, to the arms and legs without digits or claws that scratch.

The bear is harmless, flung hither and thither, neglected during the day; still by nightfall he must be hugged before the boy can sleep. Maybe the little boy imagines foraging, the parade of family members, the play of the cubs. Or right before his nap he thinks of his bear and cries to retrieve it. It is found and he tucks it under his arm as he drifts off in his mid-day slumbers, as if the bear has just eaten the fish he's caught or devoured a fresh honeycomb and is ready too for sleep.

The boy's bear never really haunts his dreams, but stays comfortably in his arms, the soft extension of all the hugs he'd ever want. It is a stoical, silent, understood reciprocity. It brings the world to the boy in this very softest, brown manufacture. There is nothing to clean up, feed, no mandatory sleep not compatible with his own. In fact, the bear is the perfect foil to the little boy, to his needs and fears, in a world adults most of the time overlook.

The bear is only to be picked up after, never tracks mud through the house, never won't eat; in a toy chest by itself it doesn't have a chance at reproduction beyond the susceptibility to being replaced by the purchase of another bear whose eyes are bigger, or whose color is an unusual blue, or maybe the pile is deeper, more furry looking, or the pink of the snout is more real, runny. Rarely is it a ferocious bear, but one that is lovable, a bear no one would consider hunting.

Until one day the boy hears the unearthly roar of the mama bear who rears up on her hind legs, and leaves the whole Goldilocks scenario behind, where the family is run away from even if they are like us, live in a house and have chairs and legs that can be broken, or porridge eaten. We want to adopt the docility of the bear into our lives. The bear is a chance to redeem ourselves, replace the worst of us with the hugs and cuddling we never show each other.

The reaction of the boy is split second to the pink mouth, the violet gums, the large white teeth, the deafening roar. The cuddliness is thousands of miles away in a British textile factory, or a Dutch loom. The snout is raised to the smell of the air; she responds unlike the stuffed animal to the proximity of human beings.

Children are amazed at the first sight of a real bear behind bars, astonished at its slow tread, the sheer thickness of its paws, the powerful immobility. They try to comprehend the lack of urgency, the busy attendance to local smells, the fact that there is nothing to cuddle, no possible bear hug. The few hundred-pound animal in the zoo has little relation with the teddy in their room.

*

134

MAN IS A big game hunter. One who can't quite tame his own personality and so has to shoot out in the wild, focus through his scope on what escapes him to make him more of a man.

He gets the giant mother bear in his sights. But before he knows it the bear rears up before the hunting party outfitted with all the modern accoutrements money can buy in 1902 and the celebrity raises his weapon, takes in the tremendous power of the roaring creature, as if out of nowhere the whole animal kingdom is at his doorstep ready to tear apart and swallow the man and his party. The man stands there frozen. His trigger finger stuck fast.

The celebrity then shoots at random into the air. The hot lead goes into the forest and strikes an oak tree, then another shot rings out and hits a poplar, a third buries itself sizzling like a beetle in the wood of a soft pine. The celebrity drops to his knees and topples on his backside, then loses his glasses at the sudden kick of the gun that he thinks is the bear's paw. Multiples of the huge animal are already above of him as he struggles in the dust for air. The bear is roaring and gesturing for all she's worth. The roars rivet the man to the spot, and he thinks it is the end.

But just as the bear lunges forward, a shot rings out and strikes her in the chest. The guide pours three rapid shots into the exceptionally large brown bear and she wobbles forward, almost falls on top of the important man but remains stubbornly standing a moment longer, hugging the air, fighting it with alternate movements of her giant paws.

Then her mouth grows slack and blood starts to spill from it as the animal drops down, shakes her head and the red blood goes everywhere. It splashes the horrified man; the former Rough Rider, who could dig his spurs relentlessly into saddle horses to regain a position, is now too petrified to get to his feet before this enormous creature drooling over him whose chest has been pumped full of hot lead. Blood oozes out her orifices, soaking her snout and interrupting every gurgling breath as the animal drowns in her own body fluids. The second guide has also fired his gun into the animal.

Someone comes and pulls the great man back as the guide stands his ground and finishes the huge animal off. The man could not move from the shock of the attack as he is dragged stiffly away, leaving his famed spectacles in the dust to be retrieved.

Then there is a giant thud as the bear crashes to the ground and groans with what seems her last breath.

The party quickly gathers round to help the personage up, but still keeps a distance lest the bear has another death throe or waves its paw at them.

"Are you all right, Mr. President?" one asks.

"Get your hands off me!"

He is soaked with sweat, spattered with blood, and his pants have a giant stain at the seat coated with dirt. A tiny ant crosses his forearm under cover of his matted body hair, when all of a sudden the man throws out an elbow that hits an aide squarely in the face. Everyone moves back.

Everything is a blur to the President until his glasses are returned in that tense moment when his dignity has to be recouped. Within seconds allowing a false move could rewrite history.

Once he puts on his spectacles the giant animal comes into focus and hits him all over again with its full force.

"What happened?" he says curtly.

"You shot the bear, Mr. President," an aide says quickly looking around at the guides.

"Good shot, Mr. President," another adds to what soon becomes a chorus of congratulations.

Just then a second party of mostly reporters arrives.

"I'm Harris from *The New York Times*. Can we get a shot of you, Mr. President, with the bear? It'll make headlines. Could you step over here? Here put your boot on the bear. Yes, like that."

"Great," says the aide, quickly, to dispel the President's hesitation, dusting the President off.

"What a shot!" the aide says.

"Why don't you sit on the animal now," the reporter says, "and hold your gun."

"Is it dead yet?" someone jumping back asks as the bear's leg suddenly twitches.

"She's not getting up again, is she?" another voice panics.

"It's dead!" pronounced the guide.

And so they aim the camera, an unwieldy tripod affair. Both parties gather round as if they all had a hand in shooting the bear, if only as witnesses.

Just then there is a rustling in the underbrush and the sound of crying. A small cub scampers through the crowd towards his mother. They make a wide swath for it. The little fellow is not to be denied. It stops before his mother, sniffs, whimpers, and seeks her nipples fully exposed to the daylight, and begins to suck the mother's milk.

The group of men stand there astonished. All of them must have remembered when they too sucked at their own mother's breast inspiring lactic dreams that all human beings participate in. The fact that we are so eager to cover the breast shows that we are trying our best to forget it. Even the President, who gets to live in the White House and seems so far away from the maternal instincts with his Rough Riders storming San Juan Hill on foot, with his big game hunting of Pronghorn antelope, cougar, and mountain goat, with all his African safaris, even the President stood with the rest in amazement at the reconstruction of their own buried infancy, and watched the muscles of the little cub's mouth working greedily, and heard every sloshing, suckling sound. Inside their own buccal cavity were muscles long unexercised that had helped develop the brain capacity that would make them grow up to rule a country and become big game hunters.

"Oh, let me take this. Stand back, all of you. Mr. President, would you get by the cub?"

The President is compliant, fearful of a dissenting word.

"Come on, let's draw it away from the mother! Just the cub, that's right, and you.

She's had enough! Anyway the mother must be dry by now."

"Yes, Mr. President, you can leave your glasses on. We can see the milky whites of your eyes, convey the full import of the rescue. What a headline, 'Teddy Rescues Bear!' That's right, now you hold the cub, like you're the mother! Wow! What copy!"

"Damnable shame she had to be shot, but great picture! It's gotta win a prize, and...another election, Mr. President!"

"Just shoot the picture," an aide says irritably.

Teddy is still dazed by the turn, the spin of events, at being given credit for killing the bear, by the implications of getting his picture taken with the cub, by in the back of his mind the true story getting out.

In fact, he is still dirty from crawling, that he looks like he could have "wrestled with the bear," one reporter suggests.

"That's an angle!" another chirps up.

What should he do? He is not a thinker, but a doer, a talker, a trustbuster, one who knows when to speak softly or not at all, for the country can always count on him to carry a big stick. But now he cannot mobilize his thoughts.

What to do, as the flash blinds him, crisscrosses his mind. The photographer underneath the black cloth is shooting the President again and the cub is just about to wriggle free.

"I want it in the Oval Office."

"What, Mr. President?"

"The rug. Thinks she can frighten me! I'll stand up to all of them! They're a pack of wild animals. I'll show 'em I'm not afraid."

The guides have left already, and the President is talking to reporters, his handlers are there fielding questions with him.

The photograph is developed, and he looks fearless and nurturing. A new angle.

"It looks like a stuffed animal!" someone says.

"Yes, let's call him 'Teddy! Teddy Bear!'"

And so children for the next hundred years sleep with their cuddly bears, the mama who was shot by a President in Yellowstone National Park, well, almost. All around the world they drift off to sleep squeezing the life out of the bear whose mother stunned a President of the United States and was quickly shot dead, bears whose population continues to dwindle, and whose solitary habits ill-match our efforts to develop the land and our own reputations at the expense of wildlife.

The President started our national park system. Could it have been out of guilt for killing that mama bear, or for the credit he took as a big game hunter rescuing her cub and having a stuffed animal named after him?

THE CHERRY TABLE

THEY SCRATCHED MY soul. Maybe that was it. That I couldn't provide a visible counterpoint to the scratches on the table. The new wood table I had taken everyone who visited to see. Cherries might have been hanging on it once. Its reddishness was little different than the bloom on the fruit. Had I robbed the yearly bushels of fruit that would now never grow out of the soft wood? Youths would never blow seeds out of their mouths reclining under the cherry tree devouring the flesh with breezes overhead rustling the leaves of branches loaded with fruit. Birds would never visit the tree. It was heaven, a tree replete with luscious cherries.

But somewhere a furniture maker was already coveting the tree and a buyer like myself was waiting for a piece of furniture to fill space in his living room. And why not oak, ash, or maple, you ask? But cherry has the most beautiful wood that I have always had an uncanny attachment to. Beyond its lightness and rich grain, even more than the soft pine that could ooze a resin that blinded. It haunted me as irreplaceable by other woods, as something I had not made my peace with.

The juice ran down our faces, staining our mouths and lips as if they were widened with some past unspeakableness, long before we'd grow up and have to give our word about purchases and the exchange of money.

And when the first scratch appeared, I thought it was the end of the world. Like telling your first lie. It was as if I were forced to walk barefoot upon the naked cherry stones that had been rolled around our mouths and blown out. Perhaps the scratch was my penance for stopping all that yearly growth as I rose early and checked the table when my wife was in bed. It stood there like the version of a story I couldn't get straight. She knew I was capable of such qualms about my purchases, yet she never gave it a thought, nor did I. It was beyond us that we could be observed by the hungry eyes of all those children deprived by the table sitting in our home of runnels of juice streaming out of their mouths every year from cherries eaten. And the birds' bellies too flew emptier now. Is it that I should have feared my eyes being pecked out, or giant talons clutching my bare shoulders from behind to lift me skyward for cutting off so much shade and food supply simply to embellish our home?

I'd sneak out and look at the table and admire its beauty when we first got it. The whorls, the rich reddish browns, the delicate traceries of black, so glossy and suggestive of a secret growth that I knew I would never revisit, yet whose lines were so wonderfully detailed challenging me to a higher, more moral life even than I lived on our lane. It was as if I had the right to cut down such trees and keep their boards in my house indefinitely as a table top, make four legs of the trunk, that I now circled so superior with my two.

The beauty actually humbled me. I didn't know how I could have ever put out of my mind the shiny tree with its yearly burden of fruit. Maybe that's it. Its burden became my own. With a gentle mixture of walnut stain and oils, wearing protective gloves, I circled the table with spirals of soft cotton rags till the luster of the wood emerged imparting a sheen to my own life. And visitors I called over to admire the table to share the shine so that we were all better for it, somehow more brilliant.

Until one day the table got scratched.

"Martha come here!" I bellowed, beside myself.

It was as if I were convinced that I had lived an unblemished life. Pleased as I was with my work, my family, my surroundings, my purchase on a tree lined lane where no one lived but us with our shiny table and bright prospects. And with the periodic furniture polish just like the daily housecleaning and yard work pruning the trees and hedges, just like the routine visits to the dentist to find the right wood, or to the doctor to upkeep our bodies, so we kept that table in a high luster, in shipshape condition as if it were emblematic of the State, or represented the underpinnings of some larger truth.

That was until the day our cat clawed its way into my conscience. It had just gotten the strength to leap on the table, but not quite.

She was inexperienced at gaining heights and so caught the tabletop with her claws and left a two-inch-long scratch deep in the surface of the wood.

That was the beginning. It seemed after that my life came unraveled. We were unable to stop the blemishes, the material misrepresentations. Thick and fast they came. Oh, it started out slow enough. I grieved, and my Martha picked up on my distress and knew the scratch had touched something deep in me. I took pride in saying that it scarified both our souls, such as they were.

Today I am sorry to say I don't believe in a soul. That's gone and all its immaculate voodoo. My mind has stuck more pins in it than I can count. At first, I thought that all the new furniture could cushion us, make up for the scratch on the table but no. Nothing could compensate for it. Nothing. Not my getting up at night and looking at it in the half light from the lamp in the hallway. That didn't erase it. Or rising early when the first rays at dawn made the room golden red with the table standing there absolutely glowing, radiant, sharing its rosy hue as if it were awakening in me an appreciation of furniture I had always had without realizing it. It was as if the wood were alive again with new growth.

But I was fooling myself. The ugly yellow scratch made me want to go after the cat who sat so smugly cleaning its paws in the next room.

"Good work, cat," I said bitterly realizing a change had come over my life so that for the first time I concluded that you can keep nothing, not the teeth in your own mouth or the furnishings in your own house, for the past followed you around disrupting the tenor of everything alive. Who are we but the sum of our misrepresentations, no matter how shiny, glossy, we make things over, no matter how we transform them with metaphors, the tree still stands. No matter how shiny the wood, the luscious fruit is always there in its darkness to torment us.

The rug was next, the weave was like an extended swirl of the wood. I won't even mention the ripped tapestry the cat had climbed up and down. One day a friend had come over and was playing with a toy mouse and lifting the string from his armrest when our cat lunged entangling its claws in the carpet tearing the weave of a seamless past I was trying to hide with the table. The carpet was woven in India and though not deeply piled was a rich maroon that puffed up like the downy feathers high on a bird's leg. Such arabesque designs I quickly realized hid an intricacy of motives that Westerners would never dream were regularized with symmetrical efficiency, not unlike the shiny cherry table top where the deed disappeared into the lesson learned. Still it surfaced in us despite how sumptuous our surroundings.

I forgot myself, yelled at the guest, later broke off all association with him, and scolded the animal. The scratches insinuate themselves into our lives despite all the tricks of camouflage to hide them, despite periodic polishing to bring out the luster of the wood.

Once I myself even knocked over our bronze Buddha on the cherry table in haste to get a sheaf of papers for a visitor and the heavy metal figure from Siam with wings on its knees bore two holes into the tabletop. I then caught a glimpse of my whole scarified, pockmarked environment that even paintings of me revealed. Artistic representation has a certain verity that can't lie. Everything left seemed nicked, marred, untruthful. Even my wooden teeth made me think of termites and the holes they'd make. Our grandchildren traipsed through the house every food stain imaginable until after the scratch all seemed smudged, just the opposite of art and craftsmanship.

The cherry table ended up with even more scratches and indentations that I have lost count and the desire to look. The only consolation I can take is that with age the wood is darkening. I'd like to write that the cherry table had initials carved in it and a tiny heart for what was never inscribed in the bark. Some mornings I wander around the house in my slippers too angry to do anything, disoriented, still hearing sounds of chopping, screams of denial, the stern reprimand of my father. I get these bouts of anguish from time to time regardless of the scratches, but then they subside.

The children, the animals, friends, the outside world has won; it always does. My wife is resigned now. The crosshatch of lines on her face tells me that passions age and furniture is an inadequate representation of all we feel, though sometimes it is more precise than body posture.

One day my cornea got scratched and it burned so badly that I was taken to the infirmary and they put a patch over my eye so that I discovered to my amazement that I had no depth perception and no matter how I thought I could still see blemishes they lost their severity. My age and public service probably has something to do with it. Even my cherry tabletop seemed smoother, restored, and I find that my wife and our grandchildren have grown closer since I have the patch. Even the pockmarks on my own face no longer seem as bad.

My wife to celebrate my return from the infirmary had a bowl of cherries waiting that she washed and placed on our table top with a coaster underneath while I read and periodically rest my one eye from not having bifocal support. I have been calmer than I have been for years. The chopping noises are less severe, and the urgency of the denials have almost completely disappeared.

The scratches did me good my wife said, and "You know what, George, that cherry tree now seems to go with you!"

THE CURTAINS

H E DOESN'T KNOW what it was. It could have been the typhoon that lasted for three days. It could have been the depression before, the empty lull where the whitest clouds are pasted to the horizon curtaining something else. It could have simply been the telephone call. That's what probably started it.

"Can I wash them?" he had asked. "It's been five years since I moved in."

"They must be dirty," she said.

"The whites are black."

She laughed.

"The whites you can wash. If they're plastic, they won't shrink."

"And the others, I better send to get dry-cleaned."

"I wash them too," she said. "They might shrink though."

"Well, maybe I'll try it."

She had given him advice before. When he added it up it had usually been wrong. About the briefcase he never used, the coat that didn't fit; she liked them, so he spent about a hundred dollars for each. And there were other things. The women half her age that the advice always seemed to make things worse, separate them.

She knew about the Philippine girl. He had showed her about twenty pictures of her.

"Is she coming?" she said.

"I think she wants to," he said.

It was a vacation and he started to clean things without even realizing it was in preparation for her, things that hadn't been touched in five years, like the fan in the kitchen, wiping the grease off it.

He got rid of the fluorescent lighting. He always wanted to get rid of it, but somehow things never seemed that important for the effort of changing the cordage and getting regular lighting. He bought two large Japanese paper lanterns that an ordinary bulb went into and they both sent out a warm yellow glow that made the night somehow more restful.

And one sunny day right before the typhoon, the last clear day, he as if by some electrical impulse got up from his writing desk and unhooked the curtains, first the whites, then the thicker green white drapes with bamboo designs on them, and plunged them one after another into the soapy water.

Then the typhoon hit. He had hung them out on his balcony railing, but the stronger the winds grew he had to take them indoors. The moisture pervaded his apartment, warped the knit binding on his paper doors so it sagged, and somehow seemed even to invade his books, already laden with the moisture of the drapes not drying.

The whites had dried the first day, but his book covers on the top shelf curled up in protest against the intrusion of the drapes, his foolishly washing them before the typhoon. And the moisture didn't stop with paper but seemed to enter his lungs. He could feel a cold coming on, his arms, his resolve, collapsing around the moisture from the drapes.

And to take the place of the drapes—they came with the apartment, not his in other words, but the University's—to take the place of the old drapes were drapes he had packed away, three pieces. The old were two heavy pieces, seemingly very expensive, that he had purchased five years ago just before he moved. They were thin by comparison, especially the one that covered the whole door window, and after five Japanese rainy seasons stuffed in a plastic bag smelled musty. Even the metal on the set of two was rusted.

He remembered buying them, how he liked the color, the rust brown, the ocher checks on the one, and the lighter stripes on the two-piece set. He remembered vaguely that he had wanted to get each set like the two-piece, but that the store didn't have it, so he settled for the checks.

146

When he put them up the first night, the old drapes were outside. He didn't use the whites even though they had dried because the windows were not yet cleaned. He was going to buy a new can of spray for that. He put them up and his apartment took on a warm reddish glow.

He didn't pay attention to the replacements then. For three days, in fact, didn't quite think about them, his life cursed with the multiple consciousness that a woman who once lived with him said he missed nothing. The drying of the curtains, the curling of the books, the degree of moisture they picked up, the sagging of the paper weave on the doors, nothing did he miss. Inadvertently his gaze searched like a light while his attention presumably slept, till of course something was out of place, or amiss, and something was. Though he didn't quite realize it till the typhoon passed, and the clouds had lifted and trailed not even one or two woolly stragglers, leaving an incomparably clear blue day.

He unwittingly hung the green curtains out. At midday he went out on his balcony and turned them over again, clothespinned them and didn't think anything of it. His life in other words proceeded as usual.

He tried to work in the morning at his desk, made some purchases that afternoon, that always involved a degree of tension, and went shopping for food, that was easy. He had that down to a science. Then he went jogging.

Towards evening he called his friend, the same one who advised him about the curtains, to find out about an economy class ticket. And, as he didn't understand the agent's Japanese well enough, would she call, and he'd call her back at a quarter to five.

Just before, he had started to hang up the white curtains. That day he had washed the windows, swept the tatami, and wiped the parquet floor on his hands and knees.

"Oh, and I washed the curtains," he said.

"Oh?" she laughed and said, "I was going to ask you about that."

"Yes, I thought it was too much trouble to take them to the dry cleaners."

"And?" she asked.

"They seem all right. I haven't put up the green ones yet, but they look OK."

"Good," she said.

He inserted the metal clasps in the green bamboo curtains and hung them up. The first one hung six inches off the ground. The whites hung to the floor, but the greens,

Jesus, they had shrunk!

And the other door window, the curtain he hung there was the same!

A panic took hold of him. He kneeled down and pulled at them to stretch them to the floor, to make up the six lost inches. He closed his eyes and went along the bottom tugging, tugging, but no go. Nothing happened!

They just hung there like pants a clown might wear, that far off the ground so his bare legs stick out like birds' feet. Crestfallen, like something whose quills had lost their stiffness, he hung his head. What now?

The uneasy feeling that they weren't even his drapes, that he'd have to buy new ones, gripped him around the throat like a panic unequal to the importance of what it should have had.

It was almost time to eat, so before what he did was take the little cloth binders and wrap them around the foot of the curtains with a book, a heavy book, one he didn't value. He had hoped that the weight of the book would extend the curtains, lengthen the shrinkage. He used *Fowler's Modern English Usage*. He never referred to it anyway, and it was out of date and a library book. And he used another book, not as heavy but hardbound, *German Without Toil*. Then he went to eat.

Halfway through the meal he got up and switched on the light, wincing as he looked at the curtains. How could he be so stupid as not to have them dry-cleaned?

"To save money," he reproved himself.

But he knew it wasn't to save money, so much as him, a man, fussing over curtains, taking them to be dry-cleaned. His friend, the old woman, had chuckled when he mentioned them each time. He had gotten over shopping, but taking curtains to be dry-cleaned, he should have a wife for that. But he lives alone. And a woman may be coming, a beautiful Filipina.

He was a little embarrassed of his apartment. He didn't really fix it up, left things simple. One friend said, Spartan. His high school was the Spartans, the cross-town rival the Trojans, so perhaps there was something to that. Another friend said he was the only person who seemed to have less in his apartment each time he came. Maybe that was because his mother's apartment was like a warehouse and had always embarrassed him. Even Japanese who visited said *kirei*, because his apartment seemed so simple, only the bare tatami, a desk and two chairs, Shinto almost.

He wanted to show a warmth of atmosphere for the Filipina but looking at the curtains after he ate turned his stomach at his folly. They were so far off the ground. And the typhoon having passed brought a mass of colder autumn air. He thought, right in under the doors the air mass would come and the girl if she came would discover me for all I am, my parsimony, the chill atmosphere of my life alone, that I couldn't even have enough material to spare that it would reach the floor and keep out the drafts. Clown that I am, he thought.

Despite his stinting, pinched nature, he had always liked clothes that had some superfluity, just the opposite of a Nehru coat, and its stingy collar, or a Chinese party member's outfit. No, he liked clothes with folds, with an excess of sleeve; bells whose bottoms kicked out and rang with a generosity he didn't have, that gave tongue to something he was not. These shortened curtains bespoke just the opposite, a lack of material.

He sat down in the soft chair, his only one, and tried to look at the curtains through other eyes, as if someone else were there. She, in fact, were looking. He even stood up and looked down at them and realized they didn't look as bad as when he was sitting. But they couldn't be standing all the time. So he sat again and looked and looked.

The books had done no good. He got up and kneeled down and stretched them, pulling again and again, harder each time. Then he got angry and worked himself into such a pitch that at one end he pulled the rod completely off the wall, and a screw dropped loose and bounced on the tatami.

He jumped up in surprise. But without a moment's thought he was in the closet for his screwdriver. He jumped up on his desk chair and twisted the screw into its former hole, but the wood threads weren't able to grip the metal again, so he twisted the screw downwards against the hole and started a new shaft in the wood. The metal bar was a little lower but was secure. He gave it a little pull and it didn't budge.

He jumped off the chair and down to the level of the shrunken curtains again. Maybe there was some principle allied to his miscalculating here, something he feared shrunken about himself, something that he wanted to be generous, giving, wasteful almost; what he was apparently not for all the need he had to manifest this in his dress, and in the curtains.

Finally he took them down and put up the rust brown curtains, looked at them, felt them. Especially the checks seemed flimsy, not substantial like the green. And what would she think of me? he thought. Two different curtains on two sets of matching door windows, and the checks made too much of a statement.

As he looked at the green and white bamboo, the color was a sea green, or rather like an algae pond that seeped through the material leaving the delicate bamboo under water almost. The curtains now, he saw, had just little enough personality that they didn't interfere with his thinking. Maybe it was because he had lived with them hanging for five years and grew not to notice them. The checks he couldn't help seeing them. Small black and white checks he despised, and especially those women who wore them; they made him dizzy. But years ago, he had even bought clothes with larger checks; of course, the color couldn't be strong, but then he favored more solid colors, became more conservative.

He thought then of the winter, and how her warm blood, her expectations wouldn't be able to take the cold, and how the cold would penetrate those flimsy brown curtains right to her bones. And he realized that they were flimsy, sheer, and see through, he said to himself. See through! Could you see through them?

He stepped out on his balcony and looked at them with both globe lights on, and no, he couldn't see through them. But for some reason without giving it a thought, he took the browns down and put the greens back up. Their thickness he supposed is what decided him, as he dropped back in his chair, thinking, Look, stupid, she's not coming for the curtains. She's coming for you! You're not the curtains, even if you did commit the folly of shrinking them.

He wondered if it couldn't have been the fact that they were not his curtains, but the school's. He had always taken care of other people's things better than his own, that was a principle of his childhood.

Finally, he managed to get into bed. But as he lay there and the light of the streetlights shone under the exposed six inches, he got the idea of placing two cushions against the bottom of the curtain and the room once more regained its customary darkness.

But things didn't end in what was an uneasy sleep. That morning he awoke trying not to think about the curtains, get down to work. But something else occurred to him. Look for a new set. Price them.

That afternoon he was out looking through the department stores and realized that it'd cost about fifty dollars to replace the curtains. But he could find no green bamboo like he had, only pine trees, and he didn't want pine trees in Japan. They were too far in the Alps, not where he lived. Bamboo, that's what was around his house. And anyway, they had given him bamboo.

He returned, went jogging, thought, especially when he ran backwards that always cleared his mind before, that he could forget the curtains, but they occurred to him with a small panic while he was back doing his sit-ups; why, because he knew he was going to put up the brown curtains again. He alternated hanging and taking down the greens and browns by turns that night. That's just the way he was, he had to see things to be able to decide on them.

And it wasn't so insignificant as the material hooked on the little white movable plastic eyelets; no, it involved a woman, and her accepting him and where he lived. He had been thinking of moving and he had told her that, and so the curtains could be only temporary.

He thought of hanging up the greens and when she came putting up the browns and letting her decide. But he knew she might think he was a little strange for that. And the browns smelled musty. The windows were so clean, they deserved better, and the whites had come out so nicely, why put the dirty browns up? But they weren't dirty, they looked almost new. OK, then musty.

That afternoon he had thought he'd get the browns dry-cleaned. One of the reasons not to get the greens dry-cleaned was the chemicals that they put in. But he wore clothes on his own body that were dry-cleaned!

Then he thought this was unnecessary. He hated getting things cleaned unnecessarily, just because some imaginary fixation with cleanliness took hold of him, even his own body, and pulled him by the wrist so to speak like the past, a whole childhood of baths that he didn't need half so much as he had taken them.

Just to fight against that he decided to hang the browns out in the sun. The sunlight would sterilize them, and not for one, but two or three days. But somehow the smell didn't go away.

He put the browns up again; maybe the musty smell was gone, and he was remembering what he smelled to find some objection in himself. He turned on the lights in both rooms.

If she came there was an additional consideration. Could people see, not from his balcony, but from further away his body movements through the thinner sheer curtains?

He walked down the path out to the narrow but main road, looked at his apartment from a distance just like a voyeur might. When he rounded the corner of one cinderblock wall a chained dog barked ferociously, made him feel a little guilty spying on himself.

He looked up at his windows and they gave off the most beautiful golden light. The windows seemed spilling over into the night just like those houses with people and feelings whose windows promised something. Now his own apartment empty of people promised so much, empty of himself.

It seemed a little strange that he could go and be part of what took place behind those windows. How was it possible? It seemed a little that she'd never come, that his pains with the curtains were for nothing; that the warm glow in the windows was something outside himself, generated with all the electricity he could muster, but that people somehow didn't attach to him. Though he kept the lights burning. He was always reprimanded for that, "Why don't you turn off the lights when you are not using them?"

He returned to his apartment, sat down, and looked at the curtains. Took them down, thought one more day in the sunlight would sterilize all his doubts about their mustiness. Put up the greens. The next day he hung out the browns.

He felt a little relief about things having been decided. And the browns made his apartment warm. The Oslo chair, its rust brown, and the bookcase the same color, and the chair cushion that he never used, he now got out. Before its corduroy seemed too hot in the summer when he bought it; now he just got it out and sat on it like there were never any doubts. Its maroon center and two light brown borders went with everything, and the yellow of the faded tatami made for flooring, the base harmony of which the curtains would complete. That evening he took them in. The must seemed to have gone, or at least he wanted to smell it as gone. And he hung them up. He had washed his sheets that day and pillowcase, and so the bedclothes gave off the smell of fresh air as his head heavy with the week's thinking about curtains sank down to a restful sleep.

He sat at his desk the next morning after breakfast and from its wooden top caught the check pattern out the corner of his eye. The pattern disrupted his concentration, the color made too much of a statement. He tried to ignore it. After all, his new dictionary was bright red, and though he couldn't completely cover it over with his scratch pad he could still write with its bold red in his eye. So why not the check brown out the other eye with only the suggestion of red? And when he looked down at the page his concentration was off the curtain, had to be, but with them still hanging he knew he couldn't get down to work, so he got up and took them down.

Yes, better curtains without any statement, the greens with the familiar pattern. He could fit their fabric into his life. And they would be drawn so people wouldn't imagine the shrinkage during the day. And people usually didn't visit him at night. The green white seeped into his life again. He began to think what all the fuss was about, and with each day there was less of a twinge at the shrinkage, as if he himself were somehow growing to accept them.

And the Filipina, she wrote and said she couldn't come. He was admittedly disappointed, but realized his curtains finally were his own affair, something that he'd have to live with himself. As a matter of fact, it's been weeks now, and he recently has been prompted with a faint desire, everyday gaining a little more outline in his mind, with a faint desire to put up the browns again.

KNICKKNACKS

WHICH ONES SHE started with it was not clear. The gift she received of the Chinese peasant woman serving tea, her husband an entirely separate figurine, but also in a broad-brimmed straw hat ready to accept it, his scythe at his side, the gift was certainly one of the earliest, but not the first. Perhaps the lace-skirted figurines on her bureau in the bedroom that went back to when she was first married were the earliest, ballet dancers of white porcelain, the shoes, the vests, a baby blue or soft pink.

There was a heavy wrought iron Pennsylvania Dutch boy and girl sitting on a bench that had always rested in the kitchen, first on the window ledge above the sink and finally cemented to the metal awning above the stove. And there were the Italian pieces, copies of the Renaissance that included finely carved chariots full of cherubs drawn by mythical white horses. And procession pieces of men and women, breastplated soldiers with spears and attending minor deities. The hands, the fingers, the noses, the folds of the eyelids were all cunningly fashioned. Also, there were two large cornucopias decorated with pastoral scenes. She marveled at the workmanship. Anything she wanted he bought. They made trips downtown to the best import houses in the city when he was alive.

Above the curtains on the carved wooden valance in the living room were the birds that she had ordered. Cardinals, blue jays, Baltimore orioles, chickadees, robins, all the colors that seemed to mock the drab gray brown sparrows outside her city window. For she loved animals and took an infinite pleasure in the representational accuracy of their depiction. Also, in the living room were a collection of Hummels that everyone who came immediately admired.

After her husband had passed away her passion for the knickknacks redoubled. The whole series of Norman Rockwell figurines gave her life a sense of purpose for almost two years. For every third week she'd be sent a new one: a freckly-nosed boy with his dog going fishing, a boy on stilts, a granny threatening someone with her umbrella, a dentist wielding his drill into his young patient's mouth, a policeman finger outstretched chastising a little boy, a barber shop scene, a cowboy twirling his lariat. Every figurine was done with beautifully rich colors, and postures expressive of an America that though no longer outside her window went right to the heartland of her memory.

The figurines were in the glass cabinets with the holiday dishes, on special tables made of Italian marble, along the maple wood console, and on platforms secured to the walls, so that visitors who came sometimes grew nervous just looking at them, much less holding them, for she told them that the Rockwells, for example, were only a limited number, and almost irreplaceable.

The most recent of her acquisitions was a line of animals, bobcats, wolves, elephants, giraffes, bears, all with a detail that looked like an exact copy of the real thing, as if the live animal itself were dwarfed to the figurine. The hair, the look on the face, the glassy-eyed ferocity, the foraging pink tongue, the long tusk slightly yellowed, all were caught like the speckled trout in the bear's paws with a workmanship that was well worth its weight in American dollars.

In the backyard were two-foot high gnomes and elves her husband had drilled and set into the ledge. One of her friends after staying overnight had written a short tale about how one night they all came alive and danced in the moonlight, and in the morning one of them was found broken on the patio tile. The man and woman in the tale couldn't explain how it happened but would never have imagined the knickknacks had a life of their own.

Out front were two large white rabbits firmly cemented on the wall next to the garage so they would not be stolen. Their long pink ears listening for every admiring compliment from passers-by. Their owner too would stand at the kitchen window every evening doing the dishes and listen for people's comments.

At the foot of the stairs stood a young deer with two tiny buds that, following the story line of the friend, one could one day imagine growing into full-blown antlers to permanently protect the house from intruders. Upstairs to the right of the entrance was a three-foot statue of St. Francis of Assisi dressed in a brown robe with three small blue birds along his arm and shoulder as he held his rosary in both clasped hands. Beside the statue one could always find a dish for the stray animals that came to the stoop.

It could have been that her sister's eye problems at first made her reluctant to take her in when she wanted to come and live with her. Her husband had just died, and her mother to whom her sister had devoted her whole life had also died six months later, so it was natural that the two sisters would finally live together, especially since their brother died the next year.

The sister and her husband when he was alive had always said, "Helen will always have a place with us if anything happens to Mama, because of her eyes."

The two sisters now found themselves alone in the world except for their sister-in-law, whom nobody got along with, and their niece.

The sister with the knickknacks had many friends, went places, visited her stepchildren, gave large dinners. The sister who had taken care of her mother all her life, who was now legally blind and had worked for the Red Cross for thirty-five years as a Dictaphone operator, only made or received an occasional telephone call, but had no visitors except for her niece who came over with her baby every Saturday afternoon, when her aunt would give her money from her limited income after each visit.

This made the other sister angry. For as she said, "Why does a full-grown woman still have to take, take, take?"

The legally blind sister was one of those rare people who are able to live with themselves contented, blessed with an inner peace that the world with all its folly is hard put to disturb. She surveys events with a wisdom that enables her to sleep late, retire early, listen to her TV programs, and patiently await her Saturday visit.

The sister who owns the house with all the friends kindness and a patient ear could have (every Christmas she proudly displays the over three hundred cards she gets) is by contrast nervous, a light sleeper, and a bit vexed at her legally blind sister's contentment. Despite the bevy of friends she herself has, the long hours she spends on the phone, despite the plays she sees with Senior Citizen groups, the stepchildren she visits, the trips upstate and to the shore, she resents the Saturday visits, resents the money the niece takes every week from her sister. Well, not robbing the blind exactly, but at least as she points out "taking advantage of her."

Maybe there's more to it; the fact that her husband died first. She couldn't for the life of her understand why her mother, whom she resented always being fondest of her brother who drank, why her mother outlived her husband. Dr. Kramer had always said she would live to be ninety, and she did. Exactly ninety. She resented that her sister had Mama while she who had married was left alone.

But soon the mother died, as if to even things up, and at first she wouldn't take her sister into her home saying she wanted to live her own life, but finally she did after her sister went with her sister-in-law and refused to talk to her.

In the beginning the sister with the house full of knickknacks complained about her sister's wigs not being up-to-date, her frumpish dresses, her inability to see so that she had to have things done for her that kept her home more than she wanted and shortened the length of the trips she took, or that when it was ten o'clock her sister promptly left the company she had and went up to her room.

But more than anything it was the Saturday visits. Her sister had loved her niece since she was an infant when soon after the adoption it was first noticed that she was cross-eyed, and later that she limped from being slightly palsied. But to everyone's surprise she grew healthy and strong enough if not to hide at least to overcome her limp. And her aunt was overjoyed when she grew up and found a boy who singled her out almost because of her limp.

And so, every Saturday when the boy was at work cleaning at the YMCA, her niece came over with the baby. She would spread out a soft blanket in the sunken living room and let the infant crawl. The beautiful pieces of Italian furniture had the same plastic covers on that they came with twenty-five years earlier, and everything porcelain was put out of the infant's reach; especially the large Dalmatian was moved up the steps going to the bedroom, so it wouldn't tip over. The Tuscany marble floor lamp which glowed inside rosy pink as the infant's little fingers, too, was moved out of reach so the child could have free play. Both sisters talked with the niece and made a fuss over the baby; then before she left the niece would go with her aunt to her room and be given something for coming to visit.

One day however the sister who owned the house, the light sleeper, the sister with so many friends, said she didn't want her niece coming every Saturday because of the knickknacks. She was afraid the child would break one. Her legally blind sister protested and couldn't see the reason except for spitefulness. That curious spite that wants to take everything from people and have them rely solely on what we allow them. That curious spite that can't tolerate affections not our own, that wants nothing going on outside itself; that curious spite that feels somehow betrayed by someone else's kindness, by love we don't share in. That curious spite that doesn't want people to live their own lives no matter how simple, and thinks with knickknacks it can bring the whole animal kingdom into their home with representations of ferocity, bellowing, screeching and song, that the imagination can evoke just by the eye resting on them.

The sizzling of a hot tea pot as it is passed from the Chinese peasant woman to her husband, the repartee of a Norman Rockwell doctor to his freckly-nosed patient, all can be evoked by the eye, the ear, or revoked no less than the Saturday visits.

For ultimately, we want life to obey us, follow like the boy's dog with its tail between its legs. We want to keep others from it, claiming we are stopping the visits for their own good. And so, it bursts out in the form of an injunction. Maybe the person doesn't know what they are saying, "I don't want her to come over every Saturday."

The elephants don't stampede, the giraffes don't scatter, only a hush prevails as mute as the hunched back of the bobcat. The Hummels continue to hold the umbrella in the rain, the Rockwells too are mute, that is another America. A Mennonite silence as heavy as the wrought iron figurines falls over the kitchen. The animals outside, the pixies in the back, don't now have a chance of moving. The imagination has been stopped cold, frozen in its tracks. An injunction has brought everything to a standstill.

No infant's cry will animate the birds with the possibility of the curtains being pulled down one Saturday afternoon. The TV goes on, the other sister goes out as usual, tries to ward off the reproaches she expects from friends, from her conscience, from the figurines. Their silence tries to give away that nothing has happened. After all it is her house, she insists.

The pet cat seems to pad around the house more quietly sensing something has been violated, some trust in the kitchen, living room, out back, on the front steps where there stands a silent reproof to St. Francis that the love stopped with the animals, their reproductions. No story is needed to show that something has been changed without the infant having visited, and is lying in the patio, in the sunken living room, on the linoleum kitchen floor.

The blind sister has nowhere to go, and so stays. The knickknacks, however, have lost their irreplaceable beauty. They are now only porcelain, paint, wrought iron, plaster and baked glaze hanging together as barely constituent elements. Nothing really to admire anymore if you know why they are standing there whole. The flights of imagination leave the birds as mere ornaments. Everything is insured like before, but somehow now valueless for the excuse they've been for keeping away the life that would endear them and make them even more valuable by the chance that they may be broken.

BEETS

THE BEETS ARE cut up almost as an afterthought. To everyone's surprise he gobbles them down immediately, avoiding all the rest of the food. They stain his plate with concentrated juice that seeps into everything. It is all but on his clothes, broadens his lips as if they have been bruised, dyes the already pink tints of his skin. Beet juice is poised to dye everything with its own peculiar metaphor.

The family is surprised at his appetite. The father cuts the little boy more beets and the boy immediately digs his fork into them as if they are the last food on earth, as if he hasn't eaten for days.

"He eats like he's starving," the mother says.

"He thinks it's candy," his six-year-old sister giggles.

Where does the gusto come from? It can't quite be that peculiar sweetness with the tart reminder that it is only a vegetable.

Is there something in his past that transports the boy back to Europe where his ancestors harvested beets? Is it embedded in his bloodstream, the pulse of blood brought over by salty ocean currents that now informs his tiny arm holding the little fork that spears another wedge of vegetable?

Undoubtedly his ancestors were on their knees in fields untold hours pulling at the taproots to dislodge them from the stubborn earth. Could their very subsistence not have depended on the one root that grew all those winters when everything else died? The swelling redness that endured a cold that destroyed all other crops. Could a mythology not have grown up around beets, conferring on them a special status that the little three-year-old now felt in his blood?

To support the harvest and give thanks to what saved their lives, did the Europeans not build altars to the beet and offer blood sacrifices to insure a good crop for the coming winter? Could the original idea of a blood brother not have been born with a food that so obviously fuels our notion of nourishment almost bleeding like us?

The little boy cries for even more beets and his family looks on amazed. Even his sister who normally stalks his high chair during the meal, bobbing up to scare him, despite her parents' admonitions, is not entirely free of the memory of having occupied what, now that the beets are consumed in such an unusual manner, seems to her an exalted seat just because she is not sitting in it. She smiles broadly at his devouring so lustily a food she doesn't like, though you can read in her eyes that she is missing out on something.

"Ugh, gross," she says, "it looks like blood, Tristan how can you eat that?"

He pays her no mind. He is leagues beyond any brother sister rivalry. In fact, he is already in the old country after a particularly harsh winter, a near famine that has taken the lives of the elderly. He is crowded amongst a group of partially clad figures, as big-boned as he is now small. They wear the skins of animals and are surrounded by baskets of beets.

They are discussing the upcoming sacrifice.

The little boy has a determined look away from his six-year-old sister, as if he is engaged in matters of more importance. She'll not torment him this evening, tying him up, operating on him, making him wait on her, give her foot massages, forcing him to bow as she pushes his head to the carpet. She can make him scream on cue, knows just what toy to take away or wave in his face, what excites his curiosity, or his rages. Any emotion she wants she can elicit from him on a moment's notice. She knows which building block to dislodge, what piece of the puzzle to hide; she's the master of misalignment, engineer of every collapse. She knows her little brother up and down with the prescience of one who senses that she herself might one day be sacrificed.

But the beets come as a stunning surprise to her. She is amazed at how comfortable he is in his highchair this evening, how content and impervious to her taunts. She can feel his elevation. She can't circle and pop up to scare him. He's too immersed in the vegetable.

The little boy is in his own world, his fingers all red, stained like his mouth, his clothes. He is merrily, gaily, chewing the beet, breaking down the clean knife lines, the wavy growth almost like the annual rings on a tree. The taproot with its pottery shape seems to contain even more nutriment than anyone realizes. The little boy is at the very root of life with his little heart beating a mile a minute, covering distances nobody dreams about.

He doesn't give his sister the time of day, not even a passing thought. Rarely has she enjoyed any food except maybe the sterile scoop of ice cream that he has always considered too cold, or the sweets that he always seemed not to have a taste for.

Suddenly the little boy appears to have had enough and his eyes close for a second. It is then that his sister is totally out of the picture, already a full-bodied adolescent that they can't get through the doorway amid screams and scratches, bites, and kicks? All the residue of fights between brother and sister come down to this, all the humiliations of any baby brother around a tormenting sister who wants to grow up before her time. The punches and pinches, the bruises and hair pulling, the blood shed between them in cuts and scratches, the floods of tears, the quick shifts of blame, all come down to this, his adolescent sister being pulled screaming bloody murder out of that crude hut in early Europe a thousand years ago, being sacrificed to the deities of beet by early ancestors determined to have a good harvest that will get the village through yet another winter. Each time the little boy takes a bite he shoots a quick glance at his little sister as if it were she who made it all possible.

For hundreds of years beet consumption for that very reason could have gone underground, as the lowly root fell to the status of a minor vegetable, an embarrassment at what used to produce a bumper crop when all other crops failed. The sacrifices promptly disappeared with the greater availability of food as Europe grew more civilized.

The quantity of blood mankind spilled was probably for other reasons than the original fascination with the lowly beet, but that may have started it all, initiating a life of sacrifice, mutilation, bloodletting. Wars, rape and rapine all may be traced to that one vegetable that worked its way so deeply into the psyches of our early ancestors that a three-year-old could now tap into it as easily as he gobbled up beets to the exclusion of all other food.

As he trained his eye on his sister who tormented him to death and took another bite, one could sense his vague premonition that she had no place even in their family except to insure the continued abundance of next year's crop of the bloody vegetable. He barely looked at her because he knew that he would soon be relieved of her tauntings.

The tiniest cut in a beet will make for an effusion little different than those scarifications, chance breaks, in our own skin. And the stubborn bulbous root with such a rough exterior is not unlike our own leathery exposure to the elements thickening with unsightly bumps that appear on our face and nose as we too age.

The first of us who ate beets and cut them open must have thought they were miniature reproductions of our bloodline. They sensed that they could keep us alive through the harsh winters long before they achieved the status of a cult. And the one or two virgins periodically sacrificed to a continued bumper crop signified little in the scheme of things that preserved the community.

And so the little boy finally looked at his sister with the dim knowledge that she might be next, for small as he was such sacrifices were already in his blood as conscious reprisals he never considered before he ate his first serving of beets.

By the third serving his sister already grown up was pulled from the hut and carried through the village screaming until she was strapped to the altar. He had to lower his eyes any number of times at her fate. He turned back to her and imagined her face a red smear of beet juice that his fingers were now involuntarily playing in. He tried to discount all her torment of him in one sympathetic glance, overcome the separation of three years by a thousand.

He looked down from his highchair and observed the marvel of his whole family at his appetite. Gone was that look of perilous survival a little boy has towards a sister who torments him day and night. For the beet juice was now coursing through his bloodstream exciting a whole history of sacrifice.

The sister looked at her little brother steady now as if studying in him her own unwitting reaction to a fate that could easily have been hers. Her hands pried from the doorway as determined as a new toy taken from him, and on her head those bumps against the floor just as he came crashing down from her pushing him off balance, and the red stains on his plate smeared for bloodying his nose so often.

He sensed she was taken to the village to be sacrificed for a food that he had just eaten with such gusto. Strong arms were already pulling her into adulthood just as she had pulled on his own arms. The red smears on his plate depicted in their vague outlines the flowing hair and the torment of her departure, the lament over not being able to enjoy what he did. The beet juice was only a trickle now where drops had run down his chin onto his highchair streaking his elbows and smearing his arms.

"Tristan," his heedless sister drawled, "you've made a mess again!"

WAITING

THEY BOTH HAD waited so long. She jumped out of bed in the dark; he bounded up from his desk. They snatched their glasses in two swift compatible movements, and before they knew it, they were at the kitchen window parting the curtains. He even commented on the way out to the kitchen, "Our lives must really be empty."

And they were. For she had tired over the months of his predictions, of everything he knew, of his being always right. Of the times even when he cooked successfully, encroaching on her domain. The nut roast a few weeks ago was the straw that broke the camel's back. She said he didn't need her. And that very night the ratatouille he insisted on making. And his overbearing knowledge of everything written. The avalanche of stories he gave her. Cheever's "Reunion!" that very day. Neither of them had thought that it would be prophetic by midnight.

Yes, they had grown apart. Averchenko's man falling past different apartment windows catching plummeting glimpses of lives other than his own didn't snap them out of it. Not the basketball games they had with each other, or the nature hikes, or the trips to Boston, the night baseball games, the museums, the walks around Harvard. Everything seemed to make her more discontented, and put him, too, somehow on edge.

They needed something from the outside, something fortuitous. Bowles' "The Delicate Prey" only isolated her more from him and his tastes. There was something dangerous out there, they both knew, but they could not speak of it. Though he thought he was winning her back with the hot, steamy incest theme in "Valley Heat"—for he was much older than she was. He too, and perhaps that was his mistake, wanted them to share the same hammock. The crowding closeness of their sweaty bodies. But how the salt or perspiration tries to separate us, he mused.

They needed something, it was clear. And he invented things for her to do, from studying massage and yoga to macrobiotics and getting her a learner's permit to drive. That very night she had come in about ten—it was still too early to sleep—and had asked him what she could read. Though she usually took refuge in the books he suggested, she was in bed promptly at eleven. His ambition kept him up burning the midnight oil, or his curiosity that wandered from story to poem, to philosophical essay, to her sleeping. When he would come to bed she'd always stir, and occasionally moan once or twice before turning away. But that was all. Sleep was her last refuge. It was where he didn't know everything, didn't anticipate her every need, or the activity of her mind, just what she would be interested in, just what would bore her.

And so, they had waited subconsciously for weeks, for months. In the back of their minds they knew it would come. Something must. And his predictions were never wide of the mark. Even the outcome of the demonstrations in China, he seemed to be able to foresee.

It was almost midnight as he gently paged through Lamb to see if there was anything worth reading when the sound of a skid started (at his "Letter to Wordsworth") and lengthened like a black streak down the page, and grew louder and louder as the vehicle at a high rate of speed grew more out of control.

There was a stop sign at the corner of Library Avenue where they lived one flight up with his books and predictions of what just might happen one day at that stop sign, and he had said it once, if he said it a hundred times, "There is going to be an accident." Often she fought his predictions, but she learned to accept them with a diplomatic grain of salt. The same salt she so assiduously kept out of his food.

The skid continued and then a gigantic crash took place that made them both jump up. He from his desk and she from her bed. She reached the kitchen first and switched on the light.

"No, no," he followed immediately and said, "turn it off, turn it off! You can see better. And open the door, open the door," he said with a sense of emergency.

She did and heard a man screaming, saw the lights of a car, and was overcome by the smell of gasoline. They both looked down into a mini inferno. The screaming and red and white lights gave the impression of eerie confusion. People started to come out.

"I'd better call the police," he said, and ran to the phone.

"We're on the way," the dispatcher had said, as if they too were ready and waiting for this.

He pulled on his shoes.

"Are you going out?"

"No, just down the steps," he said.

"I want to go, too," she said.

Once out the door they saw many people had gathered. The screams had stopped. The blue lights of police cars and ambulances still revolved, along with the red lights of the fire truck. She held his arm as they started down the steep steps.

"I knew it would happen," he said with conviction. "It was bound to, they come down Library Avenue so fast."

"And there is no stop sign on Pine," she added.

"And the slope makes them come out of nowhere over the hill," he said.

"And the large tree," she said, "you can't see around the tree."

At the middle of the intersection was a small Escort, just like the car they owned, whose engine was driven up into the driver's seat. Further up the street was a small truck turned over on its side leaking gasoline. Over on the grass a man lay attended by firemen and medics.

The red and blue lights gave an atmosphere almost of the landing of extra-terrestrials. Firemen were starting to hose down the road.

"What are they doing that for?" she asked.

"To clean off the blood and gasoline," he said, as she encircled his arm safely inside his prediction.

They both knew this would happen. And perhaps it could be said that they wanted it, or something like it, to happen in order to, if nothing else, bring them together. She wanted him to be right as much as she fought against it. But as before, he repeated himself till she grew tired of his correctness, as they wheeled the man into the ambulance.

She stepped around the tree to look.

"I don't want you to see that," he said, and blocked her until they shut the doors.

"But it's not leaving," he said after five minutes. "Why is the ambulance still there?"

"There must be a reason," she said.

"They can't have more equipment than a hospital."

"I don't know," she said.

The police were all walking around looking very busy, exercising their sense of authority, as if they thrived on such accidents.

"That's why they don't put in another stop sign, or a light," he said.

"Why?" she asked.

"So the emergency services have something to do."

"No," she said, and gripped his arm tighter. "I'm cold," she said. "I'm going home."

"OK, I'll go too," he said, as they both walked back and up the stairs to their apartment.

She went to bed, and in the darkness the blue lights of the emergency vehicles flickered on the ceiling. Out in the kitchen he listened to the radio for news of the accident, and she called out to him to come and hold her. By that time, the flashing lights had stopped.

HAWKING

"I T'S NICE TO meet someone who is not a damned tourist, but a traveler!" he said to me.

He was crippled, bent over at the waist, so that he walked perpendicular with a cane. He gained a kind of eccentric dominance looking so vulnerable. He sat there with his shirt open and his hairy white chest exposed kneading the loose flesh over and over again between his fingers as I ate and he talked between spoonfuls of my oatmeal or bites of toast when he cleared his throat, sometimes twice in the course of one swallow, breaking a simple sentence in two.

Why I went back to the same restaurant was a mystery to me. I almost stopped on the last morning seeing his car parked outside but thought there are not many other decent restaurants in town. So be brave, I told myself.

"You're late," he said to me immediately, not yet clearing his throat, and it wasn't until I sat down that he started again to pinch the loose flesh on his chest.

Now the face, the glasses and teeth inspired memories of my childhood and the respect I had always had for elders. He wasn't as intelligent as he looked, though he gave off the reminiscent smell of authority. Maybe it was the pipe tobacco, or the thousand and one prejudices that on the last day spewed over the white tablecloth like hot chili sauce. As if all the hawking and rolling of flesh between the bites I took were rolled into one bowl of oats. An antidote.

The prejudices were strewn in such profusion that it ruined my appetite for days afterwards. All I wanted to do was get away from him, having a couple of days before not responded to his suggestion that we drive to the opposite coast together, or that I go to his room to visit. Fourteen, that was the number he gave me.

Somehow, I always left first, never walked out with him. He let me leave and I left briskly walking ever faster with the curious feeling that despite his lameness, and maybe because of his large baby blue Ford, I could never get away from the crippled foot on the gas pedal. He could catch me whenever he wanted. Even if I never saw him again, I would never be entirely rid of him. He would always be there, before me, behind me. To my right and my left, above and below. I would be surrounded by him, assaulted by every opening in my body, and the hawking, the clearing of his throat between bites and my own swallows would be the least of it, and the rolling of his loose flesh between his fingers, that too could be forgotten, and the large yellow teeth stained by tobacco. Perhaps they were false, now that I think of it, they were so even.

All that could be forgotten. What couldn't be were the prejudices, how they seeped in from all sides just because I stopped my ears, just because I couldn't close my eyes to him except by always leaving first. When he surprised me by being in the restaurant the next morning after he told me he was leaving, it was I realized only a prelude to his returning to my meals again and again. My mind reliving the distortions about people, life, races and religions that he dinned into my ears and for only a few mornings, and no matter my feeble, polite disagreements, the fact that I was there was enough for him. I was the echo chamber; he heard himself through me. I didn't pounce on him and pummel him with his own cane, for I had too much respect for his age. It was enough for him that I listened.

Perhaps it would take years for what he said to overtake me, for prejudices besiege us, lay their fretwork around us, their scaffolding day by day; all that is needed is one cane and the rest of the woodwork will be joined. Just one cane to start the process. There is no hurry; it has the rest of our life; for every disappointment, every bitterness builds and bends the back.

The splinters I get under my own skin are only a diversion, but finally in my frustration and anger over them they too add, till I am surrounded by not only one lonely cane supporting a bent old man but a whole scaffolding, higher than the eye can see, outside the mind's eye, a Trojan horse. Only this time when the support is taken away after a lifetime of disappointment there is nothing to conquer, no cities, but myself, hairy and bent, with a peculiar hawking and enough flesh to roll effortlessly between my own fingers as someone decades younger sits across from me eating oatmeal.

I am the hairy old man, bent, lonely, crippled and disappointed, traveling in Mexico on my retirement money, living my life with little more reason than to corner a youth and ease my disappointments, my prejudices, that may take a lifetime to sink in and reshape themselves along the spine of my own inevitable crookedness.

Meanwhile the youth will be put off by the interrupted oatmeal, walk away in disgust from the sounds at every spoonful, the clearing of the throat while a wad of softness passes down; his own flesh will tighten, younger as the old man rolls his, and he will be unprepared for his old age when the scaffolding of youth is one day removed, and sometimes overnight, when he will wake up and find himself become the old man who laid the groundwork for him like age does for all of us, only not so graphically as in that Mexican restaurant four days running.

MATISSE

IT WAS THE Van Gogh I wanted, but not having it in stock he got me the Matisse, also a hundred dollars. He wanted to please me with the price, the nice round triple digit figure, a price unthinkable out in the marketplace. But he could get them for nothing, for he handled tens of thousands of books every day on the forklift. The cover jacket was bright pink, with Matisse's signature in navy blue letters.

I paged through it, tried to like it, picked out the illustrations I liked, lines I wanted to praise, wove in fact a whole argument of appreciation with strokes of well-placed comment that almost redid the often careless sketches. And where the lines fell right I commented, "Here's change, see it takes time for a master to develop," but nothing showed this continuity I sought, or that Matisse bore out my theory. I had remembered my art teacher commenting on his nudes, or some such technique of his, but he looked too much like an illustrator.

Still the book had well over hundreds of pages. It was about six or seven pounds, heavier than my typewriter. I was of course appreciative, tried to convince myself that I liked him so I could find something to value and revere, but deep down I felt even when I said I liked the circling dancers, that, no, I didn't like the overall impression. The movement is what he's caught, the ensemble, I said, but she only looked at me in disbelief.

And I thought too of the weeks, the months ahead, the years, my imminent move and how heavy the book was. Its weight bore down on me already, to pick it up required a singular effort. And it was so nice and glossy pink, like a baby immersed inside, having lost its features or just come out all flesh with the blue signature of Matisse like the beginnings of a tiny network of veins stamped on what must have been some thigh or other I couldn't see the rest of.

At night, the book tormented me. So heavy it weighed like the sleep I couldn't fall into, like a door that couldn't be closed, heavier than a tome that grew to almost human proportions with fastenings little different from a hardwood fist. The book was shutting on me, imprisoning me to an inability to move again; it was restricting my freedom, it bound me to an apartment where I no longer wanted to live, where I kept my books stacked in cardboard boxes ready to move, and then the pink Matisse comes, resting, almost cradled, on top, the unexpected kindness.

And would a Van Gogh have been different, would it have allowed me to cavort free of his generosity, into a field of wheat, be and not be the blackbird: what appreciation is, this freedom from canvas and at the same time oily immersion into it. Would I have frolicked in Van Gogh, or slipped on linseed oil there too? While here Matisse, his dancing figures with their incredibly pink flesh, imprisoned me as only dislike can, and shackled me as only trying to like does to a cell floor.

To acquire a taste for Matisse, I told myself, but the very weight of the book would not let me rest, the infant birth weight of six or seven pounds. No matter how much I tried to page through it again with my eyes closed, with blind acceptance, to uncover a sketch here, an illustration there, but in vain.

I woke up sweating, thinking what am I going to do with it, that it had trapped me in my own apartment, itself too heavy to move, retarding my search for a new place to live. It was due to its hundred-dollar heaviness, to the agent's fee I was unwilling to pay, and to the obligation, the very cell door, a door that only friends can fashion giving you a book that outside your tastes deprives you just because of its sheer weight of every opportunity for freedom.

I looked over at her sleeping so peacefully across from me. Reclining nude.

The next few months I knew would be spent trying to solve the tactical problem of what to do with all six hundred pages, how to protect the book that I valued only for its glossiness and color, a book whose contents didn't matter, to protect it at all costs despite the Alexandrian impulses to set fire to my whole library to solve the problem of its bulk among the lightness of the rest of my books whose weight, just because they were suspended like feathers in my mind, I felt would not go up in flames, only the Matisse!

THE STUNTMAN

H E STROLLED INTO the dirt floor restaurant in the tropics with his broad shoulders and thick barrel chest the shape of those that had taken him over countless falls in countless movies. The spring in his legs was as taut as the giant bows that he was launched bodily from, coiled for the buildings he jumped off at one go. He worked with many top stars, reeled off names like a film in progress. What, fifty, a hundred movies, the stuntman had been in them all, saving the necks of actors, breaking his own ribs instead. Now he even had his own stunt school.

Resentful of his intruding on the two women I was with, I said, "I do bonsai, and a bit of tea ceremony, when I'm not preoccupied with flower arrangement."

He smiled slowly at me, as if to say, I've come across your type before.

"Do you ever get hurt?" one of the women asked.

"Yes, you might say that," and he continued to expand on his exploits, but took an unexpected detour. "Our roles are stunted too," he said, looking at me with perspicacity, "and arranged, requiring all the strict formality of a ceremony. The stars shine and our light is little more than borrowed."

"They throw you off buildings and out of airplanes," one of the girls said.

"Yes," he said, "and into cement mixers and the jaws of wild animals."

"How do you ever escape?" the other girl asked.

"With scars," he said, "I have them all over my body."

With that the stuntman reached into his small black physician's bag and pulled out five folders of pictures, all action shots of him, as a Roman

176

centurion, a desperado flashing six-shooters, jumping off boulders five, six times his size, riding a dolphin, a samurai being hooked to a pulley that was going to carry him over a house, tumbling out of a burning race car, or rocket, a ball of fire himself.

"That one landed me two months in the hospital," he said.

"I cut myself on the *yōkan* knife recently," I said. "It's only plastic, but serrated."

The one girl who had lived in Japan smiled.

I then looked at his chest, two plateaus of muscle, and began to think that maybe he was the true star, the man behind the movies, when his self-effacing modesty threw a pail of cold water on that observation.

"I'm only the stuntman, the clown, the monkey, the lackey, the lapdog, the human cannonball."

His muscles shrank to the size of his smile. He won me over, won the women too and I let him have them.

"Go on," I said. "They're yours. You can be my stuntman tonight," I smiled.

But his large body didn't want to overpower but seduce with just the opposite of the glare a star might have. He was operating behind the scenes again, I could tell. He didn't want to take the women outright like a hero would. No, but like a stuntman, before they knew it fill in for me. In the back of their minds they pictured even his braggadocio and then his modesty as really larger than it was, so that his massive body was reduced to proportions they could love for a night, rather than cope with my bonsai thighs, the thin stems of my arms, the tepid aspect of my lovemaking that could only be sipped.

He instilled in the women the courage to star, to take if only a small part in all the roles he played, to see through them, through their borrowed light to the man behind the scenes, to someone calm, mildly boastful, beautiful-bodied, but finally modst about the false courage that gained a kind of authenticity in the fact that leading men would never do what he did in not fifty but one hundred films.

He left the scene with the two women, while I made stirring motions with my bamboo whisk brush I had forgotten back in Japan for a ceremony that I would not take part in.

All I could manage the next morning to one of the girls was, "Well, what century were you in last night?"

THE LIVER

THE LIVER GREW big in the pan, almost double its size, bloated as if it were still in the ruminant's stomach, gaseous and ready to dispel itself at the jabbing of my fork. But it remained stubborn and rubbery, outside assuming that cooked gray brown, but inside refusing the warmth I readied for my appetite. And grainy, almost with a yellowish, bilious tinge to it, it refused to acquiesce to the heat of the frying pan, gave off instead the impression of poisons still in the ungulate's body that it was processing. That it hadn't been removed from the cow, that I wasn't standing over it with a fork and knife alternately pricking and jabbing, ready to test whether it was done, edible.

It remained large, hepatic, bloated, and the veins when I tried to see if it was done inside actually stopped my knife, stubbornly elastic for the circulatory system they were no longer a part of. And the animal itself perhaps fricasseed, sold by now, or in someone's stomach, but not for the liver, the purifying instinct was still there. It still harbored the spirit of the cow; could in its shiny exterior reflect just because it was an internal organ its large amber eyes, the appreciative transparency that reached all the way down inside, past the thickest neck, under the softest velvet coat, unpoisoned by the oxides from the bell it wore, whose jaws could work despite constant clanging, despite its audible domestication and docility.

Ownership didn't break the cow's heart, even after slaughter had removed the liver. For the liver grew in the pan; it'd never take my blue eyes for the beauty of amber. I felt the cow was still half-grazing, that there was a swaying in the liver, that its rubbery resistance to my admittedly dull knife had something to do with the undulation of the cow's walk, setting out for pasture, the impurities it absorbed along the way that allowed it to take another step. I felt in the pan the freedom and instinct for survival that the liver inspired. All the tension of refusing to heat even after I turned the flame up and scorched it smoking the whole kitchen, that for a moment I completely lost sight of it.

Do you suppose that the liver then achieved the visceral satisfaction of an imagined reunion with the body, as I too was for a moment out of sight? Do you think it felt the rise of the backbone, the pendulous hindquarters, the weight of the dewlap, the hardness of the haunches, and most of all the freedom of the tail, like the gentlest of whips spread out at the bottom, all chestnut and white to swat the fly that I was to the large four-footed beauty that it inhabited? Did the liver imagine it was united with the body through the smoke, already in some underworld?

I turned the heat down to clear the air, saw that the underside was charred, cut it again, but still the dark maroon interior was not cooked, still it was grainy and yellowish, as if due to some distemper with having been separated from its live organism, as if from peevishness it refused to be cooked, as if it would rather go mushy and soft, anything not to be eaten, rather give the impression of impurities still in it that should not be devoured.

I sliced off a portion of it, put it in my mouth, but found it bitter; something about it resisted eating, some bloatedness that gave me the impression of refusal to release its poisons, as if the heat only gathered them together, more concentrated, uric, unexpelled. The liver was almost runny at the center now, like a nose that couldn't be wiped, it was breaking down inedibly.

Finally what I did was lift the frying pan off the heat and scrape the onions I had smothered the liver with (Maybe that was why it refused cooking, the vegetable surroundings. And it wasn't me at all.), scraped them onto my plate and threw the hot, rubbery, steaming organ into the trash, then deposited the pan in the sink where it sizzled in reproof for the liver having triumphed over being eaten.

THE PADDLE

I NEVER BEFORE imagined the acute pleasure he took from paddling us. The twinkle in his eye when he had us bent over, our hands outstretched, shuddering in anticipation. Our thin sixty- or seventy-pound bodies, our small backsides that he'd place his hand against measuring up and down, and sideways. Feeling about our hips to make sure we had no handkerchief or anything inside our underwear, and that our pockets were empty, before he'd bring the paddle ever so slowly back and forth to establish the distance, to let us feel the air that didn't escape through its numerous holes. It was a pneumatic anticipation unlike those large balloon men that startle you on the street all of a sudden becoming larger than life. Three or four times he did this with the paddle, and placing his hand on our buttocks he slid it up our hips, then onto our spine, where he made sure we were properly bent so he had only flesh and no bone, as we craned our necks around, our body like the empty shell of a large egg. Our heads suspended, as prominent as Hieronymus Bosch, our faces as chalky white, but without the experience to know just what was taking place inside him.

He put the paddle down, acted out the charade to the hilt, spat into his hands, blew on them and rubbed them together, cocking back his elbows like chicken wings, and working his shoulders loose. Through gold metal-rimmed glasses he looked at us, measuring every emotion to calculate just how much force to apply. He flicked his wrist with the paddle slicing the air upwards a few times. The lenses of his glasses reflected the long wood. What we had done seemed to drift into a kind of meaninglessness, to be isolated there with him, acting out this ritual of childhood. None of us would watch. Though we were all close by and could hear the cries of pain as the "swats" came, for we kept count. A count he sometimes pretended to lose. Each of us knew exactly how many the other was getting by week's end. And exactly what we had done to deserve them.

How he laughed when we jumped up and down, our backsides hot and "on fire," he'd chuckle, for it was all a big joke to him, the way he manipulated our fears, wrapped them around his little finger; he needed the paddle to show love in the only way a houseparent could to a group of twenty-one boys. Most of us felt the love behind the charade. Knew the sting, the pain we tried to make disappear by madly rubbing our buttocks, was a form of love we never received from our natural parents. Knew he was "fair." All the boys had always said, "Pop was fair," for as long as anyone could remember. We repeated this over and over again to convince ourselves of the severity of our wrongdoing, when we couldn't find a better reason for the punishment. He had been Dean of Boys and had administered swats for the whole school of fifteen hundred. His fairness kept him his job, and his "love of the boys." And so, when he was near retirement they put him out in a small farmhouse on the hill with a younger group of boys. And nobody ever suspected that all this fairness, these principles, that could tally up so exactly the swats we received for our misdeeds, had anything to do with any more than his love for us. He wanted us to grow up straight, and know when we did wrong, and admit it, to feel the sting before the punishment was applied; he wanted us to carry throughout our lives the principles of good conduct he instilled with his paddle with the air holes in it--he wanted us to forget completely the pleasure he took measuring us with his hand, a large, gentle, and by then arthritic hand that knew every bone in our backside, every muscle, that gently rode the apophyseal processes of our spine before each swing to make sure we were properly bent over.

There was a union with us in the way we accepted the pain and the pleasure with which he administered it. Some accepted it without a murmur; those he wanted in the worst way to get a response from. He smiled at them broadly to make them tremble and cry out. Those who were closest to him went through all the motions of pain, dramatically acting out the power of his paddle hitting their buttocks, jumping around as if the seat of their pants was literally on fire. Some were even brought to tears beforehand. They were his pets. But the silent ones he had to hit a little harder to get at their pride. And he then waxed serious to better place his swings, squinting to get them in his power. And involuntarily, for his own labored breath, the perspiration on his reddened brow, his face changing color, turning almost purple, left him standing there so relaxed afterwards, having wielded his paddle; it couldn't have occurred to us then how our pain infused his loins with a pleasure of exhaustion that he never received from his wife, who being large herself collected elephant figurines.

We were his pride and joy, she said, and at times she confided that he loved us more than he did their own daughter. We tried to be good for him so he would not have to swat us, but he always found something, or his wife did, and we would be called into his office. But we never for a moment imagined the heads we twisted back would one day find an analogy in Bosch's *The Garden of Delights*. Our own arms like tree limbs would harken back to the wooden paddle, that look of comprehension would understand the pain we received as not altogether behind us. That we and our clad, and sometimes naked, backsides had climbed the ladder and gone inside ourselves for the most part completely disappearing. Only this rendering and Bosch opens it up. The flat disc on his head, the past we carry like a mock graduation, the dance of fear we made music from, the musical instruments that drowned out our cries, our shrieks, all that doesn't faze us.

We look back accepting the incomprehension of Pop. We weren't damaged for not knowing any better. Though the pain that we now give women, we should know is mixed inextricably with our own pleasure in a way Pop never imagined paddling us, so exquisitely did he enjoy it. For now, we must sense as we turn our heads back to that time that we too are made of the exact same lumber as the paddle he used.

BUCK HILL FALLS

THE BUSES DROPPED them off like cattle cars every Friday night. Sometimes they would moo mocking themselves as they wheeled into the parking lot to indicate that they were fresh off the farms.

They rose with the Holsteins before six every morning for milking. In cold weather they huddled close to the animals sharing their body heat, giving their teats a gentle squeeze with their forefinger, transferred to the middle finger, then the weakest finger before the pinky finished off the last squirt of milk. They did this until the udder was almost dry, then stripped the four teats to go on to the next cow.

Sometimes their hands cracked with deep fissures from washing the teats in winter which made milking by hand impossible, so they were sent up to do housework until their hands healed.

The cows all had numbers and if one went into the wrong stall, they'd bunch at the entrance confused until we'd remove the cow to her proper stall. We grew attached to the animals and some boys named their favorites after their girlfriends in town.

Most of us were kind enough and performed our chores willingly, but the meanest took their resentment out on both the cows and younger boys.

Once Gil got so angry at a heifer that he knocked it over the head with a steel bucket and it collapsed dead.

It was rumored on one farm that a hose was inserted up the cow's rectum that it died. Some boys mixed stone dust in the meal angered at having been abandoned to the orphanage. Some punched the cows so hard that you winced to see it.

We all couldn't help being fascinated by the pink entrance to the reproductive organs so clearly visible when the tail moved. The detail was so distinct it made a few of us want to become artists just to reproduce the cow's backside.

The smaller boys were made to crawl through the drop the cows used smearing themselves with manure. It was called "playing army," after we'd stand up with our clothes stained green reeking of ammonia. Those of us who joined the army afterwards said the indignities of basic training didn't compare to their farm home experiences. Homes of twenty-one boys were scattered across the countryside to supply milk for the local chocolate factory in town.

Occasionally one of us would be assigned to climb up the metal rungs of the silo to break the hard crust of snow and fork the silage into the cart below to feed the cows. The heady fumes of fermentation cleared our respiratory tracts making colds a rarity. Surrounded by shiny round tiles it was a castle of sorts, high enough for Rapunzel's long yellow hair to be thrown out the window for some prince to climb up. The heady fumes precipitated powerful dreams of women whose bodies bore the well-defined outlines of cows tucked away inside their clothes. The silage made us amorous knowing we were such an integral part of the milk our cows produced to make the chocolate in town.

The vats of milk chocolate grew on us, their giant spatulas mixing it back and forth into the creamiest brown confectionary dreams. It both fascinated and sickened us to watch the chocolate in the vats. Like the smell of ammonia in manure it invaded our nostrils and awakened our senses. The factory touched something deep in us, exposing a giant sweet tooth that already penetrated our bodies with all the buried implications of unbrushed decay.

The way the candy kisses dropped in the factory, squeezed out in rows of fifteen to be wrapped in tinfoil and delicate paper banners, signaled a triumph of sorts. The streetlamps in town were topped with kisses that we never received. Tens of thousands of kisses were manufactured daily in the factory, but barely one was given to us.

The fifteen hundred boys in the orphanage received no candy rations like the soldiers in World War II. The kisses probably started in the amorous Fifties when the troops returned, and the birth rate soared. The one set of houseparents for twenty-one boys didn't have the time to distribute them at all. How could they? Neither did the boys receive what the factory produced, though we kissed our cows amorously as a joke.

How else could we deal with all those kisses when it was we who supplied the milk for those huge vats with their powerful spatulas and tireless machinery that dropped the most delicate sweets, as easily as two pursed lips with countless corrugated folds laying another wet one on a sheet of wax paper?

As we got older and were sent to the farm homes we dreamed of women with eyes as big as the animals we took care of, whose bodies could be as warm and soft as on those cold winter mornings when we huddled close sharing their heat and whose pink teats gave us the satisfaction of milking them dry, even on occasion squirting a fresh stream of milk into our own mouths before pasteurization. It probably made up for all the breastfeeding that was discouraged in the Fifties and built up our forearms and strengthened our grip.

On Fridays, the buses dropped us off in town around 6:30 and we'd take in a movie. The theater in the Community Building was a high two-story affair. On the ceiling when the theater lights dimmed stars appeared and clouds drifted overhead. We sat with our heads arched dreaming of a life beyond our own.

The buses loaded us up and took us back to our farm homes promptly at 9:30. They'd pull out of the parking lot with the same authority that they pulled in. And our excitement would be over just seeing a girl, but most were too awkward to talk to them.

No matter how many times we showered and scrubbed ourselves, we couldn't get past the smell of manure in our own nostrils for being called "cows," nor could we escape the stigma of dead parents and broken homes. Most girls in town kept their distance not wanting to be stigmatized in the local high school for associating with us.

Only in athletics could we equalize things by beating our crosstown rivals. We were the Spartans, after all, who routinely trounced the Trojans.

Jason was surprised when he was chosen to attend the religious conference at Buck Hill Falls, a resort in the Poconos.

I'd like to think it was for his treatment and handling of the animals, the feeding of hay and silage, and the spreading of straw bedding rather than all the teats he had pulled, but perhaps there were other reasons like the contemplative cast he wore. Maybe the Religious Director saw him in the theater just before it got dim looking at the clouds, his neck craned back as if he were a bird about to take flight. Maybe there was something of the Holy Ghost about when his mother left him, the antithesis to the streets of New York City, ending up on a farm in Central Pennsylvania with a pitchfork in hand surrounded by twenty boys tending the needs of thirty head of cattle.

He must have seen something in Jason. It couldn't have been that he was one of the few Catholics in a school of mostly Protestants. Maybe it was his innocence, or his blue eyes.

They pulled up to the ski resort in the off season where Jason found himself on the first night in a team leader's room speaking of the *nous* and other Greek words trying to unravel the abstract nature of belief. He'd never been in such a discussion. There were girls there, but he only gave them a passing attention to hide his attraction. His school was all male.

In the dining hall that night Jason found himself sitting next to a young girl from his discussion group named Janice.

Janice was intelligent, personable, with blond curls, and socially she was leagues beyond Jason who due to a natural thoughtfulness was cautious and inhibited. He was barely out of the Stone Age insofar as girls were concerned.

He wondered as Janice sat across from him if she could smell the silo, not to mention the drop on him. He quickly checked under his nails to see if there were any traces of digested debris. And his complexion too bothered him, but he spoke to her, answered her questions, almost forgot himself, but then retreated into his shell. Admittedly it must have been nacre, just like the buttons on his shirt, for the iridescent tints caught the glint of the chandeliers in his eyes giving confidence to his handling the cutlery, making use of the special training he'd received before he left.

Jason was holding his own, but unprepared for such a pretty, intelligent, and interested girl.

He kept thinking of 104 who Mac liked, who had more black on her coat than white, but who had the nicest face that he named her Gail, after his girl in town.

Jason looked at Janice chewing her food remembering 104 chewing her cud and smiled at gaining confidence around a real girl, but then pictured himself about to fall out of the silo if he did not pay attention to the cart forty feet below. Jason was losing his balance and didn't hear Janice circle the conversation back to the falls on the third night when they were standing in the lobby. They had approached the falls the night before, but Jason complained that it was too cold and had turned back.

The last night of the conference was crystalline clear and the stars and a tiny sliver of a moon were out. Patches of snow still covered the ground. Jason and Janice had talked about the spirit all day and transubstantiation. She had even asked him about the Eucharist.

When the speeches were finally over after eating, Janice repeated if Jason would like to walk to the falls.

He stood there as if with a huge rack on his head. He imagined all the heifers he'd rounded up. He imagined himself bound though free of the thirty cows they milked twice every day. He saw his eyes scouring the snowy landscape for doe. His tail in the air indicated he was primed in his search, with the falls cascading like two lovers already capitulating in a frothy embrace. The clouds he imagined overhead moved in silence like at the theater in town when he threw back his head, looked up, and wanted to laugh at the beauty of the stars.

He remembered in the reduced light once after one church service looking for the petrified forest ring set in silver his mother had bought for him in the Southwest. He never found it.

Jason sniffed Janice's perfume as he stood there abashed despite the setting in the Poconos and the considerable rack of horn imagined on his head, weighed down by a manhood he wasn't ready for despite facing the backsides of all those cows every morning.

Janice and Jason, two sides of the same face, the mating pair brought together by spiritual concerns, were now left to their bodies.

"No, I have to get back. I need a good night's sleep since we'll be leaving early tomorrow morning," Jason said.

Janice smiled as Jason bid her goodbye and walked down the corridor. He turned and immediately entered the men's room.

It was empty with marble wash basins, shiny brass faucets, large mirrors, and six stalls and five urinals. Jason moved confidently to the corner and unloosened his tie, ducked and circled it over his head. He removed his jacket and undid the buttons on his shirt one after another hoping no one would come.

He slipped out of his shirt with a deftness that a woman would admire, undressing himself almost as carefully as he'd undress her. He unbuckled his belt and his fingers then unclasped his trousers to his zipper which he worked down to the bottom where the teeth started. He slipped his trousers off one leg at a time and carefully placed his clothes on a stool. He looked again anxiously at the door. Then he took off his socks and grabbed his undershirt so deftly lifting it over his head exposing a brilliant set of rectus abdominal muscles. They were like a washboard his friends had told him. His chest revealed two distinct plateaus of pectoral muscle that like his stomach was something he had been born with, well-defined long before he did any exercise to build them up.

He then took his hands and slipped his fingers into the elastic of his underpants and eased them off his body. He stood there stark naked in the soft light.

Not even the frigid weather, the top coat back in his room, the deer whose rack must have terrified a whole forest of does standing on the hill, not even Janice occurred to him though the falls continued to plunge into the body of icy water below.

He was so vulnerable looking, but self-composed, knowing exactly what he was doing, had a purpose in mind no one would have guessed. In fact, he didn't care what anyone thought, for he knew his body needs that early on had pushed him away from the dining table.

Almost hugging himself for the cold, he embraced the tightness of his skin as his goose flesh thickened to warm him. He forgets completely where he is and about the door suddenly opening. Maybe it would have been better if he had taken a stall.

To be so alone with his own nudity and the girl outside was almost delicious, but something he approached with almost an element of defiance. The cows hundreds of miles away testified to his indifference; the buck on the promontory abutting a state forest should have been a revelation, a shiny moment, inspiring all sorts of speculation as to why Jason didn't visit the falls. Was he dreaming of his Argonauts, or the labors of Hercules, or still thinking of Janice's golden fleece? What did he strip entirely naked for? Was it that the conference promoted a ritual baptism under the rubric of the falls, or that the unfamiliar forest had been menacing? Was this the beginning of ill-understood desires that could only be addressed stark naked leaving the girl disappointed? Had three days of discussion on spirituality using those abstruse Greek words finally gotten to Jason and he realized he wasn't a mythical hero at all, or one of god's legions, but only a young boy on the brink of manhood who had just rejected the overtures of a young girl outside the men's room?

He took two steps forward completely naked as if to approach an altar. He was aware of the sacrifice, of Janice in the corridor, of his desserts half eaten, and the mashed potatoes left on his plate.

The door opened and a fresh gust of cold air blew in.

"Hey, man, what are you doing?" Peter from his discussion group asked.

Jason standing there in his own world without a stitch of clothing looked hard at him as he stepped forward, with the certainty of someone who after three days at a conference was now finally in his element, onto the scale before him and confidently balanced the two weights to indicate exactly, as if he already knew to the ounce, how much he had gained the last three days.

Startled out of a daze of rapid mental calculations, Jason finally answered, "I have to make weight by next Friday. We're wrestling the Trojans, our crosstown rivals."

THE HORROR

MY MOTHER KNOCKED at the apartment door. There was a rattling of chains, the twist of a Segal, a Medico's bolt, the removal of the police lock, and the door opened into the warm breath, the pinkish riot of smells, of what seemed a woman's boudoir.

"Oh, Elizabeth, you brought your little boy," and she bent down and took my face in her hands and squeezed my cheeks. "He's getting bigger!"

She was in a satin slip and her breasts were visible. In fact, her skin was the softest I had seen on a woman, though she must have been in her mid-forties at the time. Still my imagination ran riot.

And the erectness of her cats, their glossy fur, I must have somehow associated with her, and my later fondness for animals. In fact, that visit, with her little bed by the door and her not using her bedroom is still unclear, but like an examining table it determined me to be a gynecologist who had free access to women's bodies just awakened from their slumbers.

But mostly I recall her lying down, and the fleshy tints of her skin, the pinks, soft browns, the rouge, the papery thin full breasts, the bluest eyes, and the softest, most lilting voice I'd ever heard. One of my mother's friends when she met Mary said she had the most remarkable complexion.

Mary was a private duty nurse who had been married twice. The first she explained was because she was young and foolish, to defy her father, a Russian Greek Orthodox priest. She ran away from home in her teens, just for the sex, she said. But he was too irresponsible for them to remain together. He gambled, drank, lied, made none of the payments on the furniture, so that she was left with all the bills. The second husband just left, and she never heard from him again.

And so, Mary got a career for herself, so she'd never be dependent on men, and took up with a prominent surgeon with an airplane. On their days off she'd fly with him over New York City and up to New England. She felt she had it all. He was married, but his wife she explained was an invalid. They did everything on the sly, and that added excitement to every meeting.

Mary was taken by his importance, being at the top of his field, but she knew what men wanted, could read their every wish. Her mother who was also Russian never approved of her daughter's career choice as "a glorified maid." She refused to speak English and read only her Russian novels. She instructed Mary on how to cater to a man's needs, how to handle them, and so abetted by the most feminine voice, an incomparable skin and sparkling blue eyes, Mary could put them in their place, wrap them around her little finger, so well did she know beforehand their ups and downs.

"Take their hand when they are getting fresh and pat it twice and say, 'That's a good boy!'" her mother would say. And the men instantly fell in line every time, were indeed tamed like little boys.

Mary felt she had the best of all worlds, a romance that had none of the dreary domesticity of housework, or the inconvenience of raising children.

In fact, she claimed she didn't like children, their noisiness, their runny noses, their extraordinary selfishness, but loved animals of all kinds, even the skunks around her house in Vermont where more than once she had to bathe with tomato juice to get rid of the smell after being sprayed.

Mary had three brothers and a sister, but none of them had children either. There was Helen who worked in the state forensics lab, and who, though she was seriously courted by the Hartford banker Harold Weiss, never married. The doctor at her death confided to Mary that Helen's hymen was still intact at eighty-six.

Helen was a sweet soul, but completely regimented by Mary after she and two of her brothers moved up to Vermont. Not only Mary's strong personality, but that she "paid all the bills" too kept everyone in line.

To keep Helen from going senile, Mary would force her to read aloud from the *New York Times* every evening at the kitchen table while she prepared supper, and then she'd march them all out to view the sunset. Mary constantly criticized Helen for her bending over and would scold her even when they had company about straightening up.

And there was Leon who lived for years in a tiny room in Brooklyn, a sheltered accountant all his life, because of a bout with bone cancer on his face as an early adolescent. The doctors botched a series of operations and Leon refused to let them touch him again. And so, he walked around with a protuberance from his cheek that was always bandaged. In certain seasons the wound wept, and as a result he never had contact with women, though Mary knew he relieved himself alone in his room when he came to live with her.

Bill was the brother who worked all his life on the railroad and spoke in astonishing strings of clichés. He never married either. He drank in secret in his room and Mary pretended not to notice unless he left a bottle lying around, then she got angry. He complained about Mary's ordering everyone around, but like the others he didn't have the courage to buck his sister. No one did, for she still carried the invincibility of having been her father's favorite.

Mary and her siblings were brought up in a rectory in Hartford with servants, where the church prospered under the stewardship of her father who made shrewd stock investments. And Mary, too, gained authority by working double shifts, sixteen hours a day, to pay for her Vermont house.

Mary was even courted by Willard Willoughby, the State Senator from Vermont who had once proposed to her. Every Sunday, as they both got on in years, they traveled to the Holiday Inn in town for brunch. Mary was always invited to the Willoughby family gatherings on holidays long after Willard passed away.

There was a time in the fifties when Mary got her car and Leon and Helen and a few friends would go on drives to Bear Mountain and around the Catskills for picnics, and up into New England to visit the historical sights. Mary was the master of ceremonies, bubbly, the life of the party. She was extremely generous with her money, so that attracted everyone to her.

The third brother Eugene lived in California, but although he was married there were no children. In fact, the family line ends with this written record since there were no offspring to carry on their Russian name.

Mary was the private duty nurse at Columbia Presbyterian Hospital who would be called on first to take the highest profile cases. Anne Morrow Lindbergh and Eleanor Roosevelt were two of her more illustrious patients. She had intelligence, charm, certain habits of aristocracy that appealed to people of importance, and an elegance from her mother who was brought up in Russia with servants before the Revolution. Mary had an ease of manner that, despite her proficiency, identified her as much more than a private duty nurse. Any number of patients wanted her to come to their homes and live with them. She was so quick to anticipate each patient's needs and put them at ease.

Since my mother was her friend and we summered in Vermont when I was growing up, I too fell in love with the breathtaking scenery and went to live there between jobs. It was then that I got to know Mary better.

She would ask me if I wanted to go to dinner when I would call, and so we fell into the habit of going out to restaurants in the Vermont town where she now lived in an apartment. When they had horse and carriage races we went; when there was the State Fair she was especially interested in the pig races, so we went. When there was a violin concert by Alexander Solzhenitsyn's son, Alexis, we attended.

I would take Mary shopping periodically and drive her to feed her pigeons every few days. She spent hundreds of dollars a month feeding the birds. We'd also drive to restaurants all around the state where I'd have to dress up for brunch or dinner, or the horse and buggy ride afterwards that though I balked taking at first, I finally relented. I remember as a child meeting Mary with my mother at restaurants on Fifth Avenue at Christmas, walking through the snow, under the picturesque arch at Washington Square, leaving with that curious security of my stomach full like a taut drum.

Mary liked history and so we went to places like the Shelburne Museum, Wilson's Castle, and the Calvin Coolidge estate. We took in the Proctor marble works and even took trips out of state to Albany. All the while we talked endlessly about politics, religion, and the issues of the day. Mary had cable and so often after dinner we would go back to her apartment and watch programs and continue our talk. She'd have ice cream from Howard Johnson's, or something to sweeten our conversation.

Mary never took kindly to my girlfriends and warned me against having children whom she thought would ruin my future. Or if a relationship was getting too serious, like when Ashley came up from Miami, she discreetly warned me that Miami was the AIDS capital of the US; or Mindy's two children, she warned of the burden that would place on me. And herpes and all the STDs that'd result from loose women, she reminded me of that too. I took her admonitions in stride as the leftover fears of a nurse surrounded by sickness all her life, or the understandable concerns of someone of my mother's generation.

I left Vermont a few times to travel to Mexico, and once to move south, but came back. Mary always appeared glad when I returned, and we picked up exactly where we had left off with our periodic meetings. I had heard all about her affairs with the flying doctor, her attending Eleanor Roosevelt and Charles Lindbergh's wife, and all about her father's investments in the stock market.

"Yes," she'd sigh, "I've had a full life."

And when we'd be driving through the picture post card beauty of another Vermont autumn, she'd suddenly throw her head back at all the colors of the foliage and say, "Now, I could die!"

There were even times when she wanted to know if I'd end her life. She'd pay me, she said, if I assisted her. Perhaps it was some depressant in the cocktail of medications she took that slowed her pulse to the low forties that she'd have to have a Cherry Coke or cup of coffee to elevate it.

We continued to go on our drives, to restaurants, shopping, for ice cream afterwards at her apartment. By this time, Mary was in her early eighties. She complained about her memory all the time but was sharper and more lucid than most people.

Finally, I got a job down South, and had to leave. Mary was apparently glad for me, though I knew she was disappointed. We went out to dinner and bade farewell, and then there was something I had to pick up a day or two before I was to leave. Something was odd about the time she suggested I come, but I went over to her apartment at dusk.

I announced myself on the intercom and climbed the inside stairs, passed the bags of bird seed and loaves of bread, when on the top landing, Mary suddenly opened the door.

She was wearing a satin slip. Never in all my visits had she been so attired. Here an old woman already in her eighties stood before me in all her vulnerability. It was the nakedly bold gesture of someone who had been a teenager almost seventy years ago.

I was stunned, as it brought the last couple of years into startling focus. Every dinner she insisted on paying for, every conversation, even the fireworks we looked at together, the horse and buggy rides, the trotters we bet on, every enthusiasm, every largesse was lost in the shimmering folds of silk that shined and disappeared by turns as I dropped my eyes.

I never once thought of the voluptuous breasts that had struck me as a child when my mother took me to Mary's apartment, of memories that had so thoroughly blended into a substratum of sensuality that I no longer recognized them, certainly not associated with the old woman now standing before me.

And the eyes, they were still hers, that was the remarkable thing. How their look didn't age though the skin formed a turbulent corkscrew of wrinkles around it. The blue, piercing gimlet eyes had a focus I hadn't noticed before. Though this time I noticed they were small, a fact she had always complained about.

And the wonderfully soft skin still had something of its earlier bloom, except for the eyes and neck where the emollients could not keep up with the sagging.

All the incantation of her soft voice, the handling of men so deftly, stood there as a parody that I didn't know where to look. The dinners were a charade, the conversations, the trips. Here I had thought she was interested in me for my mind. But just the opposite seemed true as I stood there like a woman must feel when she discovers for the first time that the man only wants her for her body.

I stepped back, never entered the apartment. There was a chill between us that had everything to do with the thin petticoat that she wore and the Vermont winter coming up the stairs in gusts.

She probably had no notion of her effect on me over thirty years ago, but now as the satin petticoat shimmered, and the strap hung carelessly on one shoulder, I tried once more to negotiate my eyes away from her face that was so aggressively taking me in that all I could imagine was being on the road heading south out of this cold state.

The expression that leaped to my mind as I bade her farewell was "The Horror! The Horror!"

Mary later told my mother that I had left without saying goodbye.

CAT

HE'S GONE NOW, dead as a doornail. Almost all who knew him said, "Good riddance." They continue to shock me to this day.

He left the community of men, rested in a rusty heap of flakes, ultimately was blown away by his own enthusiasms.

Everyone turned on him in the end. I can't get that out of my mind. How decisively the women sneered at his name, had not one good word for him. They must have known something was up, something in his background.

It's almost a joke how we'll live our whole life for one encouraging word, for the pat on the back, and just when you'd expect it to come they can't even mention his name. You'd think they were forcing out a dry whisper from a parched throat on a desert three days without water, something that difficult.

I could see the loathing in their faces. How it twisted them up. They couldn't even discuss him. But they are all blind mice, and probably only feared the same thing happening to themselves. The men, they were no better. All preserved an inexplicable silence, even his best friends.

The alcohol was the big secret that everyone knew. He drank in private, all the time once they moved away. His family turned on him, and in the end not even they had a good word for him, an ounce of sympathy left. They brought him back only to bury him.

He'd wanted love, respect, a family, a community, for all of us to be a team.

This all seemed to come, but there was something irrevocable that stuck in his craw, something that gave him no rest, no contentment, the chicken bone that made us all uncomfortable as if it were in our own throats. He loved his wife and child dearly, said he felt truly blessed. He apparently loved even his colleagues, those who ended up bad-mouthing him. Maybe they couldn't handle the unease they sensed, took it personally, or believed the bouts of depression were contagious enough to establish a distance.

Maybe it was his intellect, the natural superiority, or something else in him that had nothing to do with them at all. It could have been that, for we all want to be included, until of course we are. For people are loving, accepting, will embrace you if you give them half a chance, but show them some weakness and by next Friday they'll crucify you.

Maybe he saw the odds against himself, knew Lady Luck would elude him despite his contentment with a wife and child, the boat on the lake, their newly built house. His wife whom he repeated he loved so much you sensed that maybe he was trying to convince himself.

It could have been that he saw through people too clearly and couldn't live with the transparencies, knew himself too well to criticize them. His personality was too timid for those assertions that destroy love or friendship, so his loved ones and friends were always on edge as he battled himself, knock-down drag-out battles hiding the vast deceptions, the hypocrisies that we live by. We insist on love on our own terms, and end with kisses that ultimately bore us until we give them an edge forcing ourselves on someone. From outside most saw him as a limp rag riding his John Deere, or walking stoop-shouldered, with that severely compromised posture.

Maybe the women resented that the drama never involved them, that they weren't the heroines, even in the end his wife. Most probably they suspected there was no drama associated with him at all. That was what was so mystifying, and more than anything accounted for the inconclusive feeling at his death, as if they all had been cheated of something, something directed more forcefully, more passionately elsewhere, that he ended up being ashamed of all his life. Maybe that is why they accused him of being a tyrant, sensing there was a past that they had no access to, save for the chinks in his personality that told of something unspeakable, driving him to drink.

His wife came to despise the weakness, and in the end unable to disentangle him from the refuge of alcohol grew disgusted at the appearance of respectability, at her own hiding, that he never held her down, mishandled her, but sensed that he was on the verge of such ugliness and snapped back in fear because he knew something others did not. She sensed this sometimes with a rage that tried to provoke him, as he sloshed ahead as if he were a schoolboy in galoshes being reprimanded by his mother. He was never broken, but disgracefully bent as after each drink he approached a maundering contentment with the world.

He'd become assertive and weak by turns, had that infinite sympathy that makes us all transparent after the horror is gone, until the turbidity of the will returns. But it never really did again. Maybe that is what was so frustrating, and where the sense of loss came from. Perhaps that is why he couldn't live with himself when he saw what he was capable of and shuddered beside the defenselessness of his wife and small child, whom he loved too much to escape the torment. The testosterone rush made even his naturally florid complexion blush, so he masked it in drink. He knew he was his own best camouflage, hidden from everyone without realizing they sensed only weakness in what he thought came across as simple love of humanity.

He had told me how his little daughter once scampered into his arms under a blanket in the living room during a thunderclap, as if the summit of his emotional life was sheltering her from the storm. Never had he felt so needed; afterwards, it was all downhill as the past growled, scratched, grew assertive. His daughter too grew up assertive, independent, burying her love in resentment at his drinking bouts.

"What's that?" she asked one day grabbing his hand. She had noticed the tiny scars on his knuckle. "Where did you get these?"

But she lost interest the next moment after the drink on his breath overcame her that she barely heard him say, "Nowhere."

He knew the obstacles in himself to deep feeling, the German depths, or like the vulnerable Maginot line of the French what tempts us with empty triumphs, with knotty problems of self-esteem that make life unbearable before we are like piles of ferrous ash. Maybe it was that he had never again shown his mettle or foresaw that he'd be blown away like everyone else before he made amends. Maybe he thought he still had time. But a powerful hubris sat atop too much humility that his intellect was helpless, for in the end he didn't believe in himself.

When his wife gave me these pages, I understood completely. The cat's name could have been Pluto circling the furthest reaches of the solar system, only to be discovered that it wasn't a planet after all but a dark excuse for a satellite.

A friend of mine when he first read the manuscript said it described his own love life. His wife never knew him, the stifled need to reduce her, maybe that was what drove her unconsciously away, the subtlety with which he robbed her of not even an outright assault that would have cleared the air. The evident weakness that wanted control so badly, but his lack of assertion, which is what was so insulting because it showed an absence of feeling. Such hard won reductions of the self in the end leave nothing but speechlessness at a funeral, making us wish that we at least had talked to him so we could have corrected things.

I know it wasn't the severity of his gold-framed spectacles that turned us away; the light that glinted on the lenses, the nakedness of the face after they were taken off, his unassertive rounded nose; all the burden of observing the world in the first place buries the status glasses give, protecting us while at the same time making us more vulnerable to a visual acuity. Who wants to see everything? Who could bear it? He had the habit of taking his glasses off, cleaning them in our presence, giving himself a rest from what he saw.

His stooped shoulders gave away he was too tall to be seen, that there was too much of him for his extraordinarily tormented mind. It makes you wonder what kind of body it should fit in. He wanted to cut himself down to size but grew weak-kneed just thinking about it. Little things got to him like splinters under the skin. They define us, inflame us, and then vanish from view all at once leaving more emptiness than we can reckon. Perhaps he simply pursued the vanishings too urgently; that's why he latched on to the animal and postponed marriage into his late thirties. He was frightened of just such a scenario occurring again. This time on a human being, and that accounts for the distance.

His wife hid his drinking, his rants, put on the most normal face, thought a move could salvage their marriage.

But not before she said one day, "I packed my bags this weekend and was out of the house. I thought I'd leave Bob, but I came back. He's so miserable, he makes everyone around him miserable!"

In the end he was left alone with his demons, his one demon if this manuscript is true. I'd like to say she terrified his soul, that he hung her, but no, it was calm, deliberate, about the simple control he seldom saw in himself; writing it down he thought might dispel it, so self-effacing was he, expert at it that he disarmed people with the authority with which he could denigrate himself, at the same time like all egoists handling everyone else with a velvet glove.

But why did the women turn on him? Did they know, or was it the gossip, the whispering about the drinking? Was it the odor of the animal that persisted after all those years, after his marriage and the birth of their child? Was it something his colleagues sensed? Or did it only cling to him? Was it something he alone couldn't face? Everything else he had an opinion on, but this he couldn't lay his hands on. Perhaps there is only so long that you can suppress it, that so long are you overburdened that it finally gets to the heart eventually, swells and blocks it in the end, creates the congestive heart failure that ends one day in a massive heart attack after he is rushed to the emergency room. Here is the manuscript that was placed in my hands, all that is left of his story:

I always wondered how deep is my right to dislike certain animals, as deep as to do them violence or thwart their movements?

I hold my cat, she squirms with her claws, tries to bite me, cautiously. I hold her longer, she squirms more violently and forgetting caution, bites me. I release her. A trickle of fresh blood courses out of the two puncture marks on my knuckles and down to my wrist. On my other hand I notice I am also bleeding, there she has scratched me. She is now at the opposite end of the living room alternately licking herself where I held her and looking at me. I call her but she continues washing herself. I call her once more, she stops licking and looks at me, then continues again.

I soften my voice, I entreat her with outstretched hands. Slowly and with the utmost hesitation she moves toward me, then sits down halfway. I increase my calls with unction and she moves closer, more trustingly. Suddenly at an arm's reach I grab her, my voice now changes.

I hold her tightly with my fist by the loose fur around her neck so her head cannot move. Then I squeeze her face upwards to mine, force her to make eye contact with me and ask her why she hurt me.

"Why, cat, why?"

Clenching my teeth I twice hit her rapidly with the palm of my hand and throw her down in front of me, daring her to run. But before she does I pounce on her roughly with my hands. She struggles to free herself and brings up her hind legs for assistance. Quickly I pull them back and stretch the full length of her body immobile, then repeatedly press my thumbs into the soft pads of flesh on her feet to show her the control I have over her claws. She ceases to struggle aware that she is caught. She is more docile than before. It is as if she has finally sensed that her instincts are no match for mine, for the evil schemes, the fresh torment teeming in my brain, hatching differently by the minute. And torment whose sole aim is to wrest from her a pledge of feeling, a show of unrestricted love and devotion.

I release her and wash my bleeding hands of her loose hairs. She is now sitting at the furthest corner of the room cleaning herself, recovering her dignity and composure. I call her but she doesn't come. I repeat my call, but she remains sitting. I pour her dry food and rattle it in her dish. She comes.

Swiftly I grab her from her dish, "See, you wouldn't come for me, ungrateful cat, but you would come for your food! But I tricked you!"

I hit her and she growls from somewhere deep in her throat. She leaves go a scent, but from experience dares not hiss at me. She is frightened now, so am I. I don't know how far my anger will go, or where it will end.

I look at the scratches on my hand and another outbreak of madness possesses me, and I hit her insensibly again and again until finally she is dazed.

Suddenly I realize the angry stupor of what I am doing, and that she is little more than a kitten and that her bones are so frail. I grow more frightened. I notice she isn't putting up the same resistance she did before.

I release her but she drops before me panting heavily. I quickly feel her hipbones to see if they are broken. I stand her up and push her from me to walk. But she is shaking in terror and walks unsteady. I grab her, I hug her and kiss her tenderly on her wet nose.

I mumble, "I am sorry, I am heartily sorry." I stroke her as earnestly as ever I made an act of contrition.

But then it occurs to me to test her devotion once more, just once more, and I throw her out of my room and quickly lock the door. I so much want her to meow and scratch to get back in. I listen. But she doesn't seem to want to come in. There is silence.

I wait.

Quietly I open the door.

She is sitting in the corner looking straight at me. I call her gruffly, but she doesn't move towards me. I get angry and scream at her.

She grows frightened and runs away from me down the stairs. In an access of rage I chase her, swoop her up and angrily carry her into my room, close the door and throw her down at my feet.

She remains huddled and trembling. "Escape now, cat," I say to her. But she remains.

I squeeze her tightly, "Go on, escape now!" so tightly that she coughs a man's cough and gasps for breath.

For a moment I grow frightened, she can't catch her breath, the blood races to my temples thinking this time she is permanently injured. But then she recovers, stops coughing, and catches her breath.

I don't know what is wrong with me. I take her up in my arms and kiss her with tenderness and stroke her gently. I have never been able to show the same love and tenderness to any person. But I can do this only after I have beaten her insensibly, only after I have grown angry with her and dominated her. Only after I have tried to break her will, transgress the inviolable precincts of her animal personality, break her silence, her self-possession, her inner assurance, with my noisy commands and relentless will.

Only after these efforts, after outraging her dignity, after holding her head angrily on the kitchen tile and accidentally chipping her front tooth in an access of rage (and I admit to examining the chipped tooth with remorse a hundred times afterwards), after the fear that she will become crippled from my hitting her frail hipbones so often, after my swinging her around by the tail while her small body clings desperately to a heavy throw rug until she is howling so loudly that I stop for fear of the neighbors hearing her, after my quickly feeling her tail to make sure I have not broken it in anymore places, am I able to love her with a passion and freedom I have never been able to love a friend or a woman. Far from disliking her, I love my cat. She elicits from me the very best I have to offer, but only after I am constrained to show her the very worst in me.

I have always been awkward in love, that is why I turned to my cat. Not realizing the even larger temperamental differences between us, I did my best to reconcile them. But unable to accept the slow and timely prerequisites that would win its favor and gain its confidence, I was motivated by a hasty and reckless need to prevail upon it to accept me all at once. From no dearth of love did I abuse my cat, but rather from a too great swelling of it, that I was unable to carry with me and at the same time unable to discharge, from a tension that pushed me all out of equilibrium with myself.

Perhaps I should not have ventured into the animal world in the first place, but the ill-success with my own species has driven me there. Though I find that despite their innocence, their guilelessness, and the simplicity of their instincts, I am unable to love them any more naturally. You would think that it would be easier for me, but lamentably my experiences have proven otherwise.

CRAWL SPACE

THIS IS THE bad air of a bad conscience impossible to remove. Conscience is like ductwork gnawed through, puncturing the silver lining with its small teeth. Is it the dead animal that he feels guilty about for the fallen soldier in Iraq or Afghanistan? Is it her? Is she dead yet, are they all dead with the constant daily killing? Do the numbers mount, pile up, tip over one day?

She enlisted.

Is that his responsibility, gnawing at his conscience day after day? It's summer now. One hundred degrees easily in Iraq. The ductwork is in his mind, traveling under his house.

Will she be found buried in the crawl space? How did she enter? With her naked young looking for refuge? Is it the production of a bad conscience gnawing through the silver bag, the wire, the batting of spun glass, and finally the interior black bag? Is her body bag already the wormy duct?

The paradoxes abound. She was sent over there to defend his family, his way of life. That alone should cause him to duck for cover. He can't laugh enough at that. Instead he attacks his daughter who is on crutches, broke his own toe in the angry lunge. Soldier, ha, he couldn't defend a flea, only attack it immobilized in water; but that's a different story, that's possible! He can already hear the hard carapace click under his fingernail against the porcelain wash basin and see with satisfaction the blood it sucked.

She's so standoffish with the aluminum crutches. She takes one crutch right before his eyes and thrusts it into her brother's ribs. He has marks all over his body from her. She punched him right in front of Jack and now she's in her room, where he told her to go. But he follows her.

His son gets so angry every moment Jack doesn't take his side, sets his sister up. Jack's tired of her beauty, her make-up, her long glistening hair, those eyelashes always full of glitter, the giant eyes that seduce her physical therapist, her orthopedist, every teacher and coach she's ever known, and now this stress fracture. She deserves it, just like Jack deserves his broken toe the same day the camera crew came out and the redhead crawled under the house.

Jack went under first, hunting for the smell. Something was trapped down there. He half thought she was in the cistern beneath the kitchen covered by tons of rock, but knew decay and evaporation would have taken place, though everything leaves a residue, a small stench even months later, but not this ripe smell. Could that finally be the end of her, her last hurrah? She had surely left for Iraq or Afghanistan by now. Was she every soldier, the incarnation of America's fighting man laid out despite the most modern equipment in history in a body bag? Was he the pussy who kept three cats, and she the fighting man? He was insecure enough to want only purebreds; but it was he alone who emptied the cat boxes, had the lowliest job in the house, so why wouldn't he out of spite attack his daughter on crutches. Pathetic human beings come in all shapes and sizes. Jack wasn't short but diminutive nevertheless.

Certainly he didn't put her in army fatigues. He wasn't to blame. It was her doing; she was over a decade older than his own daughter. She should have known better. Why did she have to go? Money was tight and she probably wanted the enlistment bonus to pay off the mortgage on the house, the house she claimed he never bought her. Maybe that was why her boyfriend was in prison.

Jack pictured basic training, among all those male soldiers, either threatening her emotional stability or straightening her out; her young children she must have regretted leaving.

America's finest! Would she come back with only one lovely green eye under her bangs, or both legs blown off by a roadside bomb, or with a bullet clean through the heart? Heart! He could go on forever about her heart. She got what she deserved!

So did he, it lodged in him though he never went to a doctor, walked around with it. She broke something in him, something buried under the house beyond splintered bone, and now they'd be rooting around, and he called them! The lead was probably permanent in him like Laura's graphite in fifth grade when she turned around and stabbed him with her pencil. It probably reduced his IQ a few points. Laura's parents owned the pet store on Castle Hill Avenue with two tents in the storefront where hundreds of baby chicks gathered around a 25-watt bulb. She gave him a ball point pen when he moved to Pennsylvania as if to make up for stabbing him.

Had she been promoted by now, and does she stand taller? Has she learned to spit shine her shoes and polish the brass buckle on her belt? Has she gotten over leaving her children? How could she do that? She must have been desperate. Is she like every soldier running away from something? The lead Laura deposited in him can't be found. The black dot was visible for years. But why be melodramatic, lily-livered? He never signed up to defend his country, no, he had to be drafted.

But now he descended, that much can be said for him, down into the crawl space to get her out, wanted to be a hero to his family. If only it were her, the dead animal. Her body was so alive for him that he had to deny its existence. She's probably already taken enough shrapnel to start a small junk yard. Did it penetrate her as deeply as it penetrated him?

Is there private guilt too? Is that why he wants to be permanently inside her? Is it that his mother told him that he was breast fed for only one day? Is that why he claimed getting lost inside their bodies was the object in his life, and if he couldn't remain there he'd settle for instigating a smaller version of himself.

She's a constant roadside bomb exploding in his mind throughout the day, so why shouldn't she defend him from tyranny, or take at least some of the shrapnel? She's a sadist for wanting to preserve his way of life without her. Why does he have to live with this all the time, fear harm coming to her, her heart having stopped beating, her camouflage fatigues stained with blood?

Though his wife works in the cardiac unit, she can't help. Instead she brings home stories of heart failure every day, blockages, stents, bypasses, and the like. Jack is just the opposite. His heart gallops, palpitates, registers his thoughts for Misty, beats irregularly with every memory. What a precise instrument the heart is that makes of him a shrinking violet for all the hidings on his face. His boring looks would put you to sleep if you didn't know otherwise.

His imagination runs rampant, and the patients are not even on the battlefield, just lying in the local hospital. Maybe the adrenalin rush of battle keeps her alive, like a shot of epinephrine. In the mountains of Afghanistan mopping up after entering a stunned village meeting almost no resistance suddenly all hell breaks loose, and the blood pours out a chest. Not hers this time. The heart beats freer, has a sense of relief, the air is gulped and finally she knows what freedom is living on the brink of death. Or blood oozes freely out of an arm blown off on the outskirts of Baghdad, or in Fallujah before the eyes of a resentful population. His wife tells Jack about the stent. It keeps the valves patent, his thoughts already flowing sitting at the kitchen table to the battlefields of Iraq and Afghanistan.

Jack had a sonogram of his carotid artery and a CT scan. His carotid is fine, but his brain is getting old. There are white spindles where the nerves are bundling, embracing themselves in a hug, his oxygen needs are suffering. Is she gasping for breath somewhere, lying neglected, has gangrene already set in? Will she lose the leg? Why do you want someone you love to suffer? Is it the other side of being so worried about them? Who can live life like this? A double life doesn't even describe it, it is layered pinpricks, everlasting stabbings.

Maybe her air supply has been cut. Is there a medic around?

"Medic! Medic! I need a medic!"

Has she already been evacuated?

"No choppers available! What the hell!"

"Nurse, tell me, tell me! Is she still alive? I want to know!"

His wife sits eating calmly.

Is Misty the reason for the smell?

"Let's cut to the chase," she said one afternoon in his office about a story.

I mean has something really happened to her, or has the smell been accelerated by body decay already under the house? Why couldn't she bring her children there for shelter! Attacking his daughter on crutches, could the odor of that have already reached the neighbors, kept her away? It is only right that Jack broke his foot. Who'd want to see him walking unmolested after that?

*

JACK KNEW HE was going under; it drew him like dirt did. He was a master digger, could square a hole with his eyes closed to plant a tree. He took to it like a fish to water, as if the earth was his element and he was only a transient walking above ground. He longed to sink his fingers through the dirt and wore heavy shoes to angle the shovel before dropping to his knees with his bare hands. We all shape the plots where we will eventually be dumped. Earthworms didn't even bother him, knowing their paths would permanently cross one day. He felt the intimacy of their softness against his flesh, admired their chestnut coloring, despite the unseemly yellow underbellies with the visible thread of soil inside.

He knew he had to go under and that same day took pleasure splurging on gloves, a mask, and a flashlight. He intended to buy a miner's light strapped to his forehead but settled for a cheap $3.50 lamp. Flash in the pan, that's me, he thought. It'll illuminate the darkness. He'd been trying to buy two table lamps with thick marble bellies for months. He'd looked ten, fifteen times at Lowes. The marble was beautiful. It must be Italian from Tuscany, shaped by the same tools Michelangelo used, but the switches were crooked and lacked the easy torque of uglier lamps. The line will probably be discontinued before he decides.

Just the other day before the smell he went home and looked at the two wooden lamps in the living room. He thought why couldn't he be satisfied with what he had. Buying confused him, stymied by the intricacies of an indecisive personality. Yet the greed, the tight hold of merchandise wouldn't let him go, then the insidious excuses that threatened to topple what he thought of himself. It was simpler sometimes dropping down on all fours paddling through the dirt. And of course when he purchased anything the decision was never really made, and that was why he was reluctant to entirely unpack it, even look at it for a few days, fearing he might take it back. They made everything easy today, played perfectly into his personality. Things stayed in the house for weeks before he'd decide out of the blue to return them. And her, he didn't pick her out, his feelings did.

He didn't fall in love so much as construct, embellish, invent a twinkle in the green eyes, the long legs, the darting of the neck, the tapering fingers that played the piano for him, the pointed nose, the brush strokes on canvas she applied only for him, and her delicious laughter. Today her canvases face the wall in his office to forget her. Instead his mind bangs away, creates an awful din until finally all that's left is the weak heartbeat. Who could live with the thump, thump, as if there is a camel always getting to its feet in his chest? The awkwardness of repositioning itself on a desert is a joke. It's growing out of the irregular heartbeats, rising into his throat, and periodically he's overcome by the rank smell.

He bought thick work gloves that he knew would be filthy the first five minutes. The crawl space is bone dry with about four inches of loose dirt. He needs a mask for the plumes of dust. The one he wears in real life is insufficient, not for bank jobs, but to hide from people nevertheless. If they knew he was a night crawler under his own house they'd be revolted. Nothing's fresh around him. He chews everything up like a dirt bike, hence the mask.

The smell descended upon his family all at once, coating their lives, out of the ductwork spreading through each room. His wife and two children were turning up their noses at him. Privately he felt responsible. He knew the ugly smell was brought on by a bad conscience. It had to be more than a dead animal.

"That's what it smells like, Dad!" his daughter exclaimed.

At first it never occurred to him it could be her, be tied to our military engagement overseas that had come home to roost.

It was so bad that they immediately knew it wasn't from the land of the living. Something had died down there and only Jack knew the implications of that. The wheels of his mind started spinning overtime like a Humvee. She's come back one way or another! Military brat, that's what she was. It invaded their nostrils and informed the taste of the food they ate, disturbed their sleep, and their spirits plummeted. Everything bore the taint of premature decay. It attacked the mucous membranes and invaded the sinuses.

We don't know what smell is, but these particulates gave the certainty of death. What had died? they all speculated. Only Jack knew.

His worry, his concern, had literally come home to roost. Like the huge bird he had always taken her to be. He thought of her swarming with white lice, hopelessly bandaged in the ductwork to hide her identity.

We turn away from decay with the instincts of the healthy. We can't stand flesh rotting, spoiled meat, or even the powerful gasses from a simple onion or potato.

"I'm going to throw up," his wife says lying in bed, and the kids mimic her disgust.

Jack half knew that he was being described, took everything they said personally, not as the house patriarch. Being older than they he was closer to the smell of spoiled flesh. He splashed aftershave under his arms every day to ward off the odor, but he couldn't escape the intuition of a competing woman.

He knew they were all dying, but not with such foul markers that cut like shrapnel already slicing off a foot, or exploding brain tissue, interfering with the memory of the first smile of her one year old, its pudgy fingers reaching out for her. And then the parade of organisms turning the skin putrid and swelling the organs with gasses. It was almost intolerable to bring her back to the house in that condition, hide her in the ducts, the moldy recesses of his brain. Was he GI Joe saving her in his own home before her body parts crumbled unrecognizably?

He wanted her whole under his house, even if trapped in the ductwork, in the cistern where he had placed her. Had she escaped? Does anyone really escape the memory, no matter how small the enclosure or how secure the locks? Aren't they always banging to get out, enticed by the least resemblance? And we won't let them, stubborn donkeys that we are. So they join the army or enact a prison break in our own mind in the form of a rotten animal, and then smell to high heavens! Offensive, noisome are not the words even to describe it. So what if she is dead; she didn't want him living and his mind was too full of her, spilling, oozing, bleeding, just short of bursting not to relieve itself.

He'd medivac her underneath his house. Isn't that clever? It'd relieve the pressure of his own skull. She'd be down there, moderating the pulse inside his head. What a relief! Her dead body at last! Though of course he wanted her living, but if this is the only way he could have her, why not? The stupid complexity of tying everything to himself, binding his two legs, being tongue-tied around others; he's little more than that hardness in wood that the saw has trouble with, the knot that breaks its teeth, the bump on the log feigning an unpretentious swirl of annual rings counting the years since he first saw her. He is one big bundle of denial lumbering through life. Who'd not want to take a chain saw to that like in a horror movie to finally be rid of her? No more desire, no more imagining kids with her, no pictured smiles, basking in her laughter and the sparkle of her green eyes, just once hoping she'd be pleased with his language skill, no more oil paintings for him, just the slow process of decay, even though something had to be done. Lucky the smell, lucky it was under his house, what a macabre coincidence where her body he thought had already decayed in the cistern. It's come back to life! He relished the descent into the crawl space to relieve himself. Where else could he have gone?

How did she ever get into the ductwork in the first place and blow all her hot air through the house and onto his family? Wouldn't they find out the source of the stench eventually? He'd have to move out, probably be incarcerated himself if they dug into the cistern. The worst was in the vent that had been blocked somehow. They put in a new vent saying the crawl space was too tight. People are bigger today and nobody wants the job of crawling under someone's house.

From the defunct vent the smell came, where the crawl space didn't allow you to even raise yourself. The luxury of two feet was useless except to push off with. Maybe he was tainted for the smell coming back to haunt him. He remembered trying to get hers off him, holding his hand out of the car window, airing the house out, spraying fresheners, placing the fans up at the windows and doors to get rid of her smell, but the memory lingered before reappearing in the vents like a hidden anger, or gathering below the refrigerator, inside the cistern underneath tons of rock after the strangling. Is she going to return like this all his life? Can't he be done with her, and won't his conscience rest? His nightmares plagued him when he lived in Japan that he had committed some crime he knew nothing about, was party to some ghastly violence. But she was real and haunted him daily. He had only learned about her enlistment nine months ago. But how did she already get into the ductwork? Who would come up with such an improbability to torment themselves and their family?

The dead soldier was only protecting us, folks, get over the smell. You have to make sacrifices too!

"She's Daddy's student," the kids exclaim innocently, "who went to war. She's a soldier."

She didn't quite make it into a pine box or body bag but was teleported into our ductwork directly, the youngest probably mused.

The crawl spaces of all our houses have to live with that. The blood's on our hands, the eyeball with a long piece of metal sticking through it, the ragged remainder of an ear, three fingers chewed up by machinery, and, yes, the constant smell of decay.

His wife was preoccupied up in the kitchen.

"Don't go shopping yet," Jack had told her. "I don't want to get trapped down there. I am afraid of panicking and hitting my head, my body swelling and wedging me in the crawl space! I am afraid my heartbeat will become the living underside of the house, like the noticeable rise and fall of a frog's belly."

His wife laughs at him.

He knew they could cut the tongue and groove out and release him that way, but he feared nobody being there with his vital signs giving out.

He unscrewed the outside vent into the crawl space, then lowered one shoulder and angled his arm through the opening. There were fewer spider webs than he had expected. The house was dry as bone, like Middle East sands in a burning sun, only it was pitch black.

Once in the hole Jack turned on the flashlight, but the feeble cone further darkened everything it didn't illuminate. The daylight was useless inside the hole. He pulled in the trash bag with the hammer, nails, the board for fixing the floor, and the extra flashlight, and proceeded to crawl under the house. The clouds of dust made him realize he should have bought a better mask. The ductwork lay on the ground like an obstacle course as he inched underneath the bags wedged against the rafters, barely affording him crawl space. He secured his mask any number of times against the dust. It was so tight it shortened his breaths.

He thought, what was he really crawling towards after all this time? He didn't want to think of her death, in military gear, her nakedness uniformed like any other soldier, her helmet blown off, maybe a hole through it, the bullet making a diagonal trajectory through her brain, her body limp and in the last stages of decay, neglected for days, now assaulting the nostrils of his family. He had given up fantasizing about her body, that curious torment that made his hand wander to his crotch in his sleep or in the shower, or even when he inadvertently touched his backside he'd think about her, or when in a classroom he'd stretch and touch his shoulder thinking no one was looking and back she'd come. He saw her stretched out on his couch. You have a beautiful body he had told her when she was leaving, but she said, "It's only because I am young." Despite a certain contempt for herself she loved her body, despite the brief time she had loved him. Now the smell of it was on his mind. A dead smell.

Still how could it be her in the ductwork? She's the dead animal that he'd been trying to avoid and then meeting her nine months ago; and her telling him she was going into the military shocked him like his personal IED going off. His legs were weak when he left the store. He was always broadsided in regard to her, so why not an explosion to even things up so she'd end up in the ductwork.

She knew his objection to war. He even drove to tell her that if she wanted to back out he'd pay her outstanding loans so her transcripts could be released, and he'd give her an extra thousand to get started. He forgot about the antiwar material in the back seat of his car that gave her the option of backing out with phone numbers she could call if she changed her mind. He wanted to show her she could still get out, not like she had said in Kmart. Instead of driving back and alarming her, he mailed the information.

He had surprised her passing him on the street where she lived and doubled back. She had already parked and was carrying the infant in the car seat when he entered her driveway. This time she was more composed, but still he sensed she felt under siege. Something in Jack suspected that she knew he would come. She had set him up as a bogeyman, gave her friends the idea she was afraid of him.

"They are concerned and frankly I am," she had said.

Yes, Jack had done violence against her in his fiction, but what's a coward to do? Jack barely looked at the child, never asked the sex or name, like anyone would do. It occurred to him later. Everything was thin air around him. What a simpleton! She always robbed him of intelligence, cut out all perspective around her like a scissors on paper. He stood there bereft as she went into the house, excused herself for a moment, said she'll be right out making only brief eye contact.

Her hair was curled, long, and she had a different look, displayed an attentiveness to her appearance that cast him into the nearest landfill. For he knew she fixed herself up for someone else. It is stunning how easily we assume we are garbage, tossed out a car window or over the nearest railing. What a flimsy thing ego is that it can be recouped by a smile, or the least kindness, or we are dishearteningly soiled, rotting in the nearest dump where all low esteem ends up. Jack was nobody in regard to her, the perfect candidate for crawl space. Little wonder he finds himself underneath his house. Where else could he be? Certainly not living calmly inside. He knows he'll soon be six feet under the very dust he's crawling through.

Her face was always changing. She looked beautiful, remote from him; Jack was not puzzled over what she looked like, as he had been at Kmart. There she was thrown off balance by seeing him when she said her boyfriend had been in jail the last year for armed robbery of a bank.

Her eyes had shifted. He knew he had an impact on her, that he was a precarious boulder in her mind, and she not yet the person under the tons of crushed stone poured over her in the cistern. The fate he had reserved for her in the novel. He was a force of nature, a squall, someone to duck from. The "Oh, my God!" she had exclaimed to her friends when he had called. He tried to pin her down, crowd the last year into moments. He told her of his publication, his friendship with a woman whom she'd predicted they'd get together.

Then he admitted that there is not a day that goes by that he doesn't think of her. He couldn't help himself. He commiserated about her boyfriend in prison, how hard the last year must have been for her. It was the boyfriend that threatened Jack in a message saying that he knew a State Supreme Court judge, mayors, police chiefs, deputies, the Director of Veteran Affairs for Kentucky, and drug addicts, and so he'd better stop calling Misty. Jack had only contacted her once the past nine months.

He continued crawling, looking, and listening for moving animals, but there was only dead silence. His thoughts of her should have besieged him, but nothing came, only the onerous task of crawling through the dirt. He didn't know what he'd do if attacked. He noticed holes in the ground and wondered if there were snakes. There were a few cobwebs, but he wore the bandana he had bought to protect his neck. Streaks of white light from under the wrap-around porch guided him to the back of the house as he slithered past ductwork and electric wiring. He forgot about fixing the floor with the hammer, nails, and board he had brought when he suddenly saw uncoated wiring. He made a note to call an electrician afraid the house could burn down.

But now his job was to remove the dead, like a scavenger performing cleanup operations after a failed relationship by slithering through the dust. He'd have thought himself a mite if he didn't know better, but even they knew enough to stay inside the house.

He always feared the smell of his feelings for her as she grew distant. The aftermath lodged in him somehow transferred to a dead animal. He'd grown gaunt, his cheeks hollowed compromising the focus of his eyes that no longer always looked for her. Still her facial resemblance on the giant billboard with the young girl's arms stretched behind her back advertising a phone service had pained him and made him wince for months. It had taken its toll. Where he found the energy to slither through the crawl space was from the disgust of everyone at the smell. They must have known something was up, that he, the man of the house, was somehow responsible. They sniffed secretly around him as if he had been fresh out of the lair. His wife even once claimed to identify the smell of a woman in her car after he had driven Misty to Richmond.

They could blame the heating and air service, but all knew something else had failed. Jack's nervousness was a dead giveaway. You could tell by the tic he had developed, always blinking his left eye, his inability to keep still, to stay on one topic, "Daddy's not listening!" by his need always to be fixing something or cleaning around the house, as if this smell needed expunged elsewhere by all those efforts, eschewing the decay that somehow included his own body. He had to be crawling through the dirt, processing it like an earthworm unselfconscious about his appearance with ideas that nobody listened to, insights that could have just as well evaporated into his pajamas like his night sweats. Man of the house! What kind of pathetic anachronism is that for someone so sucked up and drooled out? He had been a broken-down colloidal suspension that had sleepwalked through life without her. Follow the dead in himself, remove it and remove her. Forget Iraq, Afghanistan. It's right here, a smelly corpse beneath his own house. It's his responsibility to remove it and straighten out his life. Who else is going to do it? The plague is on him and his family. He placed it there. He's got to clean it up. They are already complaining, joking, but he is the butt, only he can't smell it they say, and he torments himself with whiffs for not wanting to confront what finally turns his stomach.

She was right, Jack didn't know her; he barely knew himself. As if we create anything new under the sun that doesn't burn us to a crisp, dry up our remains, and is carried away; nothing is more corrosive than the air we breathe and the language that fills it. It promotes cellular decomposition quicker than anything. We are awash with solutions and walk around so dignified with dry underarms, but we are all tropics inside, vats of oozing secretions. Yes, she has to be down there drying up. How is Jack ever going to get her out of his mind? There's a Cortez in him, a hobbled Ponce de Leon falling for youth. He should be condemned like a haunted house. He had finessed everything so carefully he deserved to be crawling with illusions entwining the staff he hopes will heal him.

Everything lies waiting, the molds and fungi, bacteria poised for decay, if we give it half a chance and don't move, don't vacate the premises, track it down. He'll get rid of it for his family. They know he brought it on. How she got into the ductwork he didn't know, but maybe it was from his fears for her safety.

Sometimes he imagines harm coming to his little boy from such an excess of love that he snaps his head back startled. He doesn't know what to do with himself. Living is deadly, actual death is nothing compared to the sheer torment beforehand that kills the spirit, and finally the desire to live for someone. We don't know how to care about each other enough and then are bullied into love and turn to mush overnight. We are so unfit for it that we end up alienating everyone. Look what Jack did to Misty. He never told her how much he loved her. Oh, he did, but not how thoroughly, mindlessly, that it twisted his whole life into one knot that his sense of self went out. Not having her, not seeing her, every day being plagued by memories, resemblances, regrets sent him into a tailspin, until, until the convenience of the smell! Who could have imagined it?

Certainly it'd bury the ignominy, how could it not, how could he just go on living, tormenting himself without redirecting his pain externally? The smell relieved him, the dynamic of its odd particulates was a metaphor for putting out the fire, the eternal flame, the way it floated from room to room as if the house was being redecorated anew with a curtain of disgust, saturating the carpets, the very fabric of the furniture, seeping into all their lives! Maybe he'd burn the house down in the end, for how else do you handle a contagion inside. There's no handbook for living. Oh, a ton of clichés think they apply, truckloads of stone, but they never do. Sure, you can truncate life, and most do, but look at them. They live sensibly, sober, but they're dying inside like everyone else, only faster for the embarrassingly painful slowness. The life in him was so painful he had to summon the dead to cut off the guilt. The smell was a ruse, a misty haze he was always lost in, but that he summoned for help. Maybe they could observe her snout, the little paws, the shiny incomparable coat, and the green eyes, all that is the life of her really, the way she had to scrimp and claw for everything to feel important, respected, and overcome her childhood. Of course if she had hand grenades strapped to her and blew up his life that would be another thing, or took the clean shot of an M-16 through the helmet to give away that she was a soldier. Children would play with the helmet, just like those Jack wore on the streets of the Bronx after World War II. We don't know how to deal with the fear of death and torment ourselves because we don't want them hurt or taken from us, so we imagine them shot crashing into a store window in Baghdad or stuffed somehow in our own ductwork.

What is up with him attacking his daughter? Where did that come from? Is all this just primitive behavior; are our associations just masks for vicious assaults that we temper with smiles and jokes? Are we no less focused than killer sharks knifing through the water at their targets, for Jack flew straight into his daughter despite the black boot on her leg and wrestled her with a headlock when he suddenly grew frightened at the strength in his biceps fearing he could snap her neck in an instant. He immediately let her drop limp to the floor afraid of himself. He shuddered at what he could do to her. Was he really the stalker the police had called for information about Misty when she was missing? What exactly was he capable of, strangling her in a novel, burying her in a cistern under tons of stone? And here he had his daughter's neck in a vise for going after his son with her crutch. He realized that justice couldn't be administered, that the hand lifted to correct anything exposed something uglier in us and provided a model for future attacks on her brother. A man who loved a woman he strangles now imagines her decaying in the ductwork under his house. What a monster he was, and this is all out of supposed love. She was right that he didn't love her, didn't know who she was; how could he to put his family through all this, pretending there was an outside problem, a smell, and then link it to her, when it was him all along! True he told no one but himself, was so gung-ho about going after it as if he were still in the military, not antiwar after all. But what did he want to prove? That she was dead in his heart and so could be found in the ductwork? She wasn't. She was part of the very musculature of its beating, of the chemistry of his mind, the origin of all his thoughts. She, admittedly, was his muse. He couldn't get free of her just like that, like everyone else gets over someone, unloves them by just talking themselves out of it, reasoning! What a joke. The logicians are comics that try to predict the world with their extrapolations from known information. The tangled human heart is more of a maze and so has to resort to violence if it is honest with itself.

Jack knew all this but still he forged ahead enlisting others to assist him, making them partners in crimes he imagines himself having committed. Attacking his daughter shows that he is a criminal type, so do Misty's fears. Lombroso probably has a designation for him if he looked it up. The big head, the extra bone in the forehead, the long nose, the willful chin, the eyes uneven, the crooked mouth! It's all there. He's a physiognomist's feast; they'd have a field day with such primitivity under the guise of the intellectual. What a mask, what a hoax, to pretend he knew anything, least of all the human heart, least of all his feelings for his daughter! He might as well be stranded on the barren landscape of the moon insofar as his emotions are concerned. He didn't even care about the crutches, the fractured tibia, just launched into her to shield his son's ribs and discourage future assaults. He's a heel, Achilles through and through!

Frightened he got up and let her go and grew scared of what he was capable of. He'd imagine going to jail even though he'd have the understanding of his wife who knew he'd torment himself every waking moment, or plunge a knife into his belly to relieve himself of the pain. She knew how maddening their daughter could be, was even frightened of her own response to the coldness and pitiless taunting. Logic counts for nothing; cool reflection is the tiniest part of us until the crime is done, only then can we observe ourselves.

Violence is always just around the corner, at the elbow shoved into someone, in the knuckles, dozing in biceps that just picked up a bag of potatoes; it's an explosion of starch already metabolizing. Our gluttonous appetite is the beginning, makes these spurts of anger possible, fuels a willingness to drop down on all fours, belly under our own house through dirt like a reptile.

Any complex sugar feeds the rage, forget jelly donuts or cake with icing, even the gentle fructose of plums, cherries, and peaches can lead to murder. It makes you weak just thinking about it. The sugary thoughts in the brain make vengeance sweet. You'd think it needs the protein of steak, the blood curdling screams of animals being slaughtered.

He'd been through that with her and thought it was behind him, but she returned in the ductwork. Why did he think it was her, how had she penetrated his defenses? Could it be something extra ductile in him, something escaped from the cistern under the refrigerator where he wasn't so sure he had strangled her? Could the body be chopped up, packaged, that the envelope was now wearing through and the trapped smell let out. Phew, it overpowered everyone just like she had overpowered him.

The smell doesn't leave off another human being, but clings. It's odd how our own smell never interferes with it. Smells are one way. We can't catalogue them quite like a fingerprint or the sound of a voice, but we pick them up with an immediacy that is overpowering. They excite us and arouse our disgust at the same time.

Here she was, returned, and all his anxieties about her being a soldier, killed in war, stuffed into a military uniform, came back to him inside a vent, decayed. It was an embarrassment of riches, almost an emollient for his heart. She was down there; all he had to do was find her, retrieve the body and everyone would be happy.

She had thought he was her superior, had said so. Where did you come from? she had asked after he demolished the proponents of the war, the clergyman in the panel discussion.

Oh, Misty, where are you? he thought raising another plume of dust that coated his nostrils and throat. Sometimes he turned out the flashlight for the tomblike pleasure of the dark and to observe the distant needles of white light from under the porch causing motes to swirl. Crawl space! We are made for it, like organisms limited to the world under our houses, spiders and other creatures who shy of the daylight have somewhere to hide. We descend down there on a dry run for the decay waiting for us. All smells are passing, like we are. We tempt people with our body smell until they finally turn away in disgust. It invades our clothing and seeps into our pores and our nostrils revolt at the open decay. A woman makes that more acute that he can't live with himself, though she uses body wash and perfumes until by old age she thinks she's hiding what in fact they expose. Could it be the rising of the dead from the cistern where memories of rainwater scrubbed her skeleton?

His hat cinctured under his chin was difficult to keep on his head. It was a balancing act with the flashlight in one hand, and the trash bag in the other. He wore old clothes he'd been saving for painting and worn leather shoes that had been left outside for weeks. He was dressed to meet the dead.

Was he really heading towards her? Why was she in his mind still? Did she need rescued after all, or at least retrieved? He wanted to do that in civilian life, but she didn't want anything to do with him in the end. Hadn't her ex-husband called his home after he had gone to tell her he'd pay her loans off? He said he didn't want Jack around her, that he feared for the safety of their son. Only later did the irony of her boyfriend sentenced for committing armed robbery occur to him. Those he had owed money threatened he'd never see his unborn child and threatened to burn Misty's house to the ground. She was through with Jack, but he couldn't coerce her out of his mind like he attacked his daughter who crumpled theatrically to the floor, or keep her from turning up in his vent.

"He spits on me," she screeched, "and doesn't leave me alone. I wish he'd die!"

His little boy would yell out in despair, "I wish I'd die. I hate my life!"

Was it her he was traveling towards through the fighting of his children? Who knew what he'd find?

He finally reached the entrance of their bedroom.

*

THE DUST IN his nostrils so invaded his chest that he tore off the mask for more air. The crawl space was blocked ahead with two or more large silver bags, one that went to the vent by his wife's bed and the other beside his bed. One of the further bags was the polluted vent where the smell was, where the dead animal was, Misty whom he wanted to remove.

His breathing was labored, plumes of dust coated his body and his clothes and seemed to seek his mouth. He could feel it lining his throat with every breath. He kept his hat on with difficulty. His gloves and hat were so coated as to be indistinguishable from the dirt. Protection always flew off him, hats, coat, mask. Something in him had to nakedly confront his demons. Even under his own house he started to strip. The bandana was loosened around his neck streaked with dirt. Instinctively he didn't want to be covered, anticipating a sheet already over his face. He crumpled the mask in his hand. It was full of dust anyway. Why did he buy such a cheap one? He felt for a moment relieved breathing as if he had just come up for air. Nakedness wins in the end, freely gasping for breath after a lifetime of negotiating with other people's nudity. Why this horrid game to cover what we are, not to enjoy each other? She could never look at him in the nude. Her eyes were only cast down, even clad she dropped them. Clothes and custom get their way in the end, pettiness wins out and makes us ashamed, wraps us around its little finger until finally our bodies reclaim their natural state after nobody wants them. It is a pity that we don't make use of a fraction of our bodies before the perplexities of enfeeblement and decay set in. What a sad species we are with all this shining possibility that we are so afraid of, that we deposit the seeds of disillusionment every chance we get. First the child whom we teach shame, to cover up, then religion and custom automatically take over like lead aprons fearing our feelings will get x-rayed by our neighbors. They'd rather us slip into crawl spaces under the film of dust we'll turn into than have us enjoy each other a minute above ground.

Reduce, that's what we want to do, to its smallest component parts. Not a synthetic whole of laughter and joy, but the smirking sly hints at sex, the body proposals that we nip in the bud or shave a nipple and purposely slip for the rosy bead of blood that appears. We bring out the torment, place ourselves on the rack, enjoy the colorful lacerations just because we want hugs and kisses. We love the control of mutilating ourselves, watching others cringe. We'd rather blow up a designated enemy for the postponed pleasure of a lifetime, or rationed out in the confines of marriage, or in the lamplight of an affair, or for money. Where did this ugly stinginess come from, placing a value on everything? Is it the envy of the number system, embodied by money, so everything counts? Nothing's free, man. Your desires, we'll purchase them with a lifetime of security and material surroundings. Under your very house he's crawling around like a rat, a mole, a spider. We'll make a place for ourselves, for what's rejected, make a better life for our children, harness them to our own ideas, cripple them with our outlook, give them just enough rope to hang themselves that at the last moment we yank back and send them sprawling. If their crutches are in the way, we bowl them over for they are no defense, and strangling doesn't arouse our sympathy when our pain becomes too burdensome.

The flashlight kept flickering off and on, then went out. Jack panicked scrambling through the trash bag, and in the dirt searching for the other flashlight. The hammer was there, and the board, but not the other flashlight or the nails. He shook the large flashlight and it flickered and went out, so he twisted the cap off and retightened it but that didn't help. It was seated crookedly, but he couldn't correct it. It came on again, but then went dark. He was without light, feeling through the dirt. For a moment he feared not getting out. He didn't smell the dead animal; it was confined to the vents. He was in the dark looking for her, losing his way again. The smell should have led him to her. Did he expect to find her, or did only a thread of hope like that inside the belly of an earthworm keep him crawling, breathing dust, living up to being head of the household. It sounds like a guillotine already has it rolling in the dark! He had lost his head over her, but with night crawlers you can't tell front from back. Misty's name alone evaporates his resolve, makes him weak in the knees. Was she really killed in Iraq, on the streets of Kabul, and when? Does it really say McCracken on the dog tag? Could the stink travel so far, inside a cargo plane, body bag, and now this vent with its double coating, for delivery in the house she besieged? His home was supposed to be his castle, but the vents, the floorboards, the tongue and groove were speechless besides the demands of love and vengeance. We don't even have a word for love turned upside down, shunned, except the sickly "unrequited." What is the antidote to love called, the poison that places a film over everything she doesn't feel? She marginalized the feeling, claimed he was a stalker, had him reported to the police, yet boasted how much she was loved to her friends and about the books he had written about her. Maybe the guilt and disappointment over not being able to love is so deep that what she inspires looks like bravado. That's what Jack is trying to be, a hero to his family by crawling through the dirt, tracking down the smell, thinking that will triumph over her and make him come out smelling like a rose. Outside he throws back his head and looks at the stars and thinks of her, and at the moon whose roundness and luminosity connects him to her. Day only reproduces that light in the crawl space, with a purity it doesn't have. Only the moonlight allows the privacy of his thoughts.

Smell had always pursued him. He was made to feel ashamed of himself all his childhood. He was an outsider among strangers, not part of their collaborative family smell, orphaned, not one of the lair. Her long body would be a target, her green eyes an oasis in camouflage fatigues, greener, more lovely because of the faded colors. Her eyes were more precious than the smell, trying to free himself from his own thoughts and feelings. He was using her, just as she had claimed. His own mortality was in the ductwork, though not so obvious as the dead animal inside but the principle of smell is the same. It assails the nostrils like an eternal violence, maybe in Iraq someone who couldn't care if we are dead or alive is conveyed back to us. Maybe the shivering maggots in the body animate it. What does he have to do to love her? Create a fiction that drains her blood? Anything to deal with the dead head on, armed with a malfunctioning flashlight and one that is lost, and a hat buried in the dirt, a mask coated like his bandana, and not even the smell as evidence of her these past three years, so scant that he cannot hang his hat on it; it is always dropping off, doffing itself imagining passing her or it blocks his vision to keep him from ascertaining it is not her. Still he keeps on sniffing even though the smell is now safely inside the ducts.

So much did she flash through his brain, did his heart beat for her that he had to imagine crawling to rescue the very body she wouldn't give him. We live on the phantoms we materialize. For the material insult of everything decaying in our hands we have to create. How else to elude what is, overcome what rejects us? It's the insult of a tree trunk overgrowing our initials. She doesn't come so we step on the accelerator, want to crash. Bathed in a lovely spite coated with dirt, taking those puzzling dust baths of animals, elephants rolling in the mud, thick skinned enough not to be hurt by her. The lids of his eyes are inflamed, the eyeballs constantly bloodshot because of her. You understand people kicking the corpse for not being dead enough. He should have just left her for dead, for not giving him more than he could have ever dreamed. Now he was crawling after her, rescuing her from the bad decision to enter the military. There was no proof she was harmed outside the contrary odor of his desire for her to be safe, or at least removed from the ductwork of his own house to offset the terrible burial in the cistern where he'd strangled her and covered her with tons of stone in the novel. But even then, he had loved her too much and brought her back to life.

He crawled like the army training he'd received, one night scooting under barbed wire amidst exploding shells bursting all around in the dark where he arrived before anyone else. Was it cowardice or courage that propelled him through the obstacle course, or both?

His wife called through the tongue and groove. Hers had found his on the circumcision line of absent foreskin the night before. He felt closer to her through the floorboards. He wanted to be a hero, find the dead animal, but he panicked as the crawl space narrowed and the bags of ductwork loomed larger as to be impassible when he raised his shoulders.

He decided that he couldn't get to the other side where the smell emanated from and turned around with difficulty. He feared running out of air, getting stuck, hyperventilating, hitting his head in panic, his backside swelling, getting wedged in the crawl space. He could have gone deeper and got stuck. Then he saw the naked wires again. Were they live? Was all this a bad dream? Why conjure her up? Maybe he knew love could kill and a rescue mission nullified that until the flashlight went completely out. He banged it against the rafters after calmly twisting the top. It flickered as if toying with him, but he couldn't get a sustained light. It was dark except for the daylight filtering under the porch. Everything seemed dead, the dry orange powder of the chimney most of all. Piles of deep reddish dust from the crumbling brick he feared breathing in when he passed. Like a crab he scurried out the crawl space to avoid being trapped preying on the body of a young girl.

He emerged coated in dust from head to foot; it was in his lungs for taking off his mask early on, down his neck, in his hair for removing his hat. He reached out one arm, then another before wriggling out the hole into the daylight. The air was never so refreshing. He dragged the bag out behind him and dropped the flashlight when a spasm of anger seized him for fruitlessly crawling under the house, for pursuing her smell in the vent, for the dirt in his pores, for the rat, the opossum, raccoon, woodchuck, or even cat or squirrel that he didn't find, for the simple failure of the blue flashlight that became a lightning rod for everything. It almost wasn't enough for him when the obstacle was so huge, an ocean, a continent and a half away, a hundred-year-old crawl space, its wood saturated with creosote, a broken heart, and the smell. Ironically he loved lamps, their incandescence, the Tiffany shades, their warmth, and when the flashlight didn't work it enraged him that he stomped on it repeatedly after removing the battery, broke the plastic with one swift movement so hard that it got stuck around his shoe and for a moment he feared its sharpness penetrating the leather. Then he shattered the silver bowl with his heel and crushed the bulb so decisively that it'd never shine, for the humiliation of being without her. In the clear sunlight jagged pieces of blue plastic lay on the lawn and the silver bowl reflected the broken sky.

Destroying anything makes inroads into the soul, that soft susceptible interior that he didn't even believe existed but knew it bore the imprint of the boot. Was he a Nazi that only wanted his simple pleasure after being so thoroughly stepped on himself? Was that so bad, so fascist? It was only a flashlight, after all. The barriers were considerable, they threw him back on himself making him feel guilty, shameful, coated with filth, standing there in the broad daylight, so he retaliated on what just a few hours before had sat proudly on a Wal-Mart shelf. He had removed the battery knowing it was worth the price of the flashlight. Still his heart was racing from the destruction, and he grew frightened. He didn't know himself, where it would end. The crawl space was a marker, so were the silver bags of ductwork, the dead animal too, his family's disgust, and all over his own inability to deal with a feeling that plagued him, that should have given him relief erupting through the skin with something like shingles for all to see, but the sudden spasm of violence was confusing. He had crawled through his feeling for someone who treated him like dirt, so he had to imagine her dying in the duct to save himself. How otherwise could he get her back from the Middle East except by imagining the dead animal? He couldn't leave the smell unaccountable. He'd tried to keep her by placing her under the refrigerator of his remodeled kitchen, and that had worked up to a point, calmed him with a vaguely comforting memory of her, but then the smell started. All artists are cowards elaborating their fears, embellishing their pain, gilding the very cage that love makes for them, that they have to seek allies after mindlessly stomping on a plastic flashlight.

*

THE SMALL REDHEAD emerged from the crawl space caked in dirt. Jack had followed his progress overhead and heard his groaning, his sneezing, his talking to himself through the floorboards, his coughing to expel the dust that attached to his mucous membranes, the moisture trying to stave off the stinging dryness, the smell of death.

His cough was angry, cursing himself, his condition, so it seemed when Jack heard the talking. Yet he had the strength of mind to continue towards the smell, not entertain thoughts of getting trapped like Jack. He was like the police when they called Jack about her missing, ignoring entirely his just having written about choking her to death and burying her in the cistern. They were completely oblivious to what he wrote. That's why the authorities are so despised. They have almost no access to the shadowy precincts of the mind. There they might actually do some good for once, intervene before the real event occurs. But no, they are always Johnny-come-lately. They should be ashamed of the crimes in their own hearts, but they'd never recognize them, buried in their prosecutorial fervor.

Jack had to hand it to the redhead. He persisted just where he himself had grown uncomfortable before getting to the furthest duct.

Jack didn't speak through the tongue and groove, kept mute following his progress, stepping softly overhead. Jack had had dreams of crimes he never could identify, despite the strangling he visualized in such detail more than two years ago and the smell that needed to be removed if there was to be any peace in his family. A guilty conscience will pursue you to the ends of the earth, until you throw yourself off a bridge, or crawl under your house. We all need something to look for in ourselves, to ferret out. Sometimes it enlarges so that we have to externalize it. At first, he jumped to conclusions about it coming from under the refrigerator, but everyone knew it was in the ductwork and traced it to the bedroom. The hormones to his bile duct, spleen, islets of Langerhans, thyroid were only remotely connected to the ducts beneath his house. All his life he woke from sleep with his heart pounding, his body sweats evidence that he'd murdered someone, the smell of decomposition in his nostrils, his guilt burdening his waking life. It muscled her into the cistern for rejecting him and shoveled in the gravel until she was hidden, then called in the backhoe. Maybe it involved his ancestors in a Warsaw ghetto, crimes of such proportion that hunks of hooked meat were transported in rickety covered wagons, bodies packed so closely nothing moved. His imagination of the horrors in Iraq and Afghanistan fed this imagery. How could he place her there and keep her? It was no mistake that she enlisted. The laughter of children stilled overnight, bellies slit open, limbs torn off, faces hopelessly disfigured. She didn't have to go over there to find the fault of leaving her own children. It could be corrected by Jack's crawling.

The simple evidence of the smell testified that it was dead between them. Who needed witnesses, courts-martial? His family kept complaining that he had to do something. He could have grown used to it. But day and night they complained that it had to be removed like the bad memory they didn't know they stoked.

"We can't live in this house with that smell!"

He had driven by her house three months ago, and two months before that, knowing she was gone, had entered the military like she said. He knew it, so what was he looking for?

She had asked him when she worked on the school newspaper and they still were on good terms, "Tell me, why do you drive by the south campus?"

"To see if you are there," he'd told her, "and Goody's too?"

"It comforts me," and in fact that was true and why he went by her house and work though he'd not have the courage to approach her even if she were there. The comfort came from seeing her car, or that the shades were pulled differently, or that a new toy was left outside, or the chairs on the porch were rearranged or replaced by a new set. That she was all right calmed him. Just that she was carrying on with her life was enough. It made his easier. Anyone knows it is a far cry from the crushed plastic of the flashlight, but it was true.

Now she was gone, but still he drove by and hoped there'd be a light on, some activity that would connect her to him even if she was with someone else. Otherwise he couldn't explain it. His life would just be empty, as if there were suddenly no sky overhead, or the foliage didn't have somewhere a green that matched her eye color. The transparency of her iris was more beautiful than anything he had found in nature. It was a green that he had once seen on a man's face in India. He had remarked on that beauty he had never come across again, until her.

How to account for the dead animal in his home? Of course, she was far from that. Or was it just a random dead animal that got trapped in the ductwork, nothing freshly killed on the sands of Iraq, trapped in a firefight in a mountain pass in Afghanistan, nothing whose smell rose from the cistern beneath his own kitchen, or the monstrous wish to keep her in the ductwork just to have her close-by, though he knew now his family couldn't live with that.

He was much older than anyone in his family and the dead smell was too close to him. That's why he had to remove it and find the source. Though he did it reluctantly, fearing what else it might uncover. He knew he was decaying. He tried to brush the staleness away every morning, from under his arms, clean his backside, but it was all uphill. The hygiene of a lifetime was slowly tiring him. He imagines he'll one day lose interest in himself. There is always a panic about turning into the recrement our body casts off, letting it dry, crust on our skin, losing the desire to remove it.

Not a day passed without him thinking of her in harm's way. He'd had told her in Kmart, "Not a day goes by that I don't think of you. It doesn't go away," as if describing the most subtle malady known to man.

He knew later the contempt she'd have for him afterwards. She was uncomfortable with anyone's vulnerability towards her and tried to crush it. But he couldn't help himself. So what if he were a toy to kick aside, plaything that had outlived its usefulness, placed at such a deficit that he couldn't even cope with the lowered opinion he already had of himself when he entered the crawl space beneath the house.

The panic on her face was astonishing when she met him, though he took small consolation from that. He knew he affected her, but like a scratch on the cornea, it burned only temporarily, or maybe it'd make her throw up. Only he could think of pregnancy, his giving her money for the morning after pill. She was so uncomfortable. Yes, he tried to convince himself he had an effect on her. He always did in person. That's why she wouldn't see him. Her cruelty was usually from a distance. She rarely had the courage to reason with him up close.

The redhead finally emerged from under the house, like a tortoise divested of its shell. He threw out three or four yards of silver ductwork.

"This is a bad part I have to replace," he said, and proceeded to angle out of the too small hole and stood up and shook off the dirt that coated him.

"I'm sorry," Jack said rushing into the house to get a towel.

The redhead took the towel under the carport and wiped his neck and arms, then went to the pump for water and wiped his face.

"I'm sorry you had to go under there," Jack repeated.

The redhead, later identified as Matt, told Jack that the ductwork lying on the ground reeked, but there was no animal.

Where is she? Jack thought quickly and bent down to look inside the bags.

"Ugh," he said, "the smell's powerful." He saw finger-sized leavings, but no animal.

Had she fallen yet? Jack thought. What in the world had invaded his house? Still he thought of her remains, the guilt of having fallen for her, the smell of death that he can't live without her, one step ahead of strangling her, dealing with the body beneath the refrigerator. How could anyone live with that without descending into the crawl space to remove it? We all want to strangle those we love sometimes when the feelings overwhelm us, even in dreams cutting off their air supply makes our own breathing easier.

Here she came to stop that and made him hold his breath and pinch his nose.

"Can I cut it open?" Jack asked.

"Yes," Matt said.

Jack cut into it and found it wasn't a single silver bag, but pink batting with wires running through for support, and then a second black bag with batting. He cut into the inner bag and got a better view of the droppings amidst a tangle of fiber glass, and pulled it up and looked inside to assure himself there was no dead animal. The smell was overpowering.

Misty wasn't there. Where had she gotten to? How could his mind rest with her still on the loose? Maybe she wasn't in Iraq or Afghanistan. He'd always feared that she might expose him. In fact, he half wanted to betray himself. One doesn't go through such elaborate schemes for nothing. Her decay must have been on his mind so she wouldn't give him away or be found. Had she fallen thousands of miles away, her body would stay there or be brought back in a body bag. It wouldn't turn up in the vent. Still that was no reason to stop looking.

It doesn't mean that she is not lying on the roadside somewhere in the hot sun covered by flies with huge eyes and iridescent wings long before her unit discovers her whereabouts. Notice how a body clings to "whereabouts," the thick linguistic walls it needs to attach somewhere.

"The animal is not here," Jack said.

"That's all there is," Matt said.

Matt said he'd be back to replace the duct the next day and Jack went in the house to call the camera crew who had called after Matt's arrival. Jack told them he'd call back in about an hour.

A few nights before Jack had gone out and purchased candles, and incense made in India. The candles gave the bedroom a romantic glow, especially the blue Jasmine, and the rose, gardenia, amber and lavender seemed perfect aromatics. The register was closed and the rubber backed mat trapped the smell and he and his wife made love, though at first she had coughed over the thick incense and candle smoke.

Jack felt responsible for the smell, trying to get it off him and remove it from the vents. He felt everyone depended on him. He was the man of the house with all the odd responsibilities that entailed that eat up a life until the man is a pile of bones clean of the flesh that melts with age, so that a hammer can barely be lifted for repairs and he loses the desire to wash himself so that his own odor assails everyone's nostrils until he too has to be removed. The family turns away, creating even more distance than Ivan Ilyich's fresh bosomed daughter bending over his bedside before a night on the town. Jack wanted to extract the smell from the ductwork in his mind for the protection it afforded him. Imagining her in the vent displaced her from his conscience, the military career relieved his desire for her by imagining the decay he himself dreads. She's dead and he tells himself his heart muscle is similarly necrotic.

All that remains is to remove the smell and he can go on living. He didn't realize we are always getting rid of ourselves in everything we do, though the problem is that we stubbornly lag behind. It is remarkable how we can still live with our remains, and the doddering that comes along. Every day is chock full of dying that we barely notice. Our sense of smell is not alert enough to this except for the guilt on our conscience. What Jack was really trying to do was clear the air in his own house.

Matt didn't come the next day at 3:30 as he had said. Jack called and was told he'd be out the following morning. He got all the materials, the dispatcher said.

*

WHEN JACK TALKED to the cameraman, he had the impression they'd make a movie. That's what I need, someone who can follow every inch of ductwork and find her, he told himself. She was somewhere and the idea of a film was enticing.

"We have cameras that can look into the ducts and find what you're looking for." It is operated by remote control they told him. They'll find it wherever it is, they said.

When the coast was clear after Jack hurriedly bagged the smelly portion of the silver vent that the redhead had removed, he called.

If they could find it, all the better. Everything had been like a movie before, with the huge hole out back of the house for the remodeling that uncovered the cistern.

They drove up in their white truck, not workman specializing in ductwork so much as cinematographers to bring to a head a life otherwise uneventful that now included the smell of death, conjuring up a past he had already tried to bury. The odor needed to be removed. How convenient if he could find her stretched out in the vent, reduced like a bad memory so she could be filmed, and the house treated with chemicals. That would take care of everything. Maybe they'd find her boot, scraps of torn uniform, a bobby pin, or the remainder of a leg or finger. Maybe insects had already nibbled her lower lip or the wing of her nose. The conduit through his own mind had endured similar assaults, fish nibbling her private parts in the Cumberland River when her car went off the bridge in the novel.

She plagued him with nightmares of all the animals he'd eaten, working mandibles he didn't have, waving feelers to identify another mouthful of flesh, a white strand of sclera lifted from the eyeball. He remembered her eyes were always narrowed to a pinpoint. Jack felt the absence of feeling in her look, except at those rare instances when the color went diffuse and overspilled their boundaries and a sea of green seeped into him.

He winced at the bones of animals he'd eaten all his life stacked to the ceiling. Why be so prissy about one? Why couldn't he find the body of one woman and be done with it, lodged as she already was in his bloodstream nourishing his brain tissue with memories? Why couldn't he take a scalpel to himself and cut her clean out, perform simple surgery? Why crawl on all fours under his house? Why the need to get down and dirty, and stomp on flashlights, or hire redheads, or camera crews to sniff her out to document the dead body? Was it to get his family who had turned away in such disgust back on track that he half thought it was him they were smelling, preparing to rush him off to a nursing home for soiling himself again? Our sense of smell is our least compassionate sense. We simply want to remove the source.

Jack went through a spell in the seventies of eating chicken hearts, twenty or thirty at a sitting; the rubbery texture of the small hearts had a resistance on his molars all their own. He also ate the necks of larger birds like turkeys, imagining it gave his an added flexibility. He pulled the tender pink flesh that made his mouth water to compensate the leaky urine he could never control, the drip he was always punished for as a child.

Maybe the camera crew could go back in time and catch him in the act gnawing the animals, or even loving her, film the living room scene. Confessionals too float through the ducts tempting visual recreations. Anything to relieve the mind of hoarding all the imagery for itself.

Is that why the dead revolt us, a life's worth of animals we've eaten; the smell alone hints nothing further should be devoured. Tribes of earthworms, maggots, devour the memories, the tissue of the brain that records each and every intimacy. Jack had a stake in the recovery, in her formal removal. We are all masters at displacement without realizing it, so successfully do we to mask our private life and deepest feelings. We all have them, though most fool themselves into thinking they are immune to what lurks underneath every gesture.

Jack had thought they noticed his hands, so graphically depicted in the strangulation that it tormented him when the police called, because he knew what he was capable of, that he could reach down and retrieve what he wanted if only for disposal, but the smell taught him otherwise. He was at its mercy and the past that animated it. We all dread it rearing its head. Her skeleton there where he piled stone on the cistern, could he finesse it, so she'd still seek to embrace him and get on with the story? She had a right to be scared of him. She wasn't stupid but instinctively brilliant, knew his anger before he did, and the strength of her two arms around his neck, the suffocation went both ways, his hyperventilating, catching his breath he had told the cardiologist when climbing the stairs to his office. Was it because she was waiting at the top? The palpitations imagining her standing there outside his office accelerated his heartbeat, prompting an irregularity he couldn't control even with medications.

And the deadly grip of his hands, he felt instead his kneading hers in his office, studying the scars on her arms where she'd cut herself. And her smell that time in his office, like grapefruit he told her, had now reached his whole family as decay. He was lucky he wasn't jailed. Maybe he was as she claimed a stalker, a pervert, and the police proved that by calling him up at his home when she didn't pick up her son that night. She wasn't under the refrigerator yet, though he put her there in so many sentences. She used his love to boost her credit with friends and lovers.

"He won't leave me alone, claims he loves me, wrote all these novels about me, I need my space!"

But it was she who stalked him, every time he wanted to see if she still lived in her house, when he tried to keep her out of his mind, lingering in a store to ascertain that it was not her who turned around because the body type was similar. He needed to dislodge her from living within him, from a mind compelled to play host to her. If she lived her life, was happy, that was enough. He could live with that. But something told him she'd never be happy, that all love was temporary because she never loved herself, despite an unspeakable and exhausting vanity that could never accept the genuine love of another. Maybe it was that that he was trying to reach.

Jack didn't realize that a whole year had already passed since her boyfriend was in prison, and here she had entered the military nine months already. She had a way of insinuating herself, that he wanted to put an end to this dead soldier bit. He couldn't imagine her a soldier. She had no courage, was too lightweight; it was not really cowardice as a too rapid calculation of every advantage and deficit. She'd pull out early to save herself, finishes nothing just like her mother claimed, will not place herself on the line for her buddy, for love, will not do the stupid things, or the boldly courageous gesture. She doesn't have the rashness of a good soldier.

"No, I wouldn't want to be in a foxhole with her," Jack thinks

Then he realizes nobody can calculate courage. She contacted him after all, loved him, had all the courage for such a futile gesture that Jack even now can't stop the vibrations.

The camera crew claimed they would help. Did they know about matters of the heart, how they could be displaced even in the random smell from ductwork? Could they read the movie on his face, the dual intent calling them, that it was only a dull, ineffectual way of conjuring up the past?

The boss carried an important looking giant TV inside red padding, and a smaller laptop. He appeared to be the director and grip all in one. His partner was more likeable, talked more, said he thought he knew Jack's face from somewhere. Maybe the story was so clichéd he'd seen it a hundred times before, aggrieved love needing to dispose of the remains of the beloved, though the bad smell was the novel twist.

He could have imagined Jack in pictures already. For a price anyone could be in pictures. Once in New York City Jack was taken for the Frenchman Petite who despite high winds balanced a pole and walked between the Twin Towers in defiance of city ordinances years before the two buildings collapsed.

She knew Jack was against the war in Iraq. Why did she join? He was against unnecessary death, though not in love, what had haunted him, his hands around her neck was natural, using the electrical cord, but strafing villages, gunning down civilians, blowing up babies and buildings was not.

"In here," Jack says. "It's from this one vent. The smell's strong."

The talkative partner claims to have a cold and is not be able to smell even before he enters the bedroom where Misty had gone to pick out a shirt for him, like the bedroom in her trailer that she said she wanted him to see, but then decided not.

It was her fantasy at the time, to do it on the bed, in each other's homes. He refused, better be tormented for the rest of his life and imagine her a dead animal, relieve himself that way. We are the low life pursuing our desires so undisguised, even when cobbled together with the makeshift protection of a jerry-built bunker called a home.

"Over there," Jack pointed to the vent covered with a doormat picturing Noah's ark, stylized animals prancing in front waiting to enter, and he bent down and took it up and then removed the metal register. It was as if he were genuflecting, knowing something was dead in there. But Jack wanted to smell it for himself, had always mistrusted conveying his own senses to others. Even blatant examples when he had tasted mold in the soft drink, or on fish, he never felt entirely confident others would pick it up though he knew immediately.

"Can you smell it?" he asked.

At first, they looked a trifle nonplussed. They were big men, taller than Jack. Then one bent down close. It was the boss who had placed the red encased TV and laptop on the bed already, not the one who issued the disclaimer over his cold. The heavy TV had bounced on the bed and Jack winced.

The boss took a big whiff, didn't register the smell at first, but the next moment he moaned in disgust.

"Oh, you have something there!" as if the one whiff had uncovered all Jack's private life ameliorating his conscience, sharing the pain in his heart over the dead animal in the smelly vent, as if that were enough to relieve him.

"We'll get it!" he said determined, and proceeded to tell Jack how they can suck all the air out and pump in antibacterial, antifungal, agents and completely sterilize the system. Imagine his memory washed clean of her, the ductwork sterilized and the dead girl, soldier, lover, who scorned him would be removed forever and he'd be left with what? Nothing? Isn't it infinitely better than the torment of memory?

"It's the same thing they use in hospitals," the boss said, as he opened up the laptop, but no picture came, only a snowy indistinctness.

"This isn't our usual equipment," he said. "We just grabbed it on the way out. Our set is at my house."

He worked the knobs ferociously, but nothing came. Jack looked away embarrassed for him.

The workman then assembled the rods to attach to a little car. He had described it on the phone as a toy that scanned in the vent, took pictures. Jack had imagined a remote-controlled car freely tooling through the vent.

Still there is no picture.

The camera crew was embarrassed. So was Jack who stood there like an unpaid extra. Was this really film worthy, was it a story worth telling, calling out this crew for? Dead animals, is that exciting, yeah, right, but throw a dead soldier into the mix, a lover killed by his own hands and that should get attention. It's one big fiction, man. That's all real life is. But the smell, it's real, it abides. It at least could be something.

She just went in nine months ago. Why imagine her a dead critter in his vent already. Come on, Kunkel, don't you have a better imagination than that? At least the cistern came close, but this, you're way off beam. You're not spatially challenged, are you? Is that why you poured so much rock in the cistern, had to call in the backhoe? Is this balancing act your way of taking care of things? It was crude, I know, but this is bizarre. How do they let people like you loose? You should have received more than a threatening call by the police. I know you want to be locked up, and not just by her. It'd be a relief from being trapped if it got out, if the cameras worked. Not this snow job by a motley crew. Sorry man, we need more probable cause than a smell. I know your family is revolted, but get over it, lover boy! You're past your prime. This is your last hurrah! Give it a rest.

He loved her too much to have her walking out of his life just like that. He always told her he couldn't imagine living without her, but there he goes. Despite the imagined violence, and this charade, he got on with his life, rides the pale horse every day, and imagines the Grim Reaper sharper than everything he forgets. How could he have let it happen? Eventually she denied him too much to imagine her a person. Misty was right. He didn't know her, floating up from the vent himself beneath his own house, his emanation. It was his fear of aging, of the youth he couldn't capture, who was properly scornful. How could she not be? She wouldn't be normal otherwise. Who would want age to suck her vitality? Oh, for love, but we all know how long that lasts! She'd told him that she gets bored easily. His crawling under the vent was simply the effort to split from himself in the guise of someone he loved, who genuinely loved him for a time, and try to recapture that to prove finally that love is little more than this splitting off of ourselves and then the exhausted reunion with what is distasteful, what has died, until one day we suddenly admit it is us and claim it is in the vent in the guise of someone else and we end up taking showers all the time. We even enlist our family, invent the U.S. Army. They become complicit in tracking down what didn't work. Love is a heavy magnet whose iron filings in the end leave a smudge of grease, this oleaginous fear. That is why Jack was bent on finding the dead body, to beat himself down into the dirt. The decay would end. Even the residue of himself would one day disappear.

Why would he imagine her smell through the vents of his house plaguing his family if it wasn't love? What on earth could generate such unpleasantness? Was it that he never made peace with the body buried underneath where the refrigerator now stands? Wasn't she dead enough there? Or did meeting her in Kmart erase that and hearing about her boyfriend fathering her second child before entering prison for armed robbery resurrect her, or bury her further that he needed this vent story.

Did they think he was a pervert, just like she had said so often early on? Was he sick of all this vent business, creeping into his lungs like an influenza? His kids thought so. The dead animal in the vent and the woman who swept him off his feet became one, scratching to get away from the eye of the camera, from the redhead poking his nose everywhere.

But why send people into the crawl space in the first place, go himself, or bring in a camera crew? Did he want them to discover his crime, expose the recesses of his mind, drive out the fraud that he was, always trying to be something that he is not, for her, imagine himself loveable? He'd called her a phony once, but he's the one. His time is over. Maybe that is what he can't accept. Friends rib him that he's past his prime.

That time's past. It's dead and gone. Admit it Kunkel. Why try to put up the headstone by imagining her dead with this duct business. Your mouth should be taped when talking to strangers, your right hand stomped on.

But you're paying them, Kunkel, so you deserve to talk. But are you going to rescue her from Iraq that way? You tried that before. And your antiwar letters to the editor are putting her in harm's way. Still you can't avoid carrying her out of the line of fire in Afghanistan, from the flames of a burning building? You'd sacrifice your own house for that, and your children just to forget her.

What melodrama, Kunkel, it'd turn anyone's stomach. You don't expect them to believe love lasts this long? You've been watching too many movies.

The camera crew is still fumbling.

You've hired the wrong people, Kunkel! You should have hired me! I'll get rid of them! I'll get rid of her too! Got a match?

He remembered the boy who kissed her on the Greyhound bus in a story she wrote. It was true. She took pleasure crushing him, she said. It was so decisive that Jack should have realized then just what would happen to him! People always give themselves away if our ears are pricked, or our nostrils are raised sniffing the air. A little haughtiness is more perceptive than we realize. We'll find out about them, tuck them down even in crawl spaces under our houses trying not to admit what they have done to us.

Could the animal have been electrocuted like the HVAC man who couldn't come out had said? Jack asked the cameramen if they thought she was fried? Toast? What if a firefight literally had blackened her face like a raccoon so she couldn't be recognized after it peeled off. No, they said they didn't think so.

"Here it comes," the boss says.

"Amazing!"

The coils of ductwork were like his own cylindrical intestine, no different than the view his colonoscopy gave. Truly they were in the guts of Jack. He felt exposed. Was he trying to rid his mind of precancerous polyps by calling these guys, extruding from the ceiling or the fundament of the duct? Was the cancer already embedded in the intestinal wall, had it spread stubborn thoughts of Misty throughout his brain, unbalancing his everyday life with cellular alterations, his dreams crowded by her, his most private moments, every resemblance to someone else when he was in a store or at school, influencing what he wanted to buy for her, or the restaurants he wanted to take her to, the whole lost life every day he was without her, behind the wheel in the next car, that it finally drove him into the crawl space under his own house. Where else could he take refuge?

How could he go on living without masking the odor of what's died between them, forcing it on a decaying animal whose smell would arouse the disgust of everyone? How else to create a distance on it, and get back at himself for them? Smell is a coward's outrage, that's why he resorted to it. The shame of the smell somehow made him immune. Sometimes he dreamed of a terminal illness so he could go and tell her he had only one month to live.

"People are nothing," she had once said in his office.

They are everything, he knew; without people we'd be posts, dead wood. Had she fallen already in the desert, on a mountain pass, where a dirt road ended with tethered goats and young children staring at the fallen body, a puddle of blood reflecting amazement that the American soldier was a woman?

The smell proved her absence, that the surrogate death was more real than his own life. We invest those we love with more life than they have so that even strangling revives the hurt she had caused him, but he knew she'd never experience the deserved reprisal because he was more worried now about harm coming to her.

She must have encouraged her boyfriend to rob the bank. They must have been hard up for money. Jack looks to justify her at every turn. The love must have been deep, to go out with a gun for her. It was stupid, but still Jack defends her. Yes, it took some courage, Jack admits.

He deserves the remains of a dead animal in the duct.

She's impervious to you, Jack. You have to stoop to wildlife. You'll penetrate Ft. Knox easier than get to her. You don't exist as far as she's concerned, you're every squashed bug inadvertently stepped on swinging a baseball bat. Of course they are in your vent already feeding off your bad memories of her, but the love is mixed in and colors everything. You can't help yourself. It's pink already, shading to rose like every sunset you missed and there she is with a smile on her face, for you. Imagine that, Jack!

"It seems clean," the boss says after he extends the toy car down the vent. The picture on the TV is now clear.

"It's not flexible, and can't go on its own?" Jack asks.

"No, that's as far as it goes. The rods won't bend."

"That's too bad. I thought it might be a remote car, that with wheels it'd go by itself."

"No," the boss repeats, "we just use it to show people the ductwork needs cleaning. Your vent definitely needs replaced."

"I'd replace everything," his partner says, "and really get the smell out."

"Yeah," the boss concurs.

"Our system is used by hospitals," he repeats. "It'll sanitize everything."

Jack knows he could remove Misty McCracken from his life by this so-called snuff film. Such powerful pressure they talked about would suck out her flashing green eyes, tear the long silky hair from her head by the roots, and if she had an open wound anywhere on her torso her body organs would follow, sucked out one after another. She'd be a thing of the past and wouldn't trick anyone again, and all for "How much is it?" Jack asked again.

"Eight hundred dollars."

"There, around the bend, is that a belt buckle?" She'd drop her pants for anyone in her unit, but not for me.

You know Jack, you're a low life! That is all you think about. No wonder she dumped you!

Okay, I can cut you a little slack. I know you're confined to your house, don't even have a gun, and in Kentucky, only the anger in your two hands and the extension cord you used to strangle her. Here she'll be sucked out of the bedroom, the house will no longer be vulnerable, at least the ductwork. The smell will be gone. And you keep your air filters changed, don't you? Do that and you'll be in good shape. She'll bring no more bad air to your house. You can count on them, Jack, they are not only here to take pictures, and call the redhead back if you have any more trouble. He has to come out anyway and replace the ductwork he took out.

The camera crew will find something even if their pole doesn't extend and the toy car isn't independently remote. The equipment looks like a colonoscope that can puncture your own vitals if they are not careful. They may even see gaseous remains of Misty rising like you imagined in a hot Iraq sun, or in the infrared glow at the Science Fair in Harrisburg when as a kid you couldn't decide if the representative heart was a pig's or cow's.

Jack sometimes doesn't know what to do with himself. Throw himself through the bedroom window with the camera crew right there to bring life to the movie. Let them focus on the bloody jagged glass or bend down close to hear his last words.

Kunkel, grow up! You are trapped in this infantile entertainment everywhere in your own society. You're an adult, after all. Get over her! Why do you have to put yourself through this, put her through the indignity? She's just a young girl and deserves to be left alone! I know she'll be twenty-eight on Valentine's day, but even that seems a fiction. Women don't grow old. Will you stop making all this up? Okay, I know you're hurt. I mean I have a little feeling too. But attacking the cameramen is futile. They are only trying to make a living.

*

THE QUESTION IS, was she really gone? Jack torments himself with that.

Would his family be able to live a normal life now, not turn up their noses at the smell circulating underneath the house, at the suspicions of a body in the ductwork? Jack himself felt hidden inside skin that grows more mottled, brown spots enlarging daily on his hands, permanently connecting him to old age, more incommunicable picturing the demise of someone he loved, though for the time being settling for the animal as her double and him crawling on all fours. He had to make her the opossum, woodchuck, raccoon, squirrel, feral cat even, the gray fox he'd seen on his property last winter that darted to the blackberry bushes, then stopped and turned its head knowingly, before hurrying on.

Love, it matters not. He's an old man and should accept that and ignore young women decaying in his vent. He'll follow soon enough. The smell has already alerted him. Leave her out of it!

The cameramen pull up their rods and repack their equipment.

"Okay, well, thanks for coming,' Jack says.

"It would work, the sanitizing," they repeat. "We'll let you know."

Jack walks the cameramen to the door and then goes to his son and daughter; they are still tormenting each other.

His daughter was shameless while the cameramen were in the house. His son came and hugged him more than once for refuge. They are in his son's room yelling at each other.

After she jabs her brother with the crutch, Jack yells at her, "Go to your room!" She leaves screaming that he spit on her.

Jack follows her sneering at him and rushes her and gets her in a headlock. While twisting her to the floor, he kicks her pink barbell. Immediately his toe swells protruding from the rest of his foot. He knows it is broken.

Horrified he realizes his daughter's neck could snap and he lets her go.

"You broke my ankle!" she screams, standing up erect in the black boot that houses her fractured tibia. Jack grows ashamed of himself when suddenly he hears someone at the back door.

He goes out to the kitchen and sees a cameraman waving an estimate. Had they heard the attack?

They seem oblivious, but did they catch it on camera?

"We charged you only $625. It's supposed to be $800, but we gave you a discount."

Jack takes the estimate and thanks them.

In two days Matt comes out, replaces the missing duct, and the smell leaves.

ART

I

H E ZIPPED DOWN the highway as if he were an SS officer on the Autobahn, immune to prosecution. He spoke fluent German, Russian, and Japanese. He knew all the assignments of the Nazi high command, had ferreted out their strengths and weaknesses, their culpabilities. He still walked with an erect, proud carriage, though unlike General Bradley poring over the invasion maps at Normandy, or the more relaxed Eisenhower. Maybe he had the stiffness of the British Montgomery, of his native country that he loved to hate.

When the Soviet Empire collapsed, he didn't skip a beat. After the acrimony towards Gorbachev, he redoubled his allegiance to revolutionaries all around the world. He had been in the Philippines when Aquino was shot, and when Marcos was overthrown, and twice he happened to be in Thailand when the colonels overthrew the government and forced King Bhumibol and his family to flee Bangkok. He followed Indonesian politics, too. And he could have sworn when he was in Seoul that he felt in the air the imminent invasion by the North. And there was always Cuba, the model of a successful revolution that he claimed had eliminated hunger and unemployment and had successfully educated the masses. He took pleasure in tiny Cuba being a thorn in the foot of the giant U.S., a country that he said was rotten to the core.

Yet he was drawn to something medieval in America, something dark and bloody, like in Kentucky where so many massacres sent people into the hollows to live taciturn about their crimes, about incest and other aberrations that flourished and drove them to fundamentalist religions and patriotic flag waving.

He was drawn to the vitality of the country and took up residence in Boston where he helped organize a labor union. It was where he said he had his stroke when he was only thirty and had to learn to walk all over again. There were almost no signs now. Some congenital vascular abnormality in the brain, he said, caused it. He told me he was awake the whole time watching the catheter on the monitor snake through the blood vessels in his head and dissolve the clot.

The Russians had always fascinated him, especially the 1917 Revolution, and its aftermath. That is why he learned the language. He read Dostoyevsky, Tolstoy, Gogol, though he had no time for Andreyev's "Abyss," or Lermontov's Pechorin. He introduced me to Gorky's *Fragments*, and I got him to read his Autobiography. When I first met him, we spoke about Zamatyin's *We*. Odd, how I still have not read it, though it sits over there on my bookshelf like something unresolved.

Art and I had met at Immigration at Omika Port, close to Tokai, where they have the nuclear power plant. The dangerous spill of energy that wasn't to happen until years later was always on everyone's mind. The secrecy of the society further shrouded the plant in mystery. It conditioned a certain intellectual electricity among foreigners. Somehow when we spoke, we reduced things to their essentials so they couldn't be cut further.

Once Art was burning debris outside of the apartment house he managed in Boston, and he said the police came and forced him to put it out. They told him fires were not allowed inside the city limits and gave him a summons which he interpreted as a veiled protest against his revolutionary activities. Perhaps that influenced his view that the U.S. was a police state, and the FBI, the CIA, race relations, needn't be mentioned. Perhaps too that influenced his sniffing out fires in Japan. Hundreds of yards away on the Hitachi coast where he lived, he could smell a fire burning, especially plastics. He always had his nose in the air.

"Do you smell that?" he'd say.

The polymers drove him nuts until he approached fishermen, farmers, small businessmen in town, and told them to put the fire out. In most cases he was a head taller than they were and had an expansive, commanding highbrow, white like the Dover cliffs of his homeland. Occasionally he'd wear his Mao hat with the red star that he had gotten when he had gone to China and traveled by train all the way to the Mongolian border. He actually returned shocked at how backward the country was, but still was no less a believer in communism. He had pictures of himself on The Great Wall of China, as if he too were marching through history. He even kept the faith by taking the Siberian Express across the Soviet Union back to Europe by way of Moscow, traveling through seven time zones, although at one remote border crossing his luggage was searched, and he was asked to turn over one of his books to a party officer. What he did was politely comply, and when he saw they were going to keep the book he asked for it back a moment, then tore it up before their astonished eyes and gave it to them.

Art had a will that when it was focused was powerful to watch, though most of the time there was a quiet, smoldering self-possession to him, seething below the surface that could erupt any moment at some injustice. Just like it did at the greedy Italian capitalist who owned the language school where he taught, and whom he had once threatened with a baseball bat over a discrepancy in pay.

Art had an extraordinary love of books. He was a true bibliophile and kept his best books inside glass cabinets in his Hitachi apartment high on a hill overlooking the Pacific Ocean. Many were expensive collector's editions that he lovingly took out in the course of a conversation to illustrate a point he was making. He spent all his money on trips to Tokyo to add to his collection. He had an especial fondness for arcane writers that were not yet recognized and prided himself on discovering them before they won prizes.

"Here, have you heard of this writer?" he'd invariably ask, and get out Buzzati, Csath, or Tucholsky, along with obscure works by well-known writers; any outsider he'd identify with, perhaps inspired by Colin Wilson's book of the same name. He'd translate Pushkin's romance poems, rave over the beauty of the lines and apply it to a woman he was seeing at the time. He'd marvel at how masterfully the ineffable was captured in the poetry. He translated Goethe's "Venetian Epigrams" for me, also some of Lichtenberg, affording me a glimpse of the German aphorist long before he received wider circulation. The way he held the book in his trembling hands so lovingly, with such exquisite pleasure, impressed me.

I had introduced him to Cioran, Chamfort, to Fritz Zorn's *Mars*. I brought back a copy of *Mars* for him from the Philippines, and for a while it became his vade mecum. He tried to jointly translate it with a Japanese friend, but the project never bore fruit. The notion of the artist manqué he identified with, and with the terminal illness; for all lovers of culture are complex human beings who cherish what they only have exterior access to trying to keep it from extinction. They surround their books with sweaty palms as their heads sway giddily.

I told Art he should mark up the pages, tear the book, make it his, sink his teeth into it with the sharp sprockets of thought, and like at a lumbermill, score, warp it with the twist and turns of his own thought, dogear it with constantly sticking it in and out of his pocket, until the pages drop out, bent, exhausted, yellow and beaten. I was talking about the defilement of reading, while he was a curator, and except for that one incident on the Russian border intent on preserving. He was careful with the jacket, the sartorial garb of a book. He had books in Moroccan leather, pigskin, calf and cowhide; still he thought they should be bound in fur of some sort, in ermine or mink, encrusted with precious metals and stones. He taught me how to break in his chess book once when he felt I had abused the spine and it cracked prematurely.

"Never do that with a new book!" he scolded. And snatched the book from me to hold it gently in his hands.

He had contempt for the giant publishers in the West who made books cheaply so that they fell apart and yellowed in only a few years, so the pages disintegrated in your fingers, and whose spines broke so easily because they were niggardly with the glue or careless of the stitching.

"Books should last a lifetime. Here, like this," he'd say. "You break it in from each end, gradually, gently, a few pages at a time and work towards the middle, like with a woman!"

Art must have had the largest personal library north of Tokyo. When I visited, he was constantly popping up in the course of the conversation to get a book and introduce me to some author I didn't know. There was a certain pedagogical power he exercised over my ignorance. What I finally did to gain some leverage on him was accuse him of not reading his books, of being too busy collecting them.

We walked often to the sea admiring the landscape around his apartment. The gigantic sinkhole, almost half the width of a football field. Inside it the sea was eroding the wall of earth. Against the coast it beat day and night and he harangued with it, at the passing years, at all the still unremedied social ills, himself oddly aging in a way that the general population didn't, but preserved too somehow by all his books. His passion for them gave him youth and vitality.

This indefatigable critic of the world, this closet revolutionary tucked away in nominally democratic Japan, waited for the Communist party, only a splinter group that occasionally got under the skin of the Liberal Democrats, to make a serious bid for power. He picked for his friends Japanese who showed an inclination to a radical lifestyle, but themselves didn't act, were mired in the cowardice natural to the intellect. But mostly he loved a life of books, acquiring them, cherishing them, inventorying them, showing them off, reading portions that he'd share with me.

He had so many that inevitably he bought duplicates that he'd then sell, along with books that fell out of favor. He kept a trunk for redundant books and those he lost interest in. And he opened it when I'd visit. That he could sell them was always a mystery to me who, despite my aggressive marking them up and outlining, kept regardless of the contents every book I had ever acquired. Something of the crass businessman startled me in this otherwise loving bibliophile

The rock formations around Art's apartment were stunning. Anywhere else but in this remote company town, sequestered as it was off the beaten path, they'd be a tourist attraction. Art was proud of his own private landscape, his discovery, he said, like those little-known authors he touted, like Ekelund, Pessoa, or Stirner. The local population seemed not to appreciate the landscape, while he cherished every nook and cranny, every change of foliage, every floral explosion, every new insect.

He admired most, however, the cormorants that roosted on the giant rock formations off the coast. Through the most inclement weather scores of them perched indomitably on the high rocks, heads angled into the coldest gusts of arctic air that swooped down over the Japan Alps from

Siberia. He identified them with his staunch opposition to the clot that had him clutching this precipice of earth much like the cormorant, as the neurosurgeon worked on his brain creating breezes that anticipated the cold metal instruments probing his skull. It was a cold air sensation that opened his brain to the world, and he envied the cormorants their thick feathers, their heads turned into the wind.

He liked that sturdiness and hardiness in women too, but they are a story by themselves.

Take Naomi, the Japanese girl whom Art fell head over heels in love with. At least he had all the classic symptoms. Talked of Naomi all the time, read poetry to her, tried to expand her mind, marveled at her intelligence, her language abilities, her uncanny instincts, her graceful moves across a room. He couldn't wait to see her, set up dates that were always fraught with difficulties when he brought her up to his apartment, into the world of books, of higher culture and political ideology. Naomi learned more about her own government from Art than she ever learned in all her schooling.

She had lived in Italy as a young girl and was fluent in Italian. In fact, years later she hosted an Italian language program on Japanese television, a program that Art watched wistfully. Art too studied Italian more vigorously because of Naomi. He considered Italian a secondary language, like the Polish and Portuguese that he also studied. Perhaps he was smitten with her international experience as much as her intelligence, for that was rare in Japan, despite all the lip service paid to foreign cultures. And, of course, her looks, her white skin, her riveting eyes, her long hair, also attracted him.

Art tested his women, and Naomi was no exception. One day he took her down to the beach fronted by steep cliffs. The magnetic pull of sheer rock behind and the waves in the sunlight, throwing themselves against the shore, galvanized the afternoon. Art watched Naomi peel off her clothes down to her swimsuit, like the most delicate, exotic fruit. Both were taciturn, as Art himself undressed solemnly, as if Naomi sensed that she was on trial and Art was somehow the Grand Inquisitor. All he lacked was a cone hat, a candle, a table, a jury more defined than the elements, some covert darkness in fact. The magnified light of the sun served as well, the sparkling reflection of the sea, and certainly the stern, bedimmed look on Art's face. Naomi had never seen that look before, though she had had intimations of his extraordinary resolve. In fact, Art was still an enigma to her. The designs he had on her were not predictable, and totally unlike those of younger admirers whom she didn't respect, so eager were they for her body, foaming at the mouth with no glorious ocean of books, knowledge, or seawater to back them up. Eventually Naomi was to marry a prominent Japanese novelist, though now she was entrammeled in the passions of a foreigner whom she was learning more about at every meeting. On this particular afternoon he told her bluntly it was a test.

Art had informed me that he wanted a woman who was strong, whose mettle could be tested, who could endure trying circumstances, who didn't buckle, or cave in when the difficulties became unbearable.

The waves were giant in this rocky cove that felt the full force of the open sea, so the local authorities had posted signs that read, "No Swimming. Dangerous Undertow."

Art's Japanese was good enough to read the signs. Naomi too read them, but felt somehow that she was in good hands, that Art would take care of her if she measured up.

"You can't fight the waves," Art explained. "They will only tire you out and the ocean will get the better of you and pull you under. You have to go with them, dive and swim past the full brunt of their breaking and be prepared for the undertow. It will seem to draw you out to sea. Let it. It will soon release you into calm waters and you can swim to your heart's content. You have to trust that its gentleness will come," his eyes flashed as he seemed caught up in his own explanation.

"And when you come in don't panic if you get picked up by the stronger current; you can't resist it, let it carry you and it will deliver you safely to the shore like a brightly colored sea shell."

Naomi was afraid but suppressed her fear. After all, Art knew so much that it is not surprising that he understood the physics of the waves too. She trusted him even though she waded in with some trepidation, shivering at the coldness of the water, shaking the droplets off like imaginary quills on goose flesh.

In shallow water they briefly held hands. Naomi had reached out, but then Art all at once released her to the ocean. A claw of salt water came scratching at her, then purled around her knees and disappeared behind her calves. Giant fists of water almost knocked her off her feet. She despite being only a moderately skillful swimmer braved the waves for Art, dove under one and came up only to have another throw her back, but she regained her footing after momentarily losing contact with the ocean floor. One more wave came and she dove under it, but immediately was slapped down by a second wave and somersaulted so many times that she lost her bearings, until finally she was almost washed ashore by three or four more waves. She stood up limp with seaweed hanging on her body.

Art came over and gave her a hand.

"You got caught," he said. "Do you want to go back to the blanket?"

"No," she said, "I'll try again."

Again the same thing happened. But this time Art didn't come over. The waves caught her and threw her at will, finally depositing her again on the shore. She was unable to get past the turmoil of the largest breakers, their frothy needs overpowered her and swirled around her ankles in their mad rush for land. It was as if she was in the way and easily thrown to the side like a rag. She strove to figure them out like Art had explained. But such instruction must finally be experienced. Her left arm was hanging, her shoulder almost thrown out of joint. Art came over eclipsing the late afternoon sun that outlined his body and stood like a tall silhouette of Neptune with his arms on his hips to tell her to stop. As if to say, she was not the woman he thought she was, hadn't the stuff to pass the test.

After they both sat on the shore Naomi during one long period grew strangely silent when he spoke to her, then got up in mid-sentence and walked again into the ocean. He had told her all he could. Now it was left to her to see if she could measure up.

Art sat on the blanket, very English, distant, aloof, and detached. He could have been sitting on a beach in his hometown Liverpool, watching a frogwoman start on a mission that both suspected would have a secret terminus. Something that might alter the world with a new birth. Something that all lovers must consider if they are meant to be together, between rock, seawater, and the interpenetrating sunlight.

That Naomi looked like a dishcloth negligently tossed by Mother Nature, a washerwoman ill-suited for motherhood, her own thin figure, svelte, without the hips, and with almost boyish breasts, didn't matter. The secret of motherhood that lurks in the most unassuming bodies didn't seem to affect her resolve.

And Art looked on not with the eyes of a doting lover, but as if she were a pupil following orders. Orders that Naomi internalized as the sand crunched under her feet.

She walked into the ocean not knowing how many other lovers Art had sacrificed in his need to have them prove themselves.

Wave after wave she fought and again was thrown back, tumbling over and over, getting sand inside her suit, swallowing gulps of seawater. The strings of her swimsuit came loose, one shoulder was half naked, as if she fought the desire of the sea, of Art, and almost exposed her boyish breast as she was thrown head over heels again. Quickly she righted herself and walked toward the waves, dove and came up cleanly, then the next one almost caught her unprepared, but she got under it in time. She took in another mouthful of water and quickly thought, why am I doing this, when without thinking by pure reflex she buried herself in the trough of another wave, and another, and before she knew it she was being pulled under and thought she saw Art shaking his finger at her for not being more of a woman, for not measuring up. But because she didn't fight them, the next moment she found herself popping up on the other side of the surf. She had expected to be slapped by another wave, but none came. The water was calm.

Art had entered the ocean and was swimming towards her. His powerful strokes slashed the waves, drew him under and challenged them, and in a matter of moments Naomi heard a voice behind her exulting, "You did it!"

There was a sense of exhilaration as she smiled stretching out her arms in triumph, giving her body an unexpected buoyancy under a salmon pink sky.

Art was always working to get Naomi where he wanted her, though exactly where that was was never clear, and became even vaguer the longer their courtship continued. Naomi was certainly an idealization that Art seemed to take physical pains with. He talked to me nonstop about her, related every detail of their meetings, but when I asked if they had done anything yet, he said he was preparing her for that, "softening the battlefield," he'd chuckle. His advances seemed both exhausting and frustrating.

"She'd let me do this," he'd say, of touching her breasts, massaging her feet.

"Is this all right?" he'd ask. "And this?" as his fingers wandered over her body, hesitant, deft, exploring every sensation, as if he were the first Portuguese on the mainland, only recently landed at Nagasaki."

"She has the most beautiful feet," he'd say. "Oh, were I the earth you walked on all day?" he'd exclaim. And then out the blue he'd bend down and ask to suck her toes. To my shriek of disgust, he said brushing me off like a fly haughtily with his nostrils dilated, "Obviously, you've never done it yourself!"

Then he said she let him touch her breasts, and finally one week he said he sucked them.

"They're so beautiful," he said, obviously still pained by their beauty. He told me he had found his place in the world, after traveling so aimlessly he'd established a true connection. Just being there, milkless, and small as they were, was nourishing, he'd say. But after that there seemed a hiatus. He told of no more conquests of her body, lost the serene, the intense Portuguese look in his eyes, despite the St. Francis Xavier beard he was sporting at the time. Art had always been a student of history even in his passions.

Their first kiss had been so natural, he said. Everything led up to it. The birds outside, the autumn insects, the colorful foliage, the promise of intimacy all winter sitting around the *kotatsu*, the countless tangerines they would peel together, and even the occasional winter snowfall, the dwindling orange light of the afternoon sun, the tangerines yellowing their skin, and the cut of the mouth, their saliva even had the right chemistry, he said. If samples could have been taken he explained, "I'm sure they'd find something," similar enzymes breaking down the moment of watering for each other, showing some deeper chemistry had brought them together. When he licked the perspiration off her breasts and told of their anatomy in detail, it must have contributed to a sensory overload in one of them. Something must have happened. That musky odor a woman gives off probably overcame her that she had to leave Art stretched out on the tatami smitten for hours, for days afterward.

Art took pleasure having such power over a woman's body, knowing Naomi would be back, believing women too revel in idealizations. Perhaps he slighted the body because he felt superior to it in some way, for he was able to be crudely analytical and offensive on occasion when he talked of "poking" women, or doing "rude things to their bodies," and mentioned with a certain contempt the Freudian notion of "the wound in women that won't heal."

Art claimed to have to like a woman's smell. "It is the most important thing about them," he said. If he didn't like their smell, he didn't like the woman. Maybe it was the musk smell Naomi left behind on his fingers, not unlike the smell of rotten fish he said, as he'd run his index finger across the underside of his nose and breathe deeply, sighing to remember her and give a lift to the tediousness of a day she wouldn't come. It was one of a catalogue of scents he knew later he could conjure up on command, every particular of licking their toes, breasts, nibbling on the lobes of their ears, his tongue boring into them, or washing out their belly buttons, or simply the warm smell of their head and the oils of their scalp buried in his lap as he stroked their hair. Art said when she held his head in her lap, he had finally found his place in the world.

"It's where we come from," I said dryly.

He played with her long black hair, so straight, and thick, so perfectly cut like a doll, unlike his own that was already thinning and brushed back over his bald spot. He curled it about his index finger and she even allowed him to cut some off when he asked for a sample. Perhaps he was already thinking about the future, adding to his collection of hair from women's heads and their most private parts that he kept in a lacquered box lined with golden velvet, each sample carefully labeled. He'd joke with some women about saving their body parts, for so exquisitely did he revel in their beauty that he wanted to preserve it. And he took countless photographs of them that documented every stage of their relationship, as if he would have lived in vain had they not lent such beauty to his life.

In a sense Naomi seemed to test him by simply being available, by meeting with him, reading all the books he lent her, herself studying just what he would do next. He never intimated this, but she was so hopelessly caught in the cycle of titillation that it seemed the only explanation. Surely, she was fascinated with his politics, his culture, his extraordinary collection of books, his solitude, his living on the proud eminence in Hitachi overlooking the Pacific Ocean. There was so much that was calm and reassuring about him, a life of the mind, a commitment to a higher purpose, his exquisite cherishing of beauty. And then there were those times when she was with him when he lit candles and they drank wine and then grew amorous and suddenly there was an earthquake, one of many in that part of Japan. Not always the back and forth kind, but the up and down tremors making what Art and Naomi were not doing ever more exquisitely erotic. It was as if Art had the earth too at his service, not only the spirits of the past, the high culture of the Renaissance, all the paintings and music of Europe at his fingertips, that now they were part of even larger georhythms, players in the vast undulations of the earth that signaled a larger purpose beyond their own bodies.

And the candle would sometimes fall down on the tatami, and Art would lunge for it before it'd go out or its wax would spill, and sometimes they'd both end sitting there in the dark as if a curious reality had overcome them. Or he'd rush to the stove to turn off the gas jet and return to Naomi to relight the candle. Soon after she'd have to leave. It was odd that the catastrophe of the earthquake wasn't enough to affect them and spawn the lovemaking, despite the giant chasms that opened up in the earth defying the levelness of the Kanto Plain, or out in the deep crevices of the ocean prompting fear of a tidal wave on the mainland.

We can only imagine that Naomi was receptive, odoriferous as the earth, or the sea as Sandor Ferenczi said, like the old fish smell when Art ran his fingers under his nose to revive him when he was at home studying one of his dry languages by himself. Or after he had just gotten out his magnifying glass to look up a word in his *QED* whose print was microscopic as he brought his fingers without thinking to his face. Maybe remembrance of the smell detected something in him that with the aid of the *Oxford English Dictionary* would define exactly their relationship, as if to prove that the body is the book as John Donne had said.

Sushi was a delicacy that Art indulged in weekly. The raw fish smell he compared to a woman's body and so was drawn to the shops to be served by the talkative sushi men who by complicity indulged Art's taste for the smell of women; right in under his nose he drew the smell of raw fish. He mused to himself how sushi was one of the joys of living in Japan. And his fingers could catalogue both women and fish, whether they be slippery as eel, tentacled as squid or octopus, fleshy as raw tuna, or deadly like the blowfish. Like a cat he could distinguish them at one whiff, though sometimes they merged when he was in the shop and had another Kirin beer as he stretched his long neck, expanded his chest and threw out his arms as he looked at the sushi man with a feeling of triumph, even though he was all alone in the shop eating raw fish.

"Another beer," he said.

Perhaps Marxism makes the ultimate contact with women impossible, suppressed as it was by larger causes all around the world. He had countless monographs on the exploitative sugar cane fields of the Philippines, the rubber plantations of Indonesia, the lumber harvests in the jungles of Thailand for chopsticks back in Japan, the diamond mines in South Africa, the unspeakable conditions in the textile mills of India, injustices all over the world that he envisioned one day a united front of brotherhood marching arm in arm, lockstep just as Trotsky envisioned. Art felt a kinship with the Mexican muralists, Diego Rivera and Frida Kahlo, and the émigré who was himself riddled with bullets. Art had even made a pilgrimage to Trotsky's house in Mexico City. He had felt similarly outcast, isolated for his ideas, without a constituency save for the women he met and the occasional disaffected Japanese salary man. Perhaps for true comrades physical closeness is anathema, disloyalty to the larger cause. Even though Art was linked spiritually with arms around the world, he in the end withheld himself from the very women he idealized. Perhaps until one day he felt they would be true comrades. Maybe for him Naomi was already a party member, in a uniform whose body lineaments were lost under the superfluous fabric of a common cause. Maybe it was easier for Art that way. And he was already thinking of a line of ordinary workers, the women he idealized circling the globe.

"Mr. Lovins is a romantic," one Japanese colleague had said. Implying that that was the reason he couldn't settle down with only one woman.

II

THERE WAS A Chinese girl who Art fell head over heels in love with on a trip to Taiwan. He met her on a bus and they immediately hit it off as she showed him around Taipei. She was surprised at his culture, his knowledge of Chinese, his sympathies with the mainland. He courted her for one year, had her visit him in Japan, visited Taiwan again, but soon they grew distant, even though he continued his studies of Chinese. So many Chinese characters a day he added to his vocabulary, and as if in a kind of homage to her, he redoubled the number after he met her and his studies took on an added life. And it also deepened his Japanese, he said.

And there was the Indonesian girl who came from a wealthy family. Her father was a General, just the opposite of Art's politics and working-class Liverpool background. Art wasn't supposed to get an education, much less a classical one, or become a polyglot. Maybe subconsciously that drew him to Mina, the lure of position and power deep inside every communist's heart, to be part of the very stratum that he hungers to bring down by a physical assault on its fairest representatives. It was rumored at the Japanese university, and with some amusement among Art's colleagues who knew his Marxist sympathies, that he was engaged to be married to a member of the Indonesian ruling elite, whom they knew he would have naturally opposed. The shrewder, however, must have speculated that marrying into the ruling class was Art's way of undermining their hold over the common people.

Art traveled to Jakarta to meet Mina's parents, who when he returned to Japan, he found severely disapproved of him. Mina wrote that her heart was broken, and Art for her disappeared into the batik design that she ended up sending to him in the costliest material.

Art spoke fondly and wistfully of Mina, but their affair despite the engagement had always been shrouded in mystery. Was he really rejected, or did something else occur? It seemed the closest he had seriously gotten to marriage, but finally it never came about.

Art had been waiting for when the moment was ripe to introduce me to Naomi. Perhaps he felt threatened by me and wanted to make sure that he had her where he wanted her and was absolutely sure of her affections for him. He had told her about me, intrigued her in the same way his stories about her intrigued me. Each of us embellished what the raconteur left out, so that when Naomi and I met we needed no introduction. At the party we barely looked at one another after Art introduced us.

We didn't have to. For we had met so many times through the descriptions of Art that the designs we didn't even know we had already existed, cognitive arabesques enriching each other's life like the costliest tapestries in an unseen room that has been thoroughly described beforehand. Each gold thread, each epithelial cell, our minds had already gone over countless times.

Our eyes met later in the evening from afar, and once or twice we brushed past each other with a glass in our hand while the vague suggestion of a smile hung in the air, suspended between us. So powerfully does the imagination fix the person that when we encounter the real smile we look away, and the eyes drop to avoid disappointment.

We crossed paths for a brief exchange at how boring the party was, how uninteresting the people were. We discussed Art's idiosyncrasies, his politics, his linguistic talents, his palette of colors compared to the blank canvas, Naomi said, of her own life. She smiled, modest about her own background, about her language skills. She spoke of how they almost had a brush with me once before, but Art wanted to make sure she was ready, she said. She confided that she thought Art was a little afraid of me.

"He needn't be," I said, "we are friends."

Her plans were vague, though she said she thought they'd include Art.

"He's certainly very fond of you," she said.

"He talks about you all the time," I said. To which she gave an elusive smile.

"He says you're the only one he can talk to," she said.

Her teeth did bare themselves at me, and at about two or three removes from her they were gnashing. At an Akutagawa remove, hundreds of years before. Teeth that could survive the ravages of plagues and predation, teeth that worked their way through the social debasement, that evoked the primitive appetite for life, teeth that didn't pretend, that were tucked conveniently away inside the modern smile without giving any hint that they could steal hairs for wigs from the bodies of the dead. But there she stood giving every indication that it could happen. Teeth that couldn't only lovingly nibble ears, fingers or toes, but that could peck the eyes out, or tear the flesh of a scalp or burrow into the liver, or through whatever stood between her and the heart.

And as I stood there I felt flayed already by this almost mechanical Japanese doll that I had pictured, and concluded that Art knew better, had tested and described her cultivation, her almost Heian refinement, her fluency in Italian. But she now looked with a smile like someone who could skin me alive, follow every suture on my body with a precision of vocables that had mastered diphthongs, vowels of another language, in a kind of frenzied delight. I felt as easily her language skill could turn me over in her mind with all the uncanny exactitude of a Romance language to get exactly what she desired, then spit me out like a wolf grown tired of her own cubs after having slain the nearest one.

Art stood on the other side of the room despite all his testing, his elaborate schemes, all his English, near German control, decidedly unpredatory. There was something unwild about him. Something cerebral and admittedly sensual, but he never had access to that uninhibited sensuality beyond smells and the crude talk of poking that can in a moment evoke a vast, rich history of the species that scoured the land in dire straits, fending like wild animals, crouched atop the stairs of a shrine pulling hairs out of dead bodies for wigs to feed itself. Perhaps Art feared that in getting too close to Naomi. Beneath the thick black and hopelessly saturated red lacquer of Japanese culture was when you opened one of their boxes the teeth of a Berenice. Or the sweets that would quickly isolate enamel and eat into those teeth oddly preserved by the aesthete who knew of all the outrages they had performed to evolve into a beautiful woman, dainty, measured, almost doll-like, but whose past was so horrendous that they had to be boxed up to hide the horror that made your own teeth chatter with a chill thinking about what they might have done.

Naomi smiled and asked me if she could bring me over a glass of wine and something to eat.

"How are you two getting along?" Art was suddenly heard behind us.

"Oh, fine," Naomi said, "but I think I should be getting home soon. You live in Mito, too?" she said.

"Yes, he does," Art said. "Maybe you could take her home?"

"Oh, all right," I said.

Naomi and I took our leave of the guests.

On the train to Mito we talked small talk and generalities. Everything had a subtext, spoke to something in both of us that explored each comment for why I was taking home Art's girl. Was that natural in the scheme of things? Why had Art relinquished her to me? Was he testing us? Was there something he wanted to find out from both of us, a two-edged loyalty so that he like St. George could go into battle girded with love on one side and friendship on the other, the blade annealed by the heat of experience, cooled, hardened, tempered? He could arrange for both of us to experience the buffets of fate. Was he like Archimago or Apollonius, those Spenserian, Keatsian magicians inhabiting now the brain of a live person? Was Naomi to him no more than a projection of himself, or simply an antique Biblical reference longing for home.

"I have a bicycle," she said when we got to the station.

"Oh, I'll have to take a taxi," I said.

"No, you don't," she said. "If you don't mind riding with me. Can you ride?"

"No," I said. "It's been so many years."

She unlocked her bicycle, took hold of the handlebars and straddled the seat.

"You can sit right here. Just hold on the back," she said.

So I did, as she slowly pedaled, at first a little unsteady as the bicycle wobbled away from the station into the night.

The fresh autumn air brushed against our faces.

"Hold onto me if you want," she said. And I took my arms off the back fender and put them around her waist.

"Is this all right?" she said.

"Yes." I said. "You ride well."

We went through town and past the Tokugawa Plum Gardens, past its hundreds of trees, past numerous bamboo groves arched overhead meeting at the top, and down hills as the bicycle picked up speed.

Japan for being such a small country has surprisingly massive structures. Giant trees, huge mountains, and some of the largest statuary and temples in the world. She needn't even bring on her sumo wrestlers like she did when the Portuguese landed at Nagasaki and seemed so tall.

The speed of the bicycle injected an element of danger and fear as both our bodies hurtled through space, cutting it before us as it closed up behind. Wrapping us in a cocoon of air that would remain sealed for years to come preserving the moment.

Thoughts raced through my mind with the speed of the wheels going round, thoughts of rubber crushing the gravel, cushioning us the faster we went, the friction and heat bringing our bodies closer atop the frail machine of the lightest materials. My head rested on her, my chin in the trough of her shoulder as if we had already become one body. Her hair blew in my face, inviting me further into her darkness. There I'd find a place. In this Oriental country thousands of miles from the land of my nativity. For a woman can create a home anywhere.

My fingers rested on Naomi's hips, clutching her without moving. What would have made them grab her breasts all of a sudden, reach into her crotch as the ocean snatched at the coast? She didn't have a dress on, or she might have let go of the handle bars and we'd both tumble into a ditch, a tangle of metal and bleeding bodies clutching the loose soil. The tires still spinning overhead as we opened our eyes dizzy at my letting my fingers get the best of me. For that is the only way I could have touched her, at full speed.

But she had black jeans on, so below the waist you couldn't tell where she was and where the night started as we sped through the darkness.

And the seams were so tight and reinforced with metal studs that a man was intimidated that no helpful breeze could blow the woman's skirt up.

And the loyalty to a friend, to a lover, kept us both on the road. But mostly it was the black jeans. The extra movement they required before the conscience kicked in, just like sometimes the resistant hasp of a bra humiliates the man and makes him give up trying to touch the woman's breast, and the seduction stops cold, unless the dress yields beforehand. A watery smooth, silky material, even a rayon or cotton blend, will ripple thoughtlessly exposing the woman before we realize it, lifting itself for our pleasure way ahead of the pneumatic inspiration of a cowardly hand.

The bicycle was now in another zone, going at what both of us felt was a breakneck speed. We were past the division of sexuality, well past our desire, instead one hermaphroditic union hugging metal and each other, dependent on the machine to take us around the Lake of a Thousand Waves, but first down the final hill of plum trees and stiff bamboo high over an island of a hundred million people whose black hair on one of its own blended into the night with jeans I wouldn't have dreamed of pulling off.

We slowed down round the lake as Naomi pedaled more leisurely; the moment of tension had passed. We were out of the woods. She could delight in the breezes on her face off the lake, the soft rustle of the cherry trees, as the road leveled and we breathed a sigh of relief that our loyalties were intact.

We started up the hill towards the road to my house and close to where Naomi lived when she stopped as if struck by an arrow. There was a man standing under a streetlight with his arms folded.

"That's my father," she said quickly. And I recalled the four fears in Japan of earthquake, fire, thunder, and father.

"I'll call you tomorrow," she said, and hurried off to an animated exchange of conversation with the man she had identified as her father.

Art called the next day and asked how it went.

"Oh, fine," I said. "We got home, all right. Naomi had her bike, so we rode home together."

"You did?" Art said, somewhat surprised. The wheels in his mind turning.

"She said she'd call and wanted to come over for a visit. But you don't have to worry," I said, thinking myself in the driver's seat. "She just wanted to see my apartment," I added naively. Art grew silent.

"Hey, look, Art, don't worry. I'm not that kind of person!"

"Two adults can do what they want." he said. "You're free."

"She's your girl," I said.

"Yeah," he said, paused and added, "Well, I'm glad you are both getting along fine!"

"You say you never did anything, did you?" I asked irritated, out of the blue.

"I'm priming her, getting her ready," Art said.

And the conversation ended on a sour note. I didn't know what I wanted but knew that I wouldn't make a serious play for Naomi.

Soon after I hung up the phone rang. It was Naomi. She had just gotten off the phone with Art. She had told him she was going to visit me. He had encouraged her to get to know me, she said.

"He said he didn't mind, that I was free, but I know he is a little angry."

"I know, he didn't seem too happy," I replied.

"He'll get over it," she said.

"How about Wednesday afternoon?" I said.

On Wednesday Naomi came, dressed in a wide brimmed straw hat, in a flower print dress as if she had stepped out of a European film or had read my mind. We talked about Art, about literature, painting, music, language, and as the afternoon wore on we drew closer and I offered her persimmons, then tea and sweets just before the withdrawal of daylight when she announced she was going to leave, and I kissed her, from loneliness, the semidarkness, a kind of perversity, not active pursuit. Perhaps her nose was too small for that. We both knew instinctively it would lead to nothing.

I was reminded of a girl who wanted me to kiss her before she left my apartment and said afterwards, "Now that wasn't so bad, was it?"

"No," I said, not to hurt her feelings. But it was, for I had sold myself, overcome a repugnance to kiss her.

In this case I was intrigued by Naomi, but the fatigue of so many considerations and the lack of attraction up close deprived me of the energy needed for seduction. Besides I had Art in mind when we kissed, and she must have when she recoiled. Maybe it was the strength of the kiss, or a repugnance for me, as I asked her, "Art doesn't kiss you like that, does he?"

"No," she admitted and intuitively moved away from me as the last daylight left us almost in the dark. Whether Art was more loving, or didn't have the intensity of desire, I didn't know what she thought. Perhaps she felt the kiss could have led to more. Maybe she sensed the hunger of a solitary in a strange land and didn't want to merely satisfy an appetite.

Art had asked me anxiously one time if I thought he "looked hungry." Perhaps he felt that was the worst impression anyone could give off. In Japan foreigners quickly become adept at hiding their feelings.

She left in her straw hat and flowery dress. It was early November as she waved back at me.

I was proud of myself considering the temptation of the material swirling down the steps. I almost started down to reach out for her but felt the moment had passed and I'd be rejected.

I never heard from Naomi again, and saw her only once after that in passing, long after she had broken up with Art. I was waiting on the train platform to go to Tokyo and she had just arrived.

My relationship with Art deteriorated after that meeting, or the incident was buried so deeply neither alluded to it.

Maybe the time we talked six straight hours on the phone was the last straw. Until four in morning. We didn't speak again for months. We had spoken until we were both hoarse, yelling at each for hours at a stretch. He accused me of not understanding politics, of being naive, like all Americans; I accused him of not understanding literature, aesthetics, or reading the books he loved. We were both out to wound one another and should have stopped by the third hour but kept on. I brought up the Finnish physicist who after she met Art had said he didn't understand literature. He was one of those exceptional minds who are peculiarly literal-minded, who will forever struggle to understand what comes easily to others. Perhaps by criticizing him she was trying to bring us closer together, closer than the two hundred letters we had exchanged before she died of cancer. Once in a disarming moment Art had said, "This is the kind of correspondence I would like to have."

Then just before I was going to leave Japan, Art gave me a call, and took me to a sushi restaurant.

It ended on a sour note as we were standing outside the restaurant and he told me I'd sell out once I got a little fame, and that he knew me, for I'd also probably "screw my best friend's girl!"

"Oh, that with Naomi," I said surprised. "We did nothing," and gave a little laugh at his still harboring resentment.

And so our parting was bitter. But maybe that is natural to friendship that runs its course, five years or so, and then some trifle or other destroys it, really an excuse for the exhaustion of having grown tired or jealous of each other.

III

YEARS LATER I was visiting Japan and found through a friend that Art was living in Morioka, a beautiful part of northern Japan, so I gave him a call. He was surprised to hear my voice. We caught up on what we had been doing, sounded each other out. He was teaching at the prefectural university and, "Yes," he said, "why don't we get together?"

On the train ride I thought of our conversations, our past experiences. Art had not married, but lived the life of a bachelor scholar, continuing his language studies, traveling around the world on his lengthy vacations, all the while increasing his library. He had a new girlfriend now, he said. Miya who was long-legged, taller than the average Japanese woman, and interested in Black American women writers. He was bringing her along just like he had done Naomi, and countless others.

When I arrived at the station Art was nowhere to be seen. I waited about a half hour, then called him, but got no answer. I suspected maybe he still held a grudge against me, and that I had been tricked into making the long trip when his car wheeled around.

"Sorry. I'm late," he said. "The time completely slipped my mind."

We shook hands. His hair was close-cropped to his head, and immediately I saw he looked older, gray around the temples, but with still that expansive forehead and a certain rubicund vitality to his cheeks that would always have him escaping the vicissitudes of aging. As we drove, he described the scenery, named the mountains that we passed as we crossed over each bridge. He said this was marvelous country, not like the coastline, but still bracing. There was a group of Germans that he was friendly with he said, but he was still rather isolated as a foreigner.

First he took me to the campus and showed me his office, explained about a local poet who became famous throughout Japan, about his tragic life. Told me of the history and German professors on the faculty whom he had befriended, radicals like himself, he said. Showed off his library, the books he had taken from his last position.

He was proud of the tests he was using to awaken students' consciousness. He said his contract lasted only another three years, but he was going to fight for a renewal.

We arrived at his apartment on the top floor of the building. Books lined the walls and he now had three layers of sliding bookcases for his vast collection. He had photographs on the wall of his travels to Tierra del Fuego, New Zealand and Tasmania, India, China, Kenya, even Cuba. We spoke nonstop most of the afternoon. He gave the impression of living a solitary life, of being starved for conversation. A foreigner tucked away in an alien culture who had accommodated his lifestyle to the local population to the extent that he could follow their customs outwardly, but privately pursue his own interests. He was still a diehard Marxist despite the disbanding of the Soviet Union. He loathed Gorbachev and Thatcher with a passion, and still proselytized to his students, trying to win converts to Marxism.

We continued to talk about books. "Here, have you read this?" he said and handed me Italo Svevo's *As a Man Grows Older*, and countless others.

I thought that Art had not changed. His designs on women, his need to change the world, his exquisite appreciation of his natural surroundings. I had always envied the locations where he chose to live, and the knack he had for drawing out the most beautiful aspects of his environment and impressing them on visitors.

Art asked if I liked hot springs.

"Yes," I said without much thought, although I had only been once in Izu and in Greece. Morioka was famous for its hot springs, and we could go this afternoon, he said, if we hurried. He'd call a friend who had a restaurant and could get us reduced tickets. A German friend who was a baker.

I scanned the bookshelves while he was in the other room talking to his friend. I was always fascinated by his collection. And not even his expensive books that he kept inside the glass cabinets, but the ordinary finds of relative unknowns. And perhaps I felt somewhat proud of myself that I could introduce him to some writers.

He returned and said if we hurry, he'd stay open for us.

On the highway he sped along like we were on the Autobahn. And despite his Marxist leanings when I looked over at him, at his determined grip on the steering wheel, I thought I could see as the sunlight dropped behind the overcast cumulous clouds a star or two on his stiff collar and an eagle insignia, set in a gray worsted uniform. His short hair and expansive forehead gave the impression along with the German music playing on the cassette of a Nazi officer taking off for a weekend at the hot springs.

Art asked about my wife and child, seemed somewhat suspicious of the commitment I had made since I had been so staunchly against marriage. He then spoke of his engagement to the Indonesian, and then about Miya.

He presented her like he did most women as elusive. And yes, she had stayed over, he said. She is like a bird and comes when she needs restored spiritually, he said, and help with her term papers.

"She likes being around my books. And her parents know about us," he said, "about our age difference." But somehow that revelation cast the saddest pall over everything. The futility struck me all at once, that Art would be limning women for the rest of his life, keeping them at a worshipful distance, conjuring these sylphish Platonic embodiments. On the other hand maintaining his freedom, as if he had derived the best from them, appreciated them without being worn out by daily domestic contact, without waking up every morning with them, or lapsing into that silence that results from having heard what each other has said a thousand times, and finally turning a deaf ear altogether. He could be his own boss, and continue to have all the fantasies he wanted, punctuated by the pleasant interludes of live visits, just enough to spice his life, little different than the seasonal motifs in haiku.

He tried to convey to me that his life was a poem, with a backdrop of books and the contrapuntal music on his cassette, all of which provided structure and the illusion that indeed life could be ordered the way he wanted. He had made peace with his father who out of work for many years he said had become a shell of a man. But he understood him better now and had brought to Japan both his parents who were surprised at how successful he had become. He had bought them a house in England he said as the gray uniform seemed to fade, but then reappeared when he changed the subject to the wrongs in society. How Japan was exploiting countries in Southeast Asia, no longer militarily, but economically.

There was an edge to his speech that indicated that he was still an idealist out to avenge the poor, that he still had ideas for social reform, and was a romantic, and the aging process hadn't gotten the better of him. He would have been outraged at my associating him with the SS. But after the surgery on his brain clot and learning to walk, he was as sturdy as a cormorant huddled on those rocky outcroppings off the coast of Hitachi—that too is how I saw him sitting behind the steering wheel—a bird of prey of the same feather bracing himself against the wind and rain and whatever inclemency the injustices of this life could hurl at him.

We traveled up a mountain after leaving the highway and the sun was now blood red like the setting of the Japanese empire expending its last martial rays for another day. He slowed down and pulled off the road and we got out of the car.

"Let's catch the sun going behind the mountain," he said. The mountain was an extinct volcano, he explained, that we were circling for another view like Japanese painters had depicted Mt. Fuji over the centuries. Art had timed our trip to catch the sun at this moment as its rays trembled like a woman with Art standing there with his hands on his hips until it disappeared behind the mountain, molten and oddly inflamed like an embossed carbuncle withdrawing its heat into itself at the last moment. I marveled at how Art could capture the natural beauty of his surroundings. We got back into the car and continued up into the mountains.

We passed many old Japanese houses with thatched roofs, modernized with sliding doors and large picture windows. Everything was neatly taken care of, and I thought of the Japanese and Germans, so powerful during World War II, how such neatness almost formed the basis for world domination, as did an extraordinary cultural obedience that naturally ended up ruling others. How it started with such hierarchical subservience, such neatness and precise attention to the smallest detail, was clearly evident. Although how such humble abodes could extend outward and almost conquer the whole world was still somewhat of a mystery.

Both Art and I were fascinated by such societies. That is why Art had lived in Germany, and now was living in Japan.

We pulled up to a small bakery just as it was getting dark and the dubious outline of buildings and trees in the gloaming gave the impression of a Grimm fairy tale, for I couldn't imagine what lay ahead. This was where Art said he bought his bread. From Hans and his wife.

We got out of the car and Art knocked, sliding open the door. The room with a dirt floor seemed empty, then a light came on and a tall lean man appeared from behind another sliding door.

"*Guten Abend.*" he said. "You're late."

Art introduced me, and Hans shook my hand vigorously. The handshake was a compound of vigor and mountain air, of being miles away from his homeland but assuring you and himself that he was strongly rooted to his new environment.

"*Deutsch?*" he asked.

"No, *Americajin,*" Art said.

Hans then showed us briefly where the bread was made.

"Art is one of my best customers," he said as he led us into the restaurant. It was a small room with four blue tables and chairs, and mullioned windows all around.

"What would you like? Some bread and cheese? A Heineken, or we have cider?"

"A Heineken," Art said, "and some cheese and pumpernickel bread."

"I'll just take some cider and bread," I said.

"Would you like some butter for that?" Hans asked.

"No, bread will be fine." I said.

To my surprise Hans came out with a small plate, on it was one thin slice of dark bread. In the other hand he had a small cup of cider.

Art said, "Don't worry, I'll pay for this."

Then his bread and cheese came, and the bottle of Heineken which Art immediately drank.

I didn't know if Art or Hans would take back the bread they had given me, so I thought I better eat it while it was sitting there before me. It was so oddly parsimonious that my already empty stomach shrank that I didn't know how to respond. Was it preliminary to being incarcerated and fed the same menu by both of them, only water instead of cider? Would Hans and Art, one German and the other fluent in the language, and me who spoke haltingly, an obviously American pretender, would they lock me away in the mountains of Morioka forever? Had Art told Hans some story about me? Is there anything that would release me? Anyone who would imagine where I was? My wife, would she be happy to be rid of me for some wrong I had forgotten about?

Could Hans still be angry about the humiliating defeat hidden beneath all his civility? And Art angry at the bombing, the blitzkrieg, so many air raids over London—could he be more angry at me than at the Germans, for our taking so long to come to the aid of the British? Could this be a curious alliance they have formed, a kind of Hanseatic League that stretched from Northern Germany to England, and had now relocated in Northern Japan?

Was I to be their prisoner of war after over forty years? Before either of them was born. Was that the reason for the bread and water, oops cider? I know I had refused butter. That was my fault. But it wasn't an insult, was it? And cheese. Maybe it was my fault, and my own fevered imagination that thought I'd be locked away by these two.

And had Art told Hans about Naomi, was he still smarting from the bike ride, from my taking her home that night and her visiting my apartment? Did that ruin Art and Naomi's relationship? Was I a marked man? And had I made the six-hour train ride from Tokyo just to be ganged up on in this remote village in Northern Japan, and fed this Lenten fare? I tried to taste mold in the bread, but it was fresh enough. Maybe I was thinking of the moldy past that I feared would be resuscitated just before I'd be choked. Yet though Art and Hans talked German, they were cordial enough; occasionally Art stopped to inform me what they were talking about. Often they just gazed at me forcing me, from the few words I could put together, to imagine impossible scenarios. Was it really that "*Zimmer*" they'd lock me in? And who would feed me? That his wife had the shackles, old rusty ones from the Tokugawa period, I somehow imagined, though they had the large Akita I'd seen in the front yard to watch me. Or was it my rations that the dog already coveted? I heard the dog's bark occasionally as I sat there. How much bread would keep me alive? I wouldn't even be offered butter now that I had refused it once. A few turnips, maybe uncooked potatoes, would supplement my diet. I thought I heard the word for turnip as they talked. I'd grow weaker and weaker until the food would stop altogether, and my stomach would shrink, my esophagus swell so I couldn't absorb anything, and I'd be unable to move.

Then Hans and Art would get the gray uniforms out and the black hobnailed boots that I imagined outside as I looked through the mullioned windows and the gray material of early evening turned to wool. This is the dress underneath any Marxist. The shiny lights inside the room already informed the polish of leather belts and the boots I could see my face in, already sprawled as I was on the ground. Maybe it was the blood pounding wildly against my temples that gave me these impressions. I tried to take consolation from the tiny vase of camellias on the table, until I realized their petals dropping portend death for the Japanese.

It was almost dark now. And the branches of trees seemed to reflect curious insignia in their collars that I was afraid to turn towards them and continued to look out the window when I thought I heard a convoy of trucks and tanks, phalanxes of goose-stepping soldiers growing deafening by comparison with the German I heard inside the tiny restaurant behind me, and thought if I turned around at the wrong moment that it would be their cue to jump me and bring about the very thing I feared.

Both were big enough for SS Officers.

When I heard Art, though, my reverie vanished.

"Have you had enough?"

I turned to him and smiled sheepishly.

"I suppose I could take another piece of bread and a little more cider," I said timidly.

Hans was in the other room. And his Japanese wife suddenly appeared. Art introduced us. He asked for more cheese and bread. Hans said, "Oh, I'm sorry, we only have a loaf in the freezer and in the oven."

"Okay, I'll just take one in the freezer with me." Art said.

Hans had made a special loaf for Art.

"Do you have the tickets for the hot springs?" Art asked.

"Oh, *ja, ja,*" Hans said. He called to his wife to get two tickets, initialed them, and gave them to Art. "No, charge," he said.

Art and I got up to leave, and his wife came and wished us well. Though I still sensed something wrong about all this, something damp and murky that gave the lie to this pretended bonhomie, something spare and niggardly, just short of imprisonment, some trial that involved little more than water and one slice of daily bread.

Art paid for the food, and though my stomach was empty, my head was extraordinarily clear.

I could see the life of the early peasant, whether German or Japanese, lived frugally. The simplicity that hid unspeakable crimes. So that a packet of sardines could throw everything into disarray, causing a warmth of feeling, or *gemütlichkeit,* then violent spasms of jealousy the next moment that would make everyone realize they should have stuck to bread and water. The simple staples, the gloomy time-honored grains, somehow kept the peace. Even if they provoked visions of a secret hoard.

Nevertheless, I could see Art's fascination with this lifestyle. How in today's society asceticism always confers a measure of power, controlling our rampant surplus. How easily such a diet could be transferred into the goose step of a polished boot, endless phalanxes of them, shined and so well-trained they need not travel on their stomach, for the simplicity of German or Japanese fare was enough. But I was already an ascetic. I had already tapped into its power, perhaps that is why I expected more from others, a more lavish hospitality.

Or was it only my suspicions that more was afoot? Perhaps we weren't going to a hot spring after all and the ease of our exit was only a charade.

And we would instead enter the gloomy bowels of the huge mountain behind them.

We drove down the road and were stopped at a checkpoint. The security guard in his box in the middle of the entrance told us where we could park, and then we walked down to a large wooden three-storied building looking almost like a hotel from the early twenties built with wooden slats. Beside it ran a stream, and ahead was a bridge that led to it. In fact, families and couples stayed there, Art said, and took in the waters. The famous Morioka writer would come here all the time, he explained.

We crossed over the bridge and entered the building, approached a large desk where Art presented the tickets, and we were instructed how to proceed though Art already knew the ropes. I imagined rooms full of them where hangings routinely took place.

I happened to think how I could be tied up. Not with all the people here, I countered. Still the whole place had an air of mystery about it, possessed as it was of numerous coverts and countless rooms behind sliding doors. It seemed as if there were an infinite number of them to hide all the goings on, from organized military proceedings, and political intrigues, to lovers' trysts that occasionally ended tragically with one partner strangled or mutilated.

Outside one room was a child's teddy bear whose arm had been torn that the stuffing was part way out. From another room came the moaning of a woman, a potbellied stove sat in another that seemed like the waiting room to a train station, but on the tatami I caught a glimpse of the careless arrangement of bodies of naked men. I imagined tracks up the arms of one young patron sprawled out on the floor, his body covered with bruises, that it might not be found for days since the privacy of patrons was always respected. I heard too from Art that geishas occupied a remote corner of the building, a custom that flew in the face of traditional houses. But this particular building was an assortment of social stratifications preserved for decades that seemed to function in its own time while still drawing patrons out of the present, for pleasure, public and private relief, servicing every kind of erotic perversion imaginable. From some sectors Art said he heard screams when he had stayed the night. Though he added someone probably was having a nightmare. Maybe in Morioka there were some who had been on duty in Nanking in the 1930s, he said.

He told me about this most beautiful girl he had seen one early morning when he had gone for a walk, stumbling in the snow. He'd never seen her like again. She seemed like an apparition out of the past. Her beauty was stunning, but she was dressed traditionally, a modern beauty but straight out of a woodblock print that seemed to electrify the silk of her kimono and make every design of bird and flower come alive with the passing of her beautiful face. Once in his early morning walks when he had come up in February there was blood in the snow outside the building, and later police had gathered after the sun came up. Art told me even he was questioned.

I followed Art freely. I was in his hands and if this was all the product of a giant ruse to pay for a past grudge, perhaps I deserved it. Sometimes the will all at once tires of defending itself, and purposely lets its guard down. For who can account for his sins, for all the people he has hurt in his lifetime? What insects he has stepped on, what animal's relatives he has eaten just outside earshot of slaughter. Maybe only a few days stand between the blood curdling screams and our working their flesh to our mouths with the cleanest of forks.

But the thought passed as Art gave directions.

"Take your shoes off."

Even the goose step becomes ineffectual in bare feet. But there is still the Japanese martial arts, the sole of the foot could as easily be a weapon like the open hand.

"You can put your clothes here," Art said, and we both stripped, careful not to look at each other.

"Oh, this is your towel," he said.

We took our plastic bowls to soap and rinse our bodies before entering the pools of hot steamy water. Already there were two or three families in them. Both men and women and a few young children, and a group of company men joking with each other and all bathing together. Some men were still washing themselves as Art instructed me to do at the showers against the wall. Others were squatting at knee-high faucets.

Then we got into the hot water. The first pool was not as hot as the second, Art said. We lay back and looked at the steam rising into the cool night, and I heard for the first time the stream running outside, listened to the rustle of the breezes in the trees. The huge mountain sheered magnetically behind the hotel, probably adding some pull to the waters that swirled around us after traveling out of the bowels of the earth.

Art talked of philosophy, women, politics, dilated on every subject imaginable, then lapsed into the silence of the tall trees, the water gurgling, the leaves rustling, the occasional remark of the Japanese, and then we heard the hoot of a far off owl, or cry of some distant bird, or maybe someone muttering in the bowels of the mountain.

Our skin reddened and I started to sweat profusely, got a chill that I had to dip into the water to get warm, which made me sweat more.

"Let's try the other spring," Art said.

I was getting a little lightheaded and said, "No, this is fine."

I lost all desire to talk and lapsed into the silence that is preoccupied with body functions.

"I better be getting out," I said.

Art seemed surprised. Maybe this was a test, I thought briefly. Like with Naomi at the ocean, but the thought vanished as I rinsed under the shower and could hardly think, so weak had I become, my body rapidly losing heat. Huge beads of sweat bathed me a second time. Finally I got my towel around me and headed for the locker, the soft terry cloth was something to hold onto, and I covered myself as best I could as my head was spinning. I put my clothes on and started walking when Art who had dressed came and said something to me that I couldn't hear, so intent was I on not fainting.

"I have to sit down," I said, and went to the nearest step that led up to rooms visited by those spending the night.

The woodwork spun around me with its frightening hardness, its shiny lacquer, as Art bent down and asked me if I was all right.

"Yes," I said unsure. "I just need to rest a minute. I've lost too much fluid. I'm dizzy.

"I'm sorry," I said.

I guess I didn't pass, I thought to myself.

"Take your time," he said.

After a few minutes I said, "We can go now."

"Are you sure?" Art asked.

"Yes," I said, and we started walking down the long corridor. Yellow lights assaulted my eyes, then circular prisms. We left the building and the air outside hit me with an invasive chill that went right through my body. We passed over the bridge, and the water gurgled louder now than ever.

When we go to the car, I repeated that I needed something to drink.

"There's a store over there," Art said.

"Just plain water," I said.

"Nothing else?" he asked.

"No," I said.

I waited feeling lightheaded and weak, drained, vulnerable, as I started to sweat under my clothes that in a few minutes were completely soaked.

Art came with the water and I finished the bottle off in a few gulps.

"Do you want more?" he said.

"No, no," I said, and we headed back to Morioka.

We both were somewhat quiet on the way back. Art spoke briefly about Miya and listened half-heartedly when I spoke of my work.

When we got to town, he suggested that we go for sushi. We went though I couldn't eat much. Then we went to a pub for a few beers. I nursed one the whole time. The German proprietor who had lived in Japan for twenty years argued with Art about Japan and the War, an argument they must have had many times before.

I was silent, trying to judge if the beer and green tea would restore me.

After a couple of hours we returned to Art's apartment. I started to feel better, and he launched into a discussion of literature, then painting, put some music on and asked me if I wanted some wine.

"Maybe a small glass," I said to be sociable.

"Oh, I haven't showed you the books of woodblock prints. Some of these are incredible," he said, "so at odds with today's Japan," as he went into his tatami mat room and motioned me to follow. He got a large book from under one of the glass cabinets.

"Look at this," he pushed the pictures in front of me as he stood behind.

Page after page contained erotic poses of Japanese men and women, orgies of them on swings, horseback, standing in mirrors, bathing, and twisted into every posture imaginable.

"That was before censorship," Art said. "The Americans after the war closed down all the brothels and made even these prints taboo. But of course such art always goes underground," he explained.

"Look at that pose," he said as I was standing with my back to him before a large glass covered bookcase, and then he placed his hand on my shoulder.

Immediately all his women raced through my mind, a whole parade of them, diving into the ocean, fighting the waves, leading him around Taipei, introducing him to their parents, and immediately they all fell into place in an assortment of alluringly sensual postures just like the book of erotic prints. Poses he had probably gotten them into in various states of attire, some completely naked like the pictures, but most draped in partially unraveled kimonos, or street clothes. Artistic poses in real life that he genuinely admired for the craftsmanship of their bodies and the most delicate strokes of sharp chisels liberating them from wood, prints that entered the imagination of bachelors all over the world, inspiring even the French Impressionists.

And here standing behind me was an aesthete who appreciated art with every fiber of his being, but the passion, the passion was all the while elsewhere.

And the boy in the Philippines that he told me about who accompanied him to the rice terraces in Banau came to mind, and the one he said he was surprised to wake up with in Manila, and the young man in Thailand that had been his guide around Bangkok, who had accompanied him to Chiang Mai the time he threw up the noodles that he thought were long white worms, and who hadn't deserted him. They all popped into mind.

Art's hand was still on my shoulder, a horny hand that had none of the lightness of appreciation about it, none of the aesthete, of the preoccupation he had for Naomi, the Indonesian Mina, Jor, the Taiwanese girl, or most recently Miya, and countless others passing through his life, so that he easily passed for a woman's man, embellishing his life with an exquisite appreciation of art and intellect, language, beauty and culture

After an awkward interval, I moved away, bade him good night and slept lightly, but with a curious calm. I had made my peace with our past. And a conversation came to mind when one summer at the beach in a moment of brutal honesty I said to Art, "I don't even know your sexuality. You are so closed."

"You are too," was his quick reply.

We were both glad to separate that next morning, as he accompanied me to the train station.

I did send him Strindberg's *Getting Married* that he had mentioned, refusing myself to see the irony in it, preferring to remember the old Art, and his appreciation for Strindberg's cynicism.

He never acknowledged receipt of the book, and I never heard from Art again.

THE PEARL FAMILY

THE PEARL IS a secretive growth inside an oyster. Matched in size, shape, and color, a necklace from the sea may take a lifetime to complete. Eventually it will adorn a woman's neck to bring out the glow of her skin. It shares the illumination of everything beautiful, a hard white counterpart to the complexion.

"Full fathom five my father lies. Those are pearls that were his eyes."

The concentricity built around the speck of dirt or grain of sand is visionless. The layered density of animal accretions adopts the most uncanny nacre color. The father undersea is the clammy locker of all desires turning into a blind beauty.

The oyster's body mobilizes around a grain of sand, matching the priest's surplice when he's sermonizing on a pulpit on how to rid man of the impurities embedded in his own life, and surround them with a purifying whiteness.

Jiro had little talent though he was drawn to the arts. He attended art school but being a mediocre student smeared the canvas to hide his lack of representational skills and compensate for his absence of talent. Even his wife privately had suspicions whether his smudges could be interpreted as art.

But Jiro owned his family pearl farms. The lowly oysters worked day and night for him, developed a milky opalescence tinged with the most elegant hues in the world, pastel shades for pearls to adorn a woman's bosom, or hang from an earlobe sharing with the white of the eye, an elegance that astonished onlookers like the girl at the window in Vermeer's four-hundred-year-old painting. Jiro, a disciplined man, started early every morning at five-forty-five for his shop in Tokyo at the famed Castle Inn.

His small round body fell short of corpulence, but like the oysters on his farms added layers throughout the years. He resembled more the uncultured sea life that took years to develop a pearl, growing progressively heavier despite his small frame.

Every morning he could be observed peering under his jeweler's lamp to determine the exact shape, spending days determining the compatible size for each strand, before matching the hue and luster. It sometimes took him months to settle on the remaining pearls to perfect a strand. Like a factory worker bent over his desk, Jiro grew to master the grays and yellows in every white.

It was arranged that Ralph would meet Jiro before they all dined at the revolving restaurant atop the Castle Inn. Tomoko would come later. She wanted Ralph to get to know her husband first.

Jiro's art school was a dim memory. No, he doesn't paint any more, he explained to Ralph, though his paintings of Mt. Fuji and the sea, both visible from his living room, hung in his house.

"You'll see them when you come. You will visit our home, won't you?" Jiro said.

Both were splotches of color that Ralph struggled to understand as he sat and talked. Ralph speculated what really moved Jiro, outside the bright light of his jeweler's lamp, the eyestrain of countless hours at the shop, was his fascination with his wife that though moderated over the years still provided the ballast that informed every day.

Jiro rarely dealt with the customers, though he could charm them when necessary; his obsession was clearly to produce the perfect necklace, a strand of pearls that approached the perfection of the famed Mikimoto collection each fall. Jiro was happy with two or three strands a year, or the occasional strand picked up by a new member of the royal family. He knew he could not approach the success of Mikimoto, but some days under his lamp he dreamed of the universal admiration that would come his way. Tomoko was the body he envisions his pearls on.

Mikimoto is credited with originating the cultured pearl industry, and Jiro was pleased to live in their shadow. He left his wife behind in Odawara to attend the English Language School where he had hoped she'd improve her English enough to help with the overseas customers. It was then that she met Ralph Cecil.

Ralph didn't notice the shy Mrs. Fujimori at first. She was moderately tall, rather homely he thought at first, but incomparably polite. Her face was not disagreeable but inspired little interest. She gave the impression of grace and the utmost propriety. Her nose had a gentle slope that eliminated any attention without the eyes compensating; in fact, her eyes were slightly hooded so that looking at her made Ralph sleepy. Ralph didn't have the one student in the class he could focus on and Tomoko didn't fit the bill. She was too modest for unabashed looking, but she overcame her shyness and invited Ralph to her house and then to the Castle Inn. Ralph didn't realize he was the object of her interest until everyone lamented the termination of the class. It was then when Mrs. Fujimori approached him, saying that she'd like to invite him and a couple of her classmates to her home.

"Reiko and Mrs. Ito will come too," she assured him.

That Saturday Tomoko met him at the train station in a large black car whose make Ralph didn't know. Dressed in a cobalt blue dress she had the mild discomfort of meeting someone she had known in a different setting. Nevertheless she exuded elegance and the assurance of living in a large house on the top of a hill overlooking the Pacific Ocean. Unlike most Japanese homes the house was central heated, spacious, and sumptuously furnished in the Western style. Once inside Tomoko mentioned that Ms. Ito and Reiko could not come.

Tomoko showed Ralph around and commented on her husband's paintings on the living room wall. Their mediocrity shocked Ralph as he couldn't associate them with art school; he imagined how the talentless well-to-do end up collecting art.

Tomoko offered Ralph lunch as they made small talk about the students in the class. Tomoko was surprised at Ralph's grasp of each of his students' personalities.

When they moved to the living room Tomoko looked out the window and said, "There you can see Mt. Fuji," and on the wall to augment the view was Jiro's painting.

The mountain was reduced to a puzzling splatter of color that looked like a frustrated attempt to catch the majestic peak like Hiroshige. Ralph pictured runnels of milk streaming down an exposed red breast. A quick dart of Ralph's eyes gave away what he already knew. That the splotches of paint her husband had applied showed that his wife's flat chest was not the point of departure.

Out the other window Tomoko pointed to the sea where boats could be seen in transit across the living room. At night she said the shrimp boats trawled for their catch. She sat demurely with her hands in her lap as she spoke of the sea's changing moods.

Mrs. Fujimori was justly proud of her house. She didn't ask Ralph about himself, so much as follow his every comment with something pertinent to display a quick understanding of everything he said, all the while apologizing for her English.

As the afternoon wore on Ralph did not entirely grasp why he was there, since he normally managed his time. It was as if he had willed this departure from his accustomed routine into the life of the pearl family, something undersea about needs he didn't recognize, a curious respite from his normal pursuit of pleasure.

Tomoko's two sons, one who still lived at home and the older son in Spain studying jewelry making, Ralph never saw. Her oldest daughter was away at college.

Ralph left the house imagining that he'd never return despite her invitation to meet her husband at the Castle Inn where they had their pearl shop.

Why he agreed to meet her husband baffled him. It was like he was swept away by a desire that was not his, one of those strange compulsions outside our interest. Perhaps it was the politeness, the lack of urgency, something that could string together bright spherical moments tapering into an expensive necklace. Maybe it was the way diminished sunlight strikes salmon pink beauty, or the changing of blue to purple, adding green or a faint tinge of orange, then black erasing the blue and the last remaining yellow. It was like the reflection of pearls, or the iridescence inside an oyster removed to the skyline, the way color seeps into our decision-making rendering the will inoperable. What is will anyway but the periodic exhaustion of self-interest? What a joy, a delight to be at the mercy of color. Ralph was along for the ride and surprised himself heading for the Castle Inn on the Yamanote Line circling Tokyo at sunset.

We plan our lives then one day just let ourselves be swept by an evening sky of pastels as workers travel home. Bordering the pinks is a speculative blue trying to make sense of this odd existence. What Ralph was drawn to, he didn't know. Was it the comfort of money, but that never guided his life before. Perhaps it was the simple novelty of surrendering his will, the sheer blank slate of it wiped clean. Maybe it was the politeness that drew him, or Mrs. Fujimori's elegance. The pearls were baffling, out of his orbit like so many nighttime satellites. Maybe they calmed him. Only years later would Ralph suspect their intent. He didn't then because he apparently had none himself.

Maybe the hundred-thousand-dollar pearl necklaces in the showcase of their shop were the key, something to pilfer; such a lucrative swipe would give anyone pause. Maybe he hadn't yet discovered the larceny in his own heart. But Ralph's honesty had worked to his disadvantage all his life. The pearls in the shop case were safe from him.

Ralph's mother had said "People kill for pearls," but was amused that Ralph didn't value material possessions.

When Ralph entered the arcade he spied the shop; it was small with an elegant showcase out front. He entered and a young girl who exclaimed "*Irashai!*" bowed deeply and promptly disappeared to the back of the shop.

Jack barely had time to look at the display when a short, pudgy man came out. He had the round ingratiating face of a Daruma, as unstable were it not for the jeweler's magnifying glass on his forehead, his shop, pearl farms, and wife. His smile took up all his face.

"Ah, Mr. Cecil, so nice to meet you," he said as he bowed and gave Ralph his hand at the same time. "I just have to finish up. My wife will be here in a moment."

The assistant smiled again at Ralph who surveyed the display. He felt uncomfortable resting his eyes on the pearls, like a burglar. But he always felt guilty in stores, as if he were the target of observation. He feared merchandise would somehow turn up in his pocket were he stopped by security. Maybe it was the tension of so much propriety, being known as upright, President of the Honor Society in high school. Once in Austria he was asked to open his bag in a small supermarket. He refused, pushing the bag towards the security guard, indignant at the insult, "You open it, if you want."

Tomoko finally arrived greeting him with profuse bowing. She wore an elegant salmon dress that complemented her jet-black hair. It was a tasteful pastel that was the exact opposite of the gaudy Pachinko parlors Ralph saw enroute. Tomoko brightened up the shop and the pearls in the showcases under glass seemed to attach to her. She did have a string around her neck, and oddly clutched her purse as a kind of security.

Jiro came out and instructed his assistant to close up the shop and Ralph and the couple went to the Castle Inn Lounge on the top floor that offered a glimpse of all of Tokyo. The office lights illuminated a city of golden honeycombs when night fell, enhanced by the silent perspective at the top of the Castle Inn where blue flames glowed in preparation for select dishes at each table.

Jiro asked how Ralph liked Japan. His English was rather good since he had studied in Europe and America. In fact, his spirits were measured but irrepressible, though later in the evening the weariness of the long workday began to show. He thanked Ralph profusely for teaching his wife English and honoring them with his presence.

"Tomoko has improved" he said, to which she quickly demurred, uneasy with her husband's compliments.

"My wife was so excited by her Sensei that I felt obliged to meet him," Jiro added.

Tomoko lowered her eyes.

The food astonished Ralph that the chef must have been trained in the very best schools in Europe. The most ordinary dishes were prepared with a seductive array of tastes.

Towards the end of the meal and right before dessert, Mr. Fujimori said, "Come back to our house tonight and stay. We'd enjoy your company."

After a brief equivocation, Ralph unexpectedly agreed; maybe it was the ambience that had him following their suggestion.

They left the Inn for the parking garage where Mr. Fujimori got his car, a luxurious Celica, and drove them through the bustling Tokyo night life to their home in Odawara.

Once they returned Tomoko heated up the bath water and invited Ralph to take a bath. He finally relented at both their insistence. They had laid out a kimono so that he felt he was violating some cultural taboo if he refused. As he saw himself in the mirror in the strange house he felt exposed, even before he washed his body, rinsed, and soaked in the warm bath. His mind while bathing normally roamed, but all he could focus on was his nakedness in a house of strangers. His heart beat rapidly in the hot water. What was he doing here? he asked himself. They had taken him from his thoughts, his books, his routine. Why had he agreed to return to their home? It was not like him to spend his time frivolously. The sweat beads in the dim light he couldn't stop forming.

Did Tomoko wear the pearls for him? The heat enveloped him and he had to shake free the dizziness, and the sweat soaking his eyebrows, spilling into his eyes, and dripping down his nose and chin. His heart was racing when he got out and he could not stop sweating no matter how much cold water he rinsed with.

He tried to towel the sweat off, but it left dark stains on his kimono. He remembered once at Tokyo Woman's College drinking green tea before running to class. He started to sweat and couldn't stop. His armpits and undershirt were soaked, and at the underarms of his beige sports jacket giant stains appeared before thirty girls. He looked helpless before them. It was astonishing how the sweat wouldn't stop, despite mopping his face with his handkerchief. How he got through the class was transformative, like the beads of sweat becoming pearls then losing their contour running down his body. Was the heat he didn't have for Tomoko drawn by the bath, a reprisal for his stinginess towards others?

The couple was sitting in the sunken portion of the living room when Ralph entered. The room was half lit from behind the mantle.

A light sweat still lined Ralph's upper lip. His skin was glowing from the bath and periodically perspiration trickled down his back further soaking the cotton kimono.

Jiro suddenly stood up and announced he was going to bed first. He apologized for having to get up to catch the five-forty-five train to Tokyo.

The television was on NHK following the cherry blossoms up the archipelago while Ralph and Tomoko made small talk.

Ralph was puzzled by her, beyond the simple need to improve her English.

He didn't question his unattraction to her; in fact, it was a kind of respite from pursuing beauty. Tomoko sat in her own living room, Ralph imagined years later, like a doll on a shelf. She had the classic unattractiveness of Japanese women in those woodblock prints conveying the powerful artistic grace of a two thousand-year-old civilization reduced to the stylized embellishment of almost cartoonish looks. For all its modernization, underneath was a handheld mirror that exquisitely set off the most banal features, but with an incomparable reflective elegance. What Ralph failed to realize was that Tomoko was the embodiment of this. He felt the allure but was untouched except as a matter of stylized aesthetics. The determined unattractiveness transcended itself, persistently cultural, elegant, so that he felt she might be a lady whose charm was tempered to the dress, the jewelry, of a society out of his reach. Even though he had no desire for her, the vanity of women looking in a handheld mirror, then reflected in a larger mirror, caught him in the frozen absorption of looks that transcended that vanity in particular, but captured something in himself reaching out for the permanence and safety of art, something in all women beyond their actual appearance. It was like a woodblock print without the customary clarity and distinct color, blurred by the dim lights of the Fujimori living room, and darkened by the TV's bright colors drawing all definition from the room and leaving the two figures sitting indistinct.

Tomoko was a type. The demureness, the elegant withdrawal, piqued by an interest in Ralph, attracted him even though he entertained no notion of moving closer to her. A kiss was out of the question.

He remembered a doctoral student in mathematics when he was waiting on tables in graduate school. In this house of female doctoral candidates who lived together, there was one especially who liked him. They went on a date and were sitting in his car afterwards. Miriam was unattractive, had a bad complexion, but Ralph liked her for her kindness and intelligence. What made him kiss her, beyond the obligation for her liking him and his enjoying her company, he didn't know. It immediately froze something between them, solid as a direct kiss but bulging with regret. Maybe it was the emotional dishonesty of it. That and her bad complexion and shiny black plastic glasses must have forced her to say, "You didn't have to do that."

Tomoko was different. He knew the world better.

It reminded him too of Miss Nagatsuka, a student who virtually threw herself at him after she graduated, used him as a confidant when she started teaching, one day when she was leaving his apartment asked him to kiss her. He remembered her describing her absolute resentment at having to bathe her grandmother. She fought violently against her desire to drown the old woman, admitted how her sheer impatience with the old woman tormented her, turning her insides to a shambles of guilt and resentment. She ate more meat she said to cover up what she didn't do, imagined instead the flailing limbs of animals before they were butchered for not having the courage to hold her grandmother under water.

Ralph was simply unattracted to Miss Nagatsuka. Her nose was too big, hooked like his own, even if her mouth was wide, generous, unlike his own hopelessly skinny lips. How could he overcome the nose on her when he couldn't get over his own? Why would he pick such a woman with the same exaggeration; how could he kiss past that? His nose often enough got in the way. Asian women joked gaily about his long nose, but he was mortified. That alone made kissing Miss Nagatsuka impossible. Yet she insisted.

Ralph was repulsed, that he hesitated, looked her in the eyes to dispel her request, and convey that he didn't want to kiss her.

She looked back at him with such earnestness like nothing else in the world mattered but that kiss.

Finally, as if swimming upstream against a too powerful current, drowning in an algebra equation he couldn't figure out, he lowered his head and met her lips. With the doctoral student Miriam, his eyes sought somewhere to rest like the black plastic of her glasses; in this case it was the vase of poppies at the entrance. He noticed their black centers radiating brilliant orange petals. He remembered the roughness of Miriam's complexion against the soft tissue of his lips. He felt the acne bumps, the spiral descent of tiny eczematic flakes accompanied by Miriam's "You didn't have to do that."

"I know, I wanted to," Ralph lied.

Here too he kissed Miss Nagatsuka, but something must have signaled that he looked disoriented, for her nose grew larger after the kiss, and the disharmony of her features. It's a violation he had participated in. Perhaps the aesthetic sense in him feared large noses would be passed on. It violated his search for proportion. Mating was simply to improve the look of the species. He had compromised himself. Ralph was a purist, life's worst slave. He didn't deviate from what he thought life made him for, to correct what he most of all looked like. Yes, he sought to reproduce with what would erase his own bad looks. Miss Nagatsuka and Miriam couldn't do that. They'd only exaggerate them. Who'd want to look at a big-nosed child all their life, a regular Cyrano?

So his own face just hung there, as malshapen as all his fruitless attempts to correct himself, avoided by most beauty, an embarrassment, and a failure. After the kiss Miss Nagatsuka immediately picked up on that violation of himself and what he had been put on the earth for. Maybe that was the reason he was so picky with food, fruit at supermarkets, and why he was so endlessly selective with women. He sought beauty, needed beauty to correct the error of his looks. He'd pick the roundest, the tautest fruit, the color that best represented itself. Scanning seventy plums in a bin had him quickly reaching for the one with the most bloom, with the finest shape sprinkled like the constellations that when rubbed on his clothes shared the sweetness with the stars in the night sky.

"Now that wasn't so bad," Miss Nagatsuka said right after the kiss, reading Ralph's emotions exactly.

And Ralph to summon up something within to overcome the positive repugnance of flattening his lips against her, trying to avoid her tug on his body, said simply, "No."

He could hardly withhold himself as he ushered her out the door, then quickly rinsed his mouth with Listerine. He wanted to jump in the shower as if his skin would not stop crawling no matter how many times he washed it. Miss Nagatsuka's kiss would not go away. That's the problem we're born with. I know, who are we to make those decisions? But we don't! Our distaste for others does, and who knows where that comes from but the inability to accept ourselves. We are barely responsible for our predilections, our disgusts, but have to endure their following us around dreading the touch of most people.

That was the Ralph sitting before Mrs. Fujimori, though mellowed, but essentially the same person. We all are if we admit it the same, turning on ourselves so that we can't stand to be in our own skin. I won't get into all the wretched integument of having children whose looks will make us jump off bridges or slash our wrists. Certainly Ralph by his own admission deserved whatever disaster came his way.

Their conversation trailed off and Ralph knew that Tomoko was simply glad to have him under her roof. Sitting up with him while her husband was in bed was a triumph for her. Perhaps Jiro wanted to keep her from being bored, or perhaps there was a deeper agenda.

Fatigue and the long day slowed Ralph's brain down. All he knew was that despite having bathed, and while Tomoko was still in her clothes, he had no desire to kiss her.

Certainly the thought must have traveled through his mind, but he was the same man who had such difficulty getting over the hump of kissing Miriam and Miss Nagatsuka, who was so woefully unhappy with her life for not going to America.

Finally Ralph bade Tomoko good night though her politeness could have left her sitting talking all night until her husband awoke at five.

Ralph slept to almost past ten and woke up with a sense he'd forgotten something, that at the dim reaches of his mind was something so embarrassing that he'd be ashamed to face anyone. He took a quick inventory but found nothing. It may be just around the corner, inside a lacquered box, a phrase, something dropped, and not immediately picked up, lying exposed, something that resonated beyond his understanding or ability to correct it. He reached to recall it, but nothing came.

Whenever he called the Fujimoris invited him for dinner, then back to their house. He was like an embellishment, the West incorporated into the tatami bedroom, bonsai, flower arrangement, and the tea ceremony.

Ralph felt the bare room hid something, but he couldn't tell what it was. He didn't know why he was there. The thin stalk of iris in the Japanese garden could not tell, neither could the large carp in the pond. The Fujimoris cultivated him with gourmet foods and their extraordinary politeness. His strong features, this speaker of English, his comparative youth, constituted he thought the sole passport into their world. The milky white pearls were an added embellishment that provided luster to everything. But why was he there? What exactly did they really find in him? He possessed some culture, but it couldn't be a genuine love of art, of books, and painting that attracted them. The pearls were as if the raw material of that culture. They were benefactors who once gave him a pearl, a small tie tack.

You'd think his going to their house would end in something worth telling, a dead body to create the very interest that overlooks the fact that most associations in life lack violence. The nullity is astonishing beyond the mutilated body neglected for days, the putrid decay, the scrawled ransom note, the foreigner necessary to the mix, for Asian culture isn't noteworthy without some open-door policy. The politeness quickly turns to violence for the toll of bowing, honorifics, the burden of an unexampled etiquette at home that leads to brutality in the Philippines, Singapore, and China, so why not in this solitary house on the hill? Simple, there was no apparent reason for it, or was there?

Everything ends unless the fare changes, the diet alters, and makes holes even in the brain, galleries that after the foreign element enters allows no growth. The swarm moves in, buzzing and stinging worse than an outright blow. The small attacks to the self-esteem that are almost unnoticed surpass the bludgeoning of someone in the living room. Killing with politeness, kindness, is more deadly. It is a fact of nature sealing up so much sweetness, readying the stingers. Our human nature mostly doesn't know what happened no matter how much we dramatize it in stories or film; people just slog along in their everyday life getting deeper and deeper in each other's hatred. The pearls are kept boxed away from the slime that gave them birth until society is torn apart, politeness exposed, and they roll on the floor after a period of prosperity. Japan back on its feet, overrunning the world economy for what it failed to do militarily, still licks its wounds in private. Nobody knows it. It is still the world of the Makioka sisters getting their vitamin injections while China is ravaged, while the world falls apart, only now is it rising. In Tokyo high rise restrictions are lifted and buildings shoot up overnight to sixty stories to match the West. The yen finally reaches parity with the dollar. Like an insurance scam on TV Ralph saw once as a child when a bottle of wasps was held to a leg and anaphylactic shock set in, it is time to collect.

The bees are always there, the insects waiting; we needn't always defer to human nature. When it does the sting is deadly poised behind the simplest pleasure. It needn't be brutal, the simple revenge is under the guise of good breeding, behind a string of pearls. Ralph didn't know what they desired outside Tomoko's preference for him, but her face was in the way. The veil deserved to be lifted, so much ordinariness, the actual horror of the quotidian so that underneath you suspected something, but Ralph was admittedly slightly bored. Still it pulled him out of his world and the control he relinquished over his everyday life. It must have been the pearls, even if he didn't value them. They were of unsurpassed color, an opalescence of the most delicate iridescence. They could make you do anything, he kept telling himself to explain his presence, though he only half-believed it. Did she keep the most expensive strands in the house? He almost wanted to force himself to value them just to take advantage of the situation he found himself in. Of course the strand she wore last night was dazzling. There must be many more, a string of blue, green, champagne colored pearls, for their anniversary. After all you don't own pearl farms for nothing. Did they have a wall safe behind one of the paintings on the wall? Was a foreigner buried in the backyard, or underneath the house, who had had the same thoughts drawn by the wealth Ralph denied an interest in? Isn't it the ones who don't interest us who reel us in? Was their Fujimori name really Ifuku? Did Jiro come from Okinawa? Does that explain everything? Was his family outraged by the Americans? Did three not rape the mother, then the whole platoon took turns with his sister? Slit their throats? Okinawans considered the Japanese mainlanders too soft. They didn't fight; their underbellies were always poised for surrender, flabby like white flags. Their women just turned over for the Americans, weren't hunted down, or didn't even die by their own hand.

Did they come into Jiro's house that day? Is that what is etched in his mind, memories warmed every day by his jeweler's lamp. And does that account for the splotches of color he made of Mt. Fuji? He didn't want to see things clearly. Is that what put the perennial smile on Jiro's face that told nothing of his mother's reaming, the platoon that took his sister, or his father's beheading out in the garden where it fell into the pool and the carp nibbled away his features? Did the raping of the women not determine him to be a success, develop for the small village of Hase a cove for pearls to make something out of all that muck? Did the farming hide a purpose and effectively erase the past to get the Americans back on his own terms, one by one, for the day that they stormed their home?

This gives the injection of dirt into the oyster's body a new meaning, the miraculous production of pearl a significance far beyond imagining. It provided the means for a private vendetta that would attract, seduce, then kill Americans. His wife had to be just right. Not pretty but almost homely, a dubious attraction that didn't make the Americans suspicious, but slowly hooked them by her grace and elegance so that they suspected nothing.

Is this why Ralph was there? Will he be the first one buried, or are there more until their numbers equal a platoon? How many would have to pay for his father and mother, for Naoko, his sister? What extraordinary strength it must have taken to put up with the shrill voices, the cacophony of foreigners with their greasy fingerprints, their guffaws, the breathless rudeness, especially when drunk. Even when beer or warm sake was pressed on him, Ralph kept his composure so that Tomoko grew in her fondness for him, that only increased Jiro's passion for revenge. Like the many compartments in a lacquer box, or like bamboo sticks in a trap they sharpened his instincts. He relished what seemed to seduce his wife as a more exquisite turnaround of true emotion that would one day thoroughly baffle the American.

Sachiko the old maid saw it all. Jiro only felt the horror of the violations behind her gnarled hands, heard the horrifying screams. As an adult he imagined he actually saw the blows, the shiny brass belt buckles loosened, the loins moving like giant western machinery, the too white flesh on the backsides of American soldiers, their matting of body hair, his mother and sister writhing, pleading, struggling underneath, the thump of his father's head, the remains of his face nibbled away by carp, but in fact Sachiko had covered his eyes. He never forgot the screams that constituted his lifelong soft-spokenness. You would never imagine he ever heard such helpless cries. And just as baffling were the sharp and pinpointed passageways through a pearl necklace inside so much beauty, he was at such pains to prick. Each pearl smothered another scream, overcame the initial inability to penetrate. It is remarkable how beauty hides the horror, the tearing apart of the live animal, the scraping of the insides onto the sand and the tossing of empty shells on a heap to make buttons from. And I wonder if all beauty doesn't require something live smothered. There is a criminality about beauty for not being so obviously what it is at the expense of others, hiding the original plunder, the screams that give birth to anything that crosses the path of desire the world over.

Jiro perfected his own personality as a model for foreigners. So swiftly not even realizing the retribution is administered. You don't want to face it. They don't even have to know what you are doing. It can even be hidden from yourself. The whole pearl empire could be in the dark as to its purposes, no different than the tiny specks that start the whole process. How easily soft words lop the heads of lilies off like Longfellow's minister with his cane, or Jiro's father with the family's own sword.

They weren't interested, Jiro and Tomoko, in Ralph so much as being so cordial so that he didn't know where he stood. They never introduced their own children as if that would sully the purity of their motives, and they talked of them only in the vaguest generalities. Ralph thought it was because Tomoko didn't want to give away her age. Their own children might not have known Jiro's real name was Ifuku. He wanted the past erased so that no matter what happened the motives couldn't be traced. Ralph's history they never probed, for that he was American was enough for them. When they discovered that he had been in the army that was icing on the cake. Ralph was amazed at the hospitality, the grace, the compliant husband that he thought was the effeteness of enlightened wealth that would leave his wife with a foreigner so they'd wake up in the same house alone. He thought it was a meeting of modern ideas with an ancient culture, even though Ralph had no interest in Tomoko. He could have never imagined she was the bait and he was the fish on the line every time he swallowed more of their hospitality and their courtesy went ever deeper inside him.

Tomoko would drop everything for Ralph if he called. He interpreted that as surprised astonishment before a foreigner. He called her when he needed a rest from himself. Visiting the pearl family was something he didn't have to think about. That he got himself deeper and deeper in their debt never occurred to him. Beauty guided him around Tokyo and Mrs. Fujimori was a pleasant and elegant respite from that. He wasn't caught in a nexus of desire. It was a convenient prospect that took in the mountain and the sea from their living room. It was spacious enough, and the pearls were secretive enough to tie everything together with their mysterious beauty. Perhaps too there was a shared cultural attraction, and Tomoko had a genuine interest when she asked Ralph if he'd like to go to the Munch exhibit in Kamakura.

Ralph liked Munch and so agreed to meet Tomoko. Jiro was working, and so they went alone. Ralph couldn't have known if Tomoko had an ulterior motive for inviting him. He imagined it was solely her interest in art, or him, a titillating aside to her life that Ralph's companionship provided. He had no suspicions of atrocities on Okinawa and couldn't begin to imagine what happened to Jiro's family from his friendly chuckle and broad smile. In fact, the sun had long set on his beaming face, something a westerner couldn't probe.

How could he have known what fears in *Evening on Karl Johan Street* symbolized, that they pertained to the grieving of Jiro's family, the landscape of the dead so many years later, that those who died in Okinawa still lived, never went away, that after decades they haunt the living even in Munch. Maybe Jiro knew Munch perfectly from art school and didn't have to go but wanted Ralph to taste the horror.

Did the naked couple in *The Kiss* express Tomoko's own fear of a moment with Ralph, the physical absorption that demolishes the features? Is revenge best sucked into the past, or does it surface in a paintbrush? Are our own thrusts past every woman in the end the instrument of crime associated with each blow administered that after enough generations leave us mere actors at passions whose motives are deeper than parent, lover, or spouse, or even the murder of a whole family?

And still there were the white faces on Karl Johan Street, so intimately alone, ghosts of their own conscience. Is this where we end up after revenge, where the hollows of our eyes are almost blue for the lack of oxygen?

Tomoko didn't spend long there. In fact, she didn't stay with Ralph very much but viewed at her own pace. He tried to absorb the paintings as if he'd never see them again, tack them down like his countrymen had held Okinawans, only he didn't know it for beauty casts its spell on us while we think we act independently just looking over someone's shoulder at the horror and failings that motivate art. The way Ralph woke up in Japan canvassing his mind for some guilt showed a vague but huge premonition of having done something that may elude him forever, something he had no explicit memory of but that carries the burden in the stoop in his walk, his "cat back" as Japanese say.

In *The Scream* Ralph came up silently behind Tomoko. She was clutching her pocketbook tighter in front of her. Ralph could tell the painting made the deepest impression on her. The soft tones of her husband's voice he never raised for fear of reaching the crescendo that here was deafening. She wanted to throw her own hands up, cover the sounds Jiro heard, the straightness of the boardwalk with the dying reds, blues, yellow, the backs turned, the two boats with crosses for masts, Jiro's family disappearing in the green current. Tomoko doesn't put her hands to her ears knowing she'll give herself away but is pulled down by the deafening undercurrent of her husband's past. It echoes through the history of painting. Demuth's red fire engine caught it, but Munch is the apotheosis no one else reached. Who'd imagine it in the calm smile of a prosperous merchant of pearls, a Vermeer? The bedding in the slimiest oyster would never give away that pearl of insight, not to Ralph Cecil anyway. But this interferes, the primordial scream in the painting outyells any instrument, drowns symphonies, conjures the absolute horror of human beings, what they have done that we have no voice for but in silent reproductions. We are shamed to place our hands to our ears, but we need to continue looking. When Ralph walked up and uttered some banality that Tomoko never heard, "Can you hear it?" he thought it was only the celebrity of the painting that affected her, but it was the genesis of horror, the dead bodies, the rape and beheading, Jiro's life torn apart, recaptured only in the lowly oyster, the pearls he'd find there, their reproduction out of so much slime. The human voice immobilizes us, far beyond what we see, conveys the sheer terror of existence. Jiro's wide-mouthed Daruma smile mutes it, as does Tomoko's politeness. Before Munch was the atomic bombs dropped on Nagasaki and Hiroshima, the Rape of Nanking, the Bataan Death March, and the naked horror of Jiro's family.

Puberty recalled for Tomoko her husband. Even though it was a naked girl sitting at the edge of the bed in a wide-eyed frozen look. The inability to move, dress, feel shame at what had happened was there. The sexuality had stopped as an ugly green shadow unfelicitous to every pleasure; it threw itself across the soiled sheets patient for the moment of revenge.

Was that Tomoko standing pale-faced again in *Death in a Sick Chamber* where everyone's head is bowed? Was she regretting already what would happen to Ralph like the others? Could she not really assess if he deserved it, his irrelevance to the exhibit, if he was totally out of his depth? Ralph was deaf to what Jiro heard, or what Tomoko lived with. Was the tragedy not the universal justice for crimes he had not committed? But no crimes are committed directly, despite everyone being accessories, and in the end the only evidence is our independent memories. As unreliable as they are, they alone administer justice.

The exhibit ended with *The Red Virginia Creeper*. The red blight choked the building. It was enough to stifle Tomoko who hurried away from the exhibit.

The next time Ralph called, Tomoko mentioned Hakone. They could go for a drive, she said. Again, Jiro couldn't go. Ralph agreed and Tomoko met him at the train station, and they drove to the beautiful lake region of Hakone. The ride cut through mountainous terrain where they seemed always to be going uphill, leaving the culture behind for grass-thatched huts amidst those large trees that grew in so much of Japan outside the urban areas and away from rice fields. People looked healthier, ruddier, less polished. In fact there was the suggestion of wildness beyond the society of the lowlands, as the car climbed the mountains through numerous tunnels leaving behind the refinements of a two thousand years old civilization. It was as if they were abandoning respectability the higher they climbed that had nothing to do with survival. The towering trees hovered over the elegant Tokyo car, the manners of Tomoko, with a brazenly honest peasantry that would be more than capable of seeking revenge. There was a rawness to the landscape that Tomoko and Ralph sensed inside the car. Perhaps Tomoko even considered the consequences of Ralph's wandering hand. Ralph was a foreigner, one of the invading barbarians even The Great Wall of China had been built for. If Tomoko were riding with one, she gave no hint outside his name, meaning "Wolf Power," but how could she have known? It resembled a fairy tale the deeper the forests took them, the rarer the air became, the cleaner and more forbidding the coldness, the more convincingly it chilled their bones. There would be no sympathy here, the landscape forbade it. The tourist areas, the hot springs and minshukus were consoling, but the impression was of woodcutters on the loose to correct injustices with one swing of their axe, to correct the past and present, isolated hermits who bore the brunt of a universal vendetta, the barbarity off the beaten path that promotes the species without a thought for the niceties of culture. It is where the anger lived in Japan that Ralph barely noticed, beneath even the lacquerware, the shiny black and deep, thoroughly saturated off-red that gives the impression that you have come to the end of the line, that there is no imagination left, that your neck is extended under something sharper than you can fathom by what is to be found inside the box, a dried eyeball or a set of teeth. It was evidence of guilt, something in Ralph that remained in his bloodstream, discovered around the next bend, in a forest as dense as those in central Europe.

Ralph was always amazed on August 6th and 9th that he could walk the streets unmolested. He remembered once in Jiyugoaka eating an apple in broad daylight and nobody bothered him. What was wrong with these people? That he wasn't attacked, pummeled to the ground there on the street, mildly shocked him. The Japanese went about their lives with incomparable politeness as if nothing had happened, a truly civilized people whose cultural harmony surpassed anything dreamed of in the West. No untoward remark, even to foreigners, but instead a willingness to go out of their way to help if lost. So what if *Fat Man* and *Little Boy* dropped out of the sky? That was decades ago? But there is still Munch, still Jiro Fujimori.

Even in Hiroshima the city had a broad access of tolerance, wide streets from being rebuilt. The monuments to peace are everywhere visible. The night before going to the museum Ralph had nightmares that tapped into the collective horror. But no one attacked him and the day at the museum was like any other. The past was absorbed in film, photographs, and personal accounts, woven into the present as if nothing happened, save for the screams of Munch, or behind the smiles of Mr. Fujimori. Ralph felt they were deafening enough that in a second he'd be clubbed, or some collision was in store for them as they made their way up the mountain road. Where were they going? To a panel of judges? Would Ralph be found guilty for what happened to Jiro's family? Were the pearls a huge diversion? The dead divers trapped retrieving them prior to the farms, did anyone remember them? Did they blindside Ralph with Tomoko sitting at the wheel in her blue dress wearing the pearls on her neck?

Ralph as he looked over at Tomoko thought that she was too calm, too elegant, that the wildness outside didn't bother her. Was it that translucent curtain that separates actors? Were there naked moments of truth behind her sitting there?

This was her country and nothing intervened to disturb her pleasure, Ralph thought. That was the only explanation of her being with him. Or was she taking him somewhere that he should be concerned about? Was there more menace than Ralph imagined? Did she want to stop at a hot spring, or inn? Having no desire Ralph couldn't imagine it clearly until years later. Tomoko was like a porcelain figure, moving and breathing, but still Ralph imagined breakable, subject to a precipitous toppling. Everything could come crashing down if he reached over and touched her. But that was far from Ralph's mind. The elegance gave the impression that he'd be toppling a priceless figurine whose value he only vaguely understood outside the string of expensive pearls.

They drove out of the mountains to an open valley of breathless beauty, rolling hills and lakes offering multiple perspectives as they circled down and then up a small hill to what looked like an inn, but was a restaurant of endless sophistication. The building had the studied architecture of the most elegant Japanese design and the food came in small colorful portions, arranged similar to Tomoko, the thrust of her motives Ralph could not gauge except to imagine the clarity of an ancient culture where the ragged edges of human behavior were smoothed by lacquerware, where the most untoward emotions were tantalizingly out of reach of what was brought to the palate.

What did Tomoko have in store for him? He could not betray her husband, but why was she with him? What did she want? Was Jiro behind it? The uxorious husband acting the puppeteer that only wanted to please his wife, or was it something pernicious wrapped up in a furoshiki he hadn't opened yet, or the kimono not there to unravel so that the one piece of dress was too easy a challenge? Ralph left the meal unsatisfied, as if unequal to the politeness of so many flavors, when Tomoko mentioned the open-air museum.

Over acres of land were modern sculptures, thick-bodied Moores that conveyed the idea of interlocking families from encircled arms giving the impression of the strongest links in an isolated chain. Wedlock occurred to Ralph and the striking off of those chains, but the links seemed permanent despite the screaming from rape and beheading.

So many bodies fascinated Ralph, for the different shapes and the exaggerated breasts Japanese women admire compared with their own modest bosoms, lack of hips, despite sumptuous backsides. There were marbles and bronzes and all manner of postures. The human form was captured, immobilizing Ralph; all the naked boldness outdoors unsettling in that it exposed something in him. Tomoko's hand always across her pocketbook, her dress below her knees, was at odds with the freedom of the body postures from all over the world. How we free our movements in art, stepping, reaching, eyeing, grasping. Screams issued from some of pleasure and pain, but there was also the deep cradled sleep of an infant in another. Ralph and Tomoko stood clothed lacking the freedom of emotion and deprived of gesture, the very preliminaries to horror. Civilization had chastened them until what is hidden breaks out and the residents of Hiroshima and Nagasaki, their bodies enflamed, scorched, run nude or drop in the river screaming from their skin blistering, peeling, but here all is so calm, bronzed, marble, and outside the horror of a few, unrepresented. You have to go to Munch for that or make a beeline to Hiroshima to see the survivors' art. The bodies here are too big, substantial, lacking, but for a few, an emaciated delicacy too thin to mention. The pleasure they could take could nullify the pain of everyone tearing their clothes off. Nudity on the spot. A thermonuclear explosion's all it takes for people to be free, to get their priorities in order. All their lives they are so stuffy, *Little Boy* and *Fat Man* is all it takes. The sculpture at Hakone showed that we'd not need another nuclear war, the overrunning of Okinawa, or the brutal resistance of what happened to the Ifuku family. We can do all this in secret, carry pocketbooks and secret codes, where our layers of clothing give a false impression of being satisfied observing giant larger-than-life sculptures.

Our eyes covered don't keep us from growing up and grasping the rape despite the American Occupation seducing the local population with their PXs after the war, their canned Fruit Cocktail and Campbell soups. The Japanese were so hungry and showed they could live with the screams of war, but what if we truly touched each other; then rape would be redundant, old hat, pointless, at what is so freely given?

The deceit, the hospitality and smiling, shown each other is not enough. We need art that diminishes us living until we ignore it altogether. Still the murder and screaming deadens all sounds, makes Mrs. Fujimori dress up with perfect taste, adorn herself with pearls to observe a nude sitting on the bed? What exactly has Mrs. Fujimori come to see? Certainly not the pearls yanked from the jaws of sea life pried open countless times for the exact size and color. We are accessories to such an expensive piece of jewelry. Our nudity is inconsequential if the necklace is expensive enough. The attention to size and color exceeds the desire for flesh. The pearls alone satisfy the greed for pillaged oyster beds to beautify a woman.

Mrs. Fujimori wore one of her best strands that day. There was an odd inland connection to the sea life. Everything here will one day be underwater. What did Tomoko want? The thought passed through Ralph's mind among all the nude representations. The sculptures with clothes on were never so interesting, detracting somehow from the body's bold three-dimensionality.

On the way back Tomoko made a vague reference that it was good they could get back in time and didn't have to stay in one of the inns, so far from Tokyo. Or did she say that?

Ralph brushed her comment off and to her question about whether he had a girlfriend he mentioned Yuki, gushed out what must have thrown cold water on any thoughts Tomoko was having as they made their way around bends and down slopes from Hakone, like it was a sensuous body they were leaving behind. They finally reached Odawara station.

Years later Ralph thought about an opportunity missed. She must have mentioned the inn intentionally, but he had work to do. There was no desire at the time. It comes when it wants, sometimes years after the fact, when of course we are different.

Zorba said it is a violation not to service a woman who wants you. It goes against God.

But who put the pernicious selectivity in Ralph, the deadly pursuit of beauty that made him a monster for all the simple desires he overlooked? Maybe the desires are not meant to be simple, but to complicate us, ball us up in such entanglements that other people can strike at will, or we at them, in this shameful blitzkrieg of preferences. Why should anyone have the luxury of choosing, leaving a strewn battlefield of rejection? Who are we to shun others? A woman who wants you is a gift, but Ralph was deadly in the selectivity, the prissiness of his choice. No, he wasn't a man, but a sheep slavishly following beauty all his life no matter where it led, bleating when he couldn't have it. It was the artist in him pathetically bound to his prey. He'd be slaughtered for all he passed up. Sacrificial creature, that's what he was, someone else's scapegoat. Their sins would be cast on him. He'd be sacrificed for them. If he could have given himself, he'd complicate the simple revenge; otherwise he deserved what he got.

He remembered Kelly in Mexico who liked him, a freckled, fair-skinned, redhead like his mother with the beautiful biracial child. As much as he disliked his own mother, he still desired her. But she went with Fernando that night. He felt hurt. The next night she wanted him. But he denied her. He still remembers her. The denials come back. And Susan Matsuyama naked on the tatami calling him to come back. He was hurt by her over Brad who moved in. She wanted Ralph but he remembered gently closing the door on her. Youth makes its choices and we pay later. Life is long and loving short.

Mitsumi whom he gave money to when she was going to Europe and told her if she met someone nice to go for it. He hurt her and immediately saw it on her face. She had wanted to meet him in London, but he never went. When she returned, he saw her, but it was never the same, the wound was too deep.

Why does the tepid memory of the Pearl family come and remind him of what he once threw away? He didn't have to die for it. Though how close he came he didn't realize. Maybe he was making it all up. Maybe Jiro didn't have those designs, but only the simple dedication to his shop, and pride in his pearl farms. What does a man work for but the simple revenge on life, for the humiliation of childhood where he is so helpless, left alone in a bus station for hours waiting for his mother to return, sent to live with strangers, denied love so casually, shuttled from home to home after the father dies. Who knows what happened to the unprotected womenfolk? The Okinawans were stunned by the savagery of the fighting and had to take it out on someone. Americans were convenient, uncultured; they'd never dream of the power of the pearl. How the Fujimori pearls spanned the globe, conquered it with the waste, the secretions, of what was rendered a dead animal. Like the bodies left on the beaches, the women raped repeatedly that they lost count, were the pearls extracted leaving piles of endless shells. For years people were empty of content. But Jiro plodded along until he had the lowly oyster doing his bidding. He knew that would confer power, a sense of destiny not subject to the whims of big-boned westerners wearing their needs crudely on their sleeves where etiquette, bowing, was brushed aside, and they took what they wanted. But they would be distracted by beauty decades later, when the fashion for pearls monopolized the world. What a Japanese thing to do, enlist the support of laboring sea life, countless oysters to get a people back in the guise of one foreigner at a time, the representative of a country that invaded the motherland. They were a superpower, but Jiro would show individually they were weak, susceptible to his pearls. Maybe Ralph was not a perfect candidate, but he was better than nothing.

Tomoko herself wasn't a pearl at the time, but she wore them. Different necklaces, chokers, that Ralph saw at different times and imagined Jiro transferring to his wife a corresponding beauty to trap him. Still he wondered at the tie tack they gave him. Don't all pearls torn from sliminess eventually leave us pallid, wasting away before their spectacular hardness?

Our sins follow us down the most diverse channels. Like the Filipina who when Ralph brought her back to his hotel room unclasped her dress in the back and out popped the two most enormous breasts in the world like a seed pod after one too many rays of sunlight bursts open so that Ralph immediately grew disappointed at the gross exaggeration of the breast not given him as a child. He averted his eyes and stepped back.

"What, you don't like big breasts?" the girl said.

"Uh," Ralph hedged not to make her feel bad.

Or the Korean girl, the one who after being coy with him he slowly positioned and then thrust so hard he knew he must have hurt her. He remembered her screams, and he kept up more pitilessly than the invasion at Inchon. It was an assault on her body for himself having been dumped on strangers at eleven months, for the one day of breastfeeding his mother cackled about decades later. It was pure anger. Could it be that we are all paying someone back and may not know it, that we are all corrections to even completely imaginary wrongs? What a sad state of affairs if it's true. The pearl family amassed wealth for what they couldn't do outright, but under the table, paying someone back. Isn't that what all wealth is, a reprisal somewhere, the hoarding assurance of that? We are all simple corrections. The scars and pain of rejection that Ralph took out on an innocent Korean girl are passed on. Ralph deserved everything he got. Too bad he didn't fall in love with Tomoko. That would have taken the cake.

With the Pearl family he got off easily, apparently. It was just a mildly disconcerting memory. Not like the Korean girl. Where did she take the pain?

So many others he pleased, they wanted him. Like Khanjana, the sadness of her showing him her apartment in Bangkok that she was so proud of though it was nothing but exposed cement, hard, cold and gray, unlike her exquisitely warm body.

Or Suthirat banging on the door of his room and he wouldn't let her in because someone else was there. She was gorgeous, with a sumptuously attractive body. She knew it. But he buried his head in the pillow, holding on to the girl until Suthirat left.

Memories intertwine in their complexity, break down or remain hard and singular. They have an unspoken durability. The garrulous memory doesn't know when to stop talking and descends quickly into lies. Who knows the thorns that are pushed out, how they enter us? We don't hurt enough, pain enough, feel guilty enough. We get away almost scot free with our poor memories only retaining the best or the worst in a specious melodrama that ends up afflicting us but mildly; still we suspect the hiding of something even more painful, deadly. How Ralph fit into the Fujimori's family pain, he couldn't have suspected; he could only imagine behind the racial impassivity, the nuclear holocaust, the terrible fear of fires, the residue of broken lives so miraculously reassembled. He didn't know how to probe. His simplistic desires covered up everything. Pleasure is a palliative. There he stood, beneficiary of this family that he had the least suspicions about. But they kept their children away; he knew there was something suspicious in that.

In fact, Ralph never knew how close he'd come to being the reprisal for the horrors of Okinawa.

The Fujimoris asked Ralph when he was leaving Japan to stay with them. He could live in the apartment below the house. It looked like a bunker, all concrete, but half-finished. Their son who was in Europe they said had stayed there.

Ralph put two and two together, the pearls that were his eyes and teeth, the bones, hues of health, a whole body of iridescence, flesh that once moved through daily life on Okinawa that loved and laughed and wept. All was caught now in the beauty of pearl necklaces adorning beautiful women around the world, pried from the jaws of oysters tossed on the refuse heaps. Its privacy was most compelling, hiding the pain, building on the detritus. The pearl is a sad gem that ends in disappointment yet empowering the secrecy of Okinawans bent on revenge. Or was that in Ralph's mind? Did he tap into a universal guilt? Had the rape and beheading never happened, had the mainland never been overrun? Did Ralph only dream this? Was there no resistance, no abdomens that bayonets plunged through? Are Hiroshima and Nagasaki now only puffs of cigarette smoke? Can all be forgotten? What's wrong with Ralph wanting to bring this up, tell tales?

Let sleeping dogs lie! Let the dead rest in peace, and let bygones be bygones.

It's an unhealthy emotion. Let's get on with our lives. This family is innocent, Ralph. They didn't do anything, plan anything. It is all in your own sick mind. You need the holocaust to return, to relive the horrors of

Okinawa. Why? They don't think about such things. They're too polite! It is all your own worm-eaten way to give your own life meaning! Who knows what crawls through your mind when it has nothing to do? There are just empty galleries, face it Ralph, motivated by envy for someone's pearl farms. You can invent the island, catalogue the dead secreted in caves where the vendetta started, the familial atrocities to account for a world-class business, but you are only blowing smoke! Their success is what you resent, Ralph, that they are better off than you. Or Jiro's immersion in his job for your own lack of discipline? Isn't he big-hearted to allow his wife to spend so much time with you? Why read more into it, you little monkey, ingrate! Is it a jungle you're missing, the thick foliage, trees you need to climb, bananas absent from your potassium depleted heart? Do you resent the move towards luxury, imagining the wherewithal for reprisal? Could it be too that Mikimoto has its own stories just like the Fujimoris and all gems are connected to pain, grief, and reprisal? Go on, make that up too, Ralph.

Mr. Fujimori is such a model of restraint, modesty, propriety; the ironies of the narrative of all gems connect us to their power where we have been shamefully dispossessed, humiliated, raped, made the object of physical violence in an orphanage, among the spoils and heinous acts of war. Ralph, you have too much imagination for your own good. Growing up in an orphanage, leave that scenario of revenge alone. Why foist your own vendetta on a perfectly innocent family? I know you are going to say no family is innocent! What a dolt, jackass. Ralph, you have a lot of learning to do! I know the secret gems inside the earth are subject to enormous pressure, and so are those inside the oyster. Something's got to give. The labor of ages produces them, but the motives of people who buy, manufacture them, keep them in safes, wear them, flaunt them, often having overcome the poverty of the past themselves, the outrages and humiliations of war, the slaughter of family members, surely that can't be discounted.

But why here, Ralph, on an innocent family?

Did Jiro think the rape of his sister could be compensated by amassing some of the most expensive necklaces in the world every year, waiting a lifetime for compatible shapes and color to dispel such horrors, and would the purchasing power enable him and Tomoko to lure the unwitting to their house, into their lives with favors, the promise of living below them in a bunker? Get real. Would that satisfy them, make them safer? Would Ralph pay for the beheading? Did it even really happen? Could the amassing of so much wealth, the idea of farms in the first place, the need to triumph for all big business that wants to control people not be for a permanent sense of powerlessness and outrage? No, Ralph.

Ralph did get away, left Japan, some might say with a fevered imagination, and perhaps there were others buried in the Fujimori backyard; nevertheless, he didn't take them up on moving in. Perhaps there were no outrages, though anyone can google Ifuku on the internet and more than likely view the graphic footage of what happened to the people of Okinawa, to the one family that Ralph was almost sacrificed for, like those tag ends of the root canal of almost anyone's ailing tooth that refuses to die.

ABOUT THE AUTHOR

RICHARD KRAUSE'S collection of fiction, *Studies in Insignificance*, was published by Livingston Press, and Unsolicited Press published his second collection, *The Horror of the Ordinary*. His epigram collection, *Optical Biases*, was published by EyeCorner Press in Denmark, and Propertius Press published his second collection, *Eye Exams*. Fomite Press will publish another collection of his epigrams, *Blind Insights into the Writing Process*, in January 2022. Krause grew up in the Bronx and on farms in Pennsylvania. He drove a taxi in NYC for five years and taught English for nine years in Japan. Currently, he is retired from teaching at a community college in Kentucky.

ABOUT THE PRESS

UNSOLICITED PRESS is a small publisher in Portland, Oregon. The team is made up of incredible volunteers that seek to produce the highest quality poetry, fiction, and nonfiction. Follow the press on Twitter (@unsolicitedP), Instagram (@unsolicitedpress). Learn more at unsolicitedpress.com

CPSIA information can be obtained
at www.ICGtesting.com
Printed in the USA
BVHW081937051121
620879BV00003B/17